Tree-House Comix Proudly Presents

DOG MAN
GRIME AND PUNISHMENT

WRITTEN AND ILLUSTRATED BY **DAV PILKEY**
AS GEORGE BEARD AND HAROLD HUTCHINS
WITH COLOR BY JOSE GARIBALDI

graphix

AN IMPRINT OF

SCHOLASTIC

TO AMY BERKOWER, WHO ONCE TOLD ME, "WRITE THE BOOKS THAT MAKE YOU HAPPY." THANK YOU FOR BELIEVING IN ME.

Library of Congress Control Number 2020930257

978-1-338-53562-4 (POB)
978-1-338-53563-1 (Library)

10 9 8 7 6 5 4 3 2 1   20 21 22 23 24

Printed in China   62
First edition, September 2020

Edited by Ken Geist
Book design by Dav Pilkey and Phil Falco
Color by Jose Garibaldi
Color flatting by Aaron Polk
Publisher: David Saylor

CHAPTERS

CHAPTERS

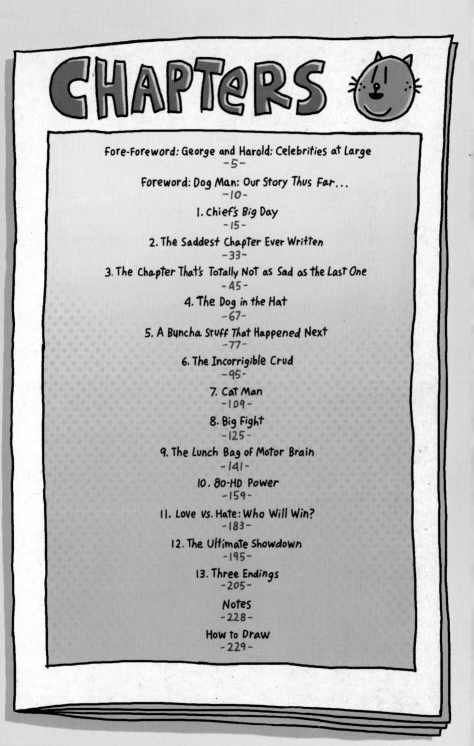

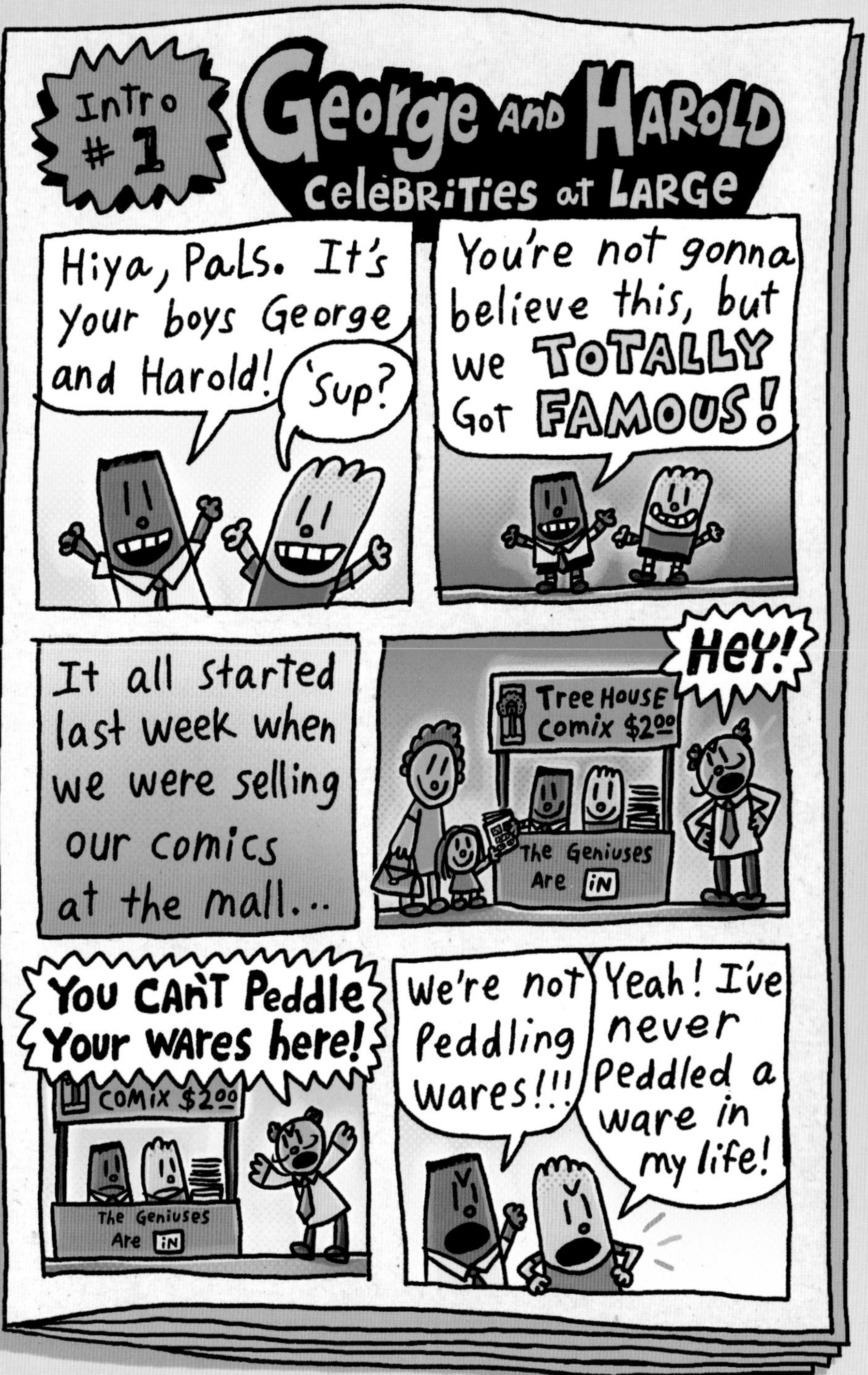
Intro #1
George and Harold
Celebrities at Large
Hiya, Pals. It's your boys George and Harold!
'Sup?
You're not gonna believe this, but we TOTALLY Got FAMOUS!
It all started last week when we were selling our comics at the mall...
Tree House Comix $2.00
The Geniuses Are IN
HEY!
You CAN'T Peddle Your wares here!
COMIX $2.00
The Geniuses Are IN
We're not Peddling wares!!!
Yeah! I've never Peddled a ware in my life!

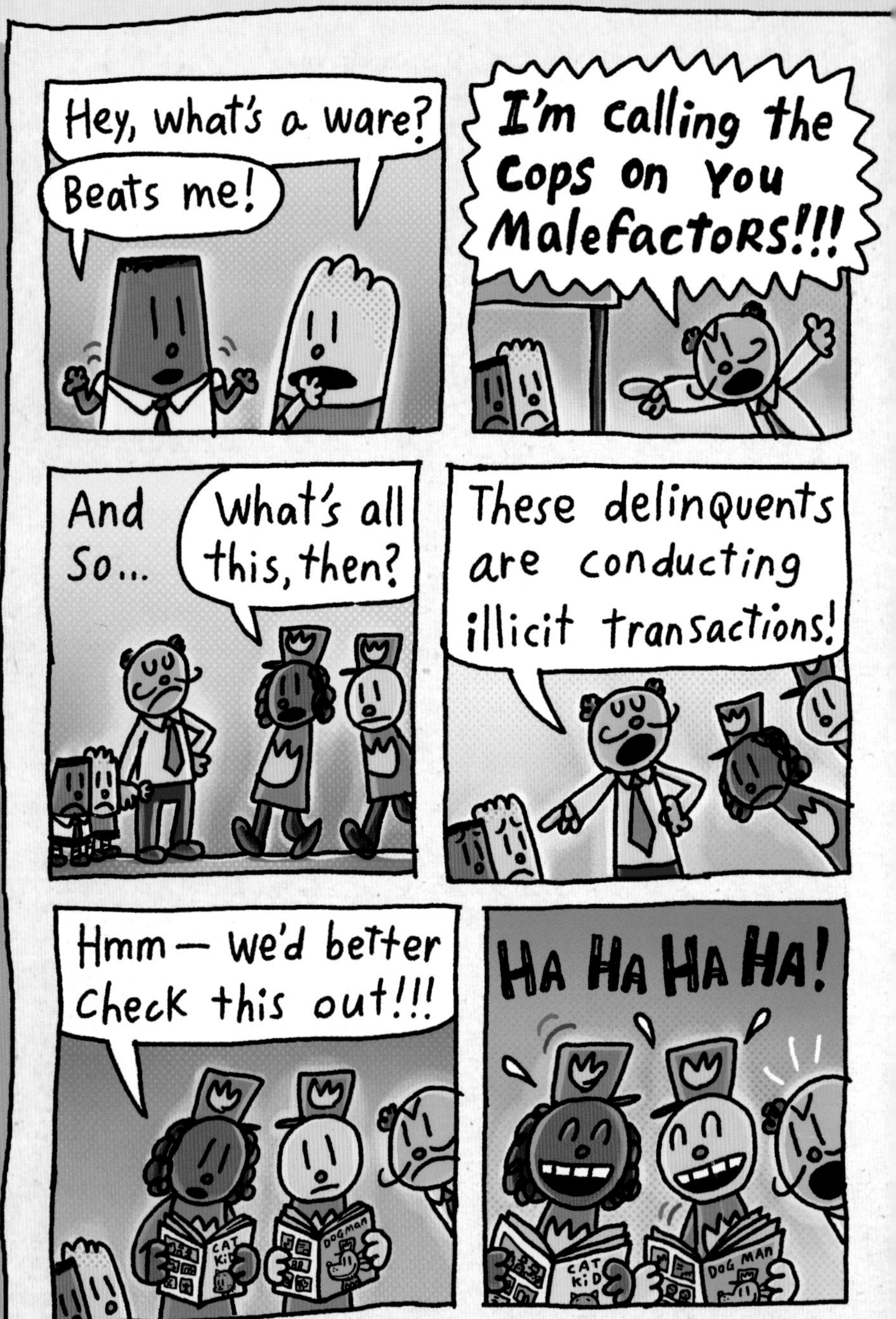
Hey, what's a ware?
Beats me!
I'm calling the Cops on you Malefactors!!!
And So...
What's all this, then?
These delinquents are conducting illicit transactions!
Hmm— We'd better Check this out!!!
HA HA HA HA!
CAT KID
DOG MAN

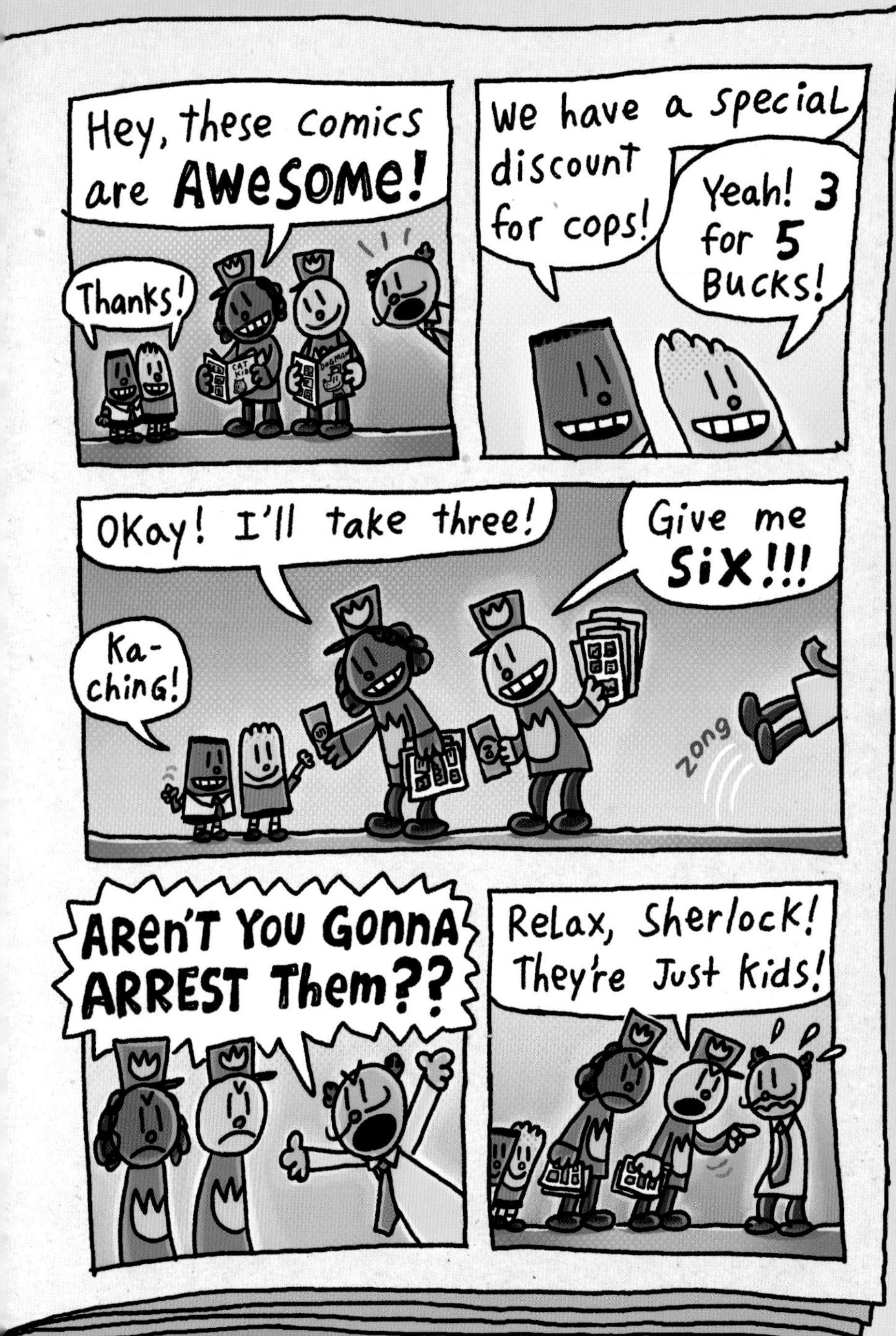
Hey, these comics are AWESOME!
Thanks!
We have a special discount for cops!
Yeah! 3 for 5 Bucks!
OKay! I'll take three!
Give me SIX!!!
Ka-chinG!
ZONG
AREN'T YOU GONNA ARREST Them??
Relax, Sherlock! They're Just Kids!

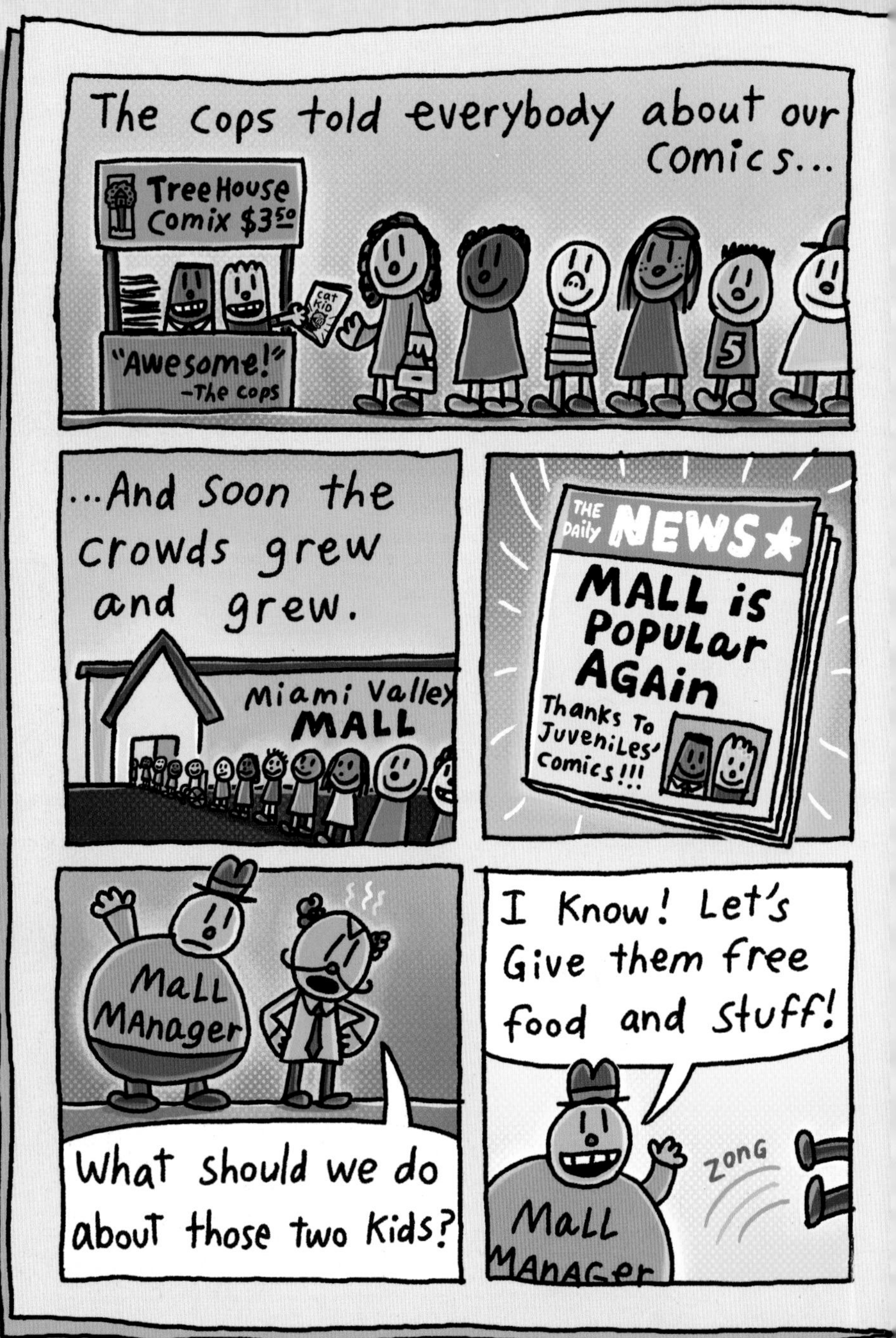
The cops told everybody about our comics...
TreeHouse Comix $3.50
Cat Kid
"Awesome!" –The cops
5
...And soon the crowds grew and grew.
Miami Valley MALL
THE DAILY NEWS
MALL is POPULAR AGAIN
Thanks To Juveniles' Comics!!!
MaLL MAnager
What should we do about those two kids?
I Know! Let's Give them free food and stuff!
ZONG
MaLL MANAGer

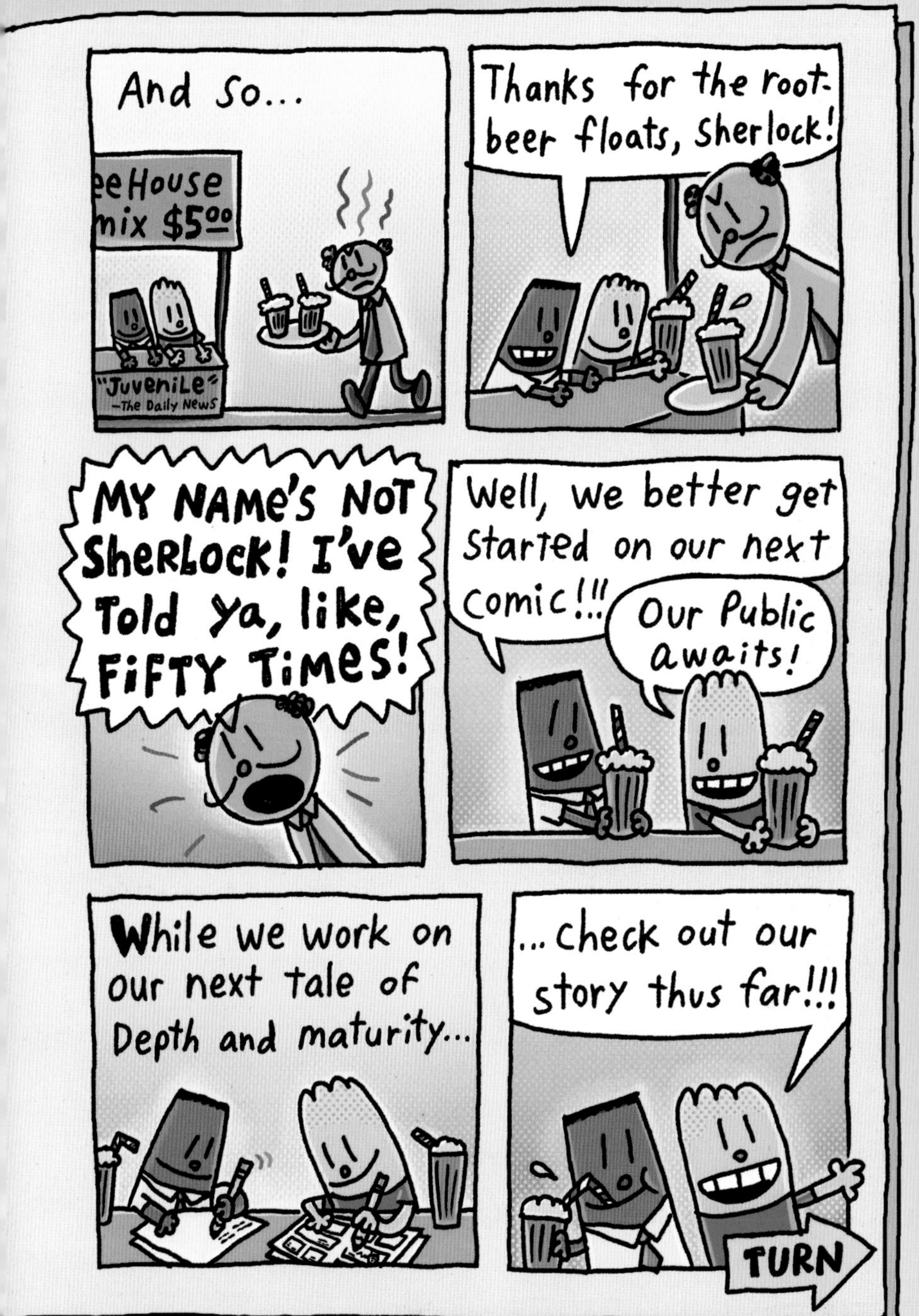

And so...
eeHouse
mix $5.00
"JUVENILE"
—The Daily News
Thanks for the root-beer floats, Sherlock!
MY NAME'S NOT SHERLOCK! I've Told ya, like, FIFTY TIMES!
Well, we better get started on our next comic!!!
Our Public awaits!
While we work on our next tale of depth and maturity...
...check out our story thus far!!!
TURN

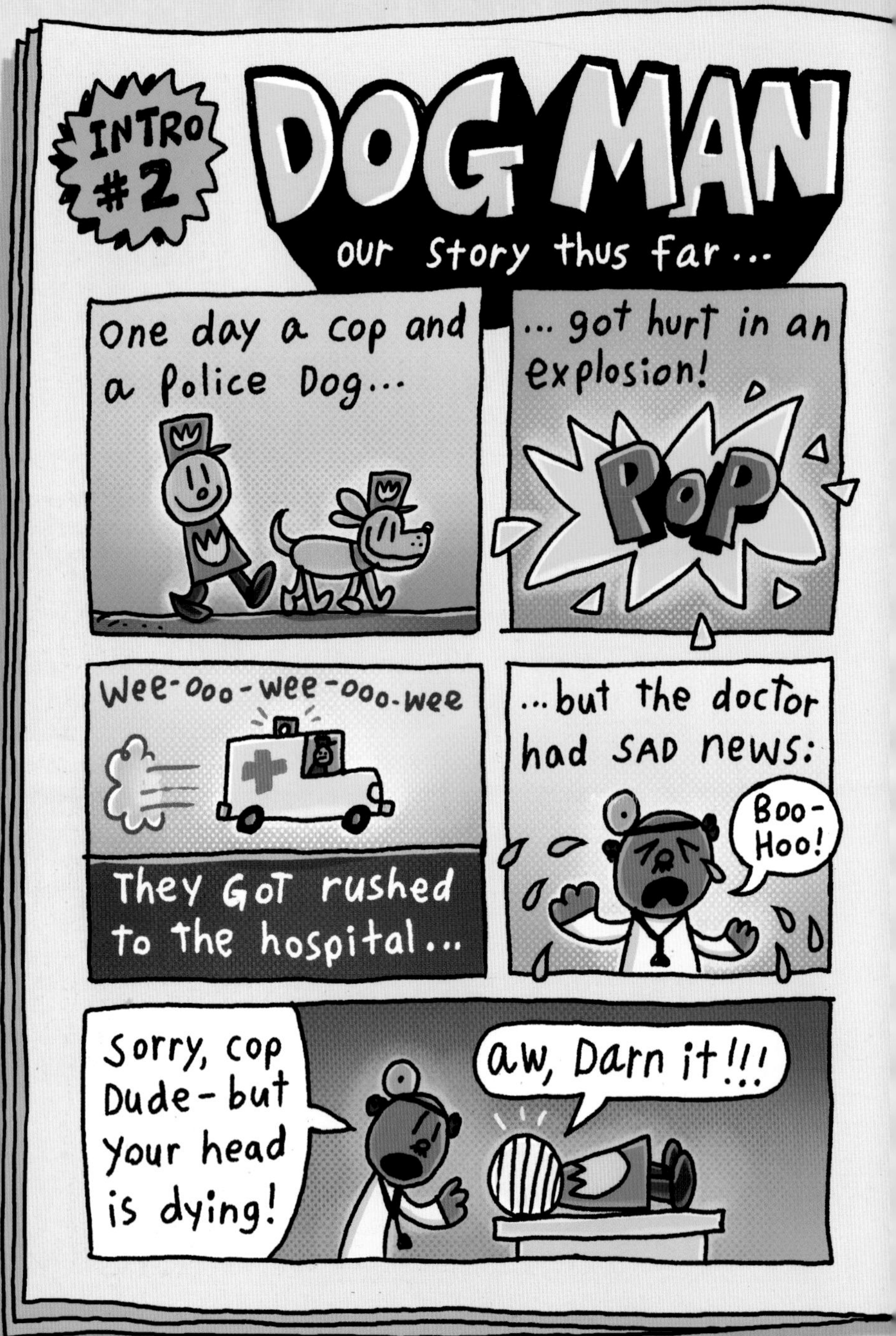
INTRO #2
DOG MAN
our Story thus far...
One day a cop and a Police Dog...
... got hurt in an explosion!
POP
Wee-ooo-wee-ooo-wee
They GOT rushed to the hospital...
...but the doctor had SAD news:
Boo-Hoo!
Sorry, cop Dude-but your head is dying!
aw, Darn it!!!

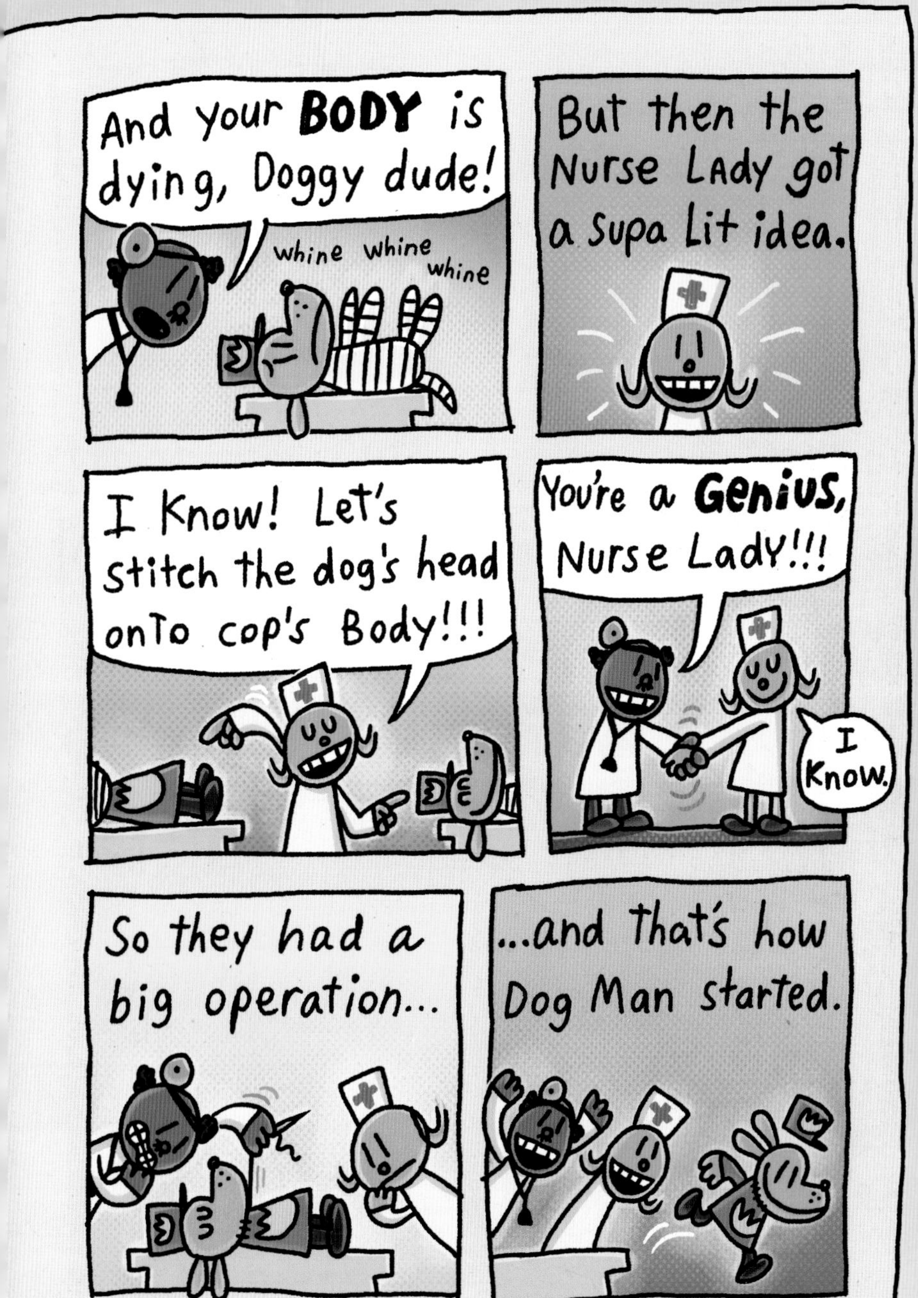

And your BODY is dying, Doggy dude!
whine whine whine
But then the Nurse Lady got a Supa Lit idea.
I Know! Let's stitch the dog's head onTo cop's Body!!!
You're a GENIUS, Nurse Lady!!!
I Know.
So they had a big operation...
...and that's how Dog Man started.

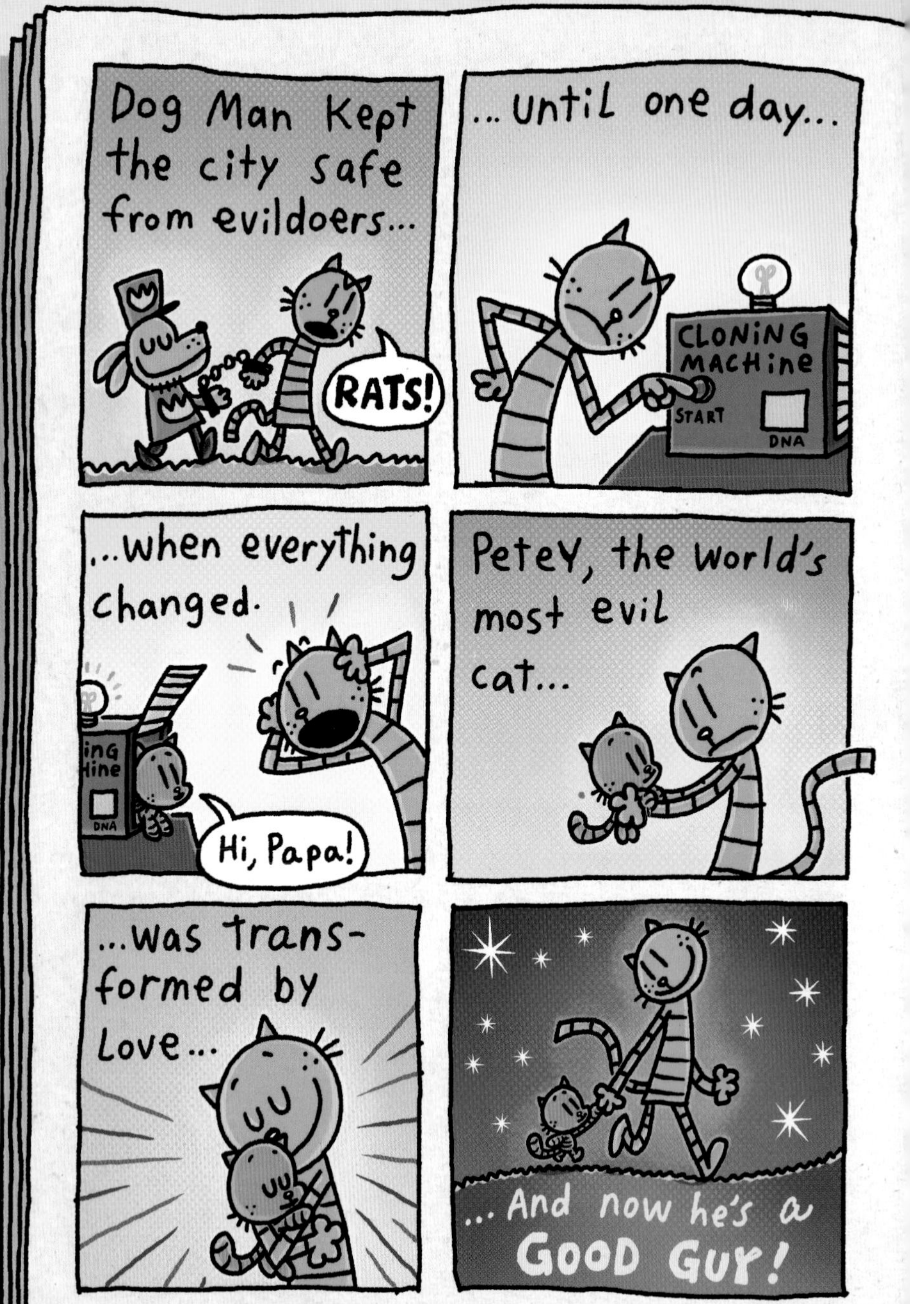
Dog Man kept the city safe from evildoers...
RATS!
...until one day...
CLONING MACHINE
START
DNA
...when everything changed.
Hi, Papa!
DNA
Petey, the world's most evil cat...
...was trans-formed by Love...
...And now he's a GOOD GUY!

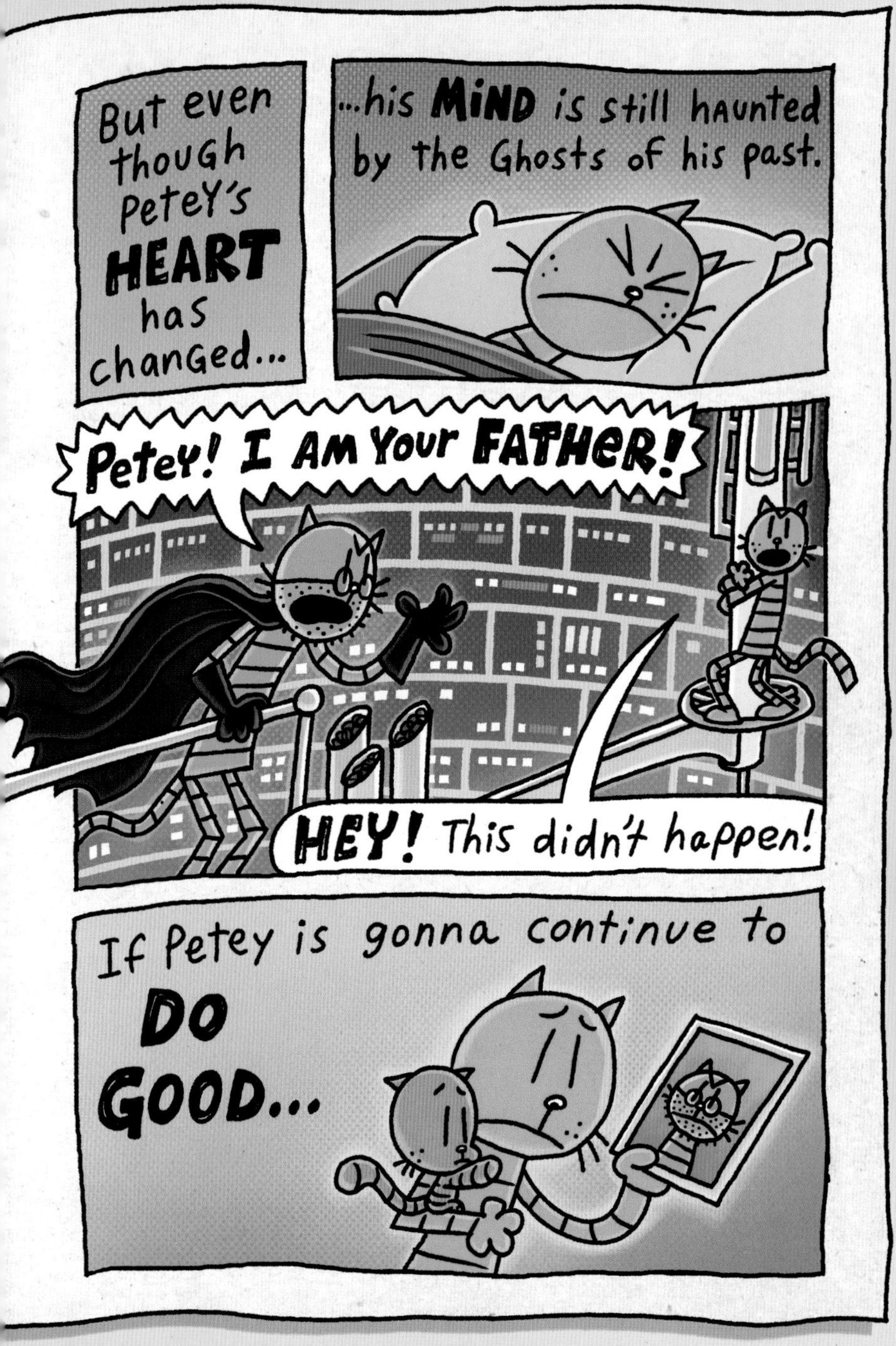
But even though Petey's HEART has changed...
...his MIND is still haunted by the Ghosts of his past.
Petey! I AM YOUR FATHER!
HEY! This didn't happen!
If Petey is gonna continue to DO GOOD...

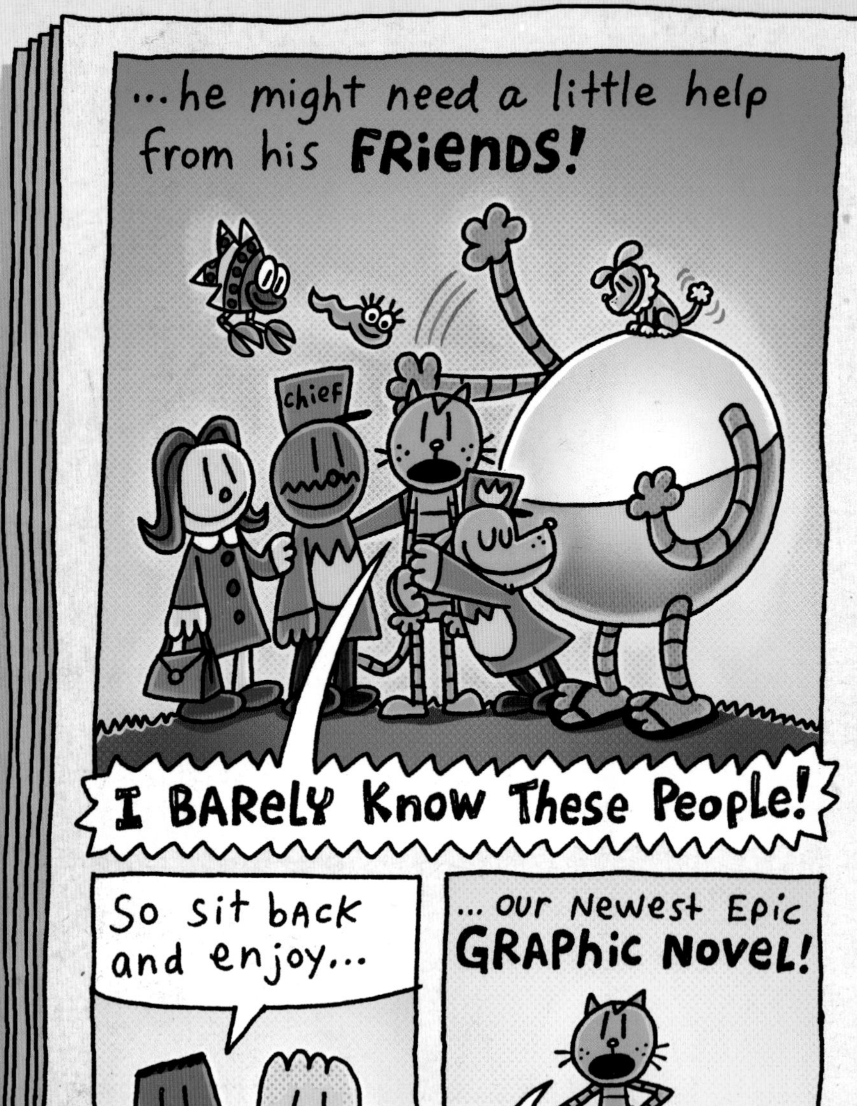
...he might need a little help from his FRIENDS!
chief
I BARELY Know These People!
So sit back and enjoy...
... our Newest Epic GRAPHIC NOVEL!
IT'S ONLY A COMIC BOOK!

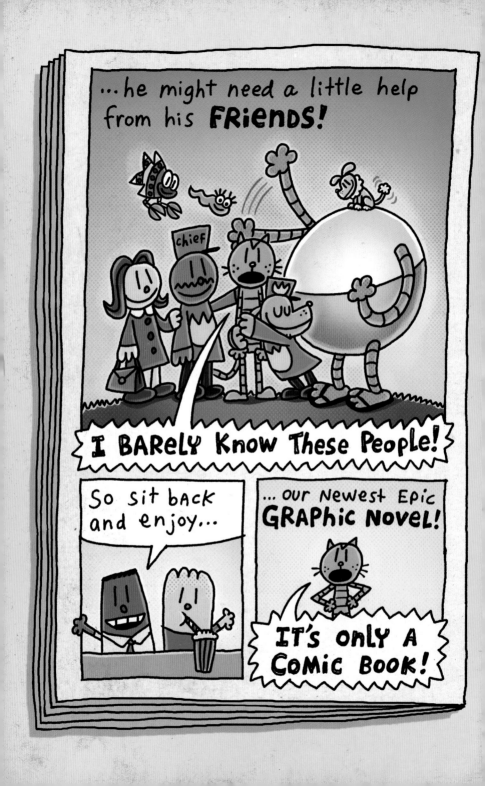

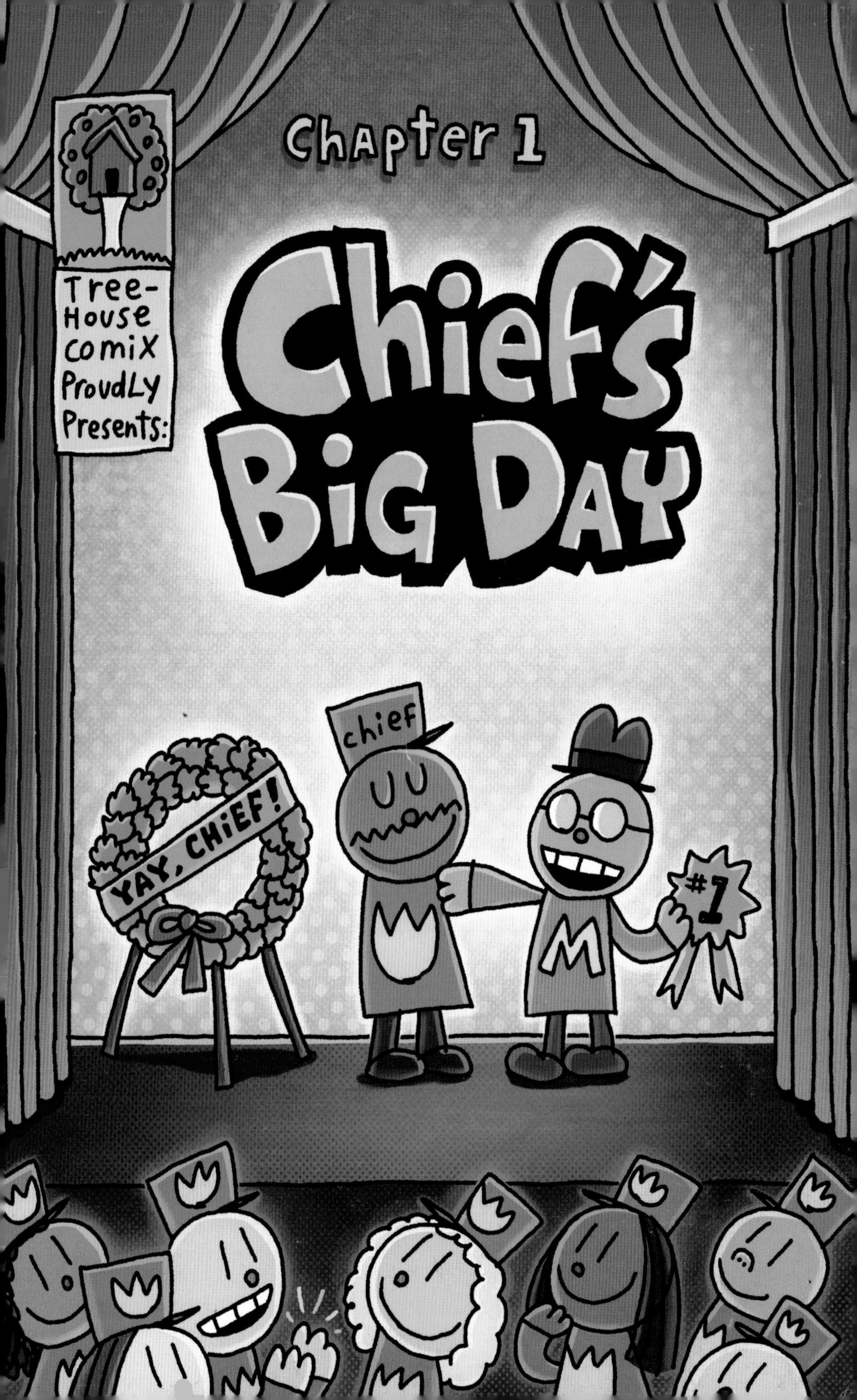
Tree-House comix Proudly Presents:
Chapter 1
Chief's Big Day
chief
YAY, CHIEF!
#1

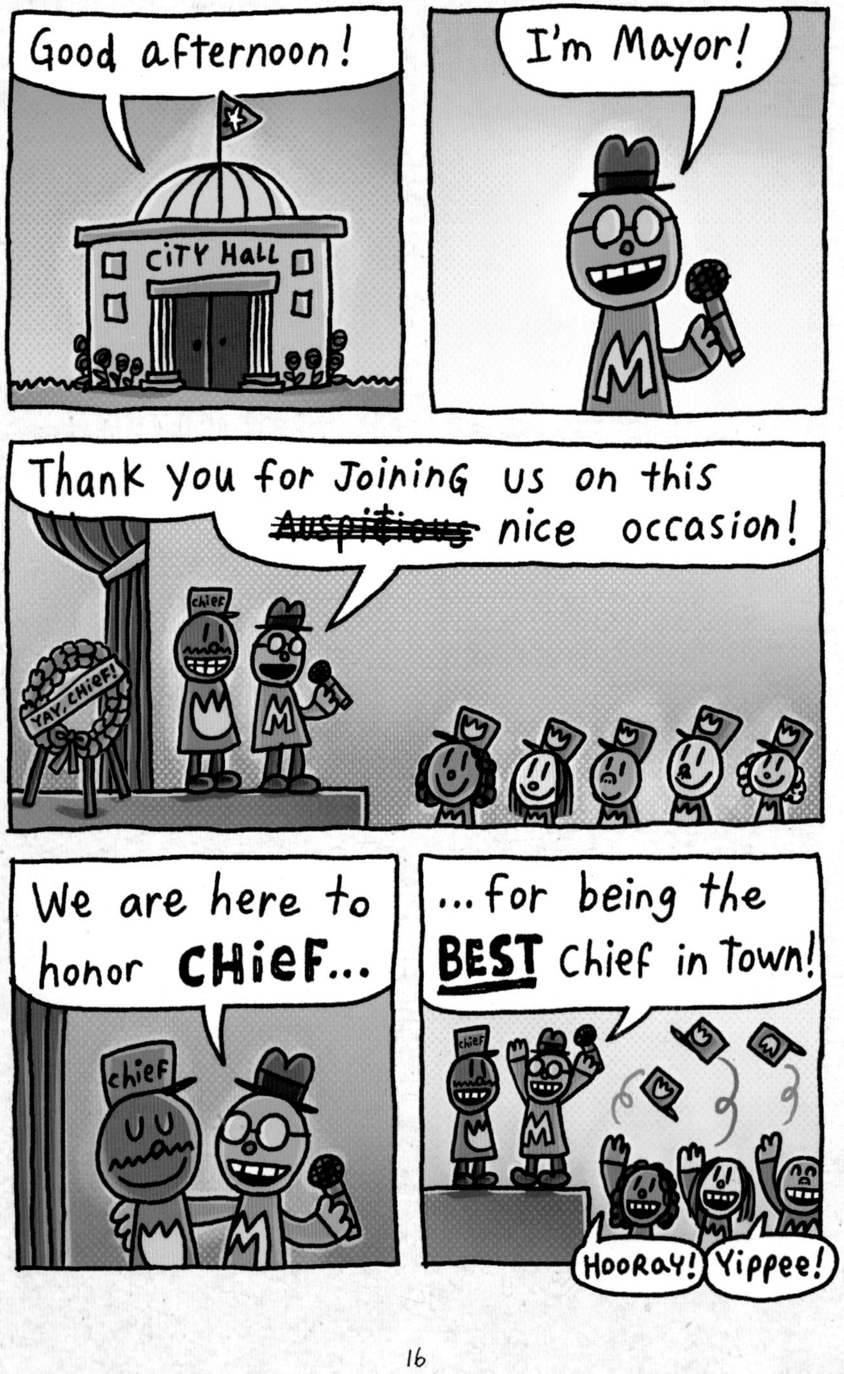
Good afternoon!
CITY HALL
I'm Mayor!
Thank you for Joining us on this ~~Auspicious~~ nice occasion!
chief
YAY, CHIEF!
We are here to honor CHIEF...
chief
...for being the BEST Chief in town!
chief
HOORAY!
Yippee!

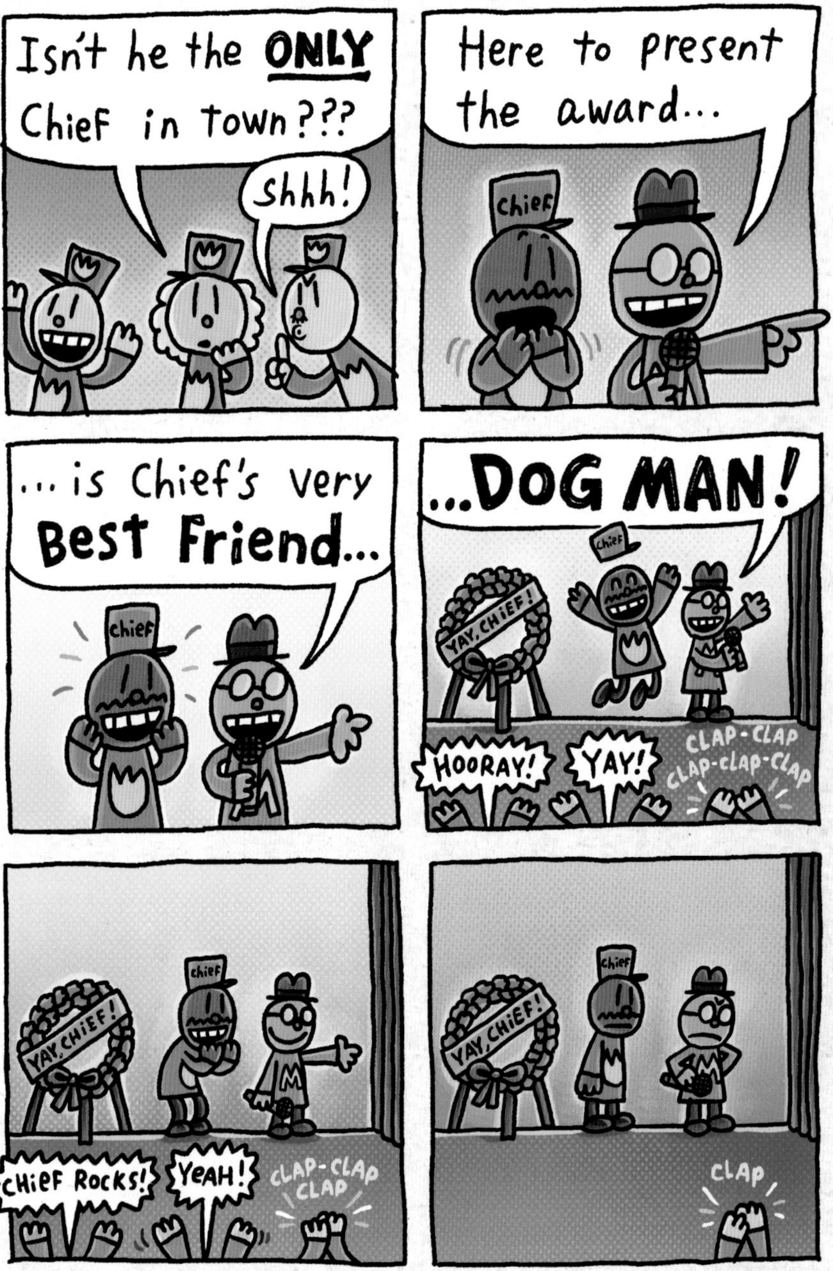

Isn't he the ONLY Chief in town???
Shhh!
Here to present the award...
chief
... is Chief's very Best Friend...
chief
...DOG MAN!
chief
YAY, CHIEF!
HOORAY!
YAY!
CLAP-CLAP CLAP-CLAP-CLAP
chief
YAY, CHIEF!
CHIEF ROCKS!
YEAH!
CLAP-CLAP CLAP
chief
YAY, CHIEF!
CLAP

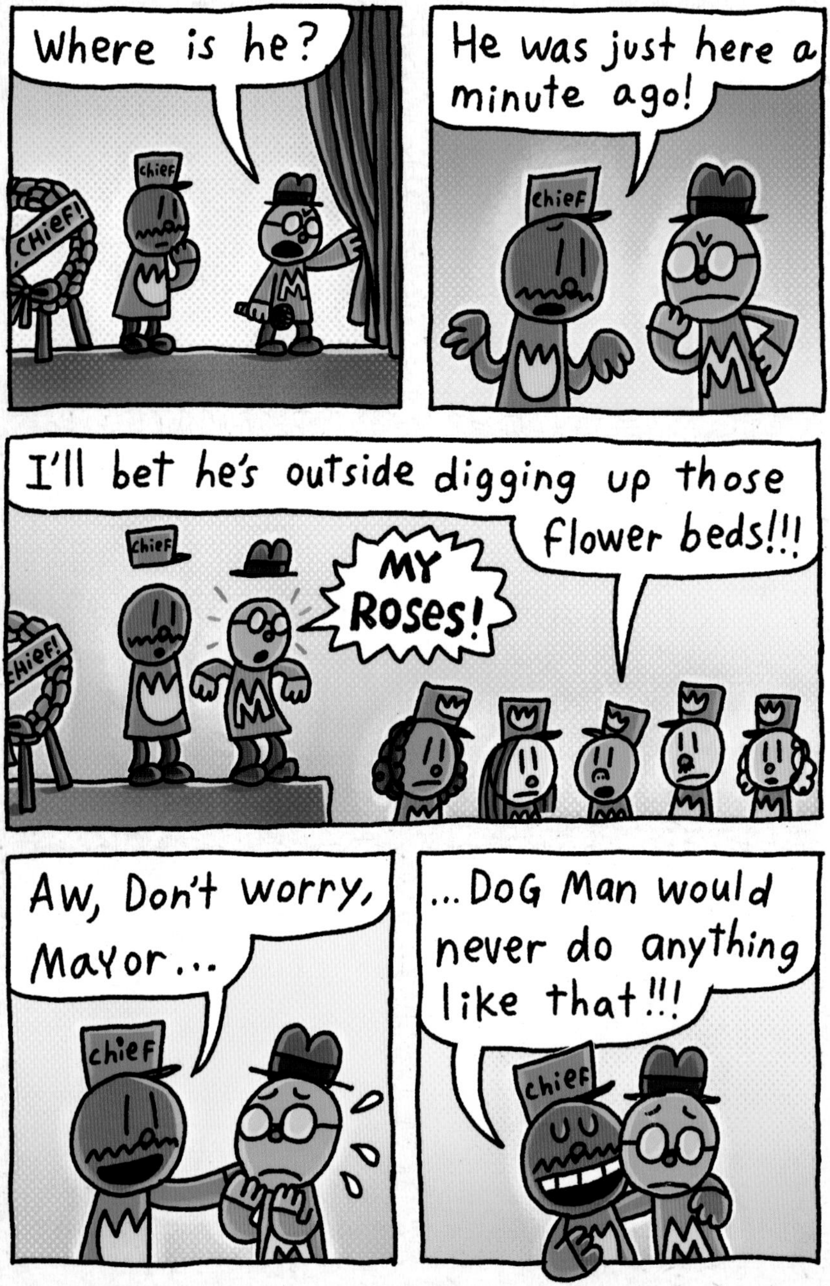
Where is he?
CHIEF!
chief
He was just here a minute ago!
chief
I'll bet he's outside digging up those flower beds!!!
chief
CHIEF!
MY ROSES!
Aw, Don't worry, Mayor...
chief
...DOG Man would never do anything like that!!!
chief

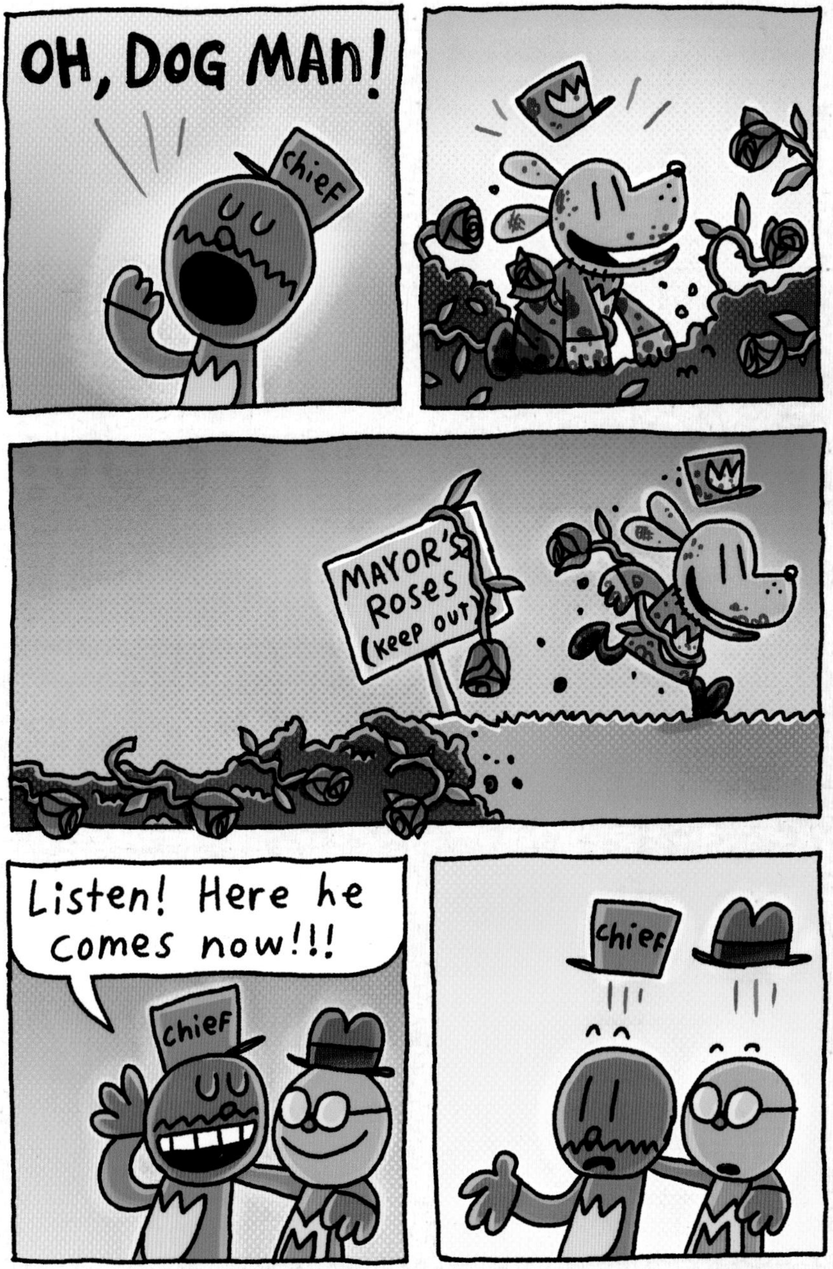
OH, DOG MAN!
chief
MAYOR'S Roses (keep out)
Listen! Here he comes now!!!
chief
chief

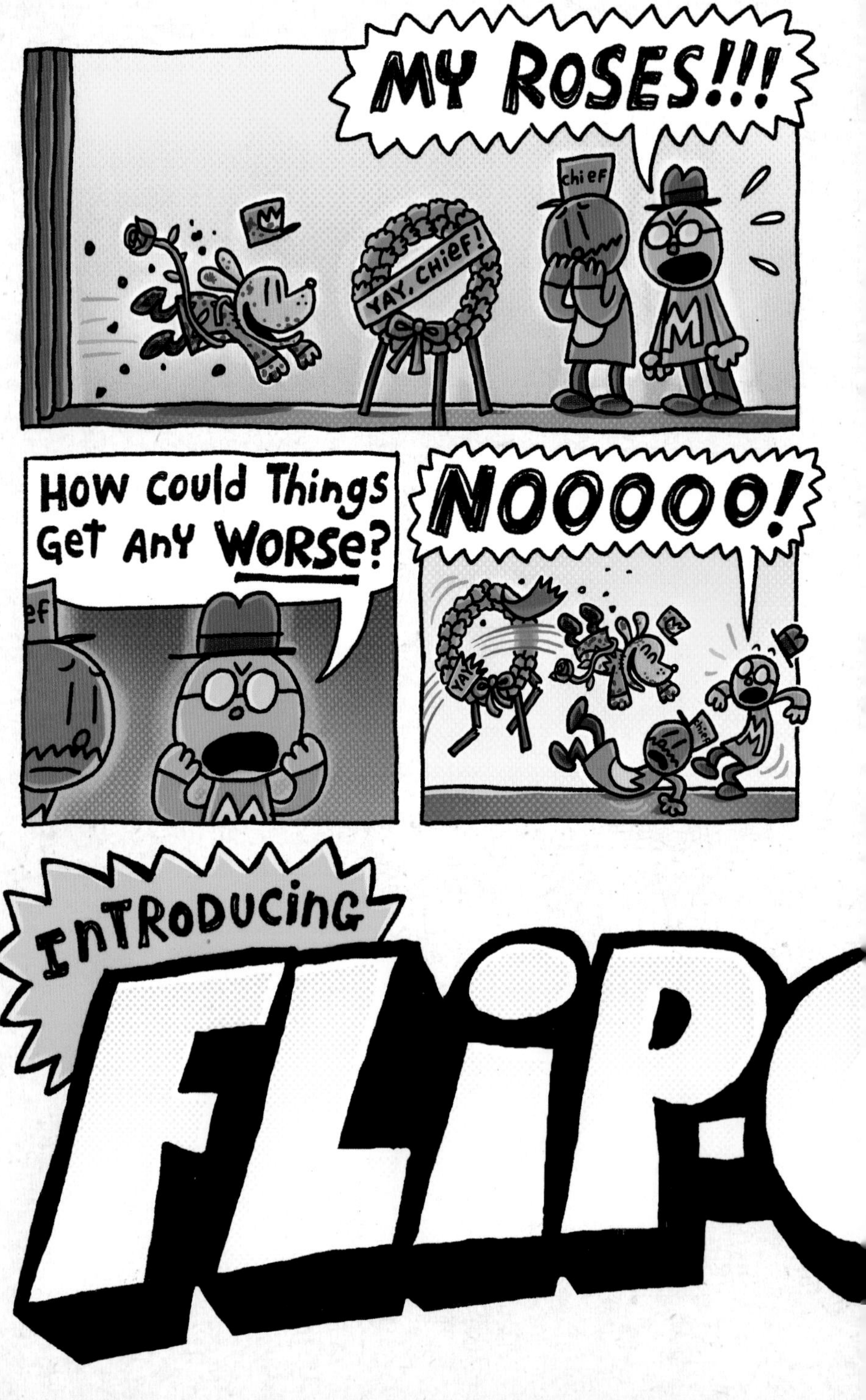
MY ROSES!!!
chief
YAY, CHIEF!
How Could Things Get Any WORSE?
NOOOOO!
YAY
Introducing
FLIP

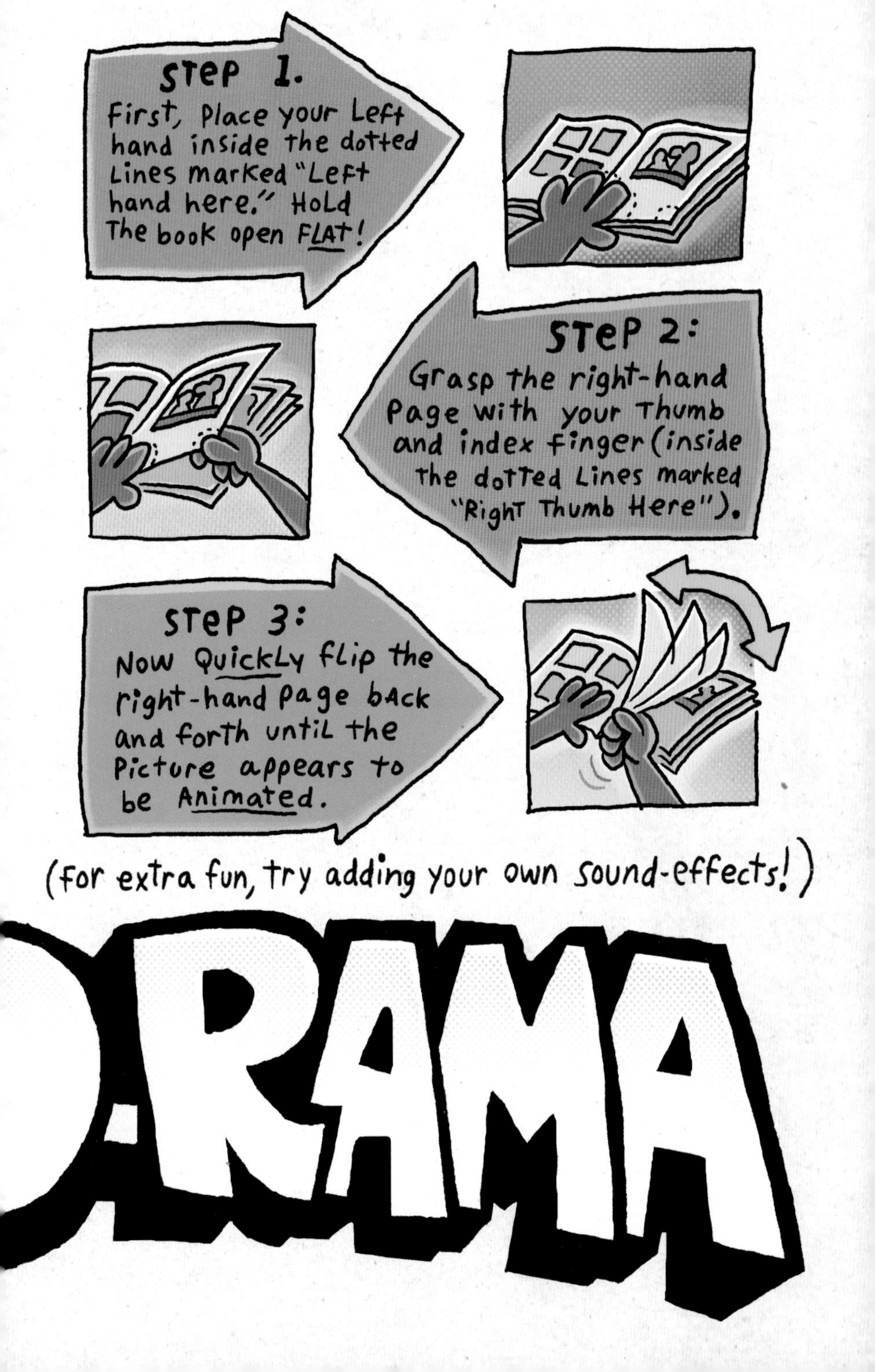
STEP 1.
First, Place your Left hand inside the dotted Lines marked "Left hand here." HoLd The book open FLAT!
STEP 2:
Grasp the right-hand Page with your Thumb and index finger (inside the dotted Lines marked "Right Thumb Here").
STEP 3:
Now QUICKLY flip the right-hand page back and forth until the Picture appears to be Animated.
(for extra fun, try adding your own sound-effects!)
RAMA

REMEMBER,

While you are flipping,
be sure you can see
the image on page **23**
AND the image on page **25**.

If you flip quickly,
the two pictures will
start to look like **ONE**
ANIMATED cartoon.

Don't forget to
add your own
sound-effects!!!

Left
hand here.

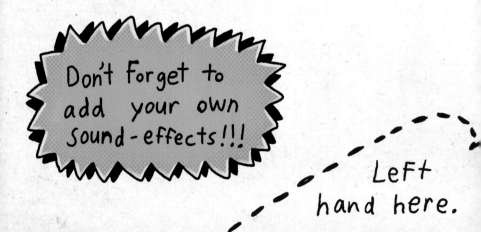

Don't forget to
add your own
sound-effects!!!

Left
hand here.

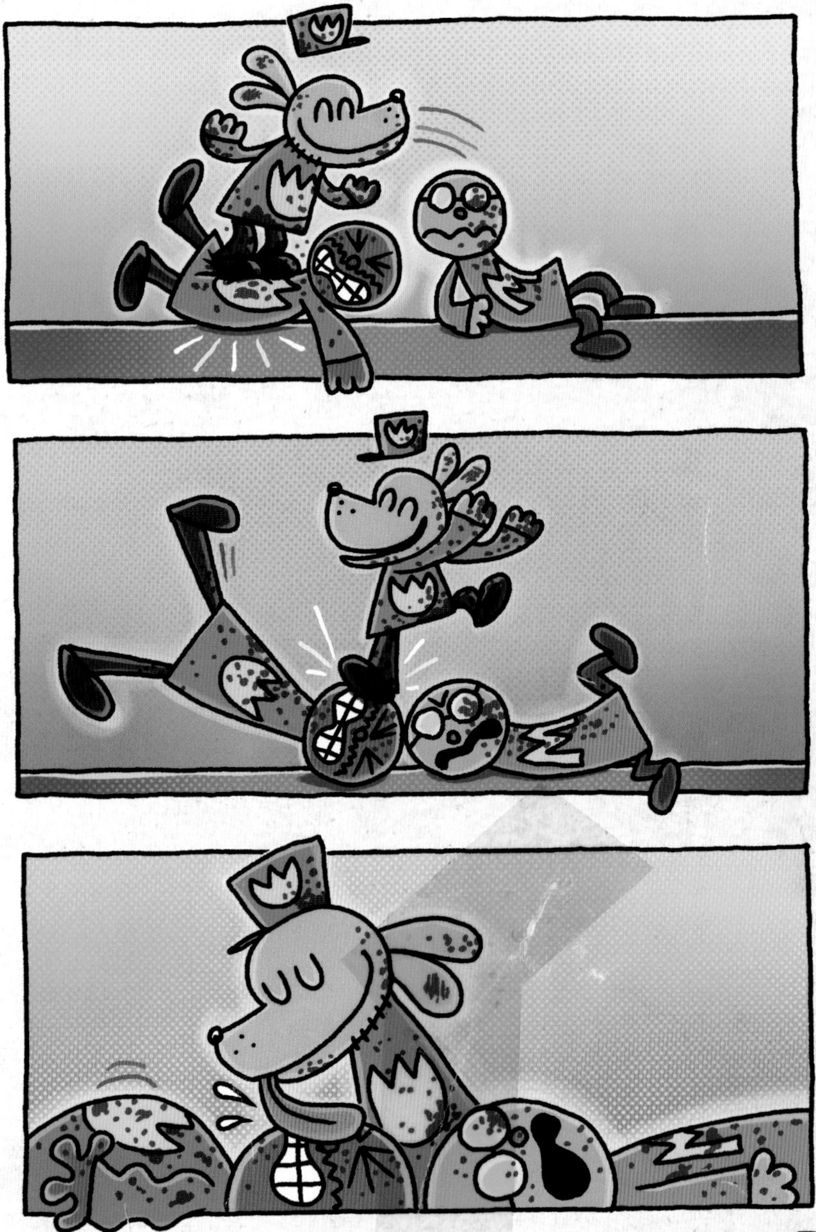

Right Thumb here.

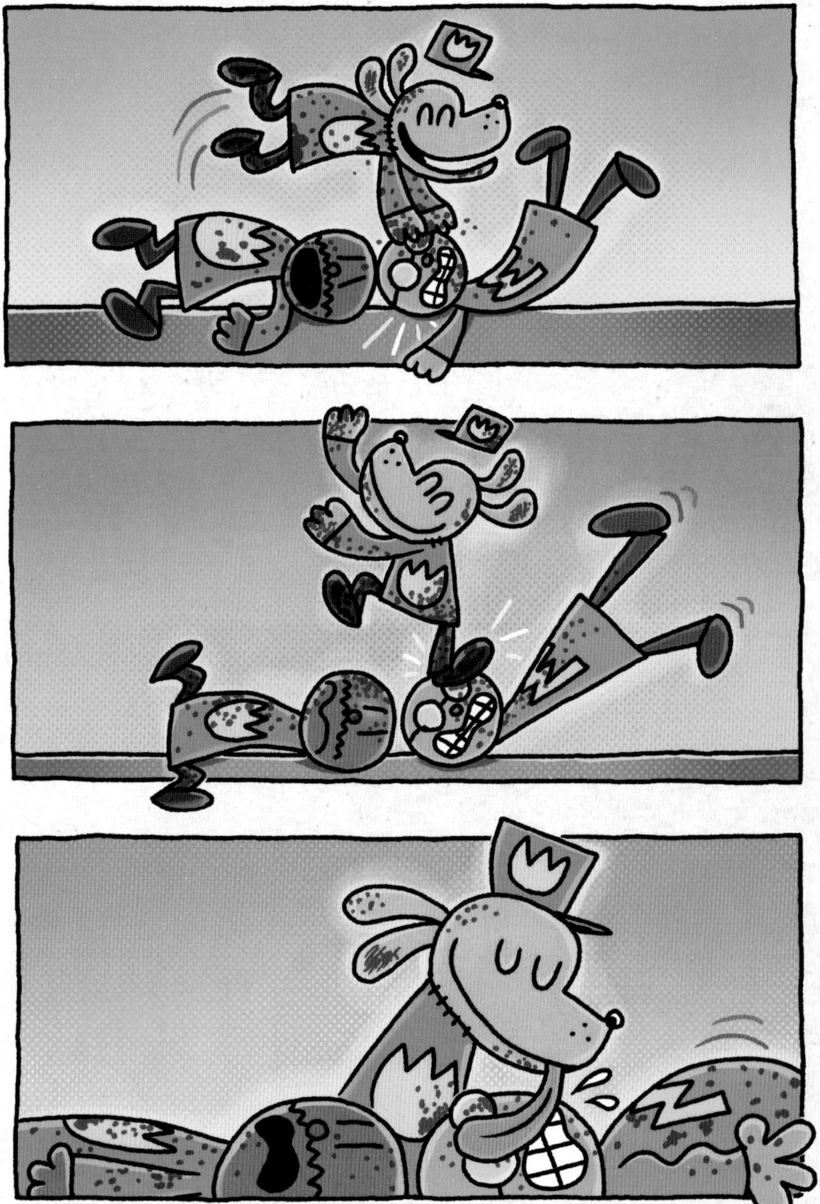

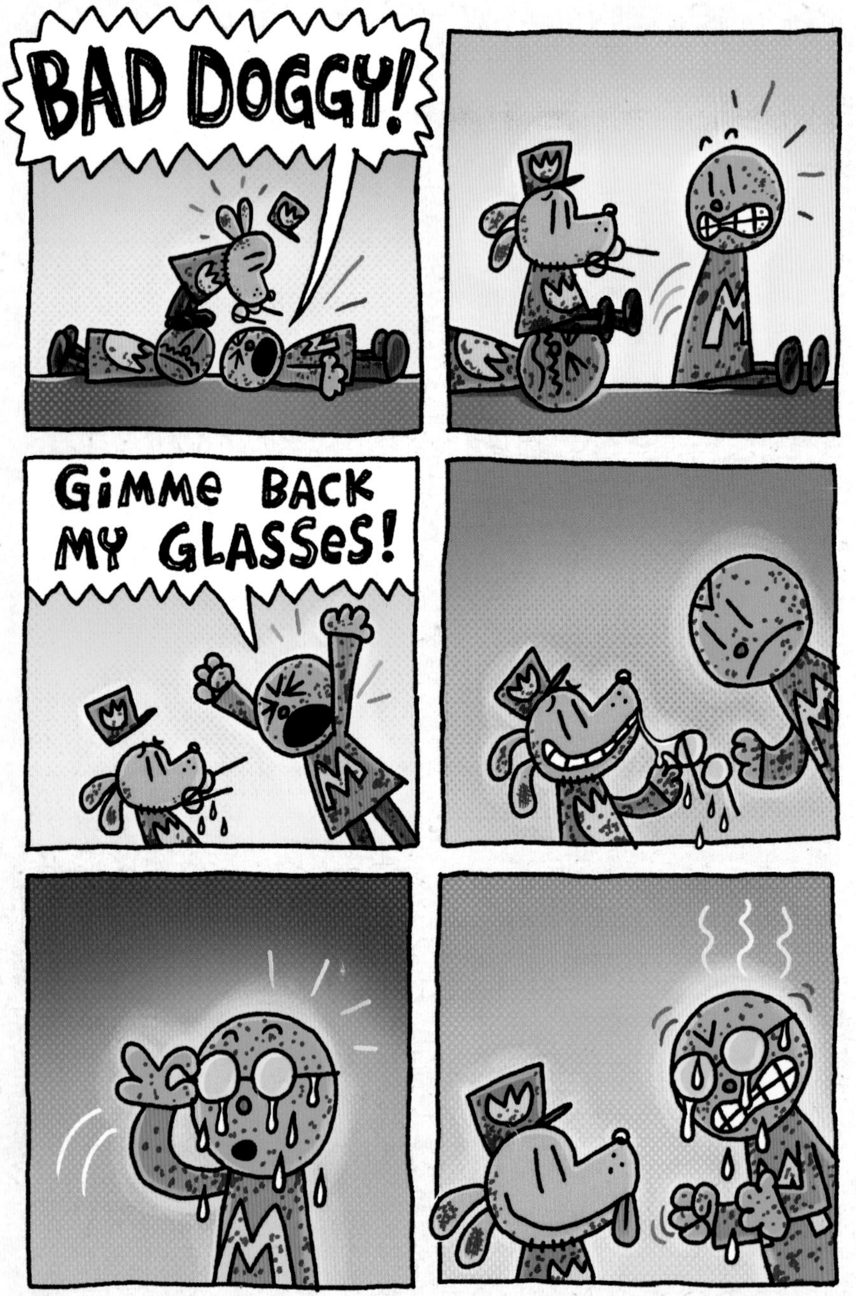

BAD DOGGY!
GIMME BACK MY GLASSES!

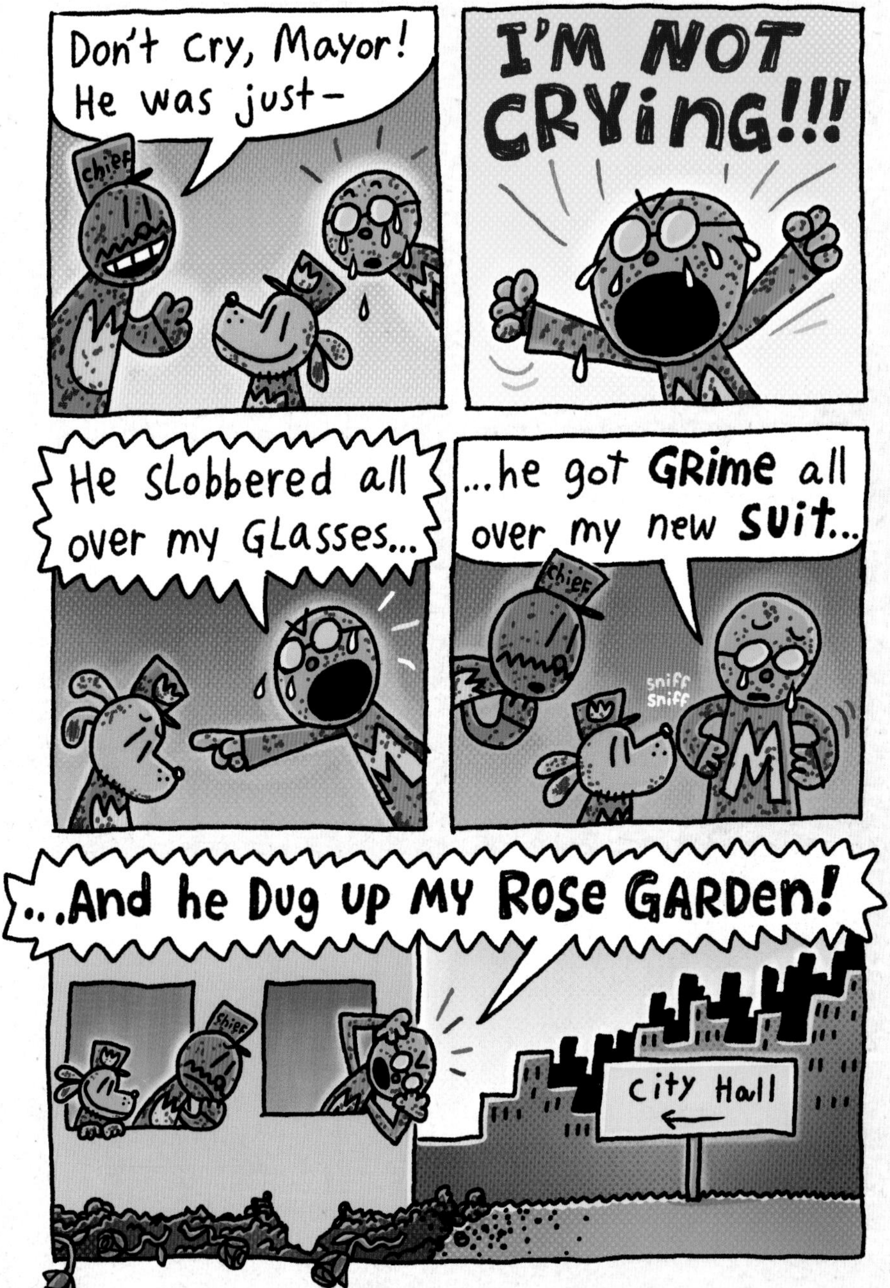
Don't cry, Mayor! He was just—
I'M NOT CRYinG!!!
He sLobbered all over my GLasses...
...he got GRime all over my new SUiT...
chief
sniff sniff
...And he Dug up MY Rose GARDen!
chief
city Hall

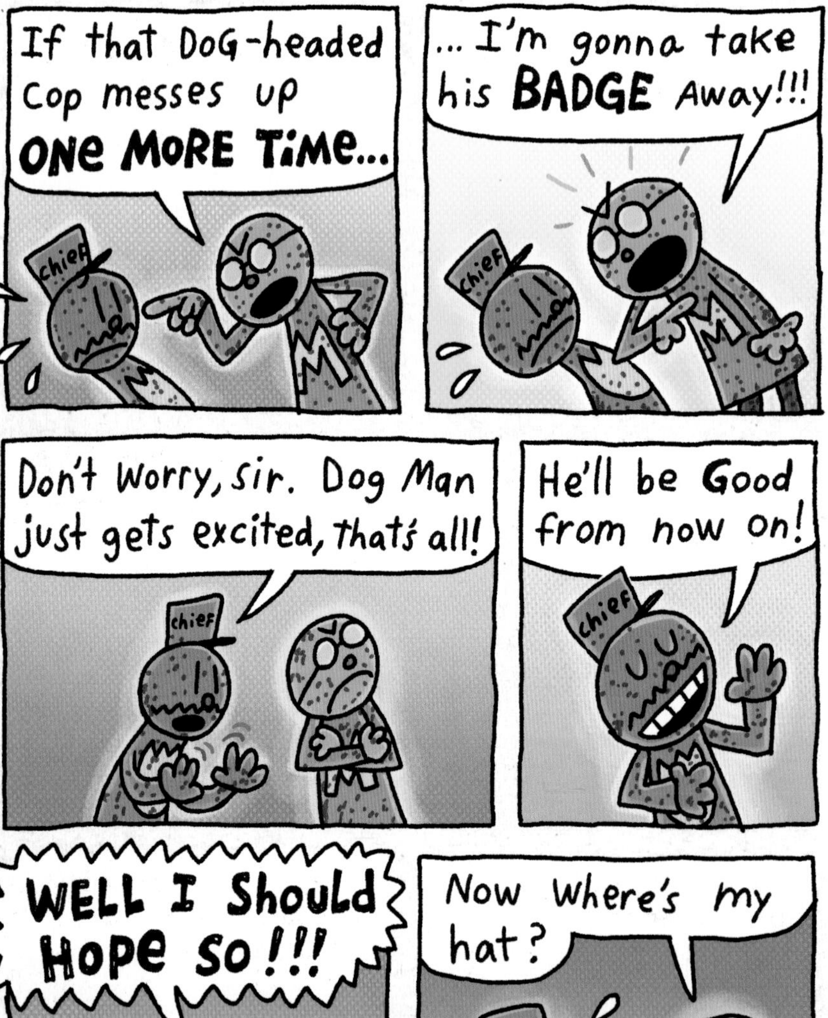
If that DoG-headed Cop messes up ONE MORE TiMe...
... I'm gonna take his BADGE Away!!!
chief
Don't worry, sir. Dog Man just gets excited, that's all!
He'll be Good from now on!
WELL I Should HOPe so!!!
Now where's my hat?

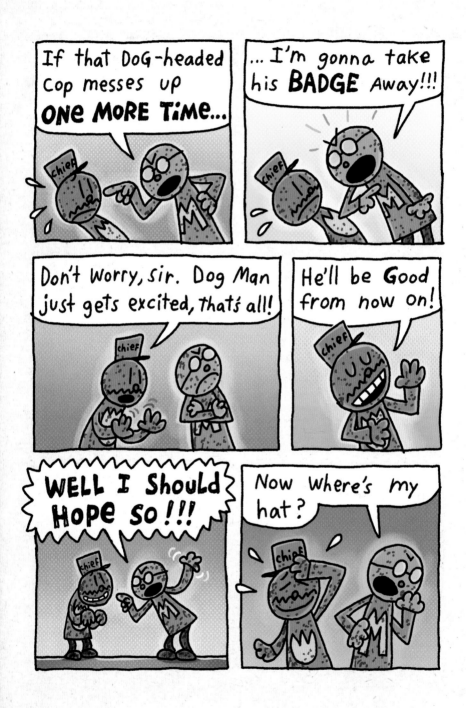

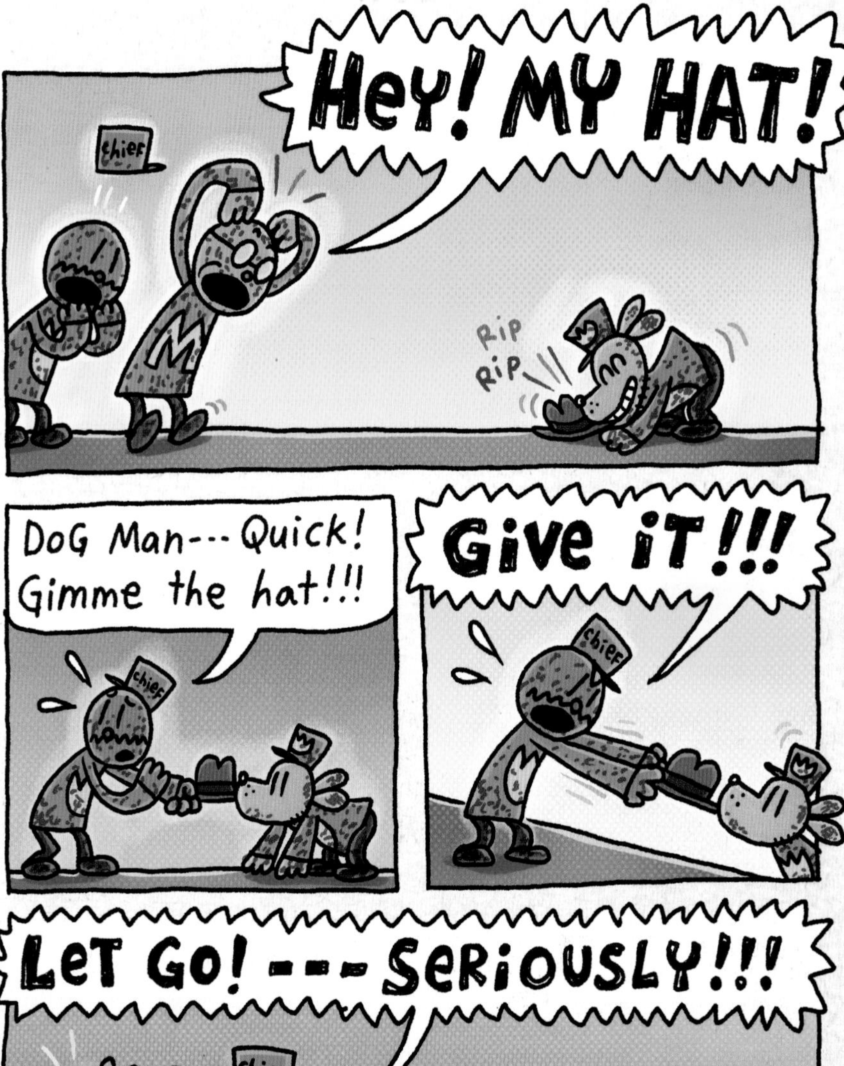
Hey! MY HAT!
chief
Rip
Rip
DoG Man--- Quick! Gimme the hat!!!
chief
Give iT!!!
chief
Let Go! --- Seriously!!!
chief

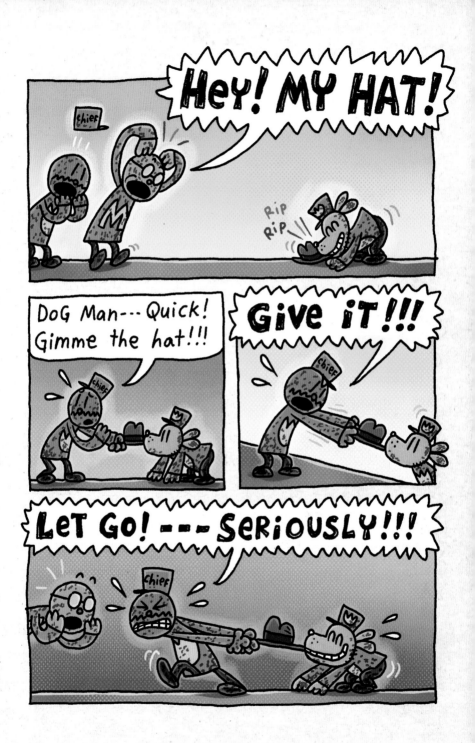

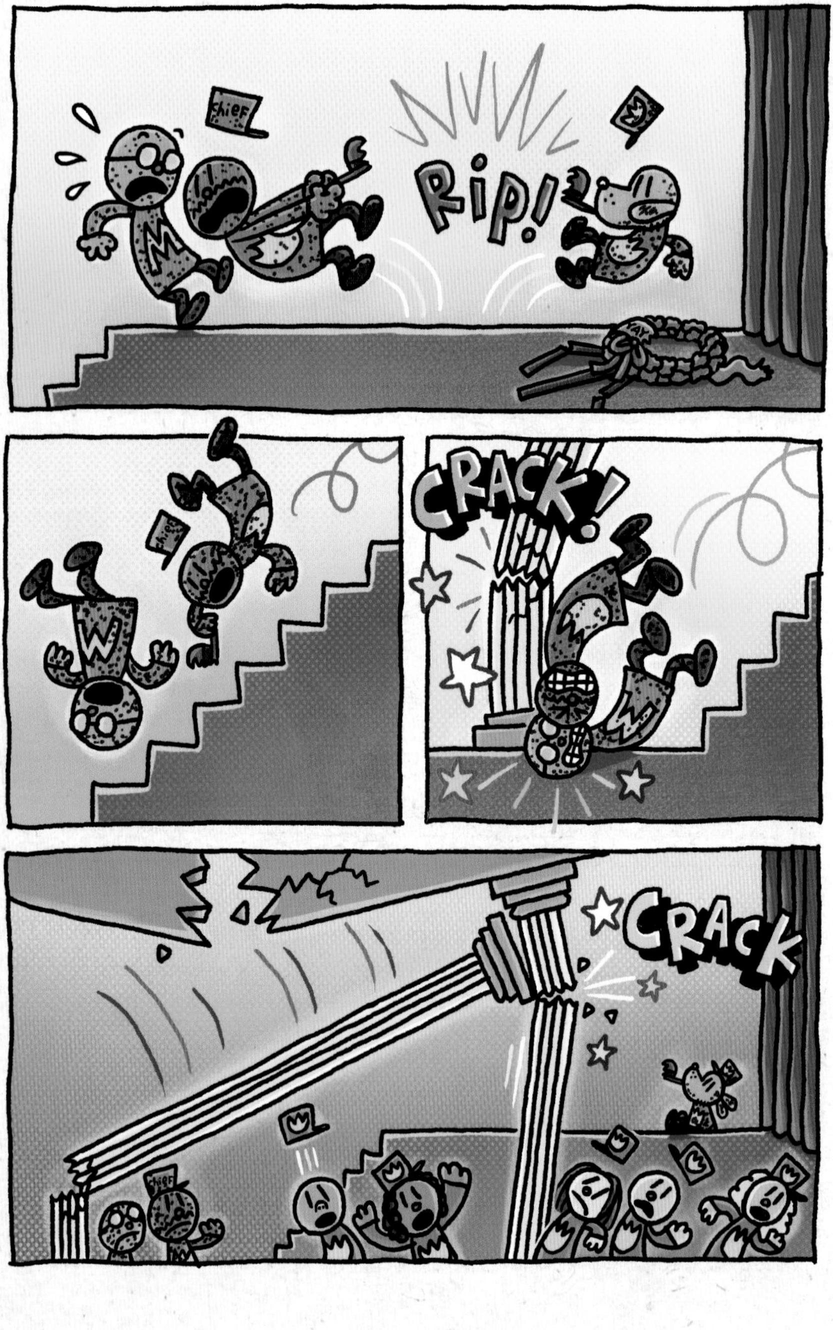
CHIEF
RIP!
CRACK!
CRACK
CHIEF

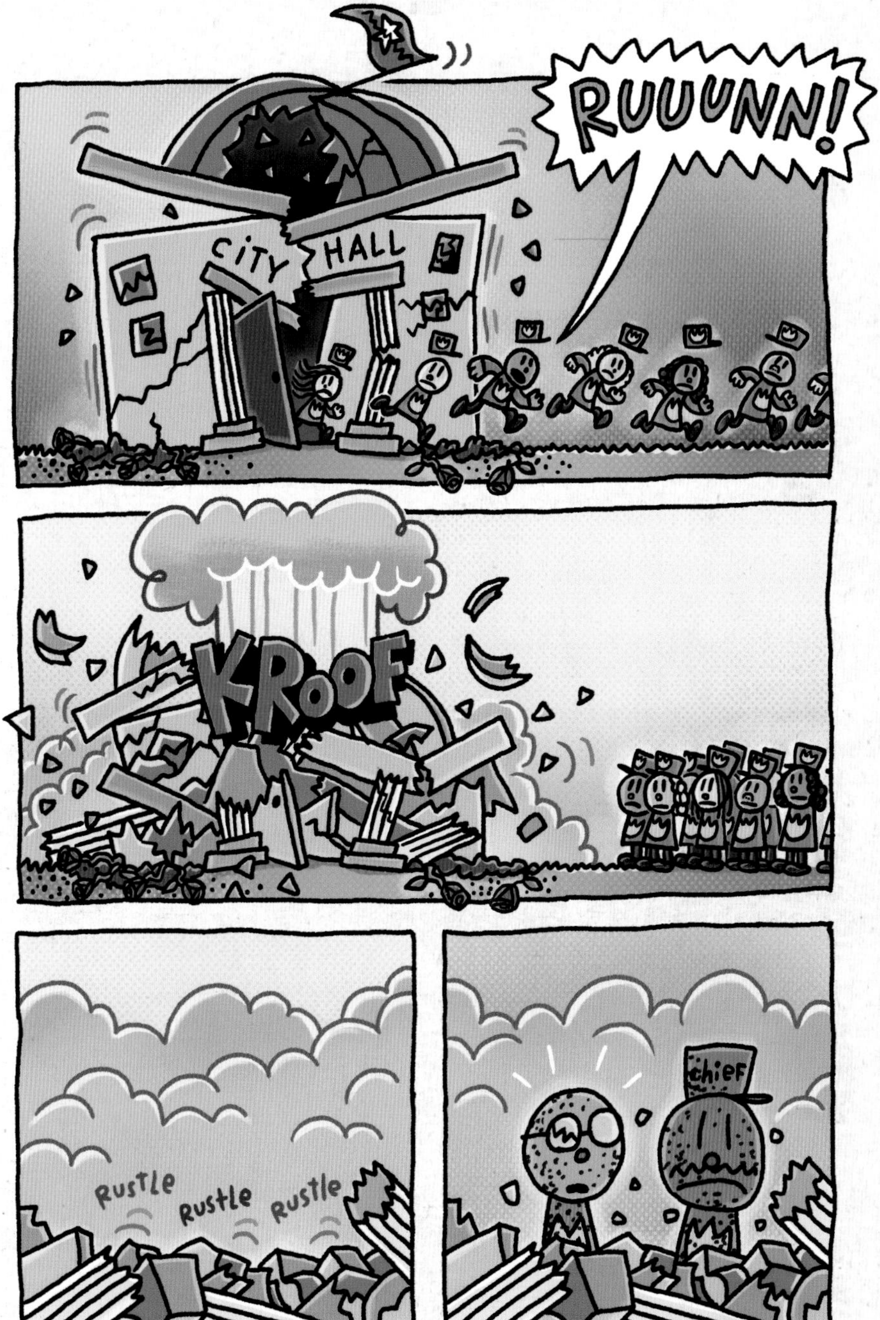
RUUUNN!
CITY HALL
KROOF
RUSTLE
RUSTLE
RUSTLE
CHIEF

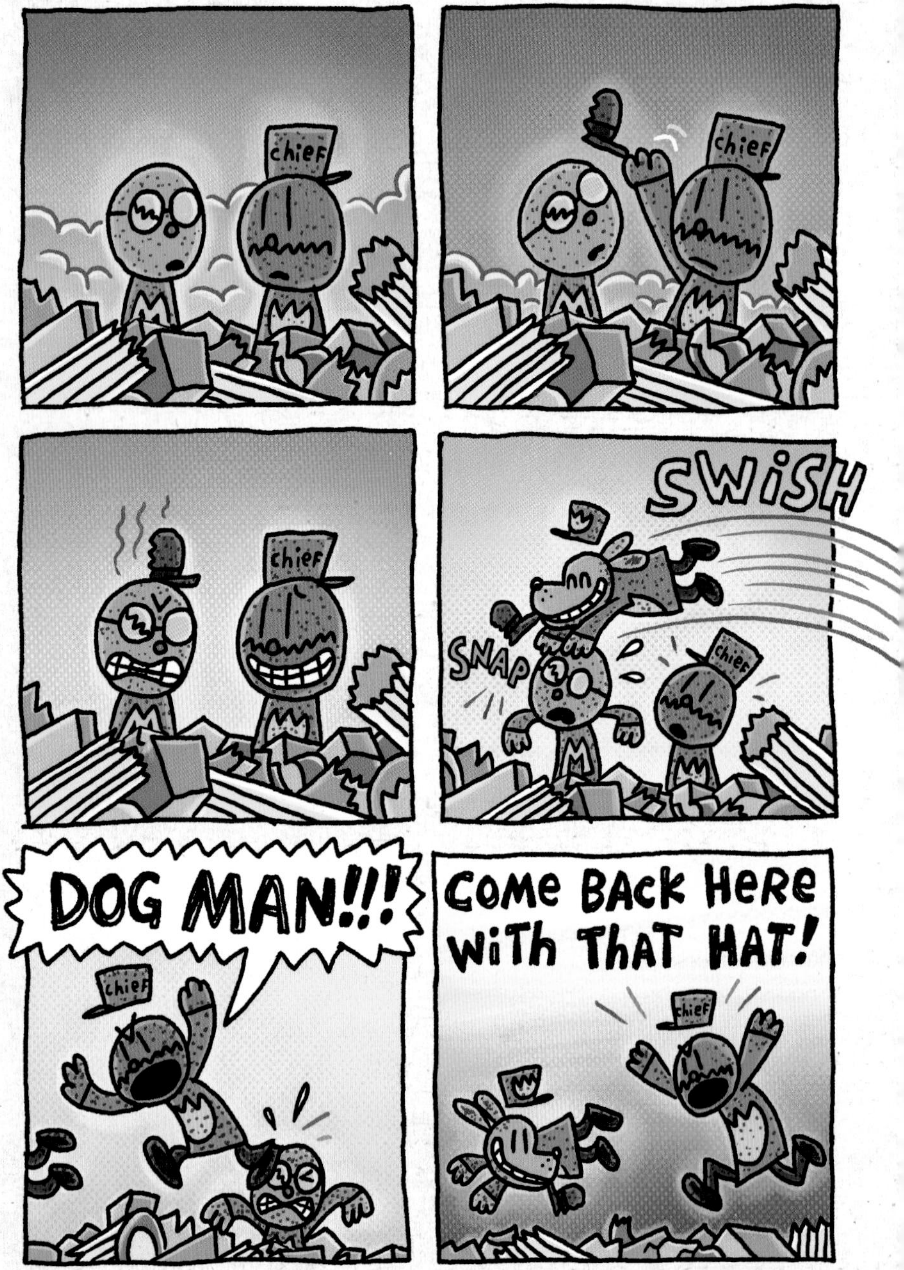
chief
chief
chief
SWISH
SNAP
chief
DOG MAN!!!
chief
COME BACK HERE WITH THAT HAT!
chief

CHAPTER 2

The Saddest CHAPTER Ever Written

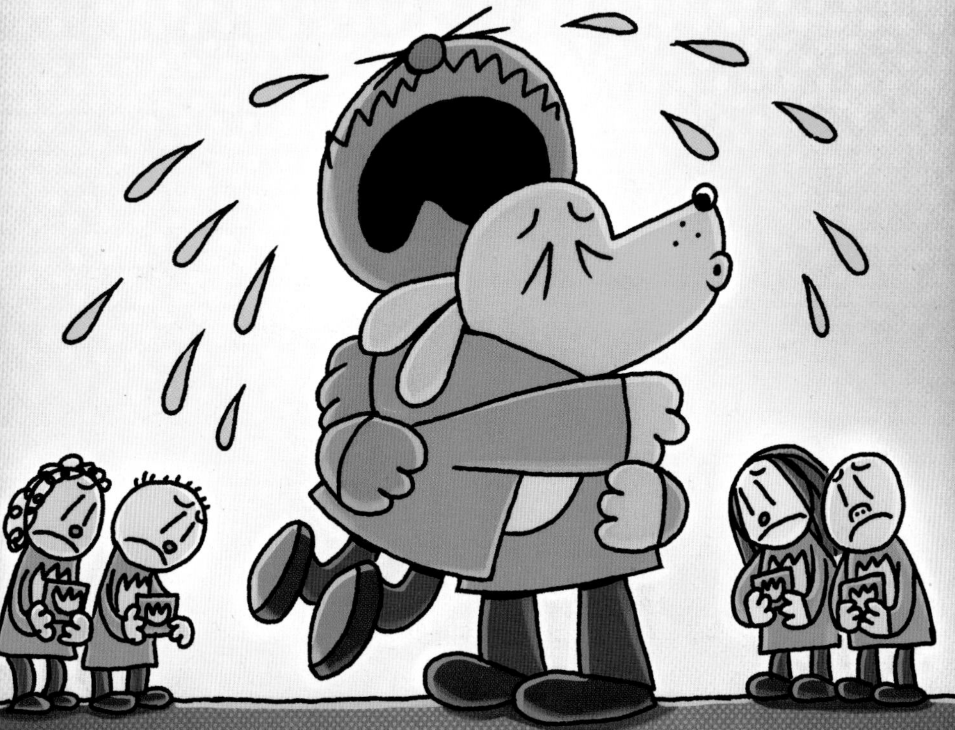

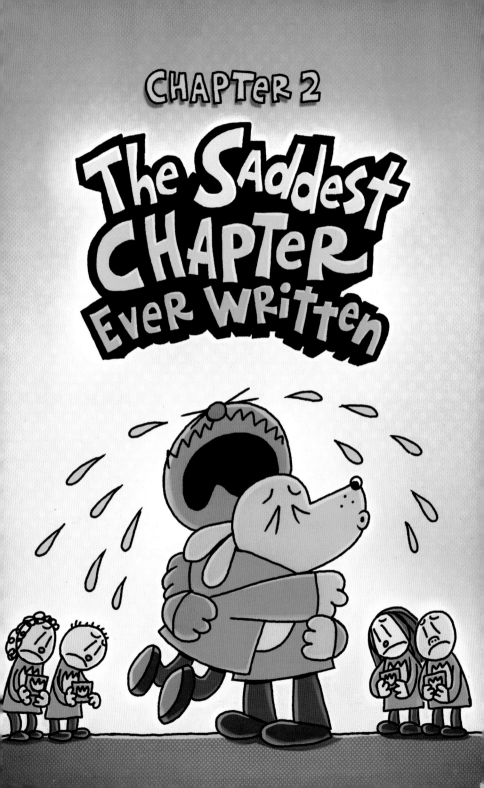

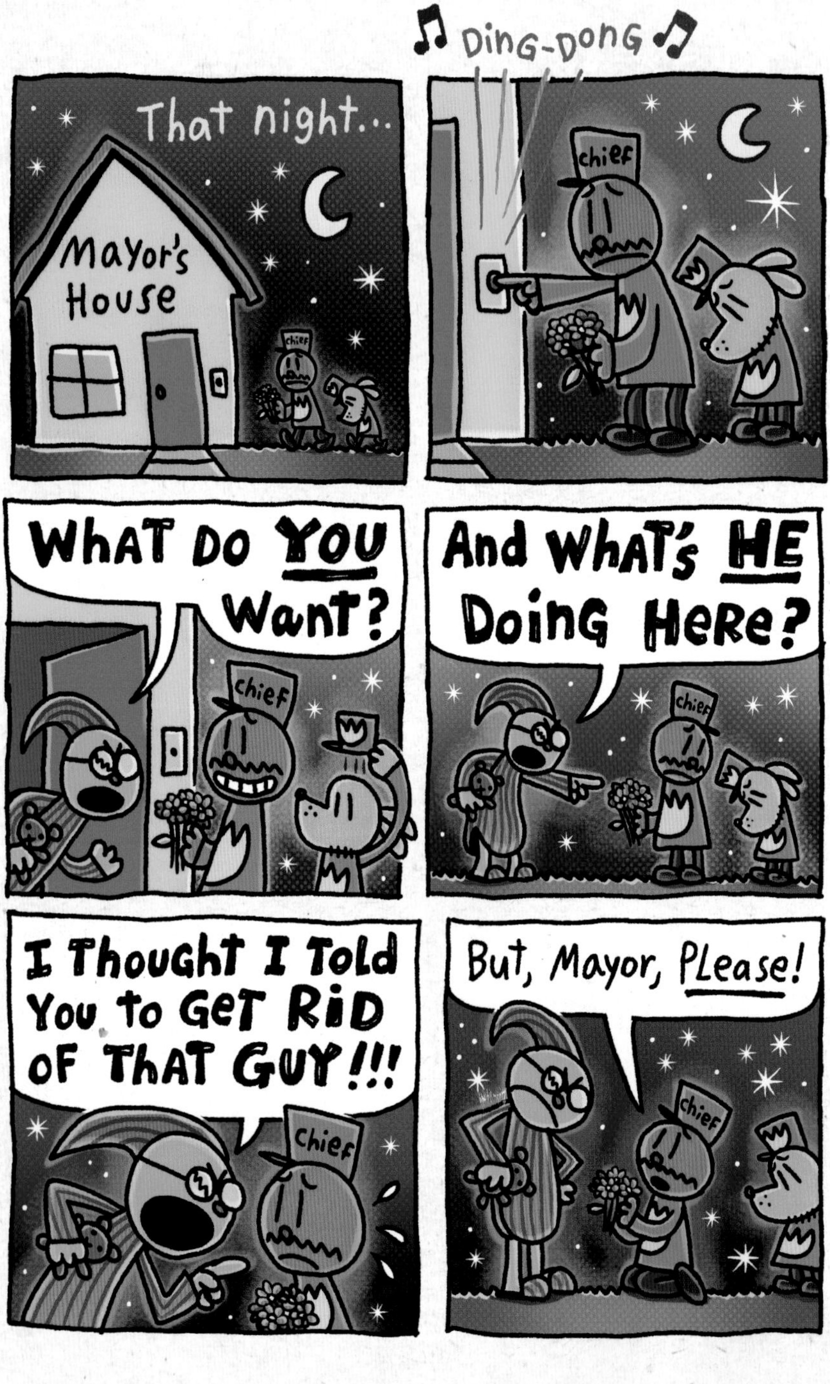
♫ DING-DONG ♫
That night...
Mayor's House
chief
WHAT DO YOU Want?
And WHAT's HE Doing Here?
I Thought I Told You to GET RID OF THAT GUY!!!
But, Mayor, PLease!

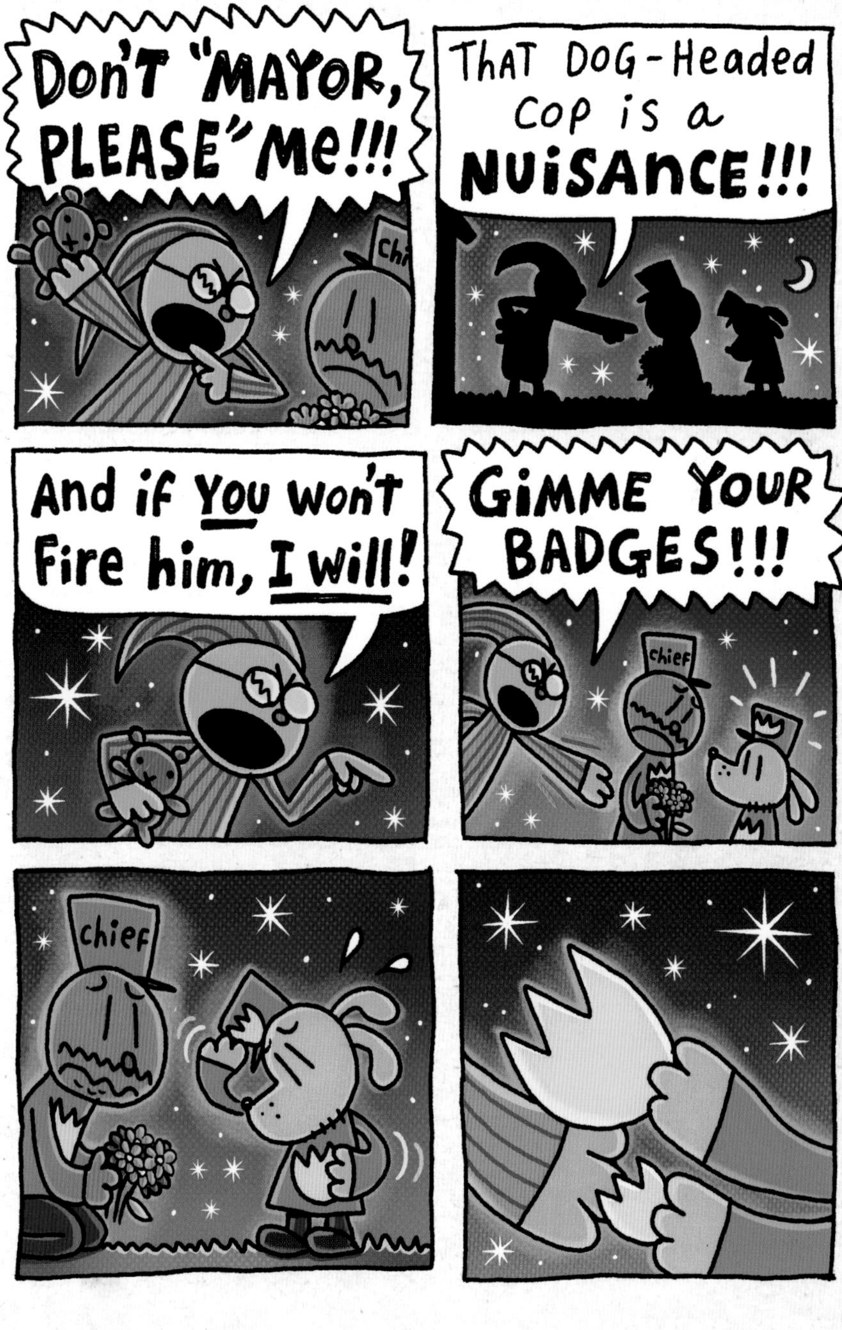
DON'T "MAYOR, PLEASE" ME!!!
THAT DOG-Headed Cop is a NUISANCE!!!
And if YOU won't Fire him, I will!
GIMME YOUR BADGES!!!
chief
chief

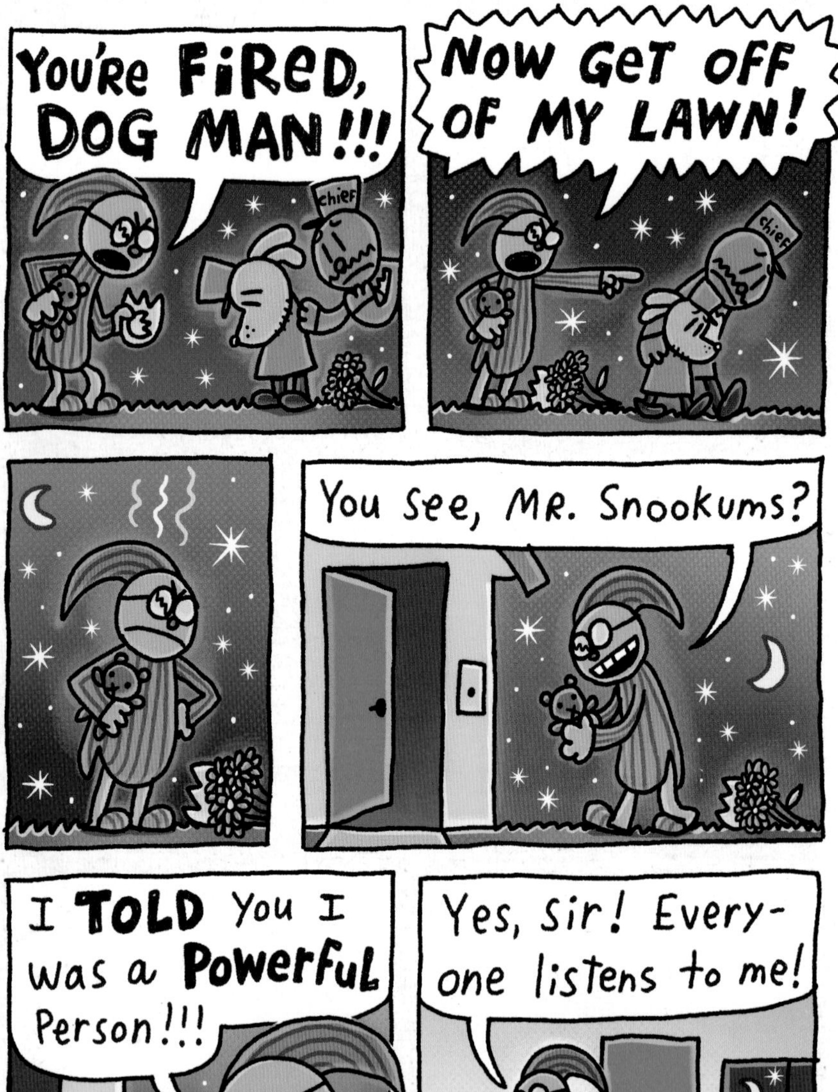
YOU'RE FIRED, DOG MAN!!!
chief
NOW GET OFF OF MY LAWN!
chief
You see, Mr. Snookums?
I TOLD you I was a Powerful Person!!!
Yes, sir! Every-one listens to me!

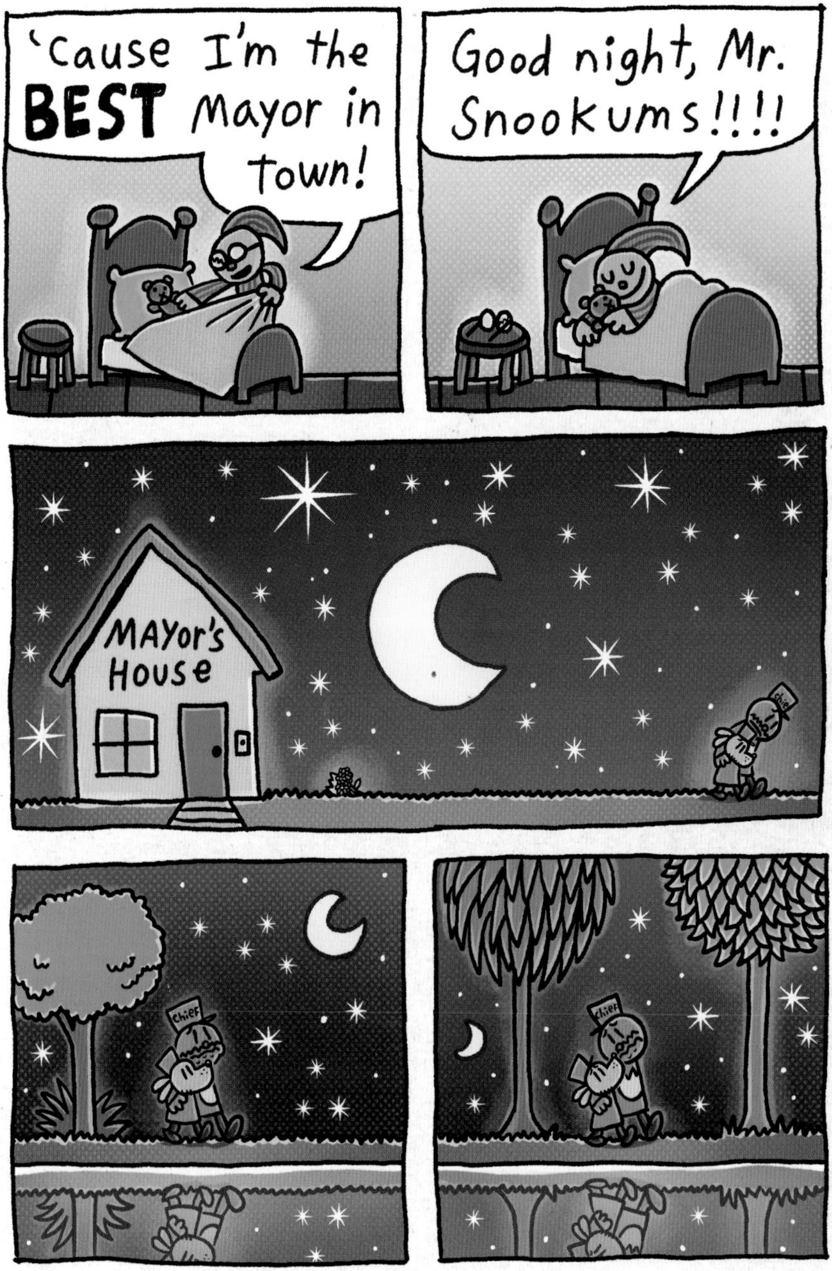
'Cause I'm the **BEST** Mayor in town!
Good night, Mr. Snookums!!!!
MAYor's House
Chief

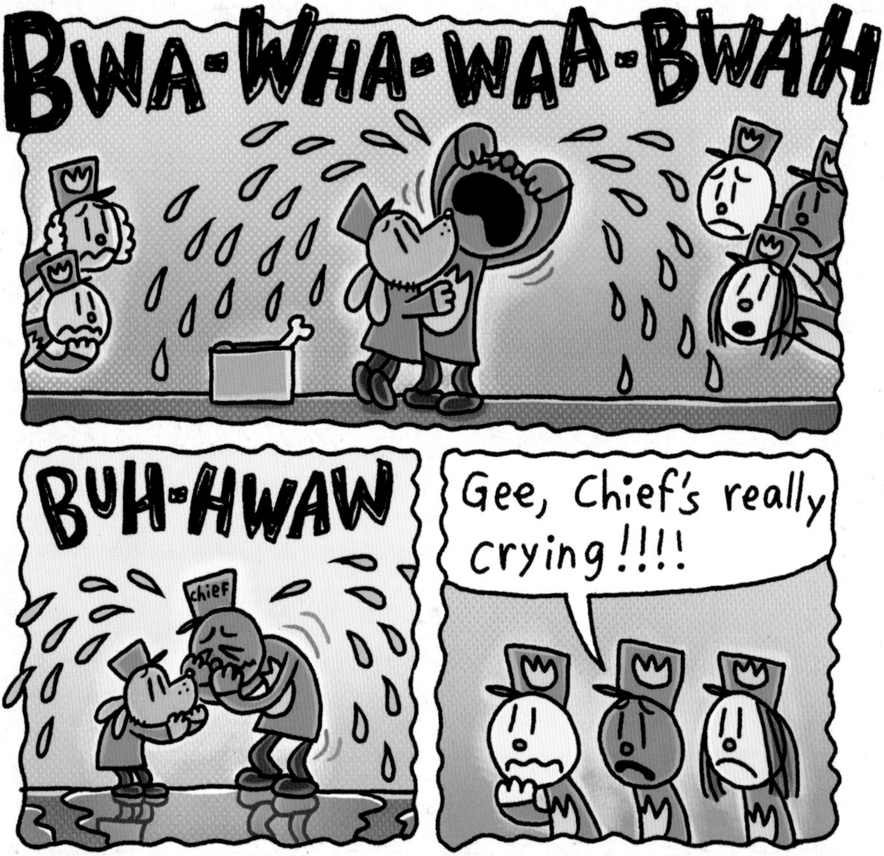
BWA-WHA-WAA-BWAH
BUH-HWAW
chief
Gee, Chief's really crying!!!!
I'm-I'm-I'm n-n-not crying!
chief
It's just allergies!!!
chief

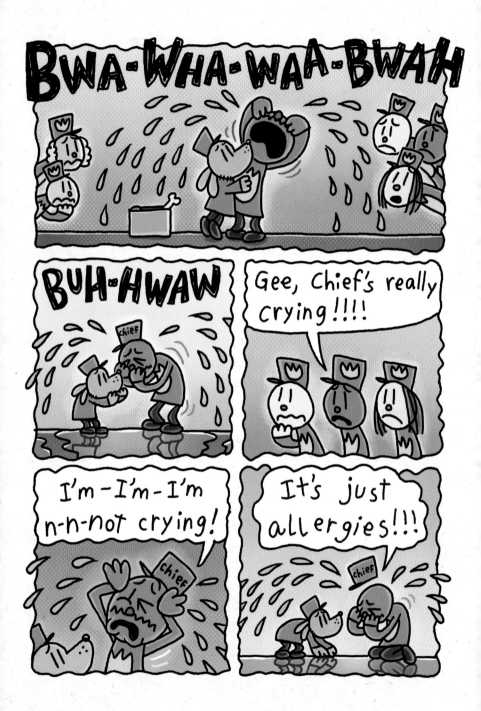

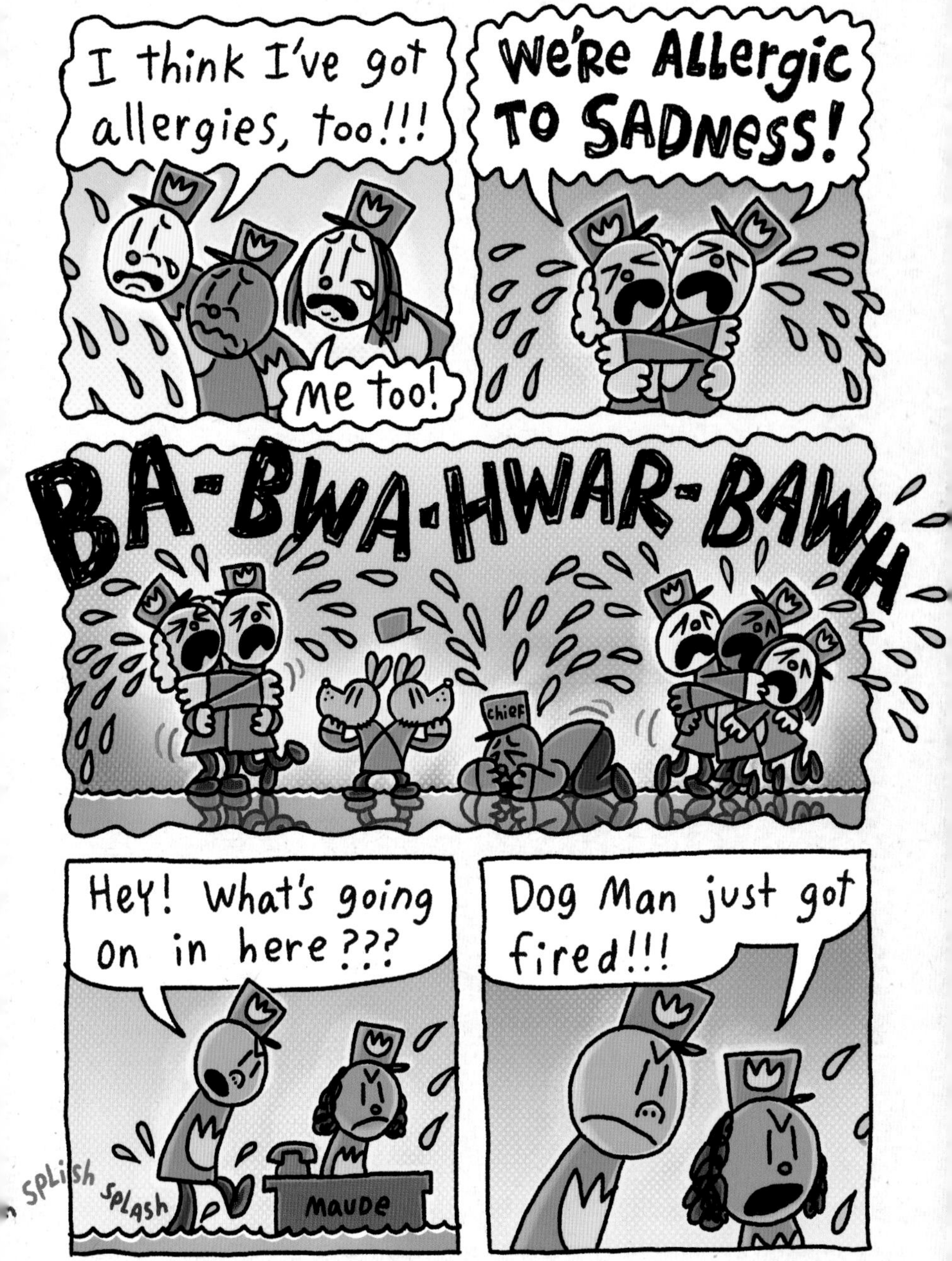
I think I've got allergies, too!!!
Me too!
We're Allergic TO SADNESS!
BA-BWA-HWAR-BAWH
chief
Hey! What's going on in here???
SPLish SPLASh
MAUDE
Dog Man just got fired!!!

lish splash splish splash

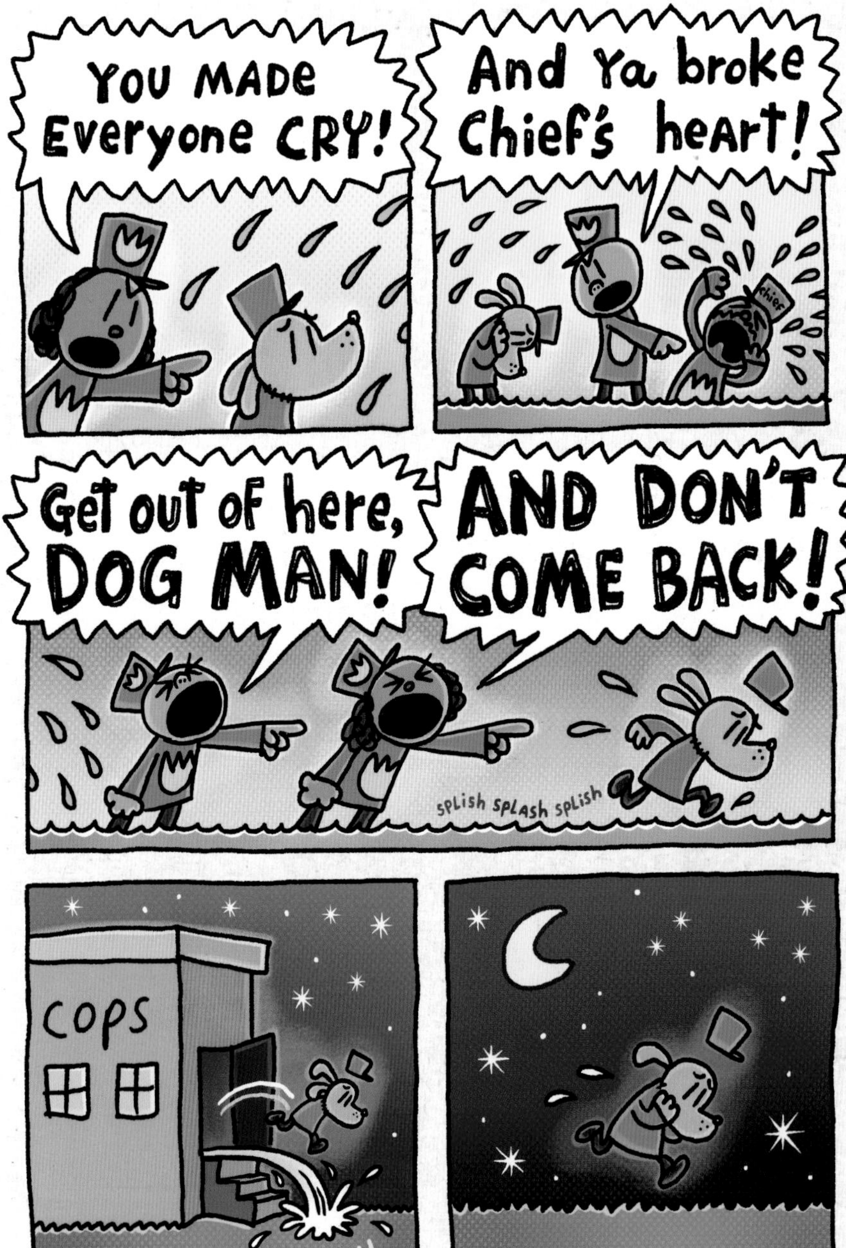
YOU MADE Everyone CRY!
And Ya broke Chief's heart!
Chief
Get out of here, DOG MAN!
AND DON'T COME BACK!
SPLish SPLAsh SPLiSh
COPS
SPLaSH!

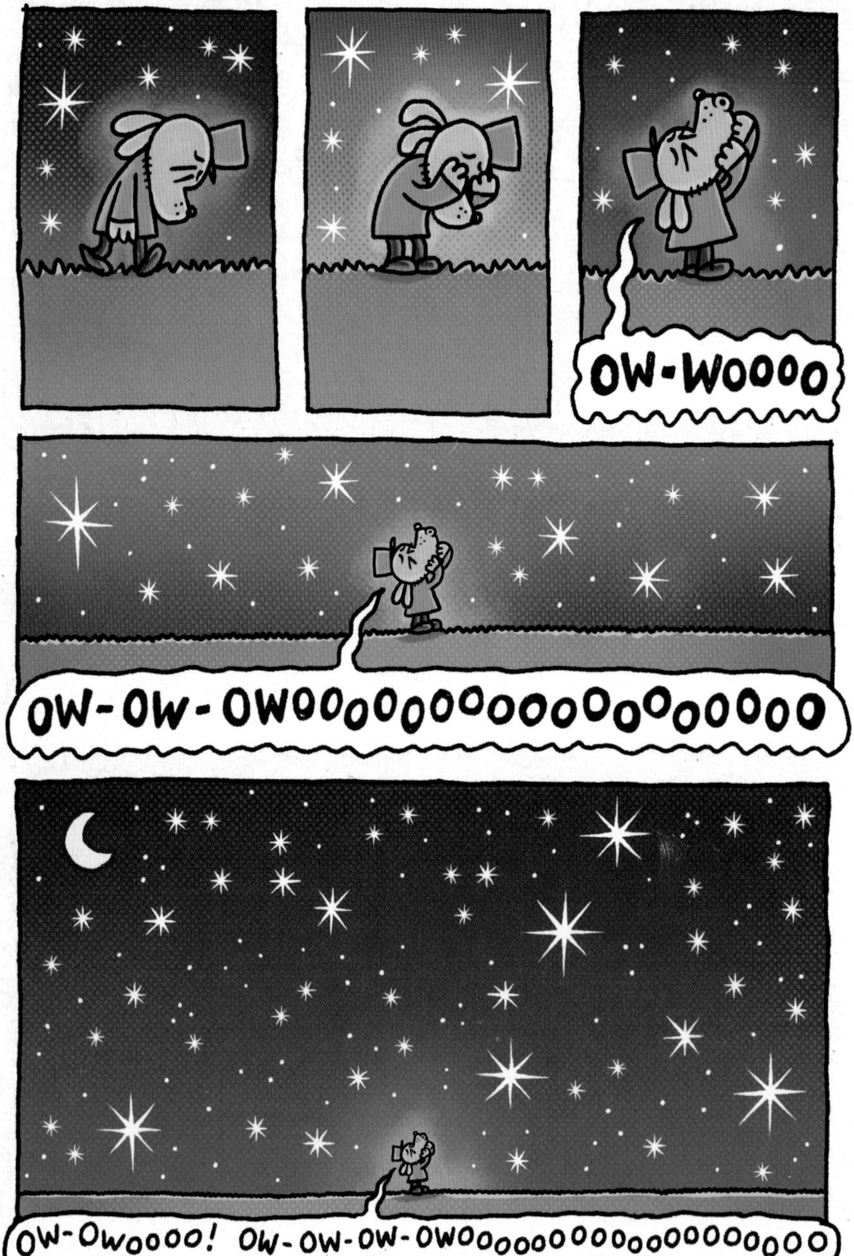
OW-WOOOO
OW-OW-OWOOOOOOOOOOOOOOOOOO
OW-OWOOOO! OW-OW-OW-OWOOOOOOOOOOOOOOOOO

CHAPTER 3

The Chapter That's Totally Not as Sad as the Last One

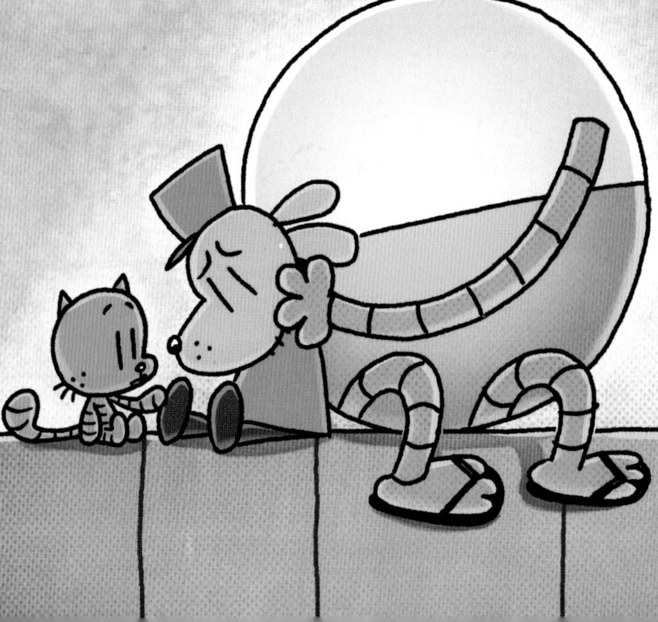

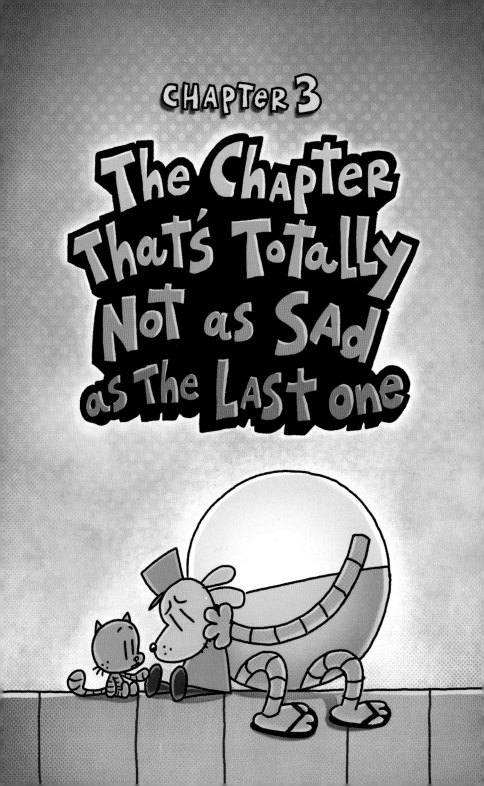

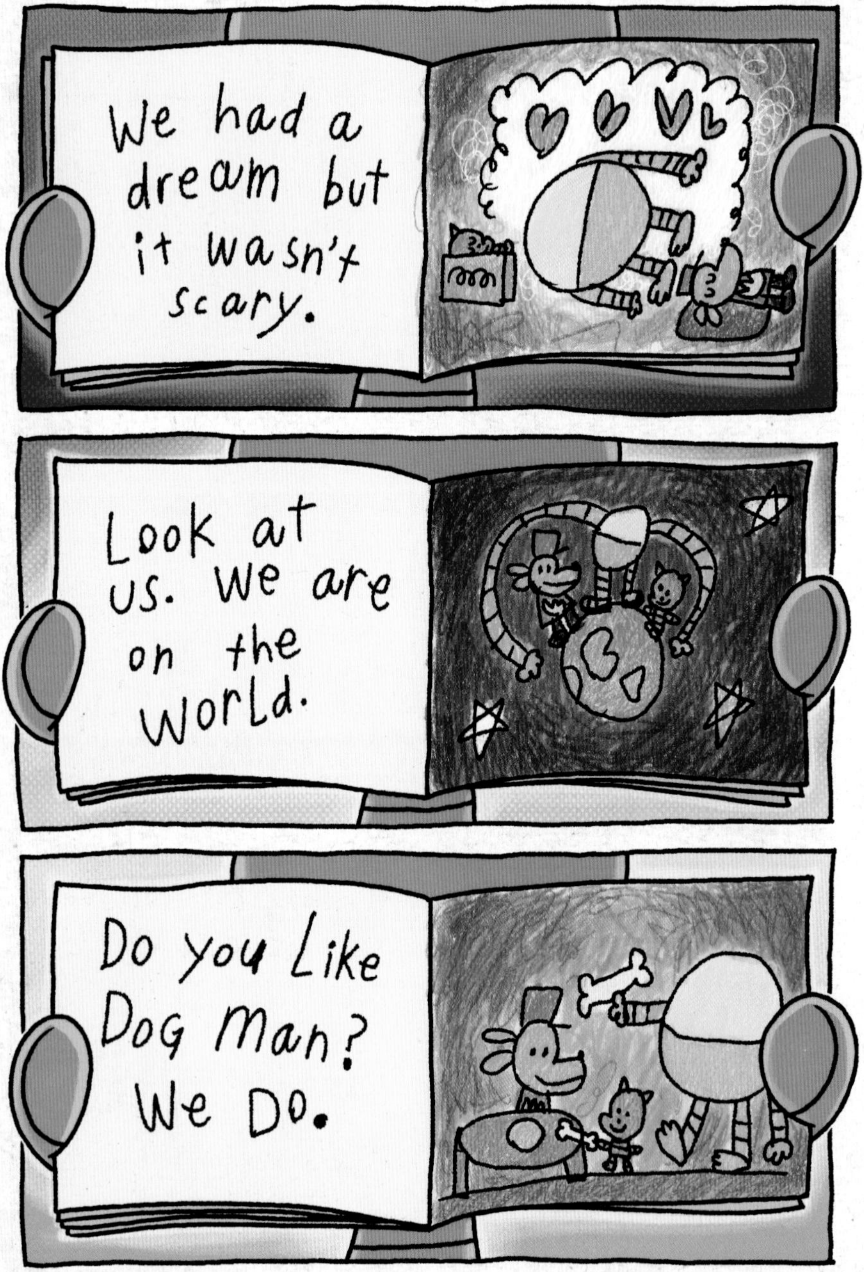
We had a dream but it wasn't scary.
Look at us. We are on the world.
Do you Like Dog Man? We Do.

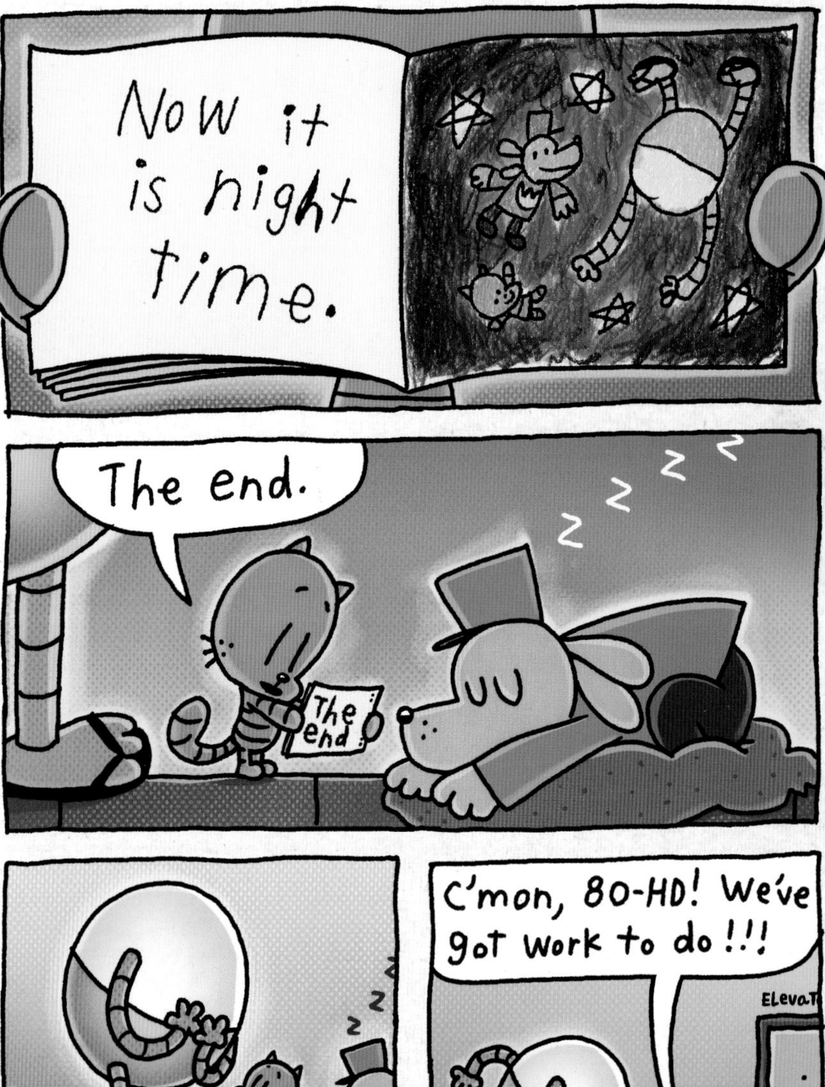
Now it is night time.
The end.
The end
Z Z Z Z
Sleepy Kitty
He's asleep!
C'mon, 80-HD! We've got work to do!!!
ELevaT
FLip FLop FLip

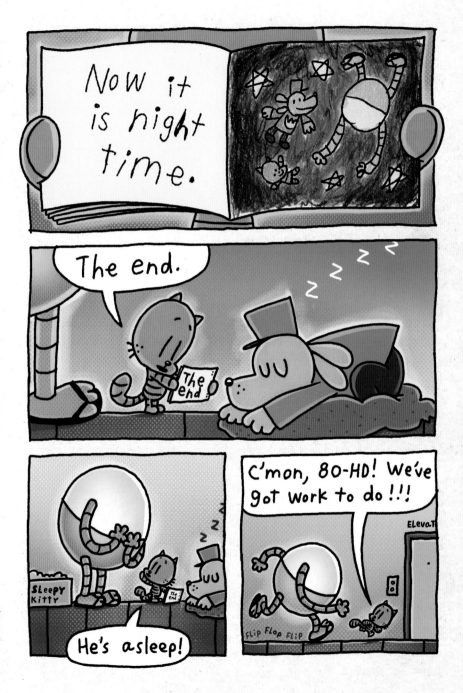

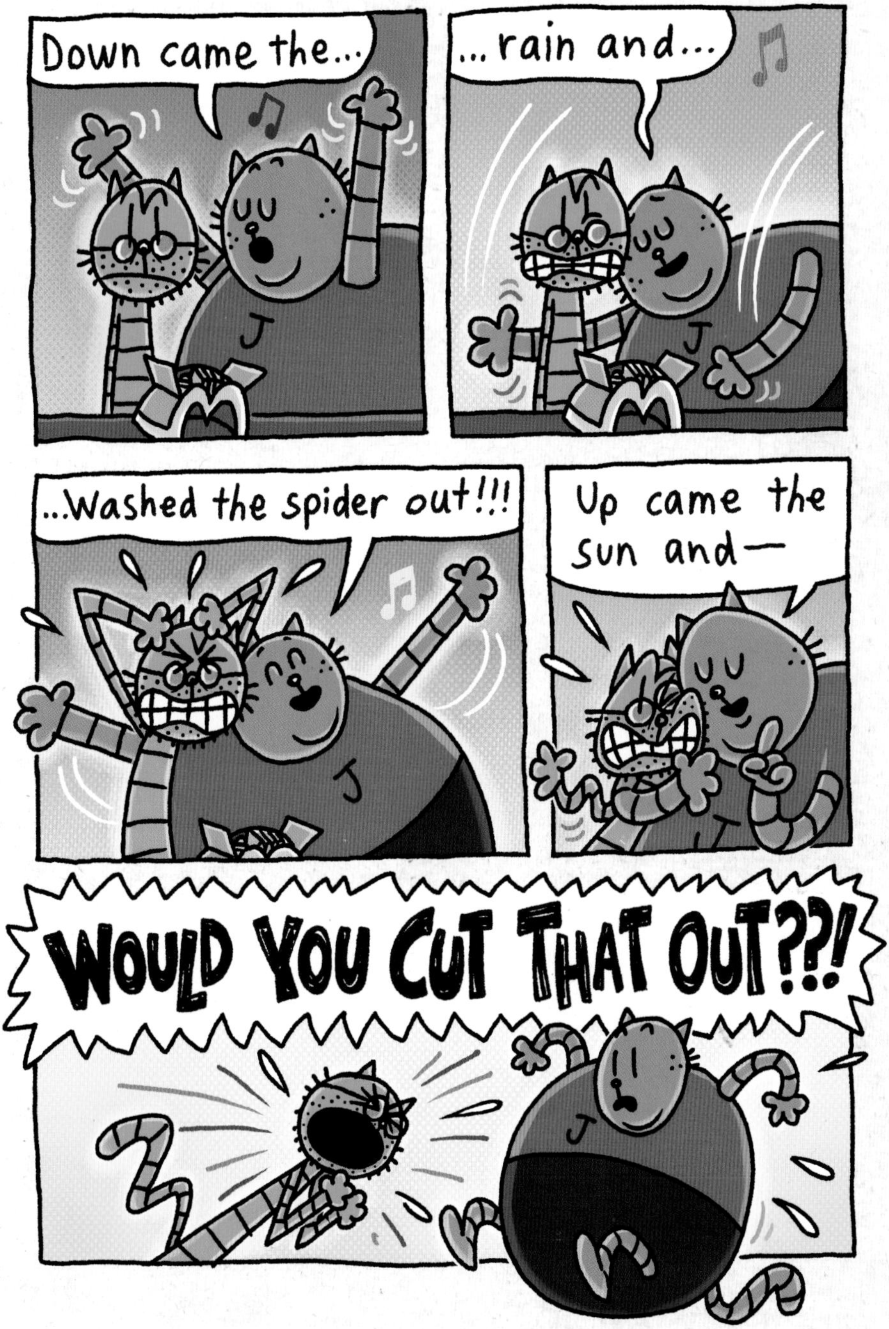
Down came the...
...rain and...
...Washed the spider out!!!
Up came the sun and—
WOULD YOU CUT THAT OUT??!

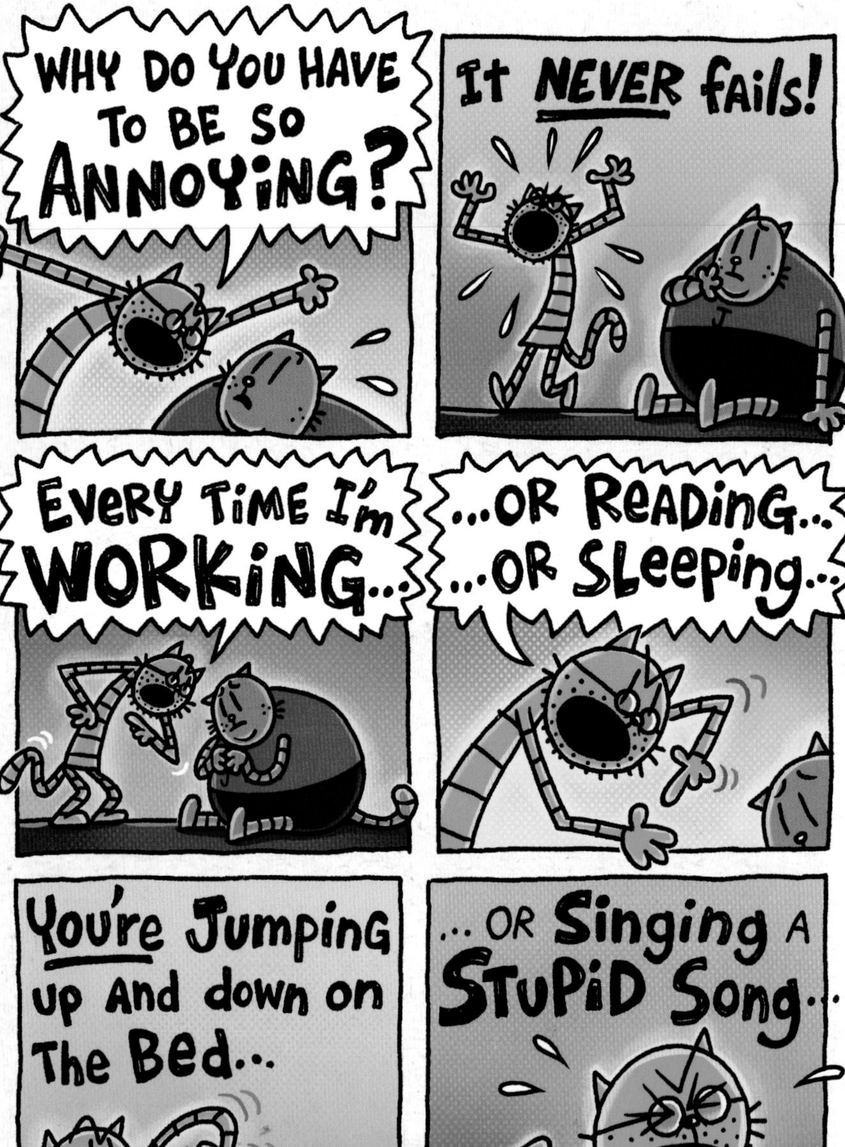
WHY DO YOU HAVE TO BE SO ANNOYING?
It NEVER fails!
EVERY TIME I'm WORKING...
...OR READING... ...OR SLEEPING...
YOU'RE JUMPING up And down on The Bed...
... OR Singing A STUPID Song...

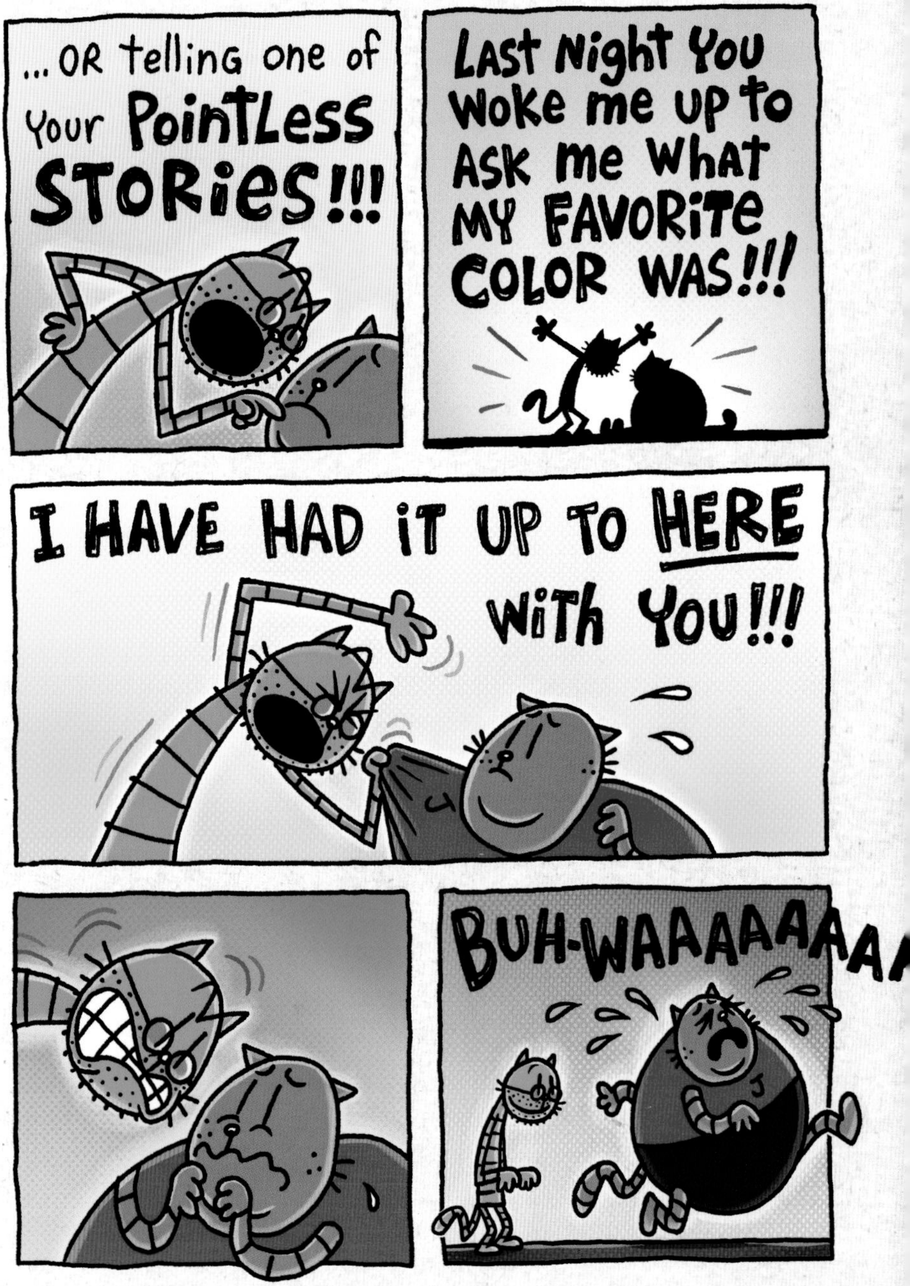
...OR telling one of your POINTLESS STORIES!!!
LAST NIGHT YOU WOKE ME UP TO ASK ME WHAT MY FAVORITE COLOR WAS!!!
I HAVE HAD IT UP TO HERE WITH YOU!!!
BUH-WAAAAAAA

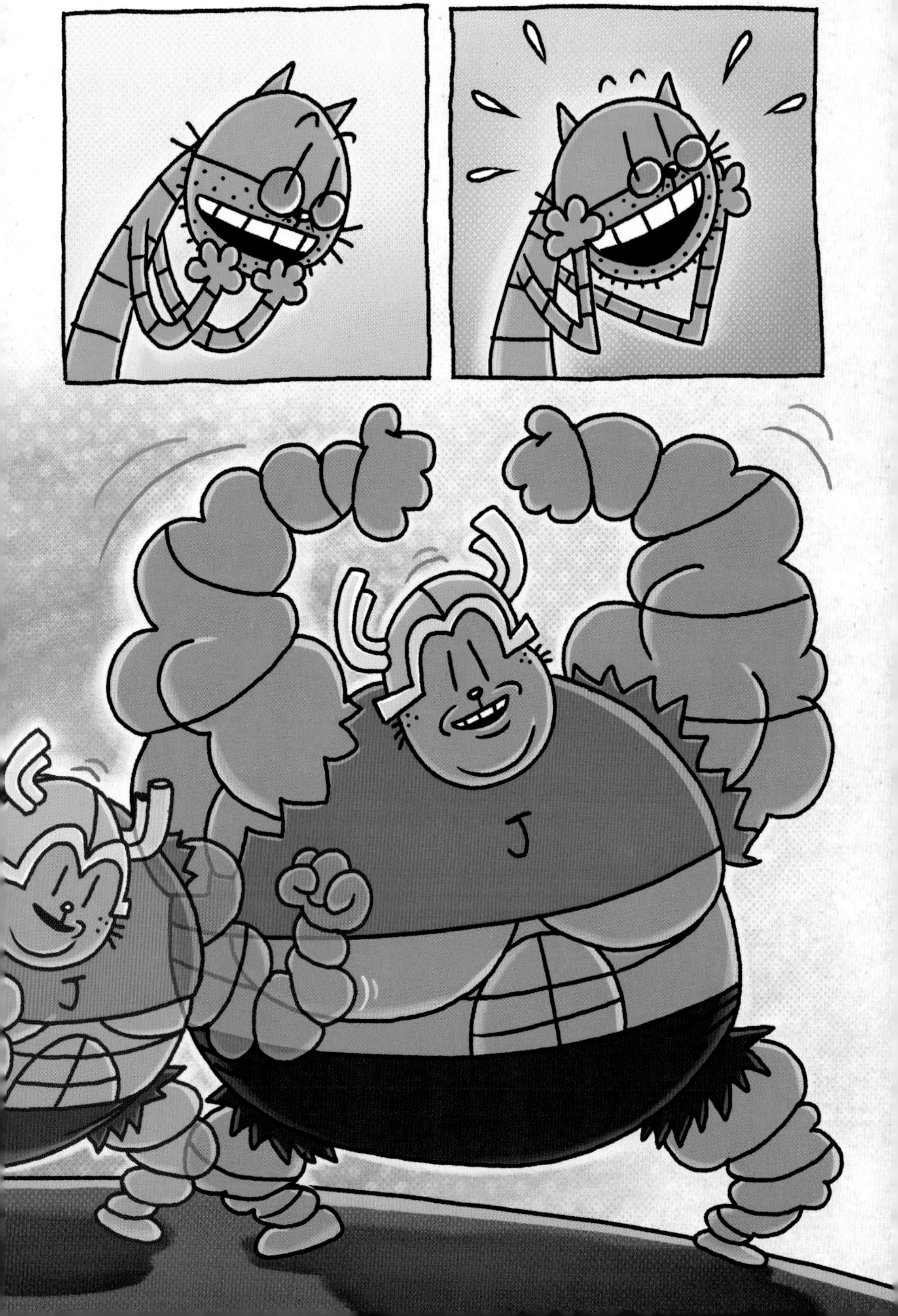

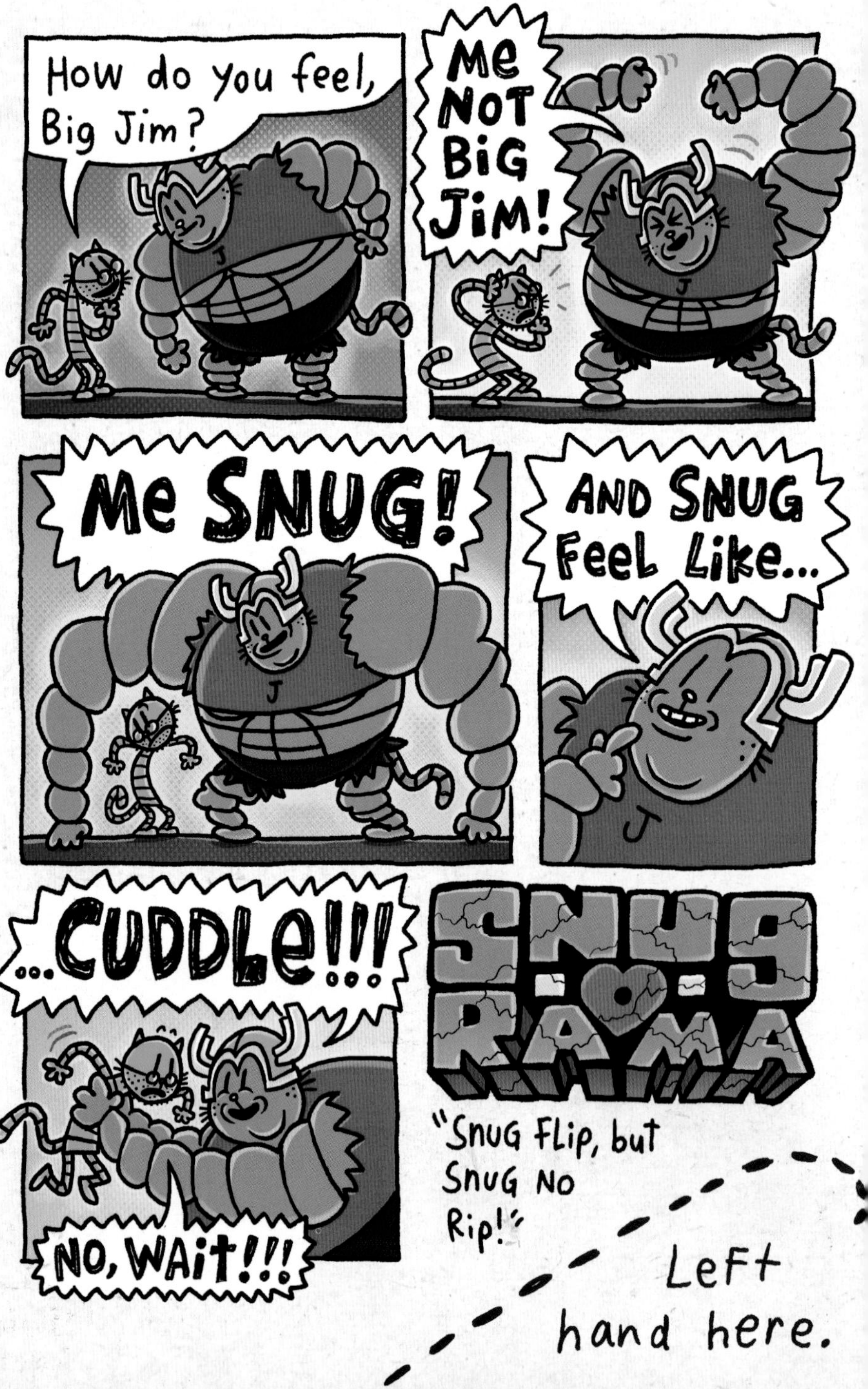

How do you feel, Big Jim?
Me NOT BiG JiM!
Me SNUG!
AND SNUG Feel Like...
...CUDDLe!!!
NO, WAiT!!!
SNUG-O-RAMA
"SNUG FLip, but SNUG NO Rip!"
Left hand here.

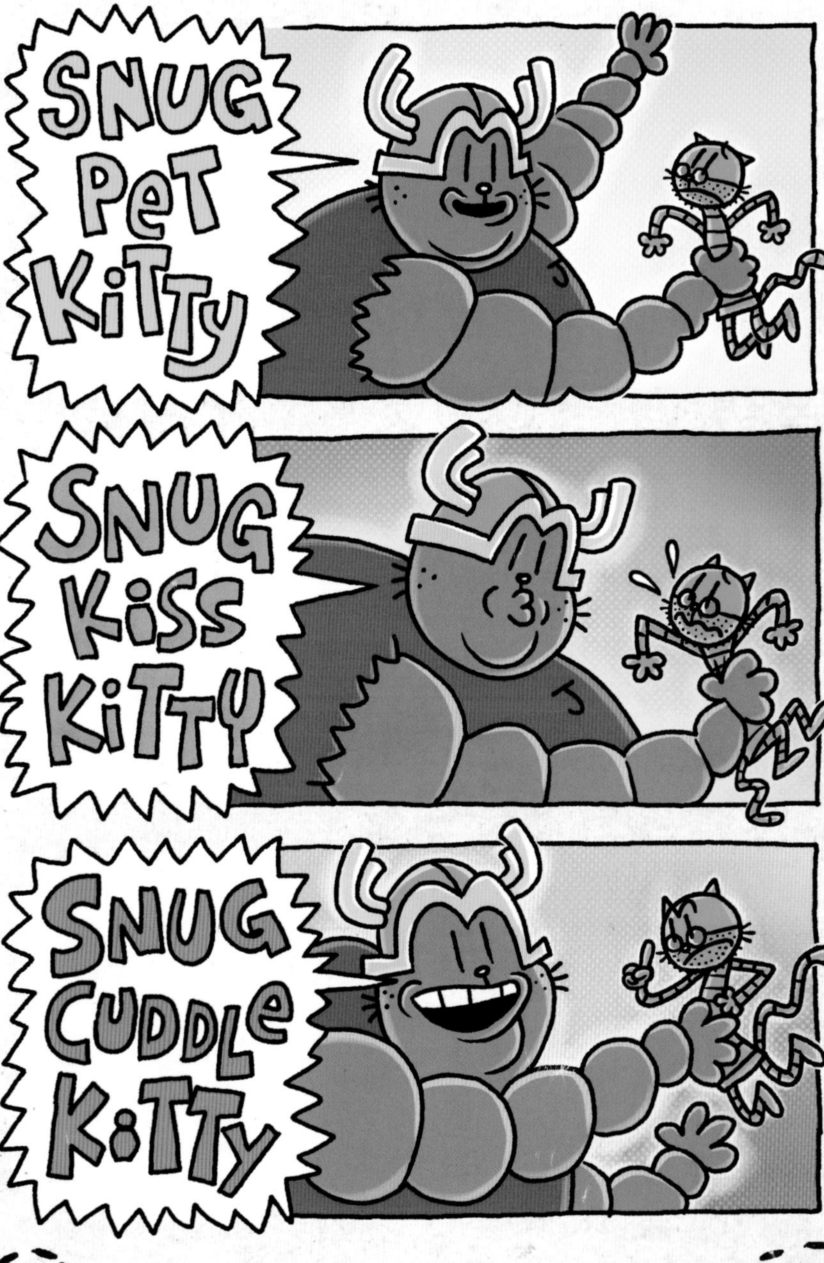
SNUG PET KITTY
SNUG KISS KITTY
SNUG CUDDLE KITTY

Right Thumb here.

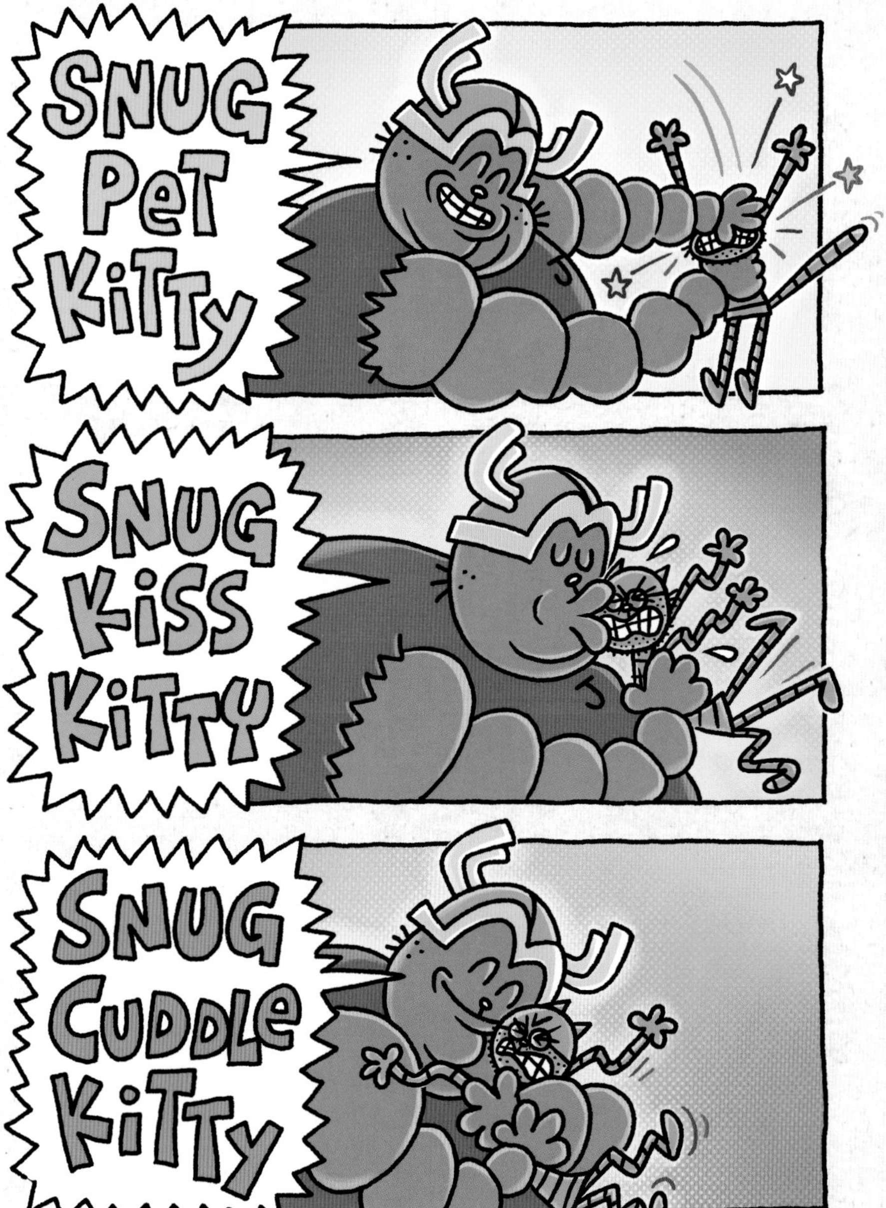
SNUG PET KITTY
SNUG KISS KITTY
SNUG CUDDLE KITTY

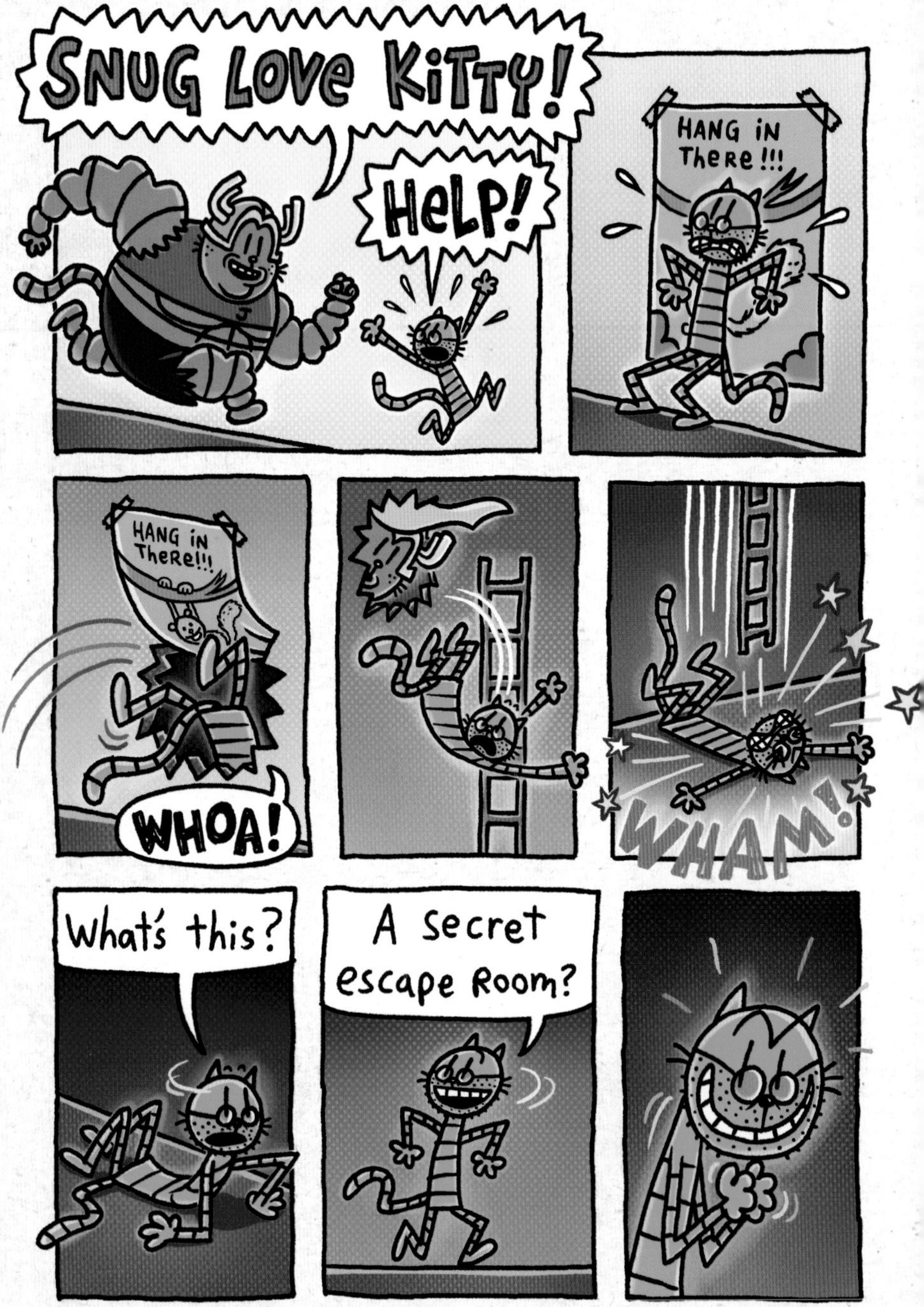
SNUG LOVE KITTY!
HELP!
HANG IN There!!!
HANG IN There!!!
WHOA!
WHAM!
What's this?
A secret escape Room?

CHAPTER 4

The DOG in The HAT

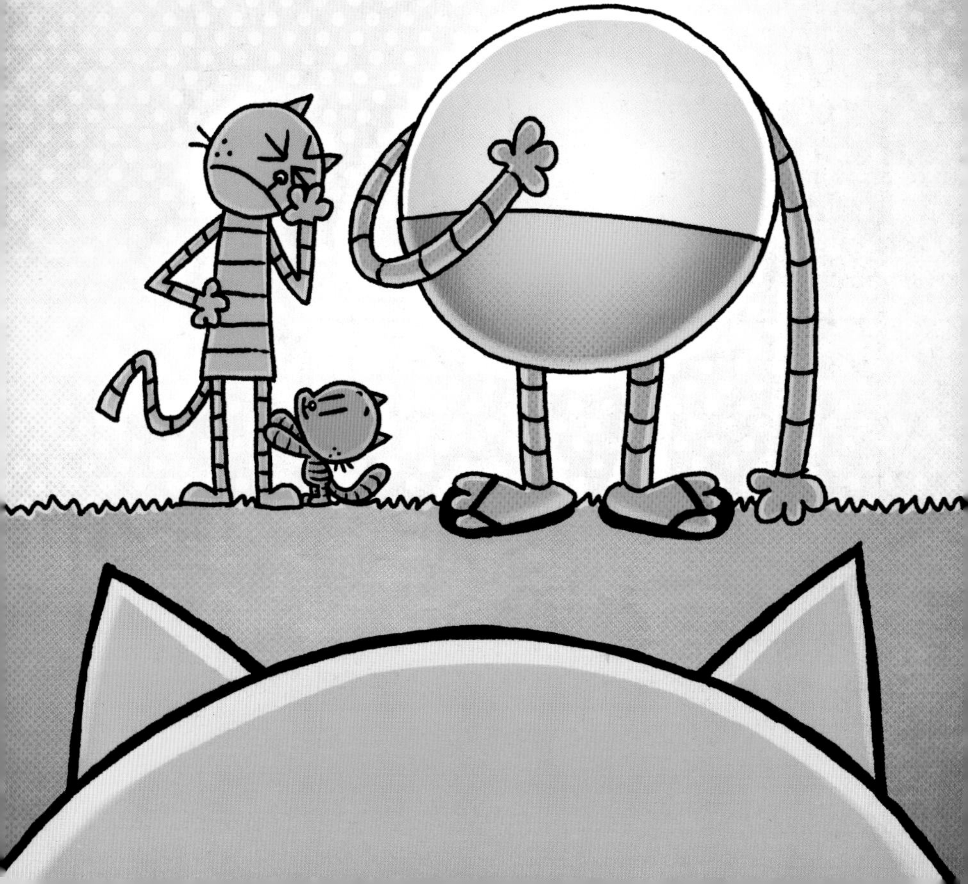

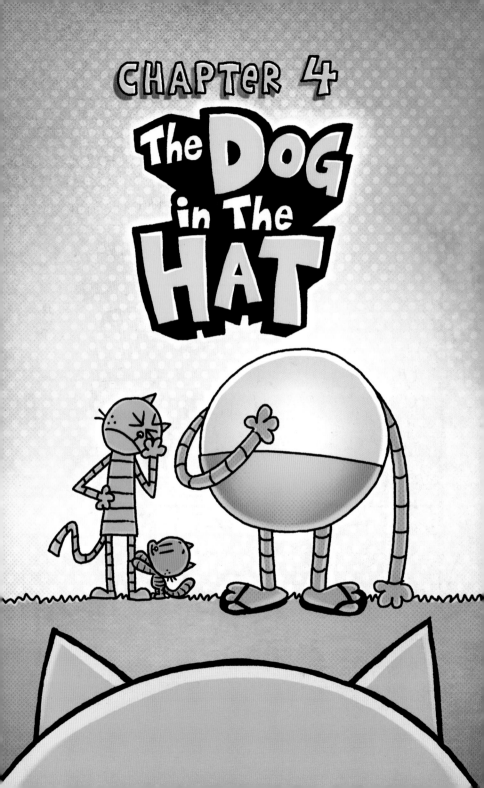

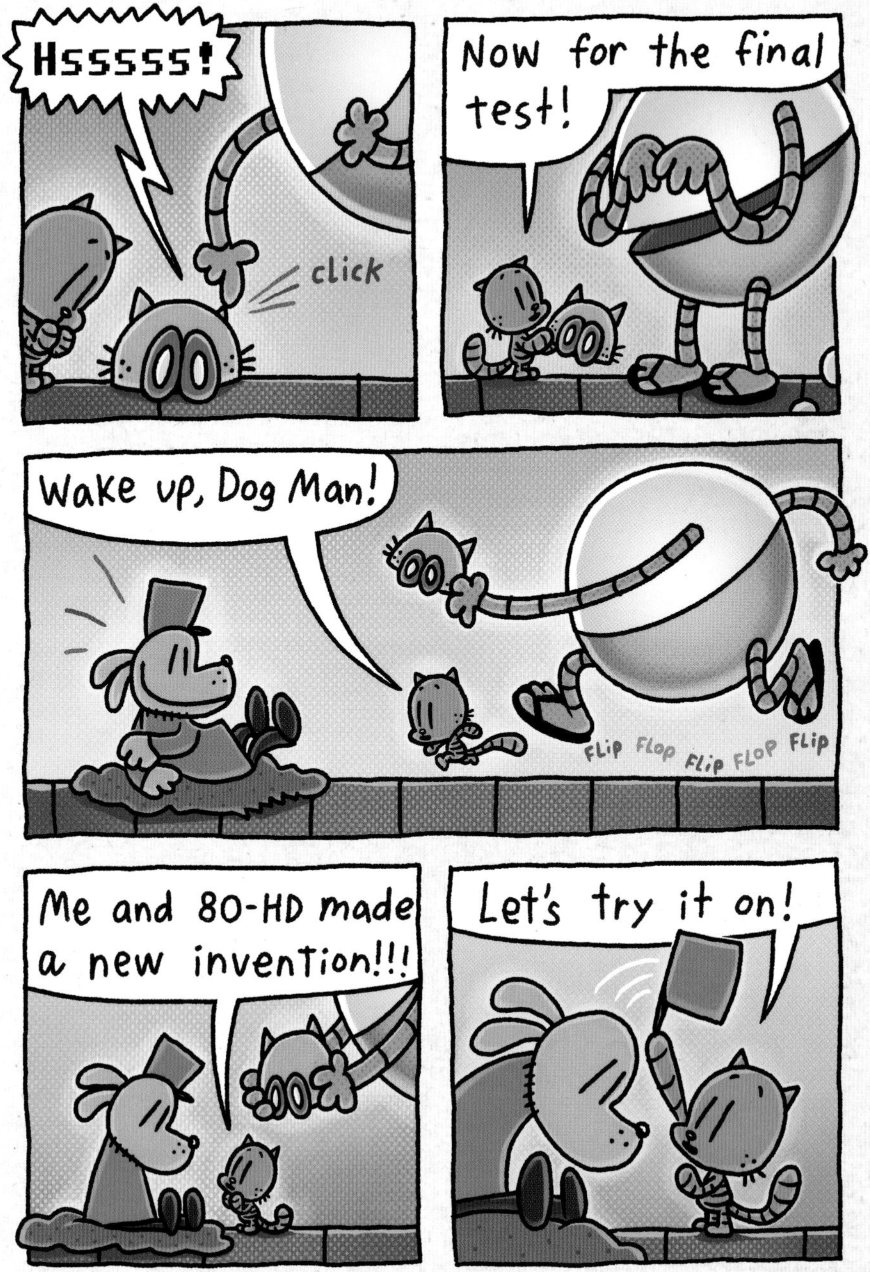
Hsssss!
click
Now for the final test!
Wake up, Dog Man!
FLip Flop FLip FLoP FLip
Me and 80-HD made a new invention!!!
Let's try it on!

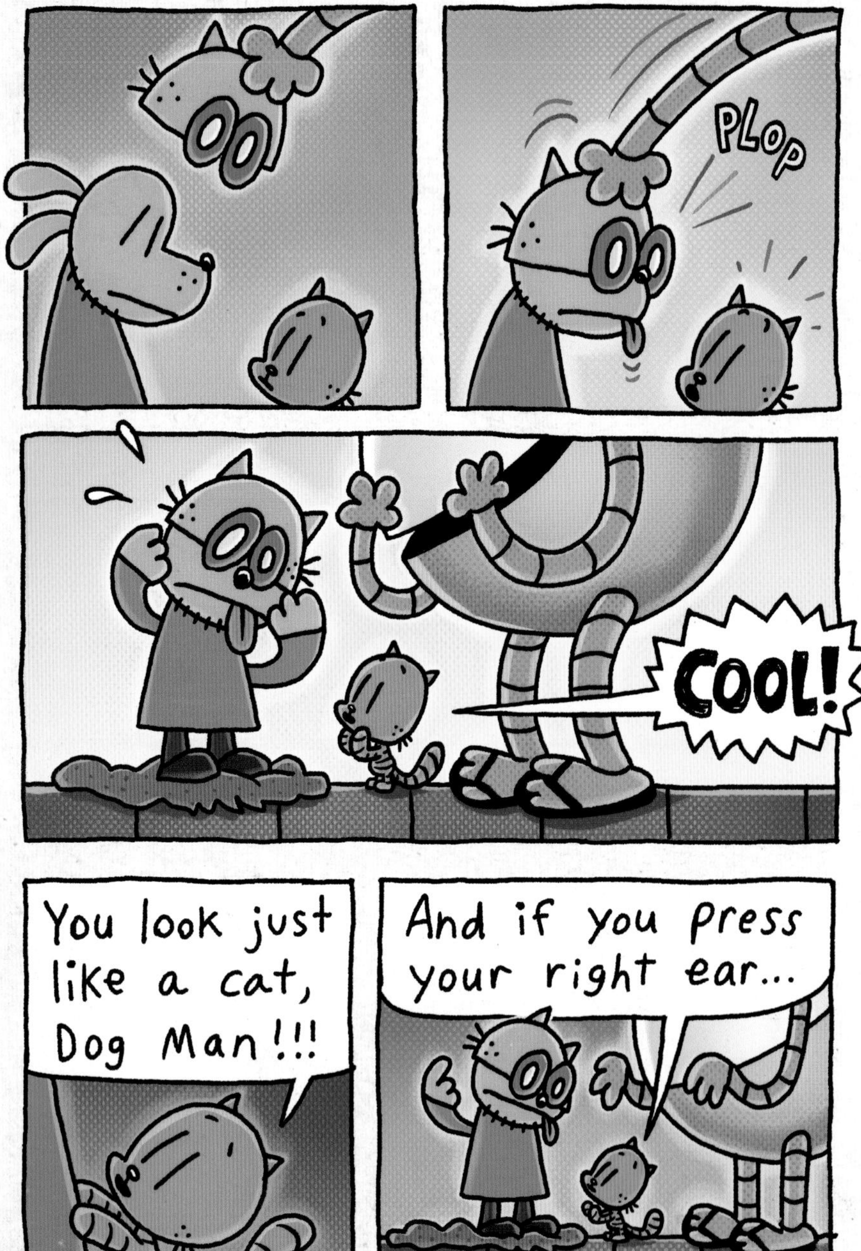
PLOP
COOL!
You look just like a cat, Dog Man!!!
And if you press your right ear...

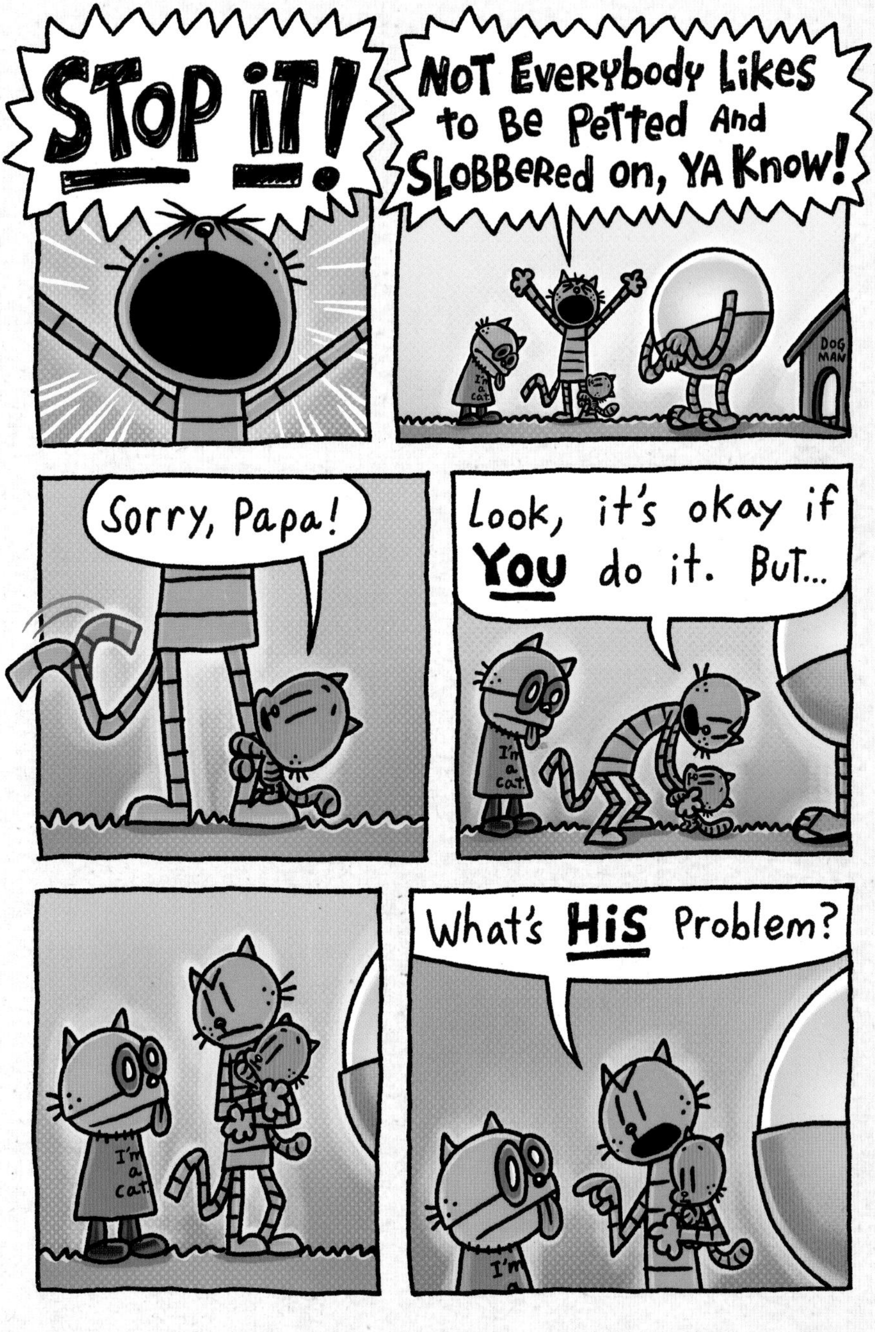
STOP iT!
NOT Everybody Likes to Be Petted And SLOBBered on, YA Know!
DOG MAN
I'm a cat.
Sorry, Papa!
Look, it's okay if YOU do it. BuT...
I'm a cat.
I'm a cat.
What's HiS Problem?

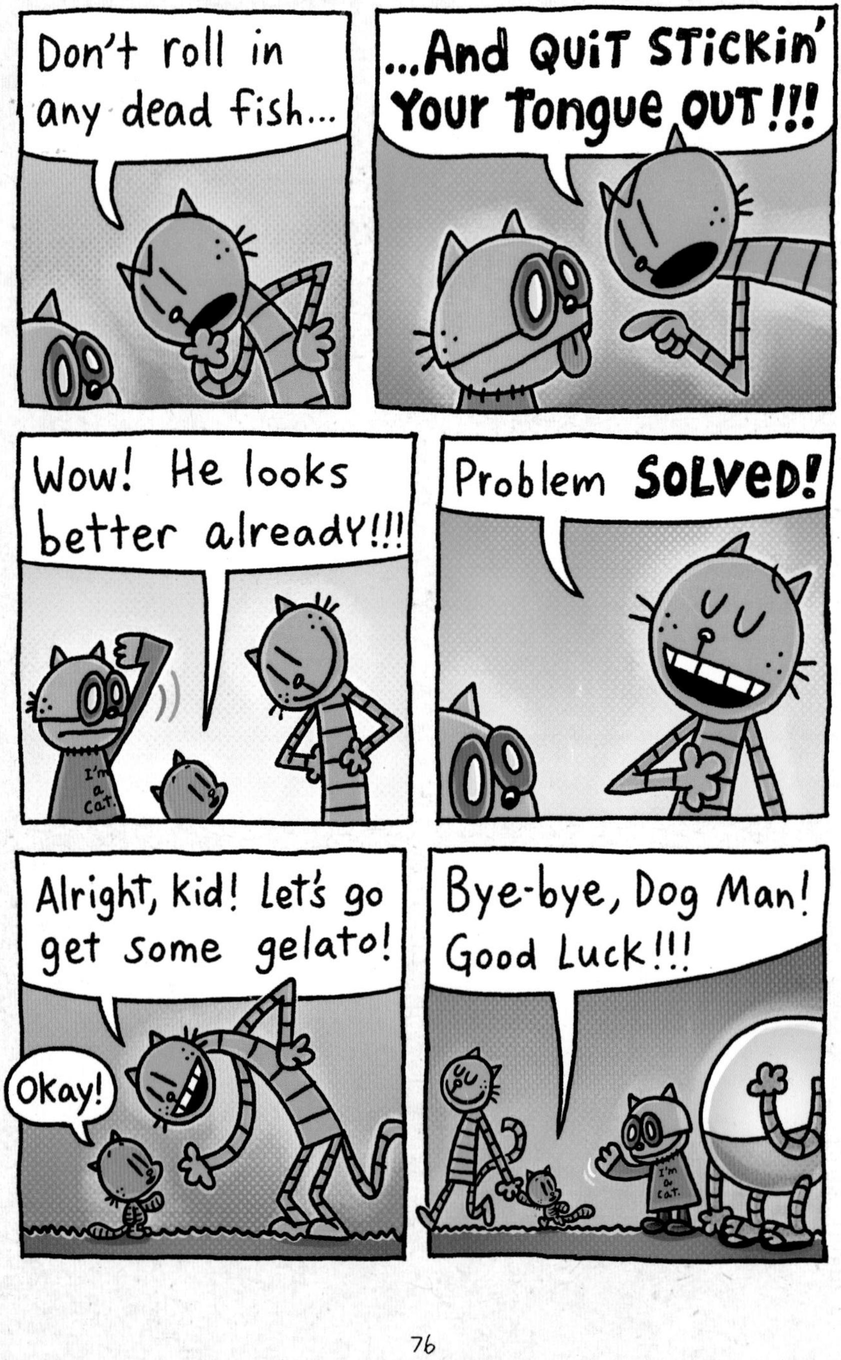
Don't roll in any dead fish...
...And QUIT STICKIN' YOUR TONGUE OUT!!!
Wow! He looks better already!!!
I'm a Cat.
Problem SOLVED!
Alright, kid! Let's go get some gelato!
Okay!
Bye-bye, Dog Man! Good Luck!!!

CHAPTER 5

A Buncha Stuff That Happened Next

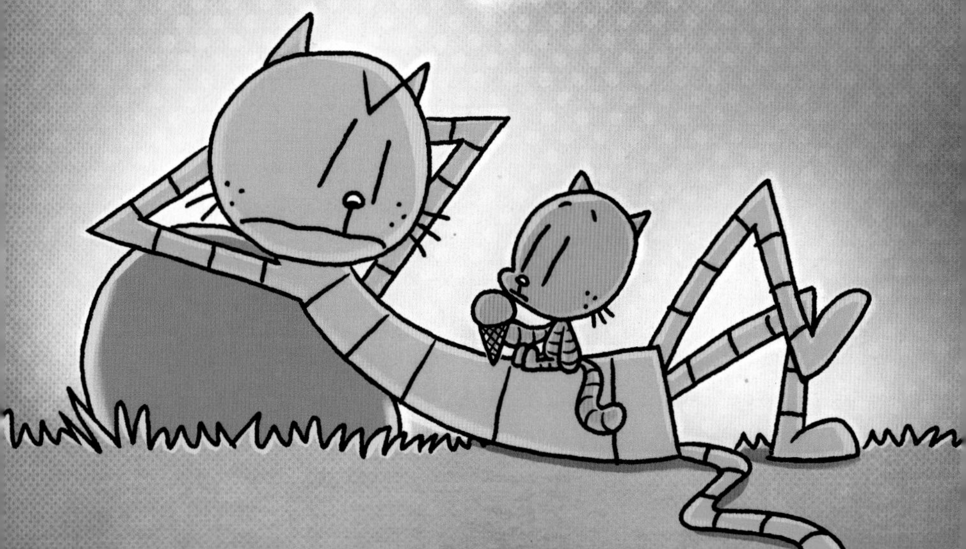

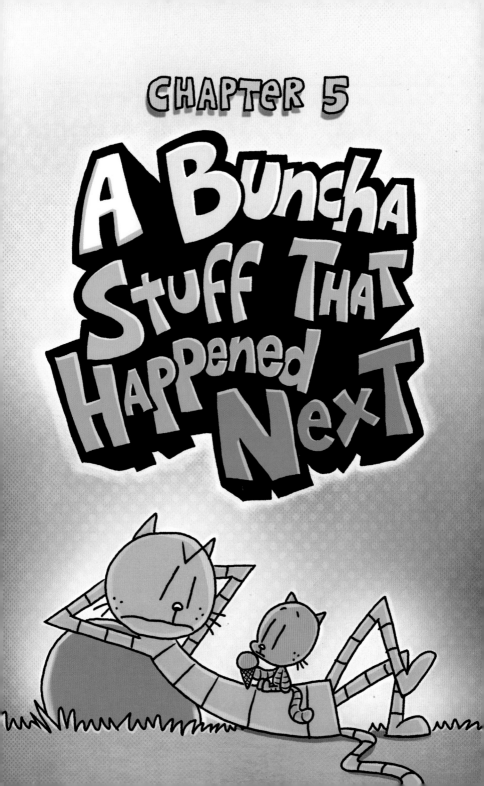

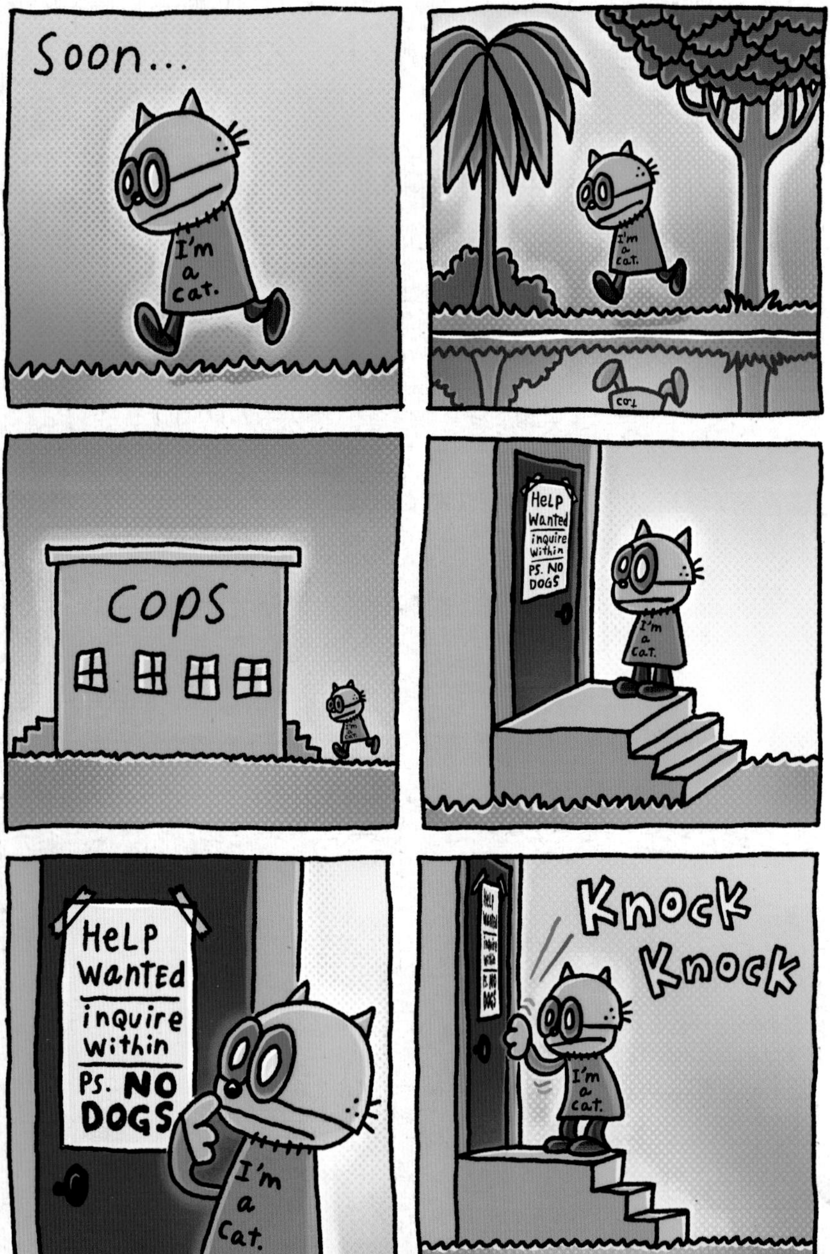
Soon...
I'm a cat.
I'm a cat.
COPS
HELP WANTED inquire within PS. NO DOGS
I'm a cat.
HELP WANTED inquire within PS. NO DOGS
I'm a cat.
Knock Knock
I'm a cat.

79

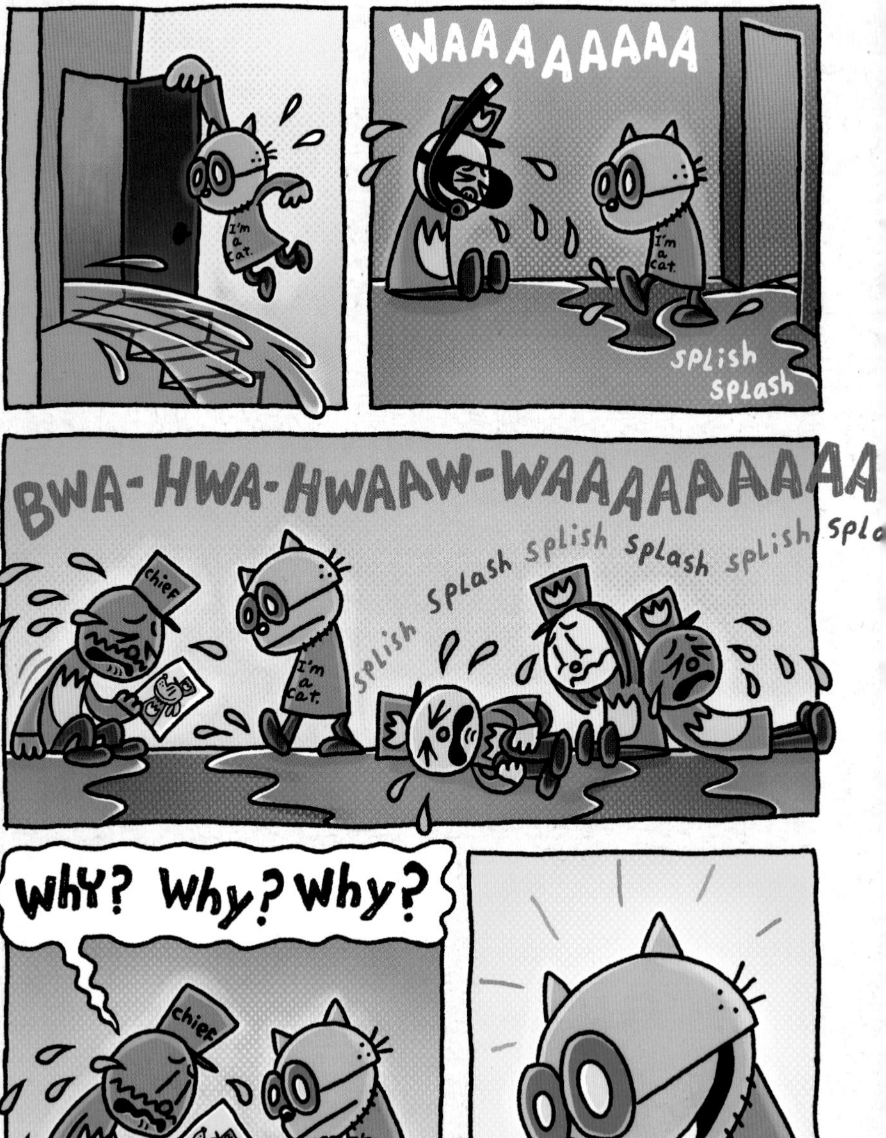

I'm a cat.
WAAAAAAAA
I'm a cat.
splish splash
BWA-HWA-HWAAW-WAAAAAAAAA
chief
I'm a cat.
splish splash splish splash splish spla
Why? Why? Why?
chief
I'm a cat.
I'm a

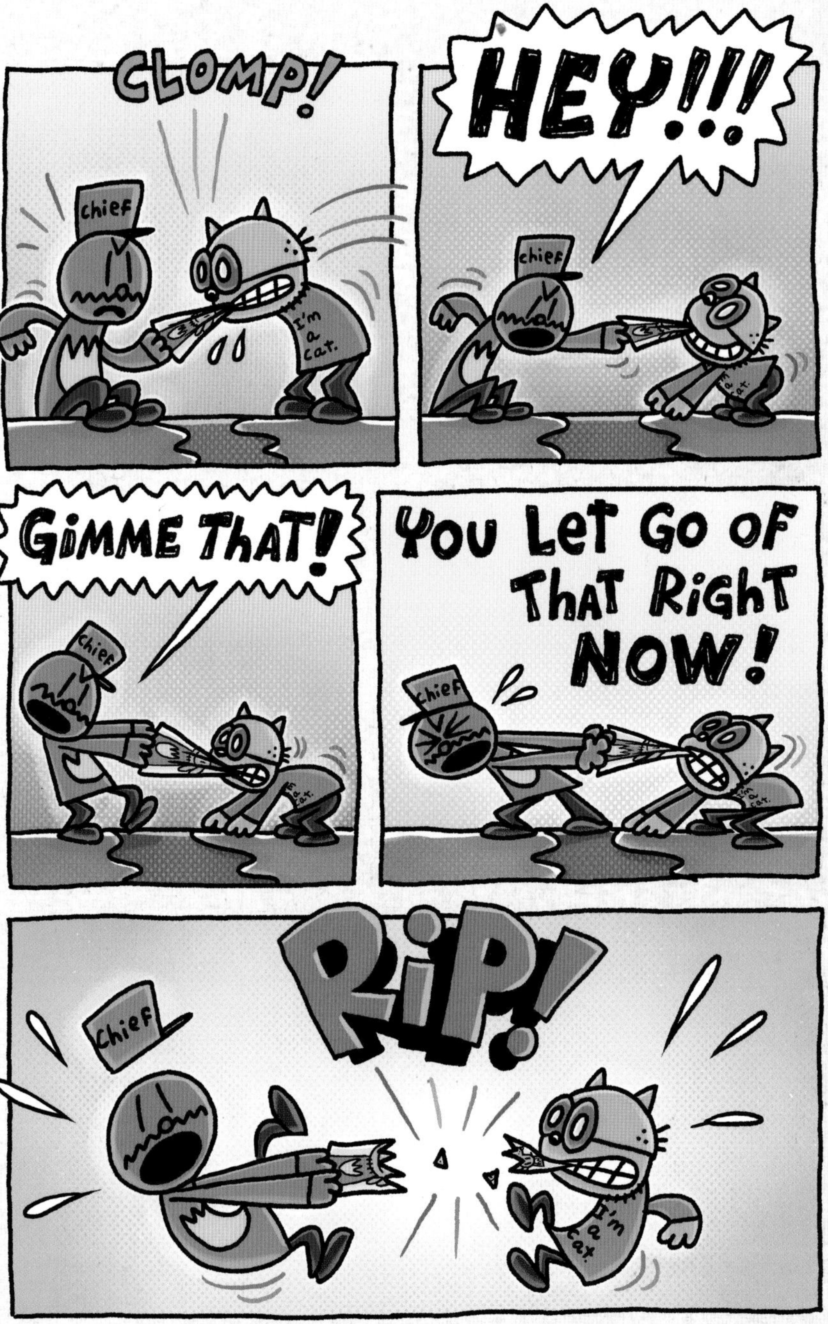
CLOMP!
Chief
I'm a cat.
HEY!!!
Chief
GIMME THAT!
Chief
YOU LET GO OF THAT RIGHT NOW!
Chief
RIP!
Chief
I'm a cat.

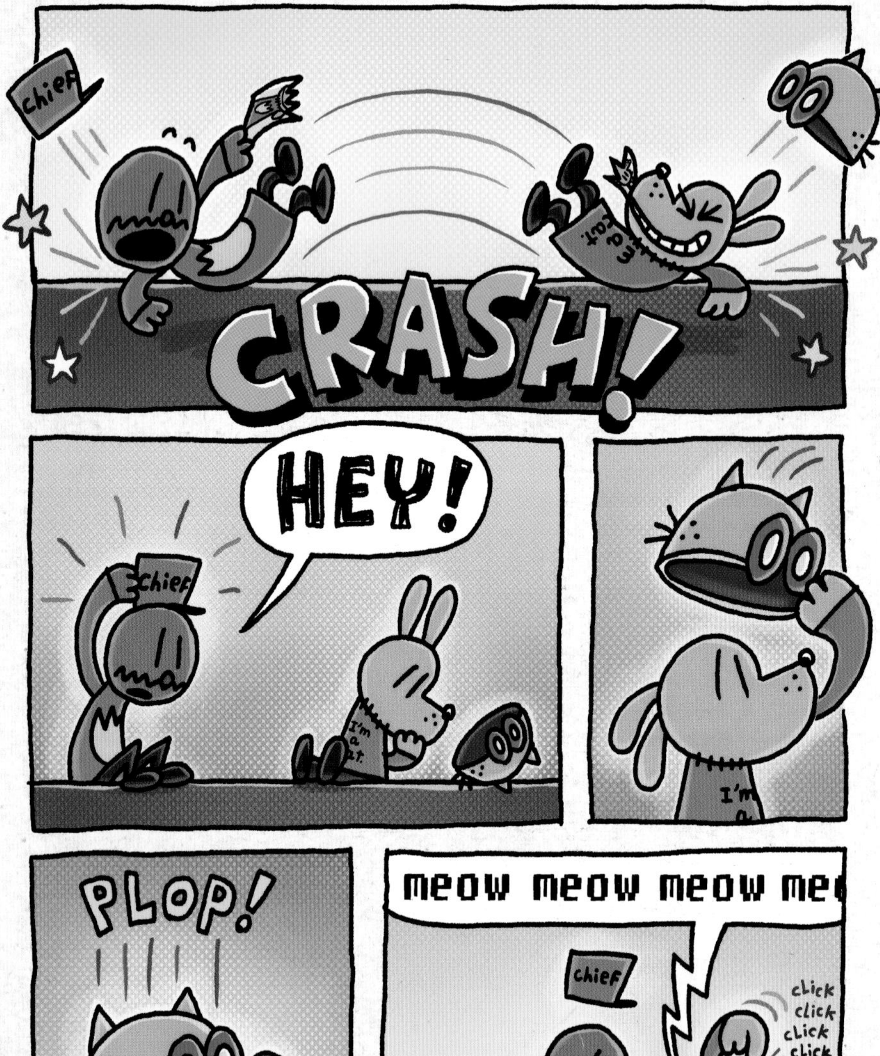
chief
Eat.
CRASH!
HEY!
Chief
I'm a cat.
I'm a
PLOP!
I'm a cat.
meow meow meow me
chief
click click click click
I'm a cat.

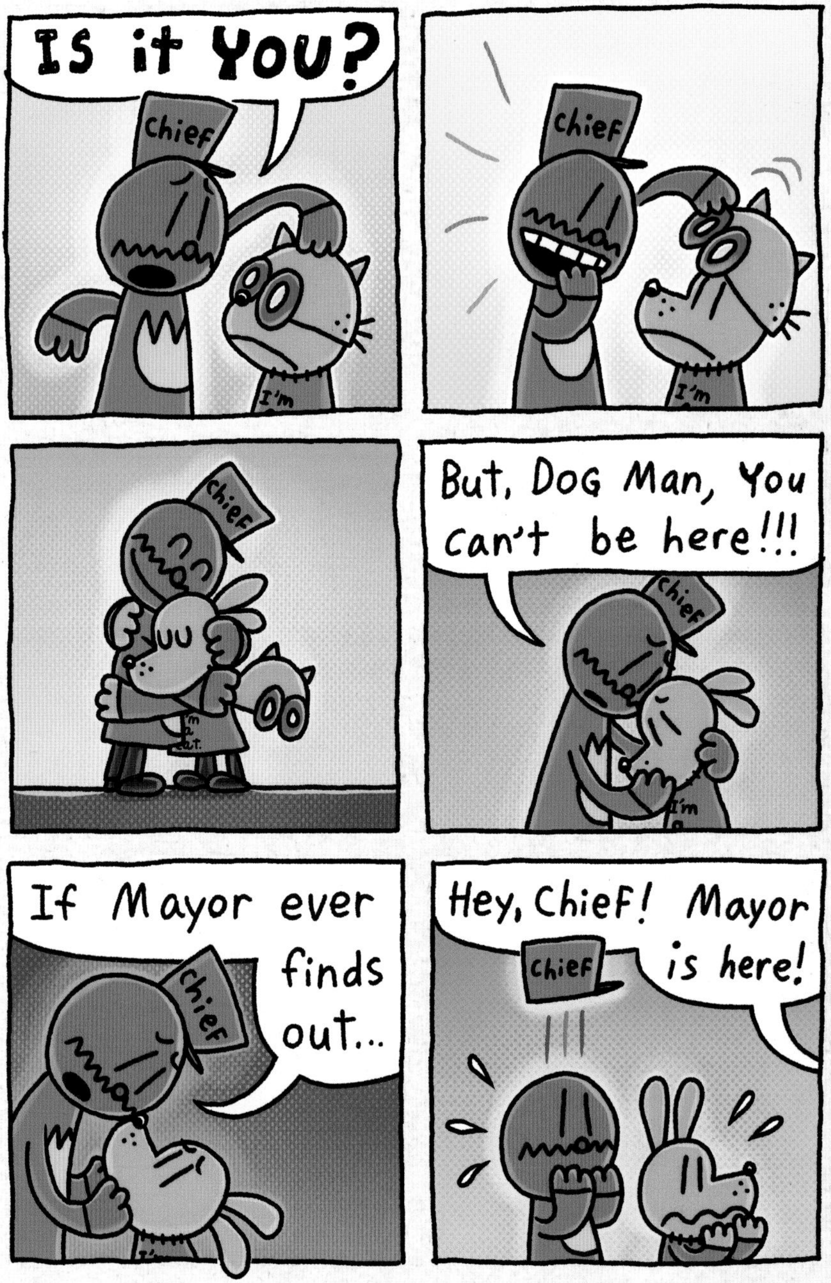
IS it YOU?
Chief
Chief
I'm
I'm
Chief
I'm a cat.
But, DOG Man, You can't be here!!!
Chief
I'm
If Mayor ever finds out...
Chief
Hey, Chief! Mayor is here!
Chief

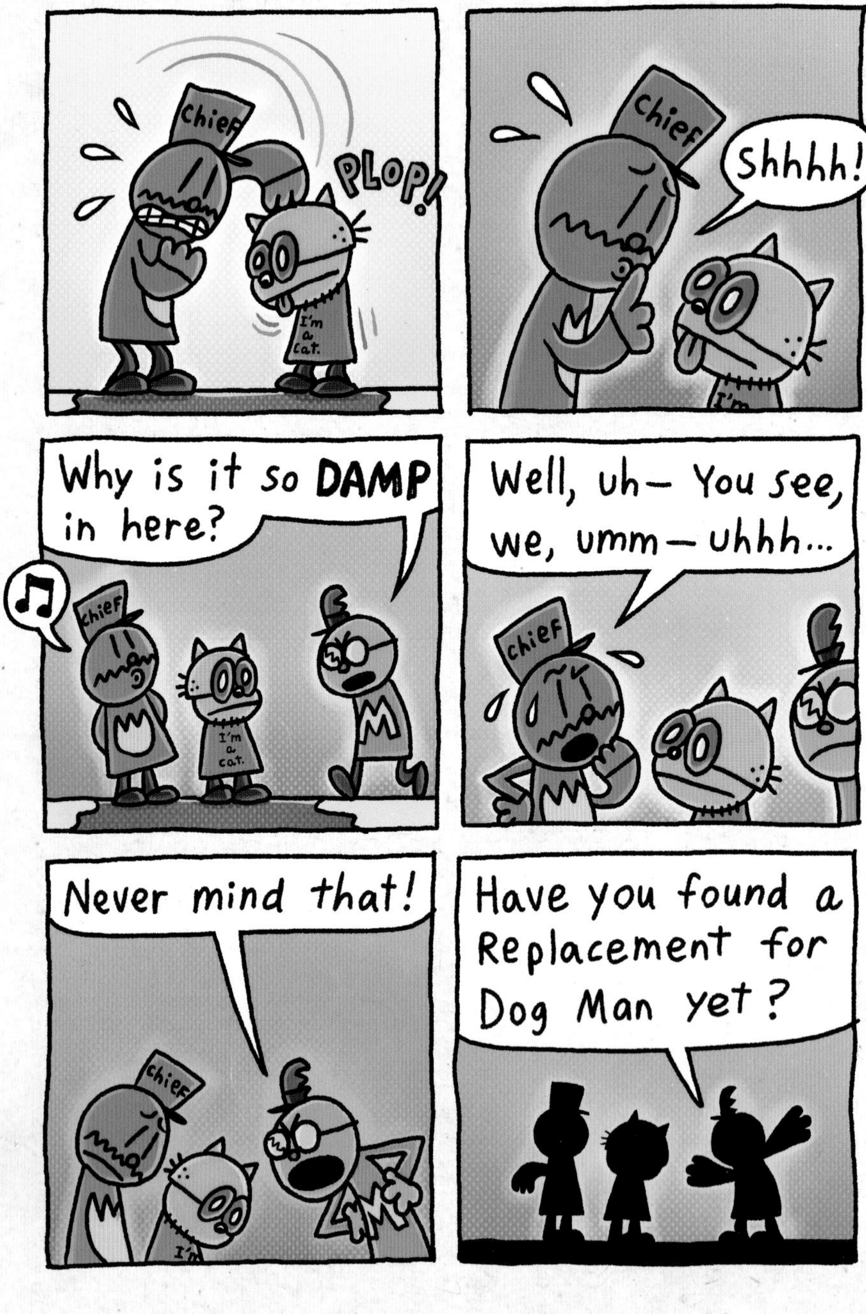
Chief
PLOP!
I'm a cat.
Chief
Shhhh!
I'm
Why is it so **DAMP** in here?
Chief
I'm a cat.
Well, uh– You see, we, umm– uhhh...
Chief
Never mind that!
Chief
Have you found a Replacement for Dog Man yet?

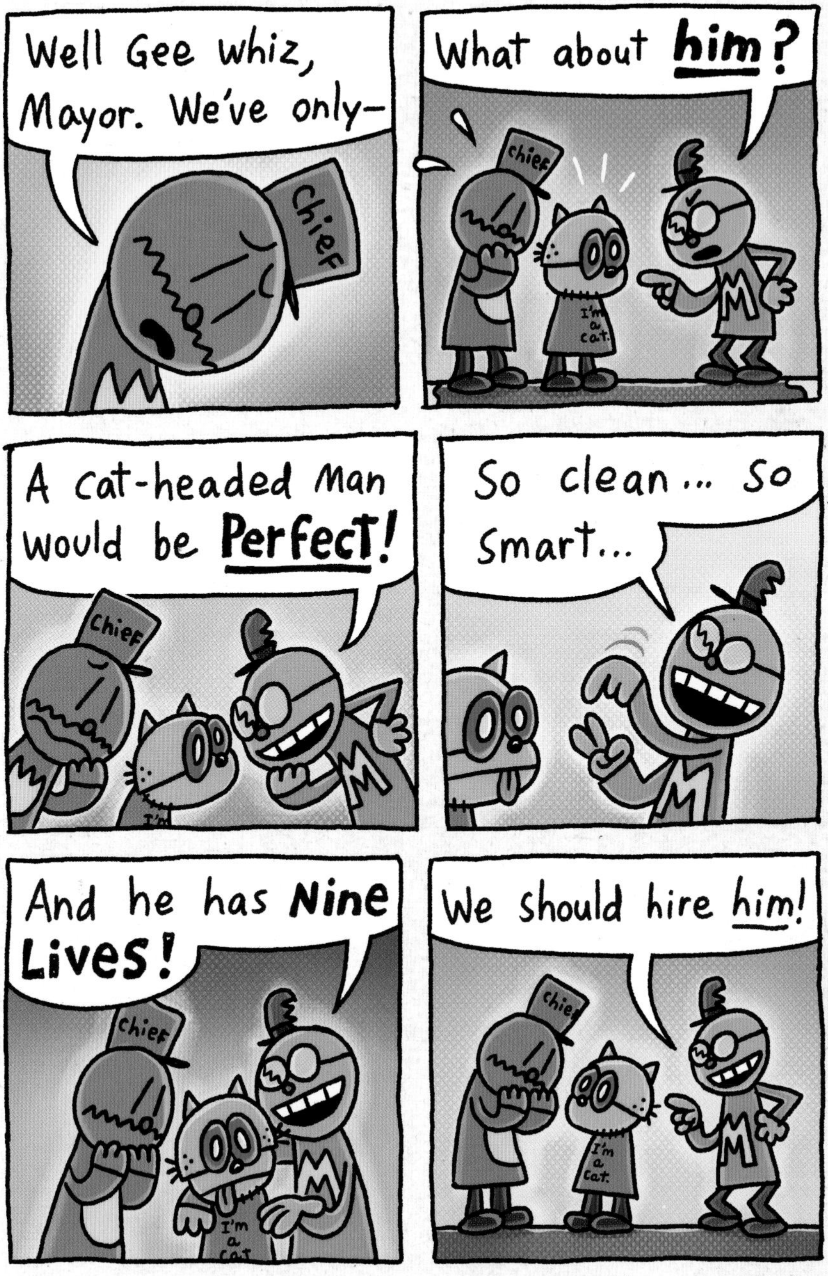
Well Gee whiz, Mayor. We've only—
What about **him**?
I'm a cat.
A cat-headed Man would be **PerfecT**!
So clean... So smart...
And he has **Nine Lives**!
We should hire him!
I'm a cat.

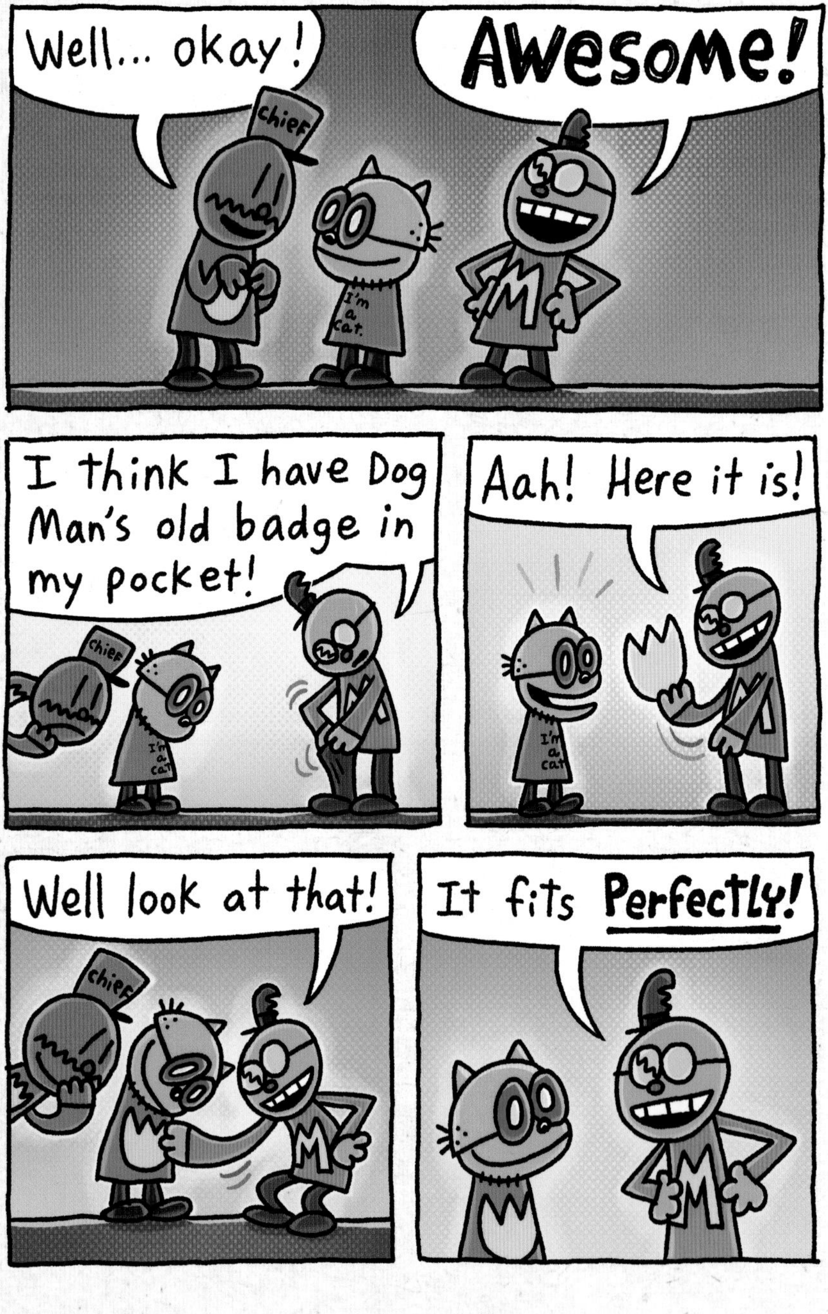
Well... okay!
AWESOME!
chief
I'm a cat.
M
I think I have Dog Man's old badge in my pocket!
chief
I'm a cat
Aah! Here it is!
I'm a cat
Well look at that!
chief
M
It fits PERFECTLY!
M

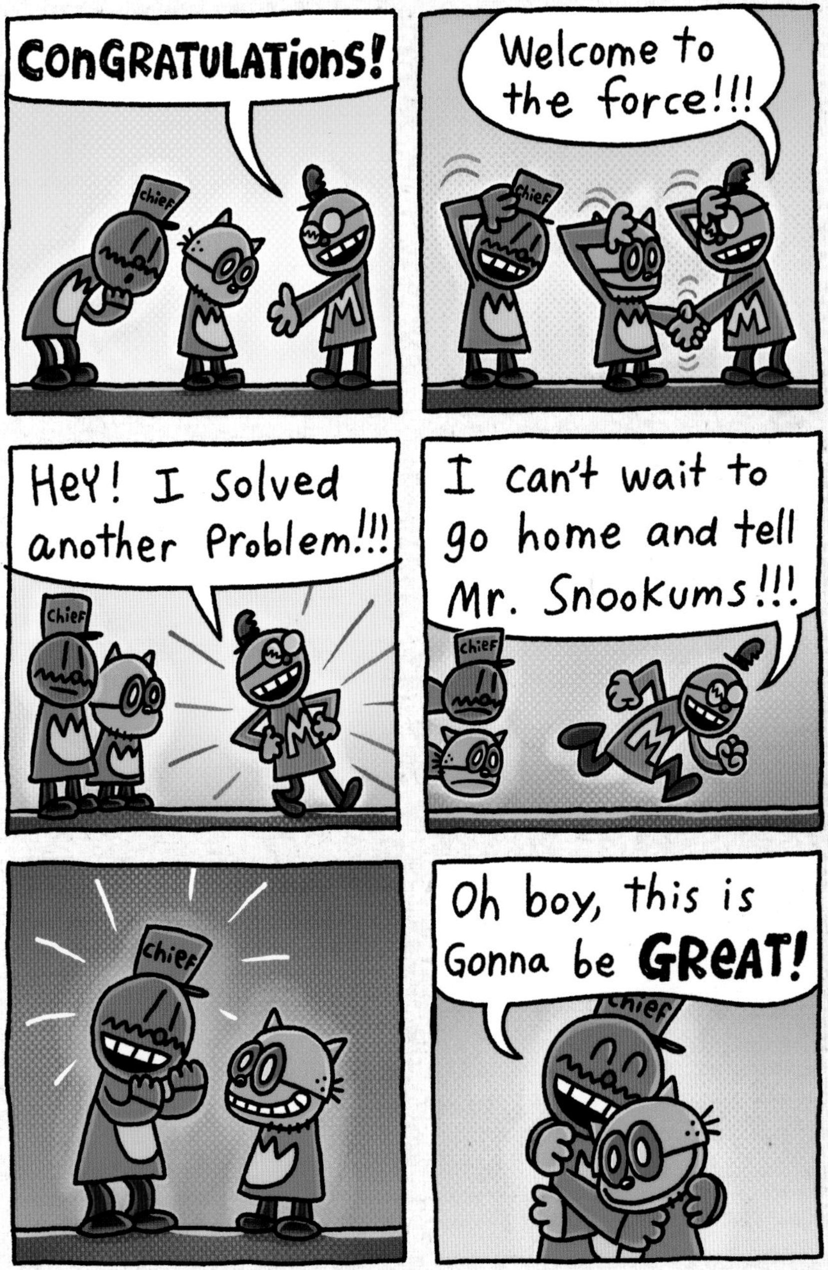
CONGRATULATIONS!
chief
Welcome to the force!!!
chief
Hey! I solved another problem!!!
chief
I can't wait to go home and tell Mr. Snookums!!!
chief
chief
Oh boy, this is gonna be GREAT!
chief

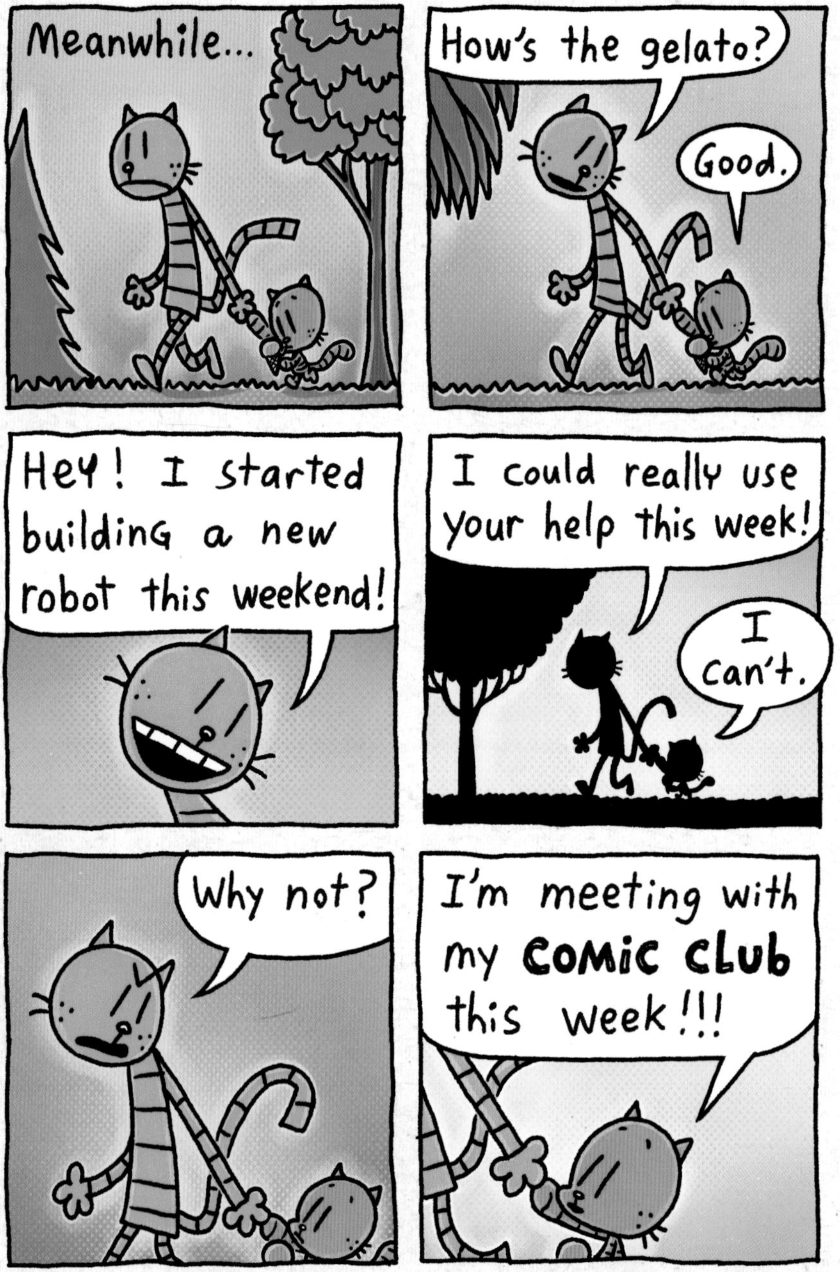
Meanwhile...
How's the gelato?
Good.
Hey! I started building a new robot this weekend!
I could really use your help this week!
I can't.
Why not?
I'm meeting with my COMIC CLUB this week!!!

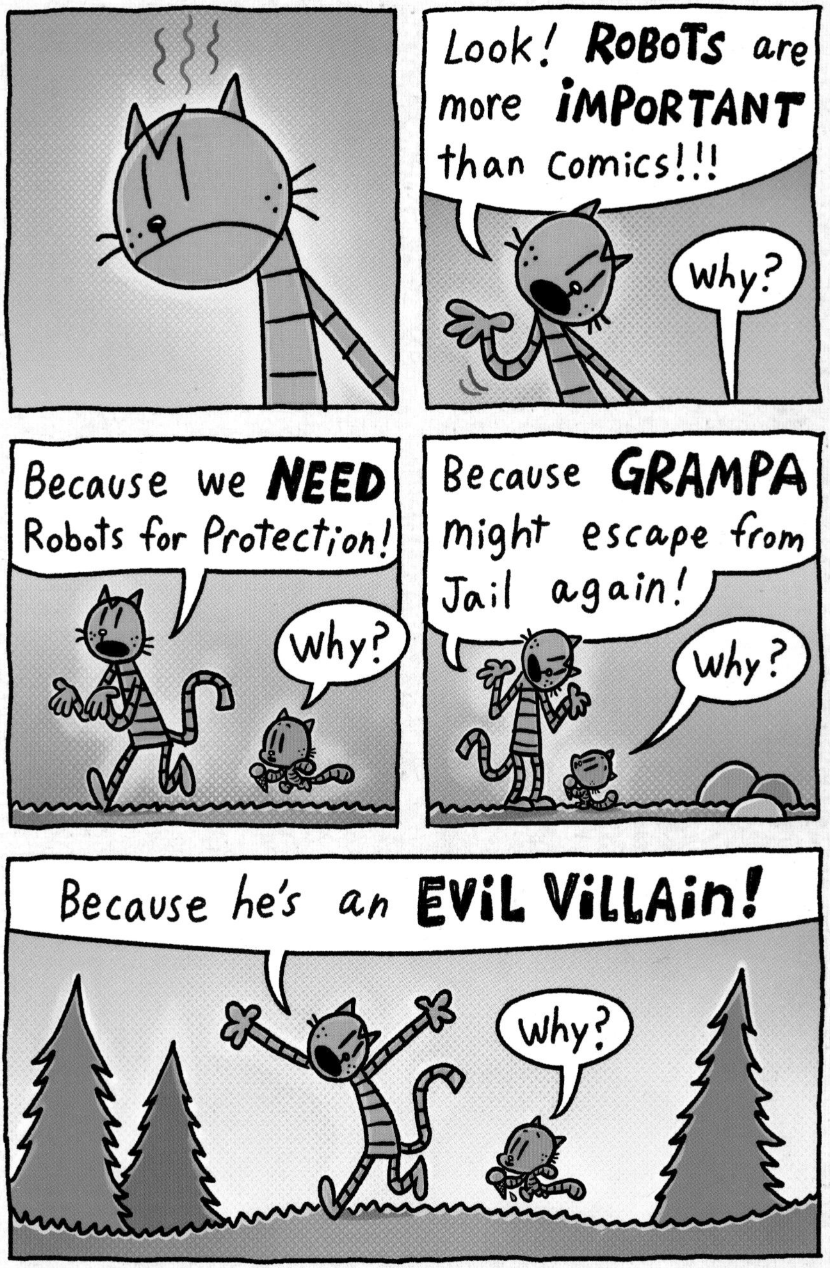
Look! ROBOTS are more IMPORTANT than Comics!!!
Why?
Because we NEED Robots for Protection!
Why?
Because GRAMPA might escape from Jail again!
Why?
Because he's an EViL ViLLAin!
Why?

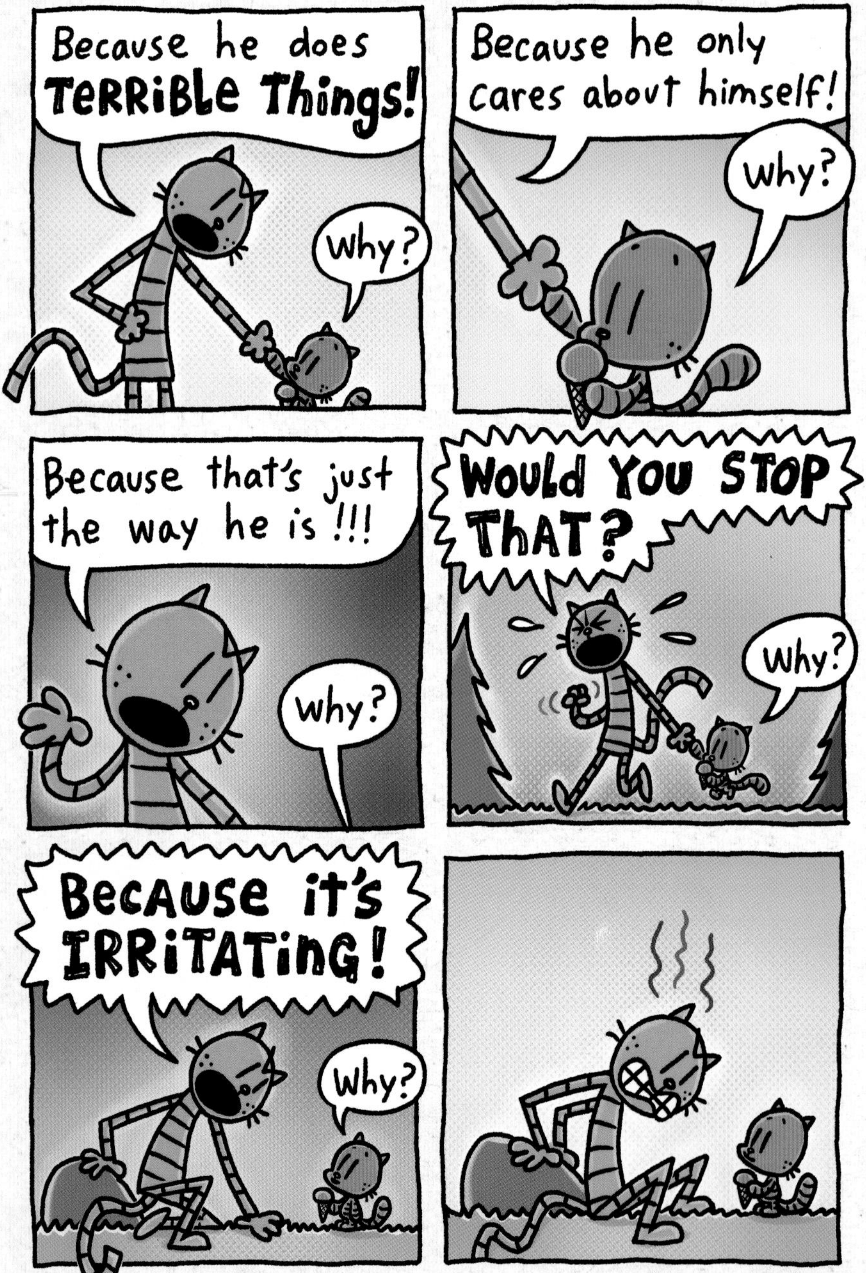
Because he does TERRIBLE Things!
Why?
Because he only cares about himself!
Why?
Because that's just the way he is!!!
Why?
WOULD YOU STOP THAT?
Why?
BECAUSE it's IRRITATING!
Why?

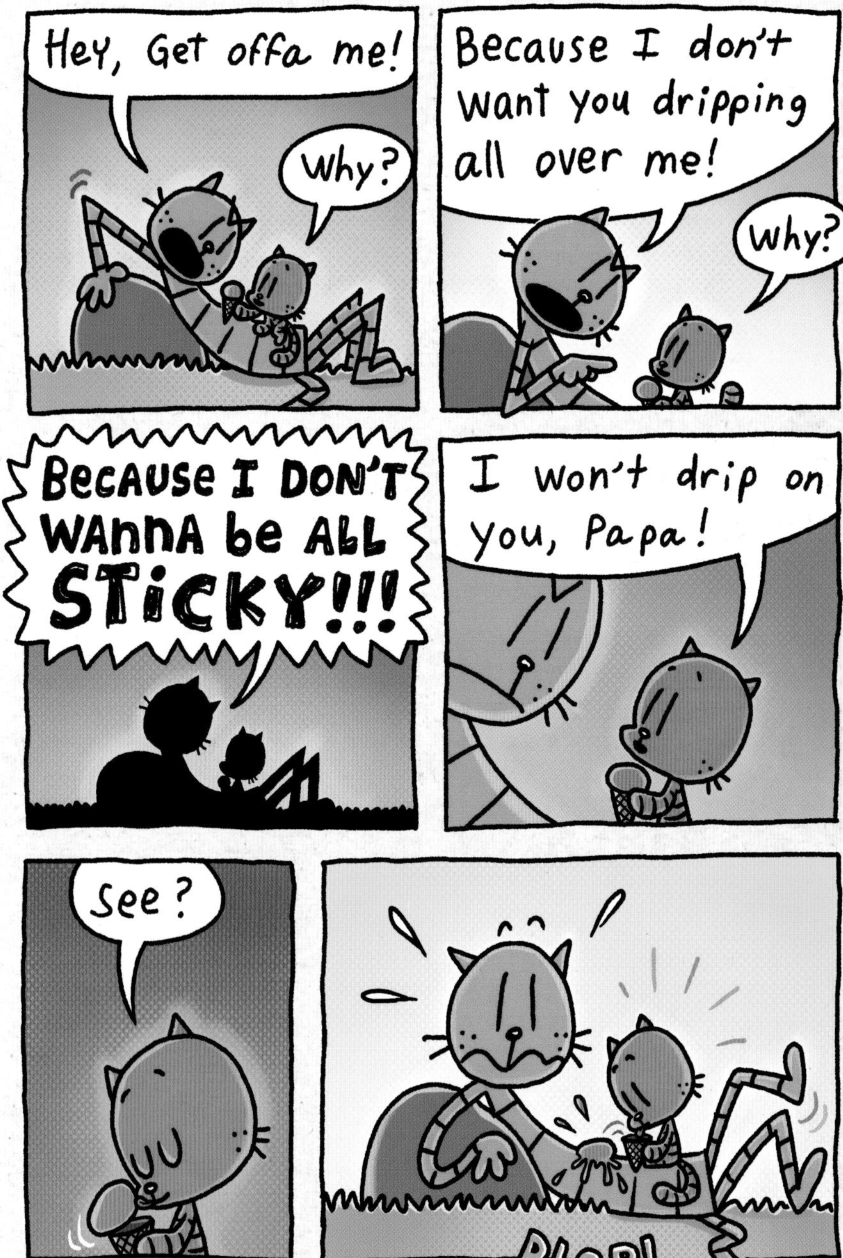
Hey, Get offa me!
Why?
Because I don't want you dripping all over me!
Why?
BECAUSE I DON'T WANNA be ALL STICKY!!!
I won't drip on you, Papa!
See?
PLOP!

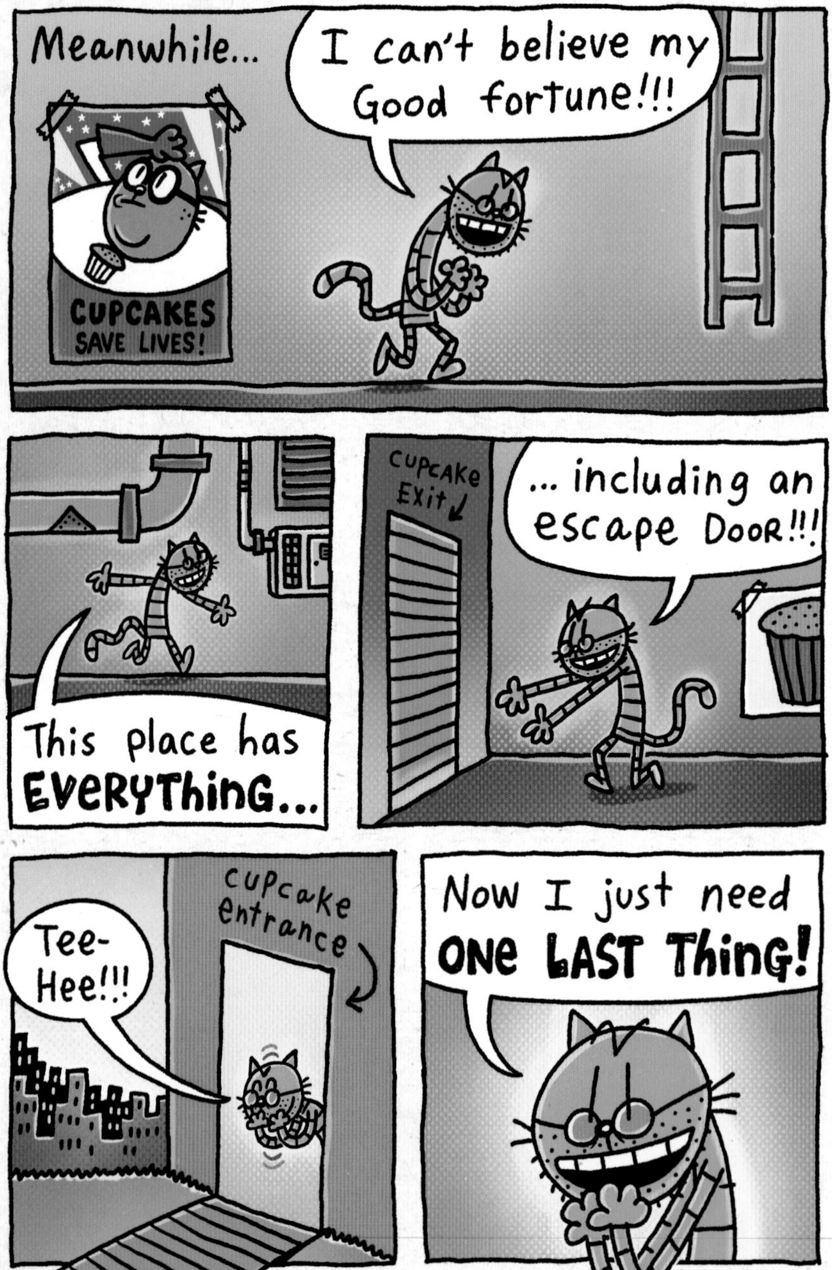
Meanwhile...
I can't believe my Good fortune!!!
CUPCAKES SAVE LIVES!
This place has EVERYThinG...
CUPCAKE EXIT
... including an escape DOOR!!!
Tee-Hee!!!
cupcake entrance
Now I just need ONE LAST Thing!

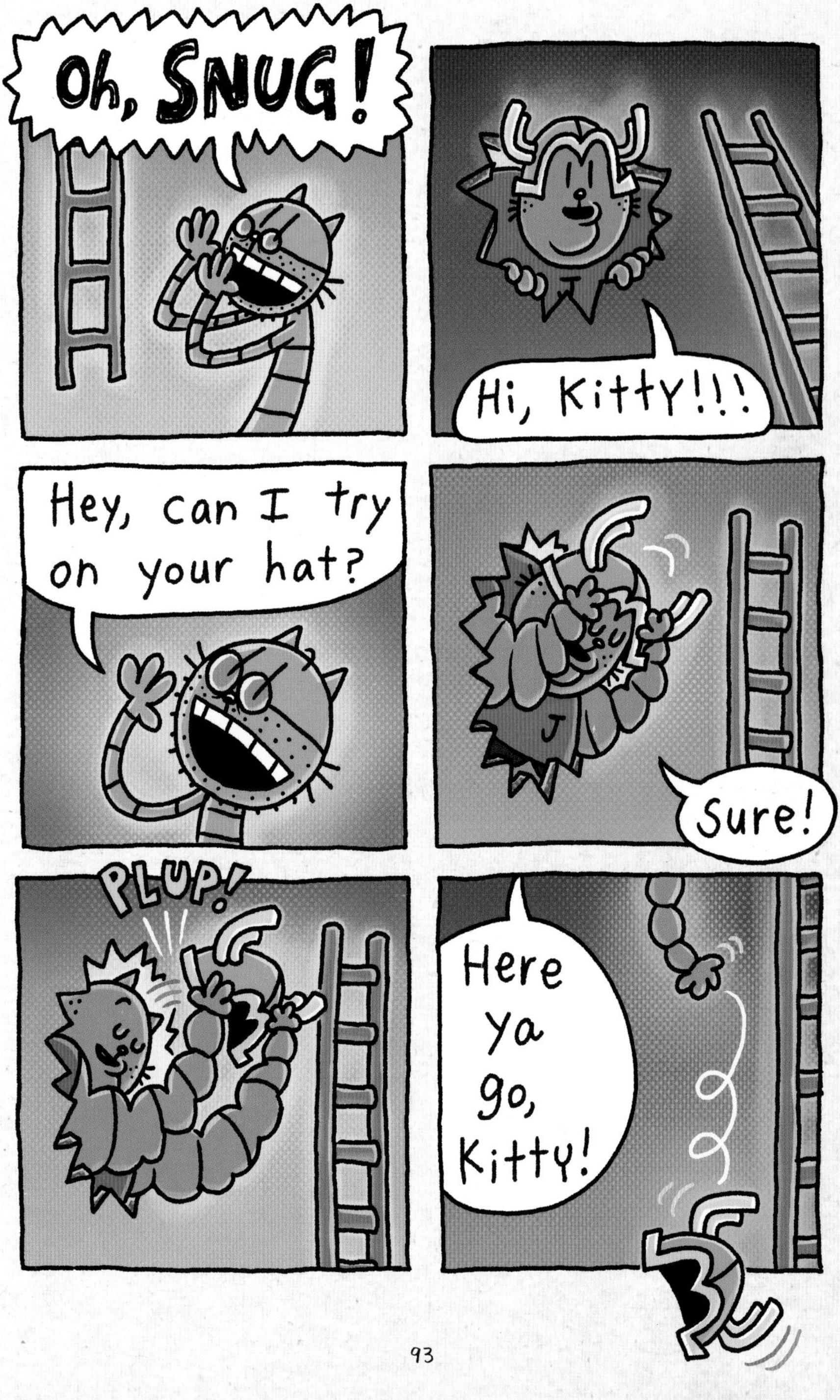
Oh, SNUG!
Hi, Kitty!!!
Hey, can I try on your hat?
Sure!
PLUP!
Here ya go, Kitty!

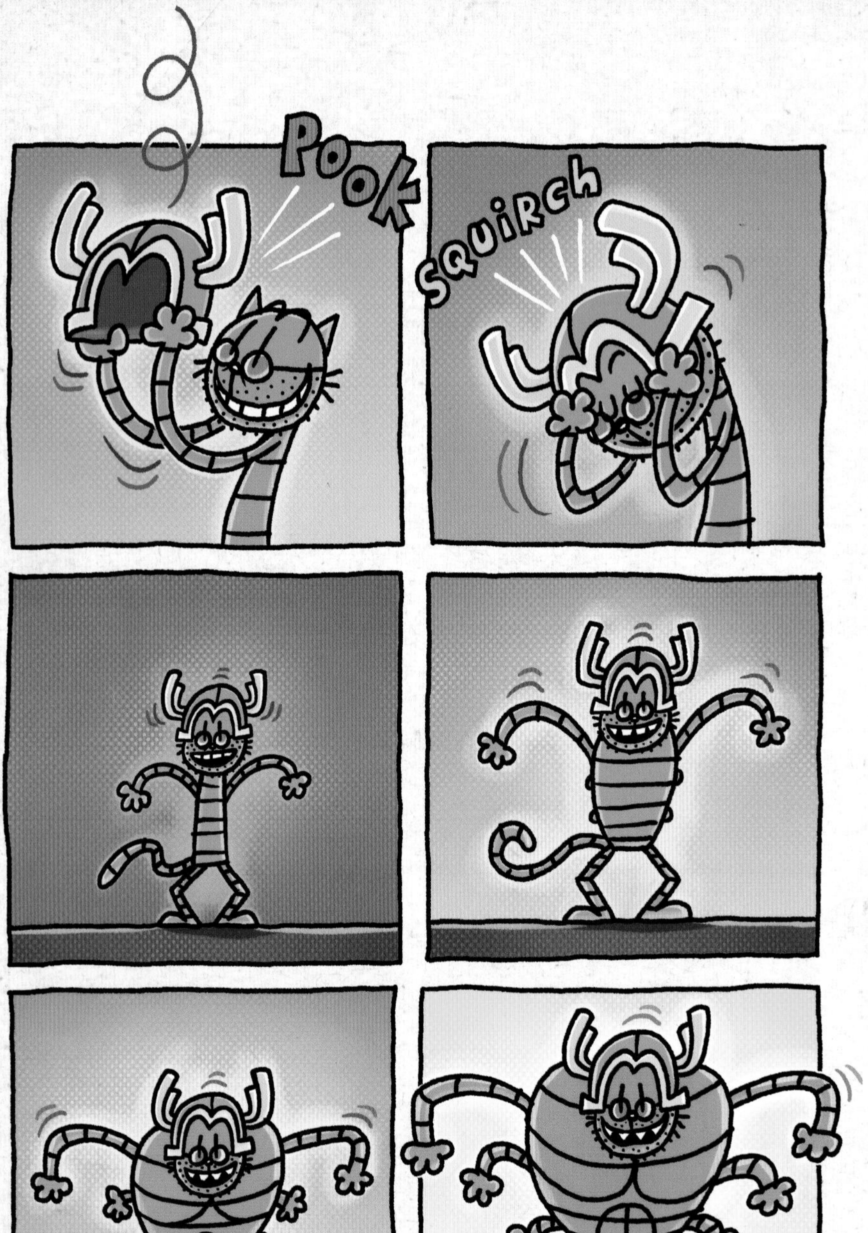
POOK
SQUIRCH

CHAPTER 6

THE INCORRIGIBLE CRUD

By George Beard and Harold Hutchins

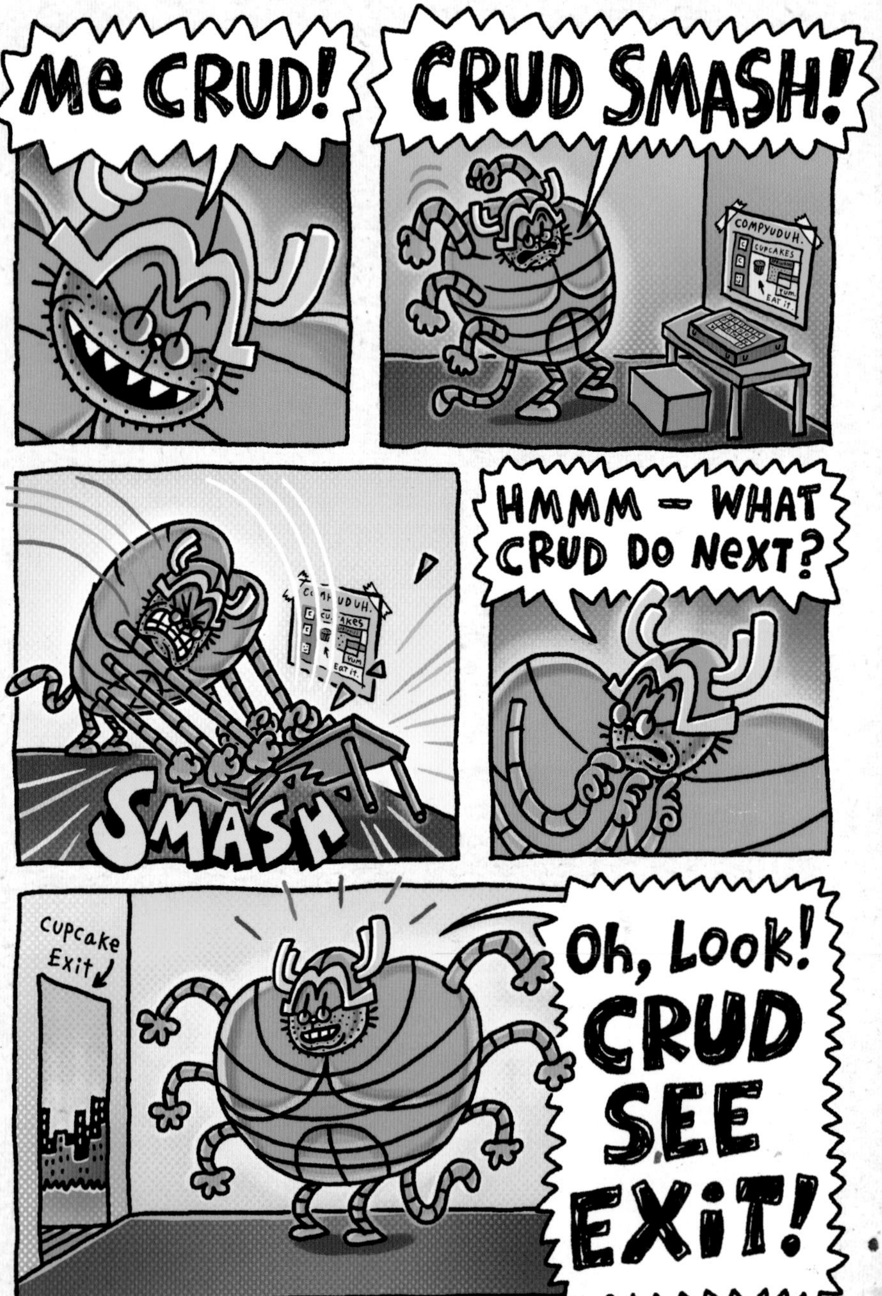
ME CRUD!
CRUD SMASH!
COMPYUDUH.
CUPCAKES
YUM.
EAT IT.
SMASH
HMMM — WHAT CRUD DO NEXT?
CUPCAKE EXIT
OH, LOOK! CRUD SEE EXIT!

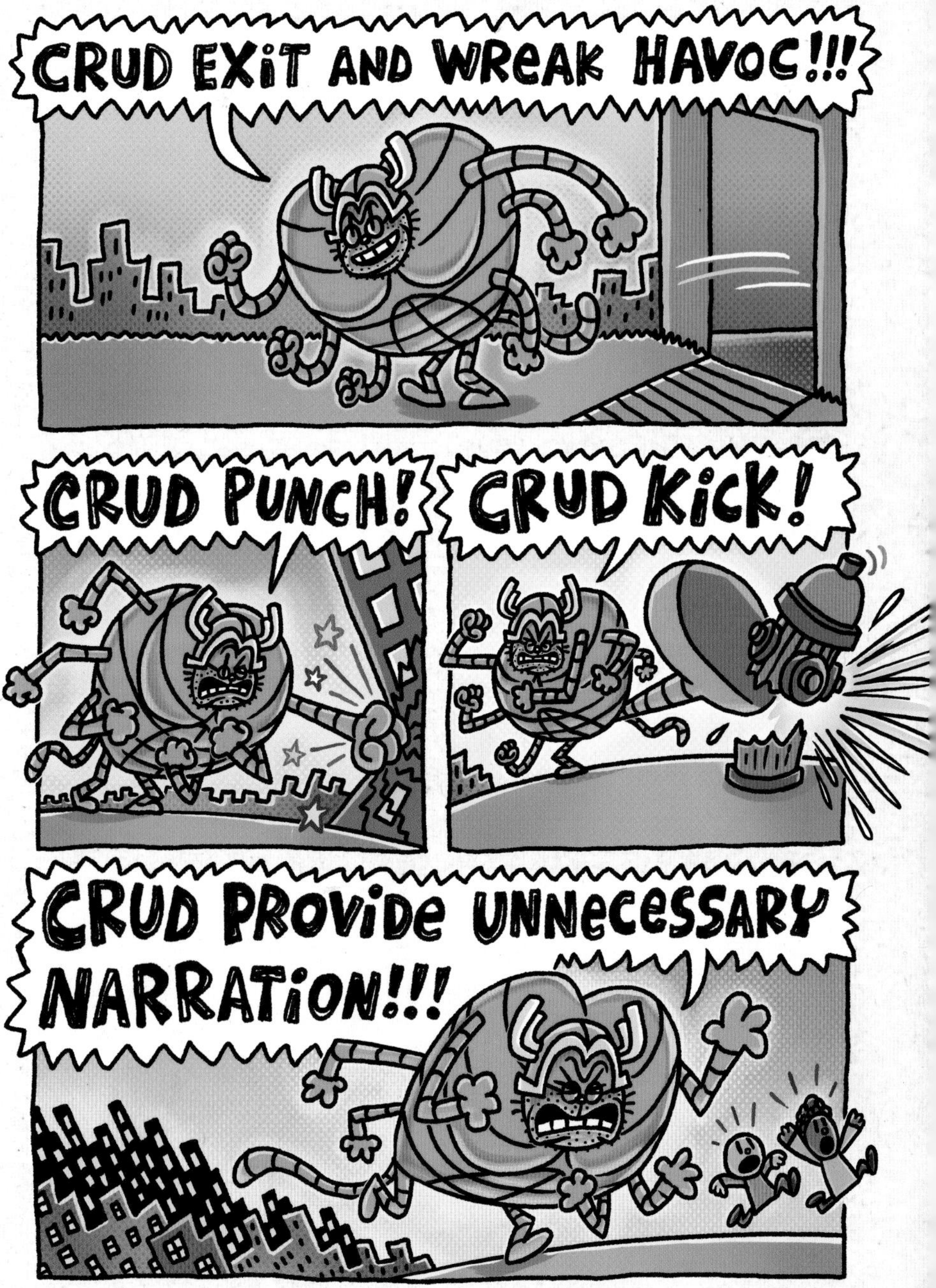
CRUD EXIT AND WREAK HAVOC!!!
CRUD PUNCH!
CRUD KICK!
CRUD PROVIDE UNNECESSARY NARRATION!!!

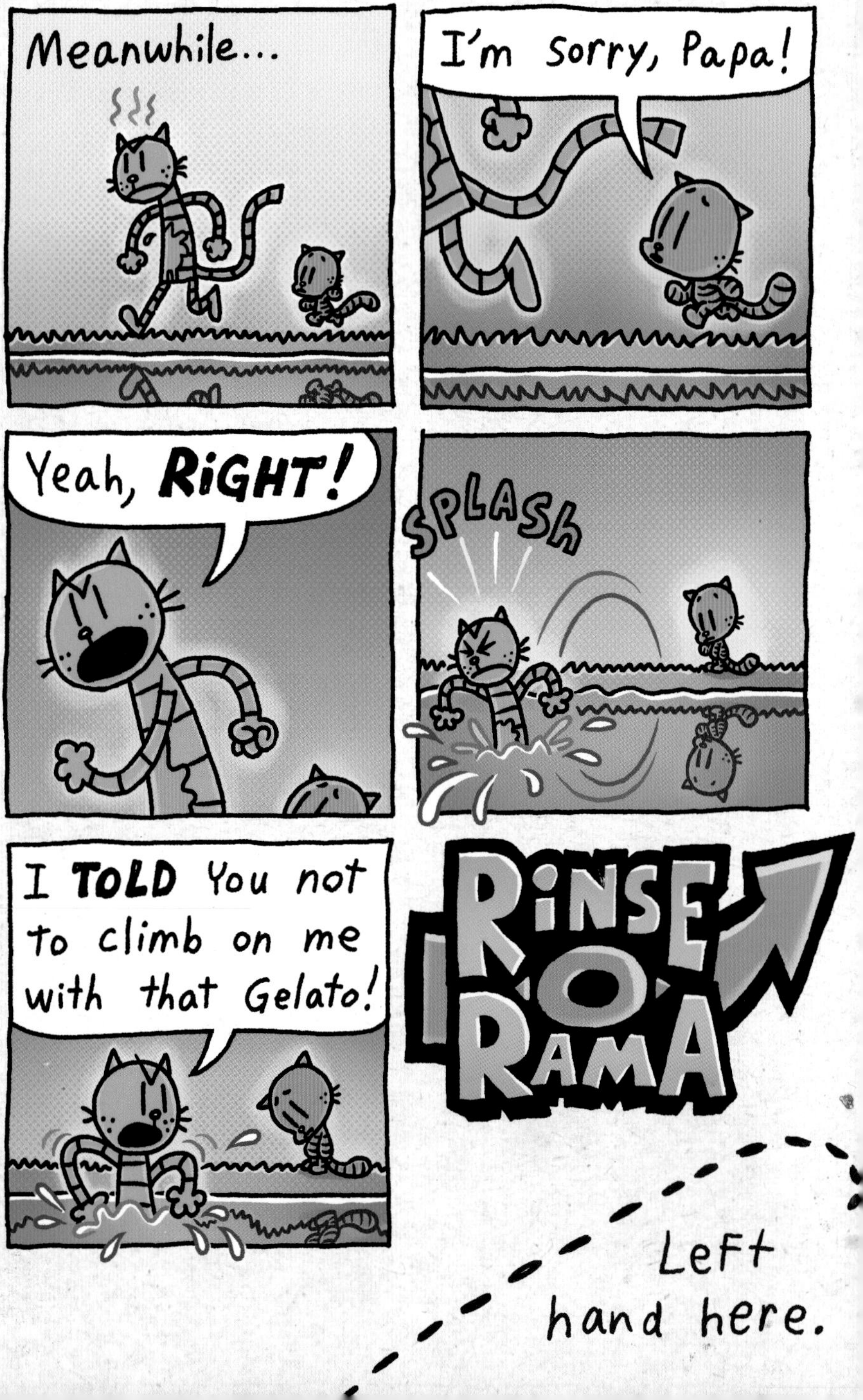

Meanwhile...
I'm sorry, Papa!
Yeah, RIGHT!
SPLASH
I TOLD you not to climb on me with that Gelato!
RINSE-O-RAMA
Left hand here.

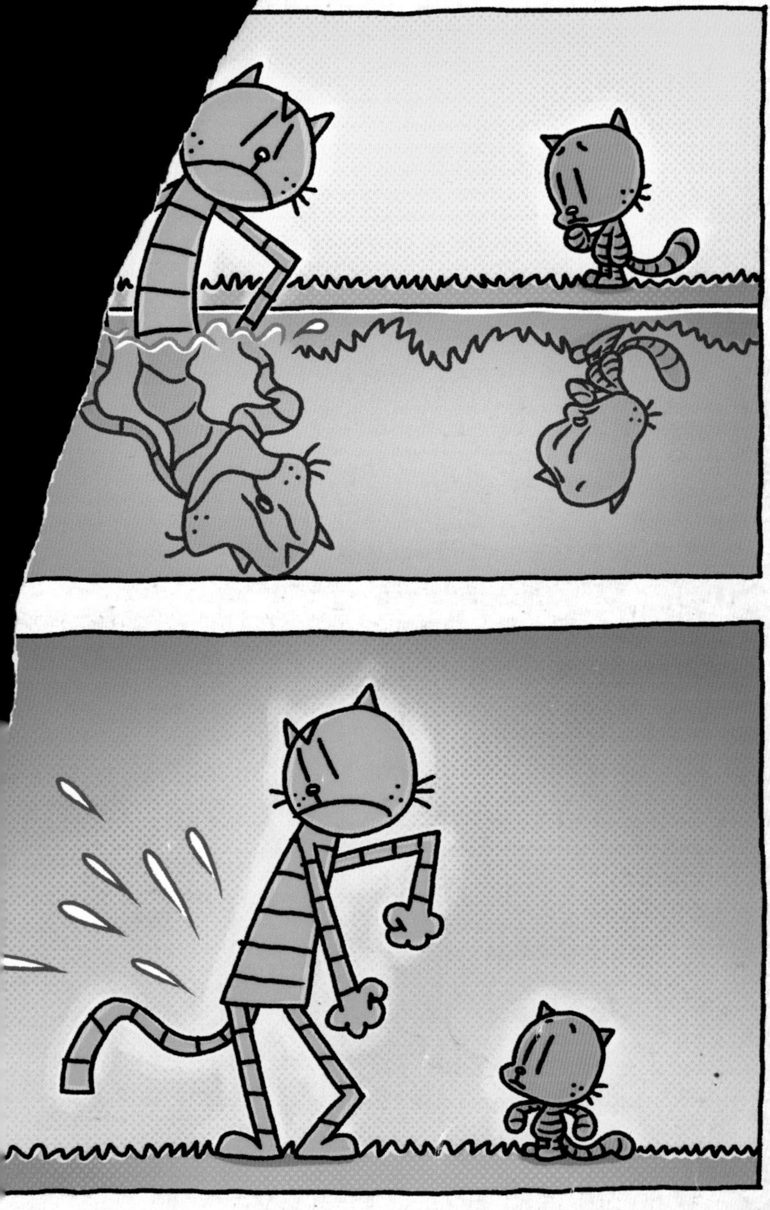

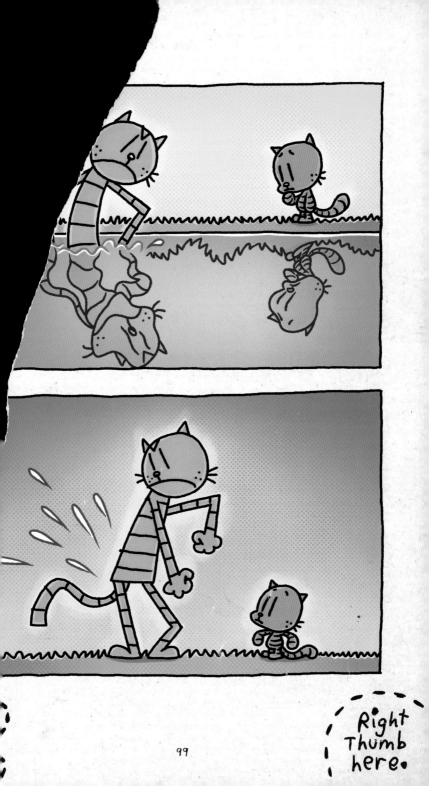

Right Thumb here.

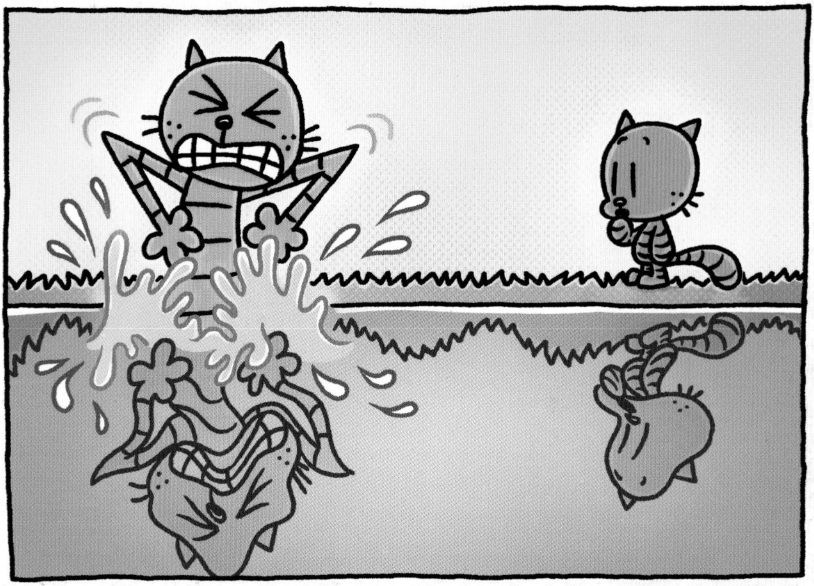

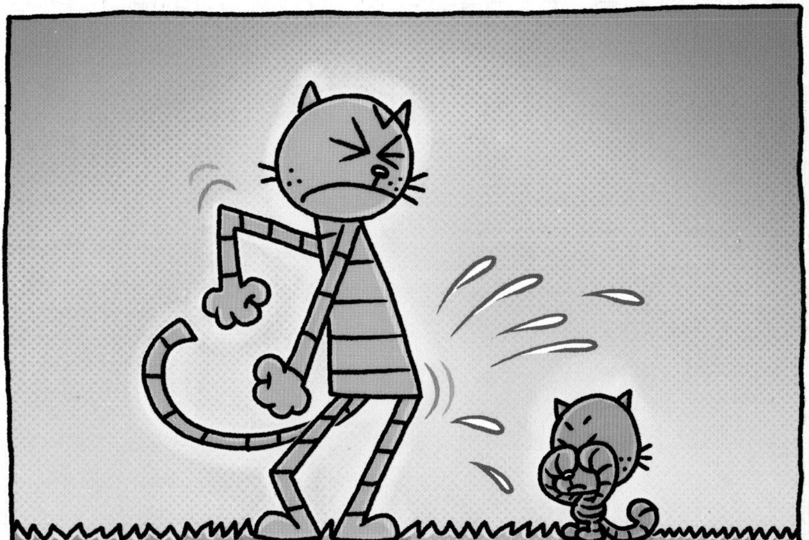

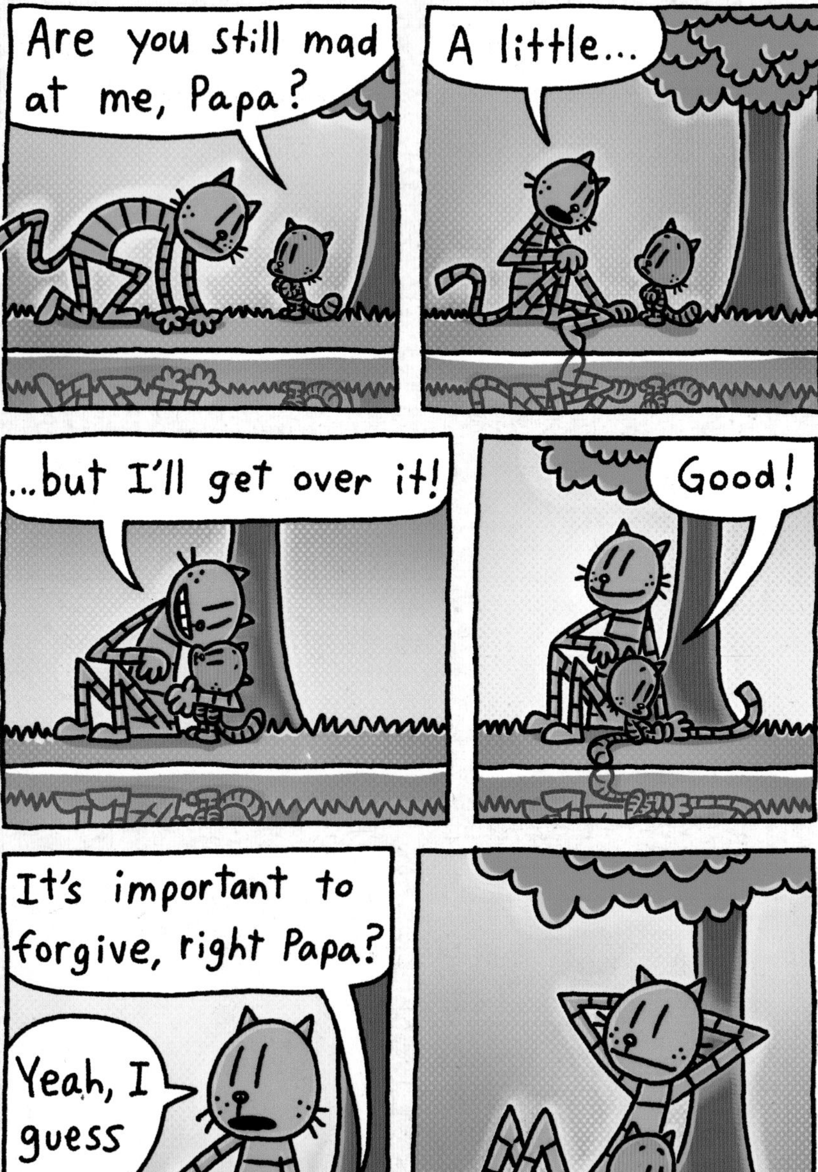
Are you still mad at me, Papa?
A little...
...but I'll get over it!
Good!
It's important to forgive, right Papa?
Yeah, I guess so.

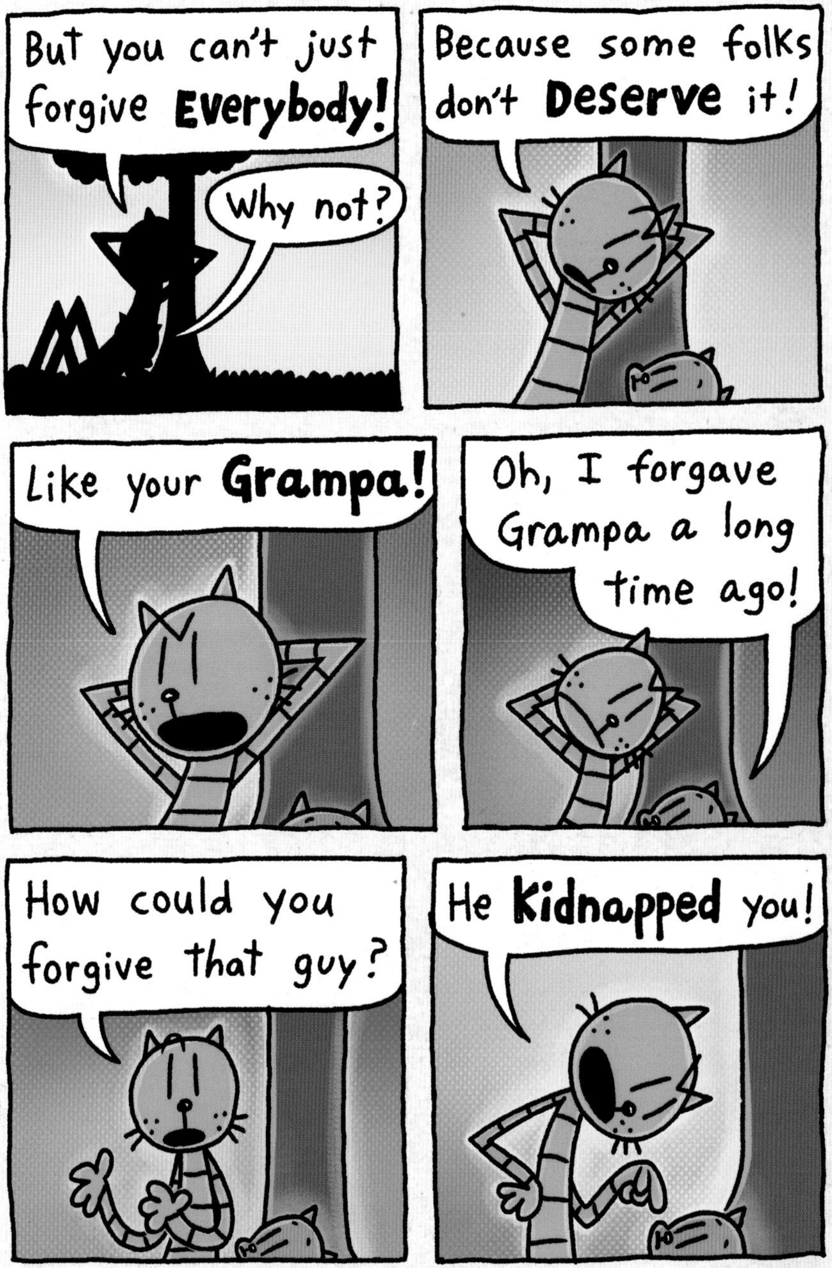
But you can't just forgive Everybody!
Why not?
Because some folks don't Deserve it!
Like your Grampa!
Oh, I forgave Grampa a long time ago!
How could you forgive that guy?
He Kidnapped you!

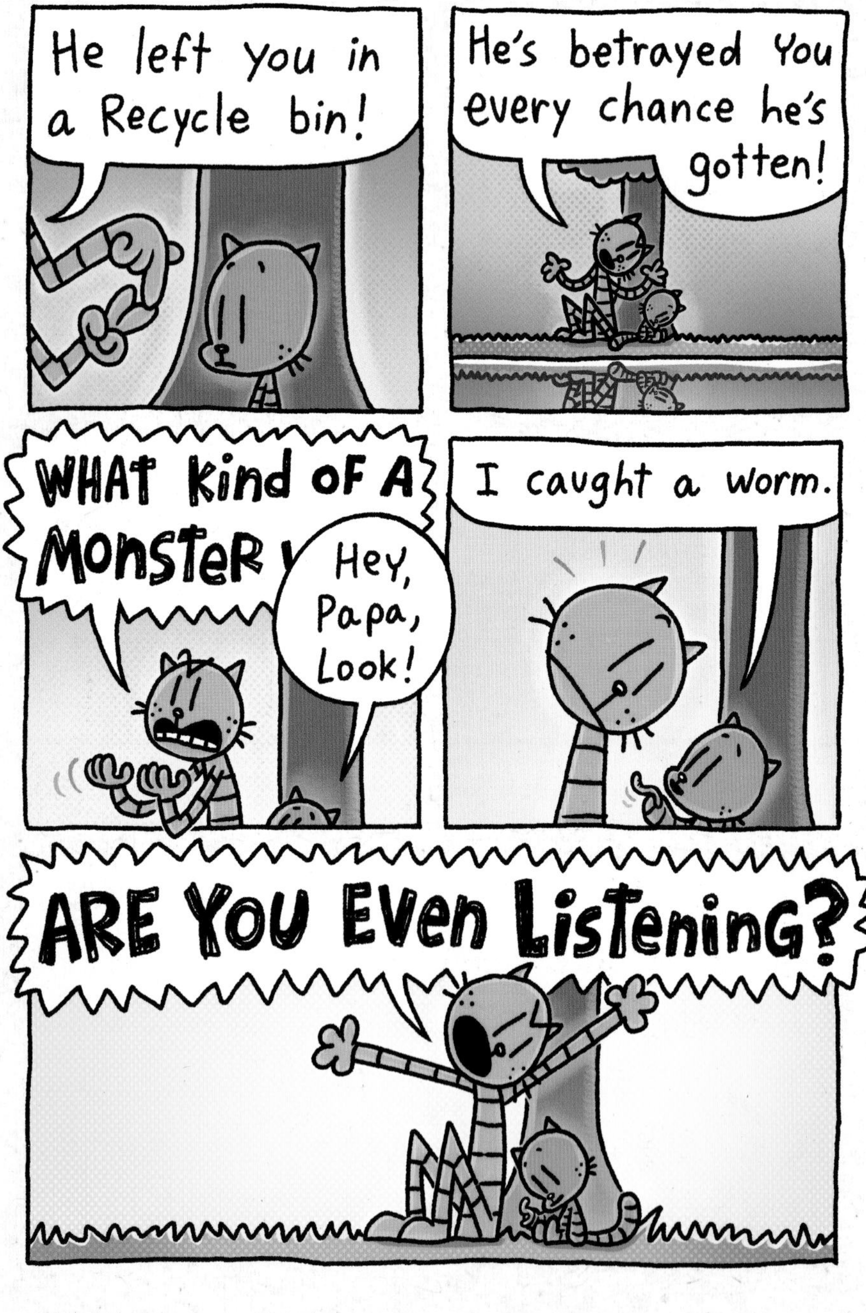
He left you in a Recycle bin!
He's betrayed You every chance he's gotten!
WHAT Kind OF A MONSTER
Hey, Papa, Look!
I caught a worm.
ARE YOU EVEN LISTENING?

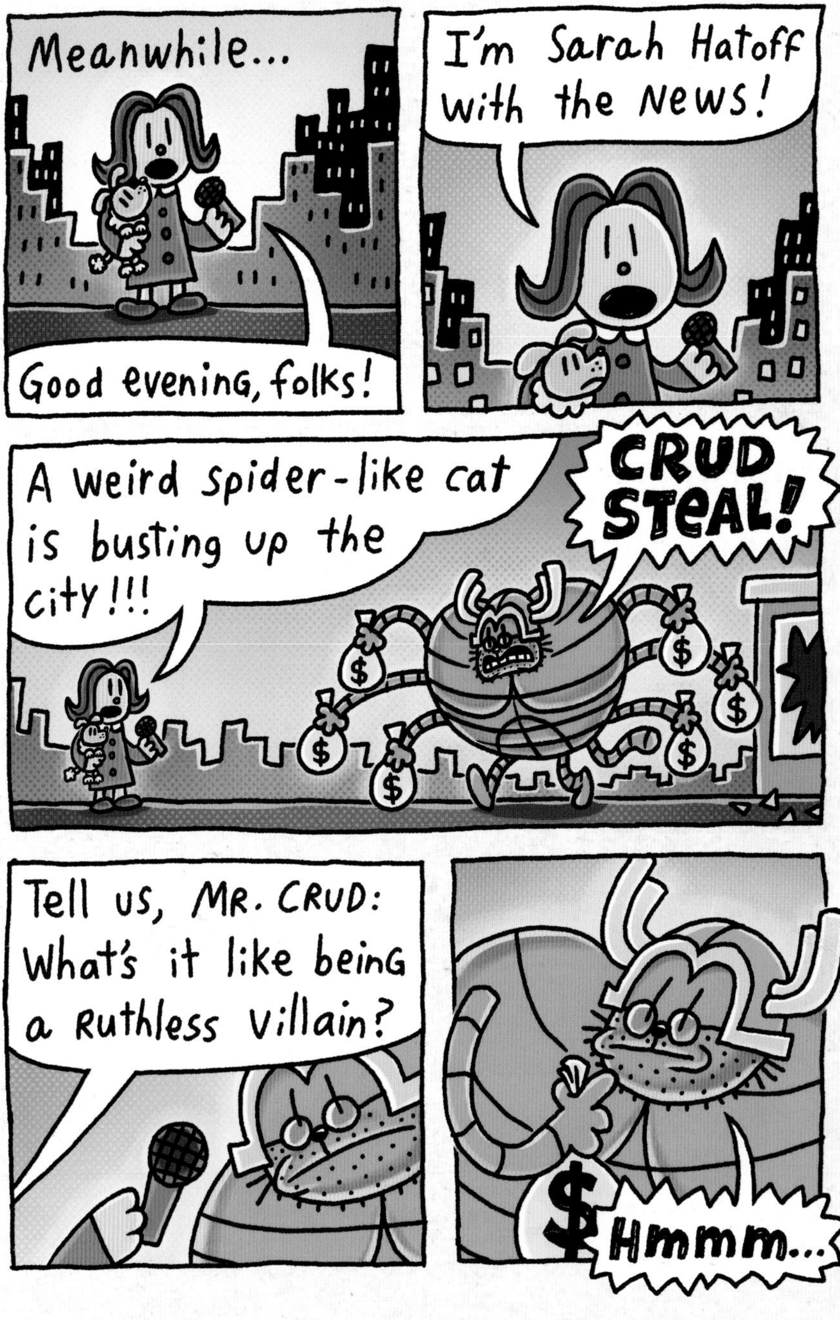
Meanwhile...
Good evening, folks!
I'm Sarah Hatoff with the News!
A weird spider-like cat is busting up the city!!!
CRUD STEAL!
Tell us, MR. CRUD: What's it like being a Ruthless villain?
Hmmm...

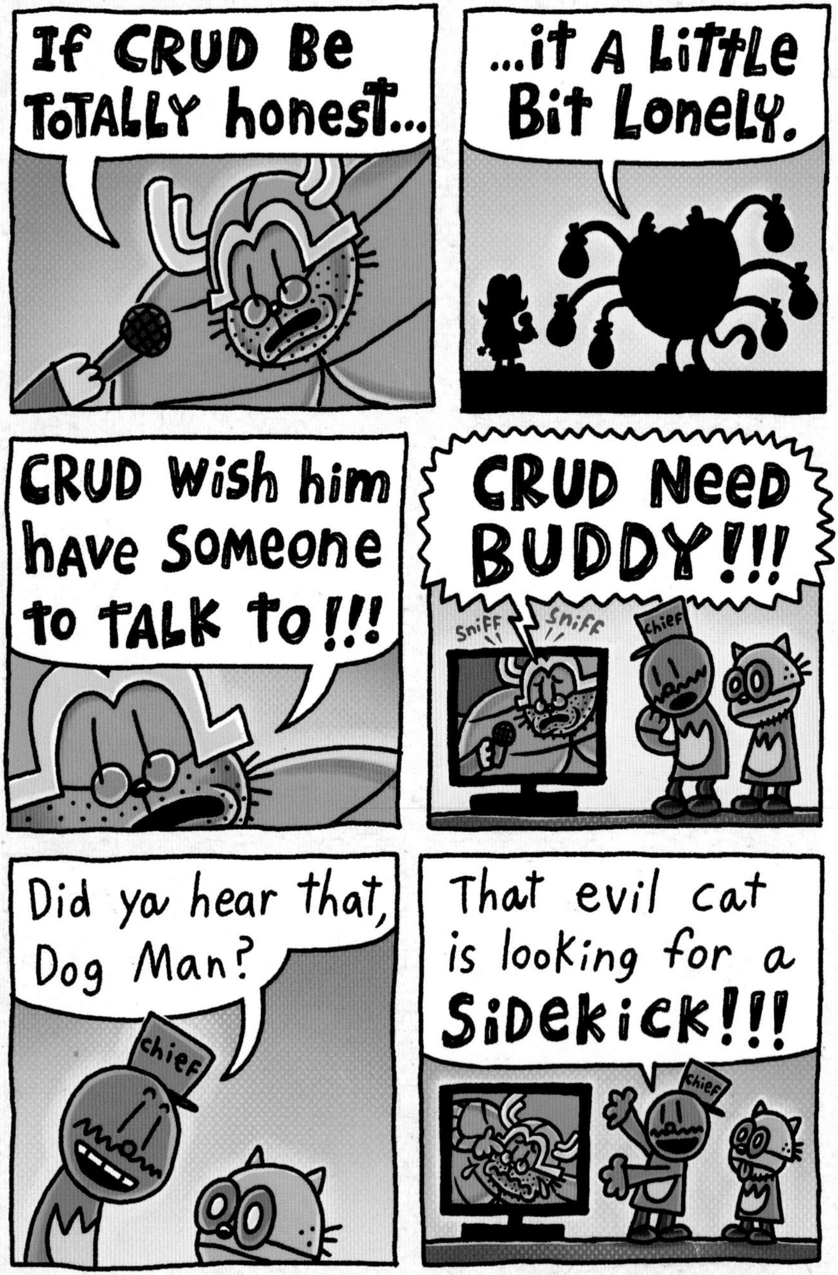
If CRUD Be TOTALLY honest...
...it A Little Bit Lonely.
CRUD Wish him have Someone to TALK TO!!!
CRUD NEED BUDDY!!!
Sniff
Sniff
chief
Did ya hear that, Dog Man?
chief
That evil cat is looking for a SiDEKICK!!!
chief

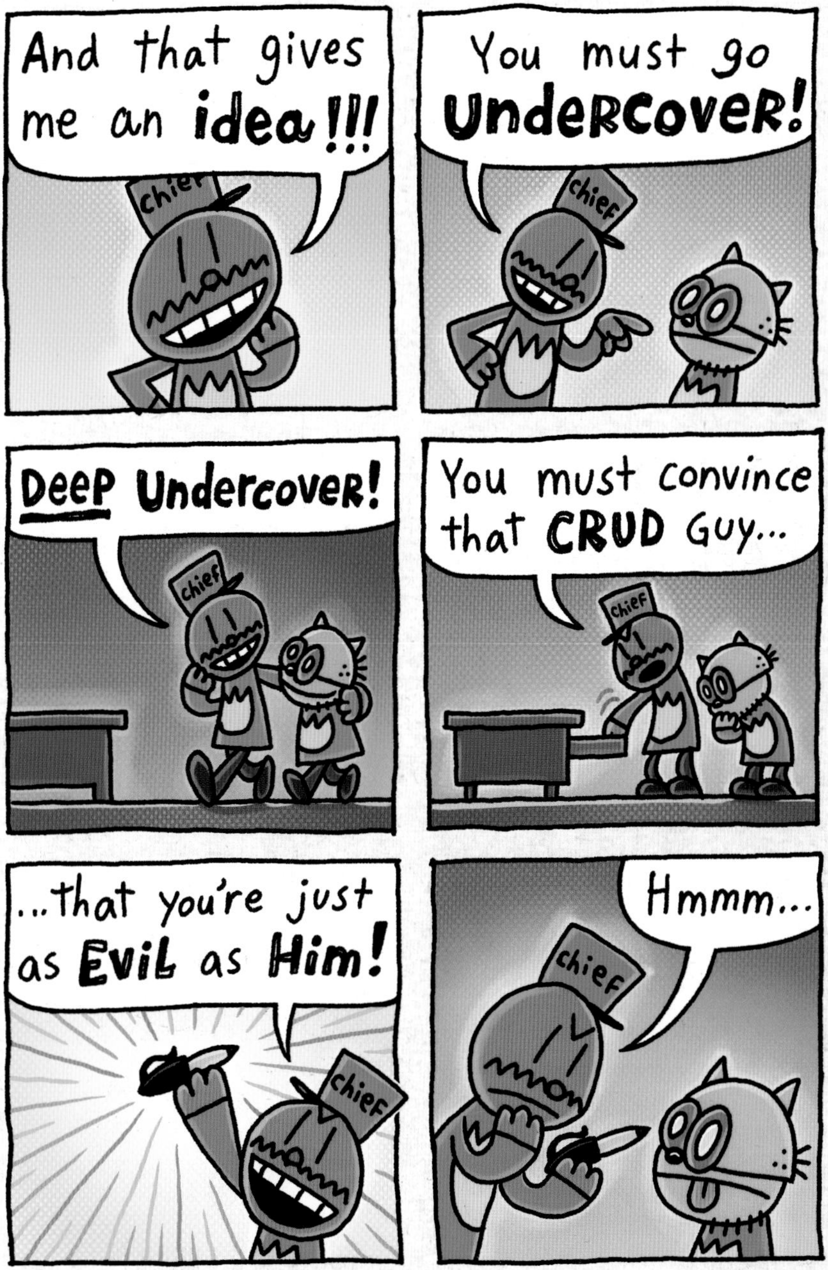
And that gives me an idea!!!
You must go UNDERCOVER!
DEEP Undercover!
You must convince that CRUD Guy...
...that you're just as EVIL as Him!
Hmmm...

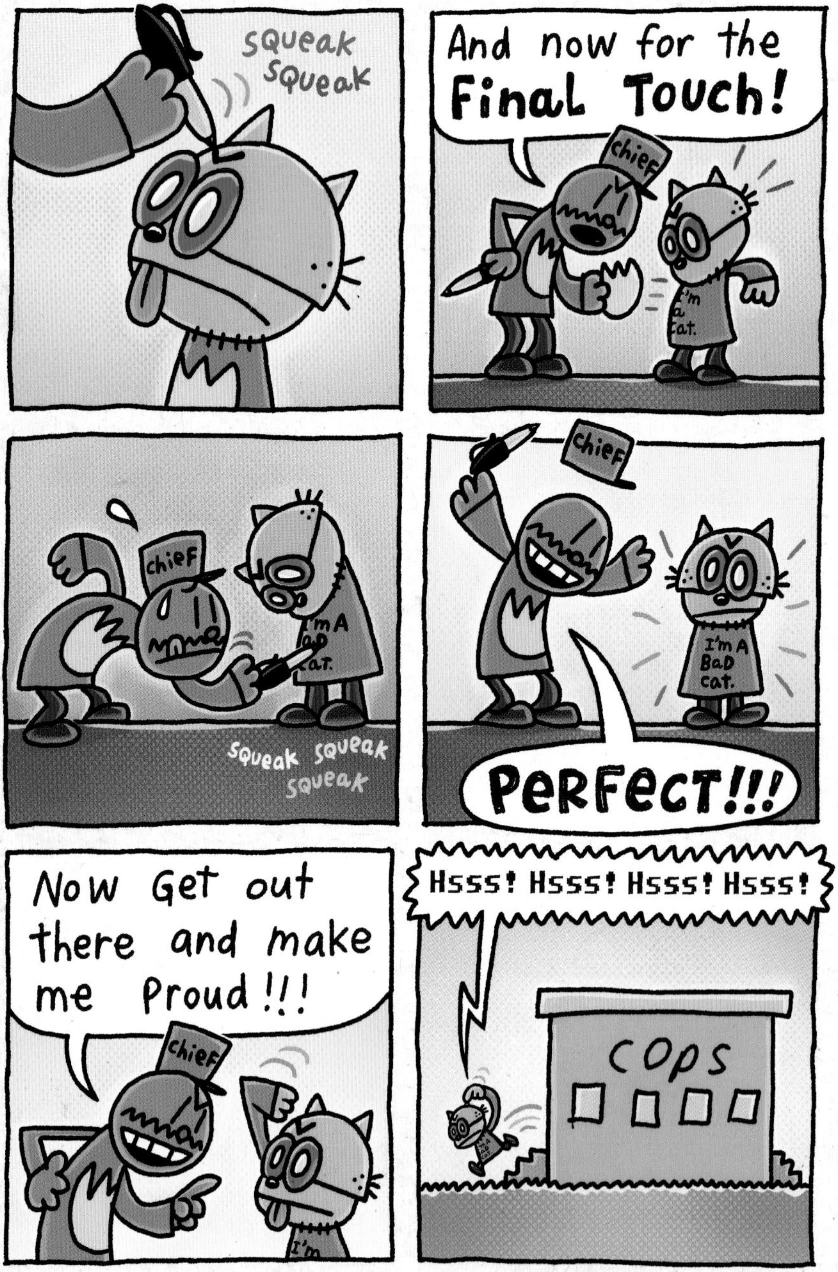
squeak squeak
And now for the Final Touch!
chief
I'm a cat.
chief
I'm A BaD cat.
squeak squeak squeak
chief
I'm A BaD cat.
PERFECT!!!
Now Get out there and make me Proud!!!
chief
I'm
Hsss! Hsss! Hsss! Hsss!
cops

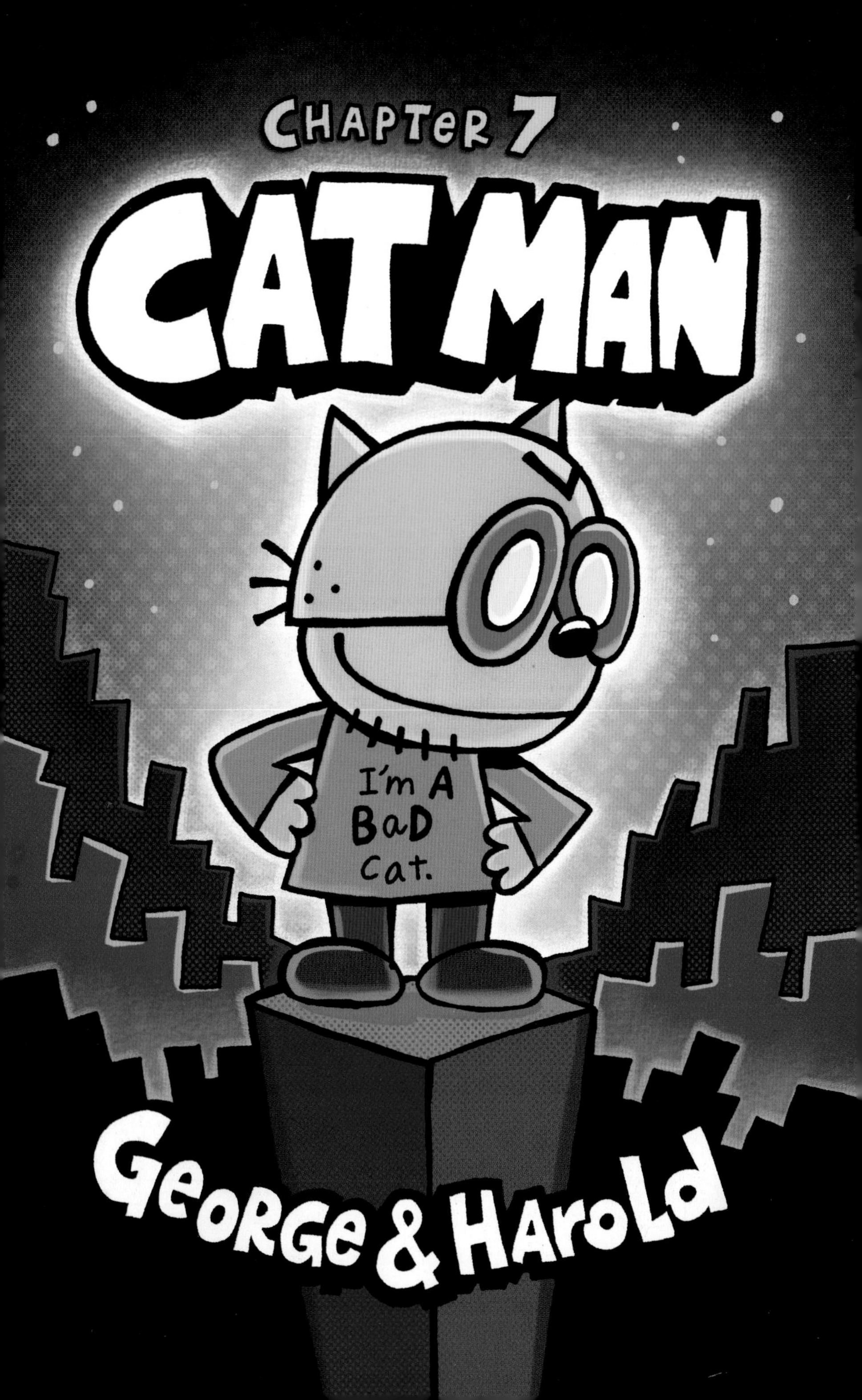

CHAPTER 7
CAT MAN
I'm A BaD cat.
George & Harold

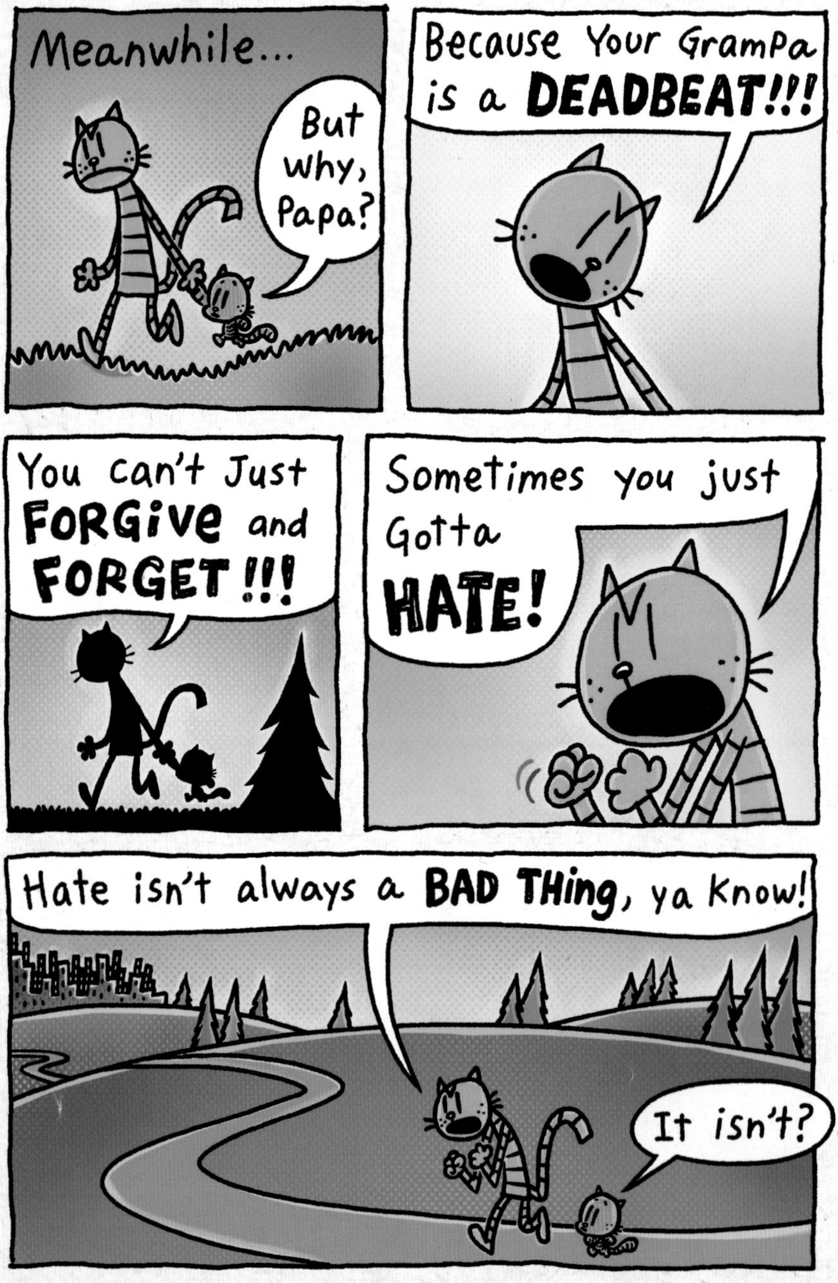
Meanwhile...
But why, Papa?
Because Your GramPa is a DEADBEAT!!!
You can't Just FORGive and FORGET!!!
Sometimes you just Gotta HATE!
Hate isn't always a BAD THing, ya Know!
It isn't?

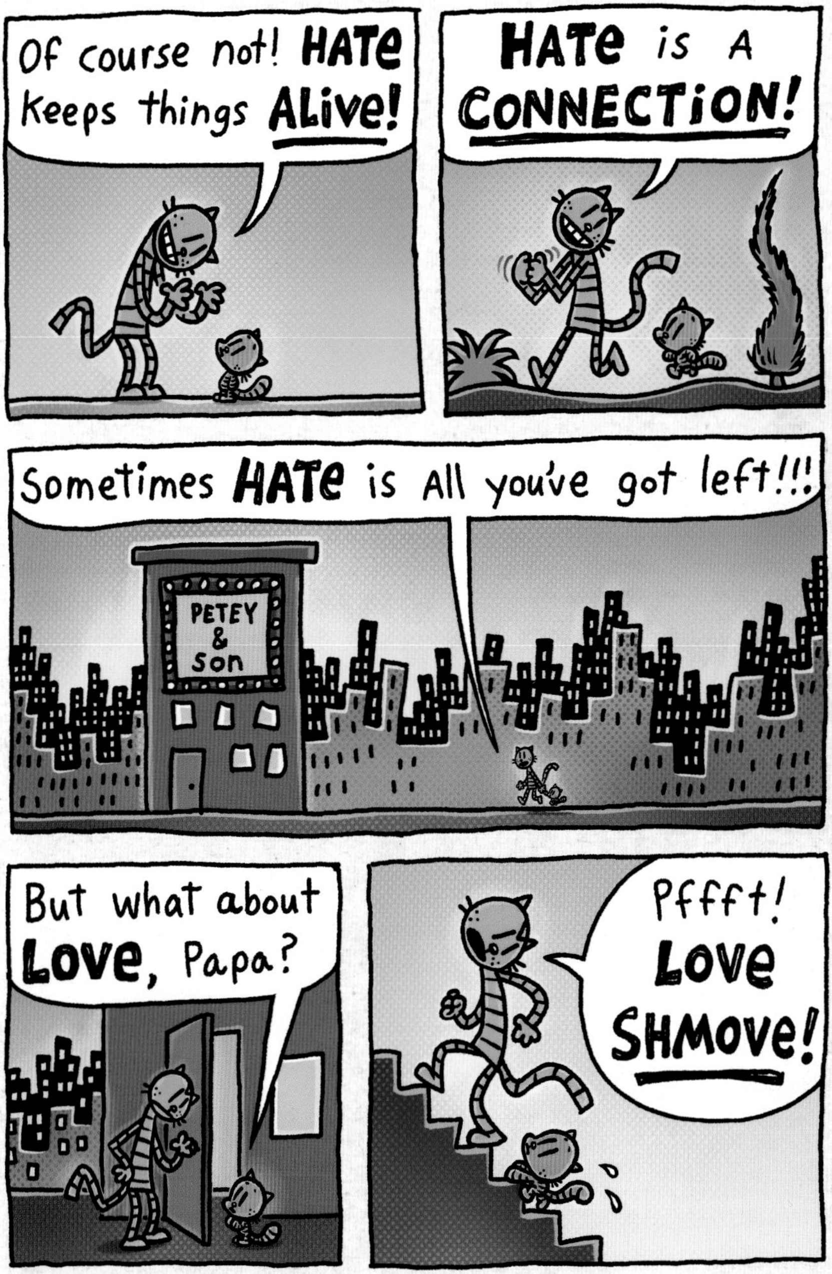
Of course not! HATE Keeps things ALive!
HATE is A CONNECTION!
Sometimes HATE is All you've got left!!!
PETEY & Son
But what about LOVE, Papa?
Pffft! LOVE SHMOVE!

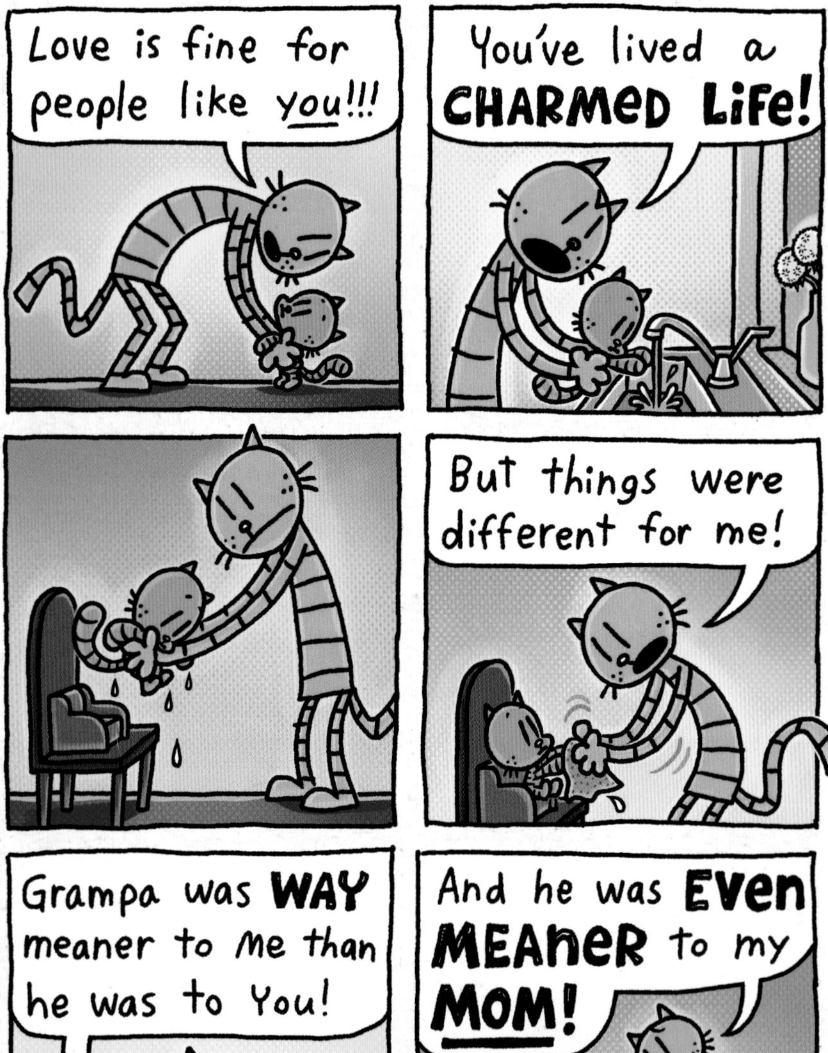
Love is fine for people like you!!!
You've lived a CHARMED LIFE!
But things were different for me!
Grampa was WAY meaner to me than he was to You!
And he was EVEN MEANER to my MOM!

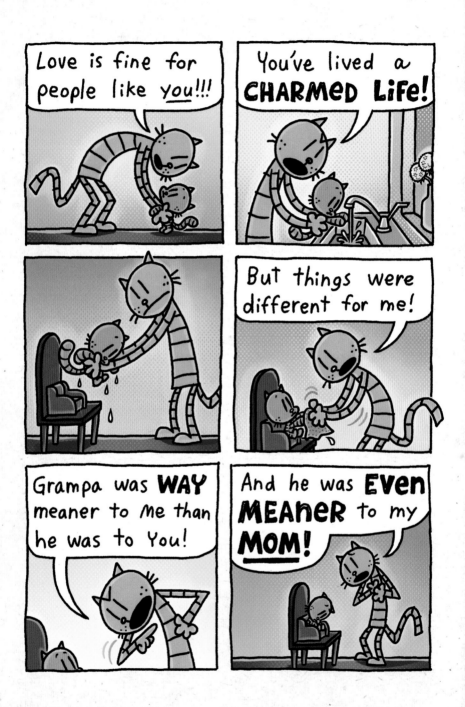

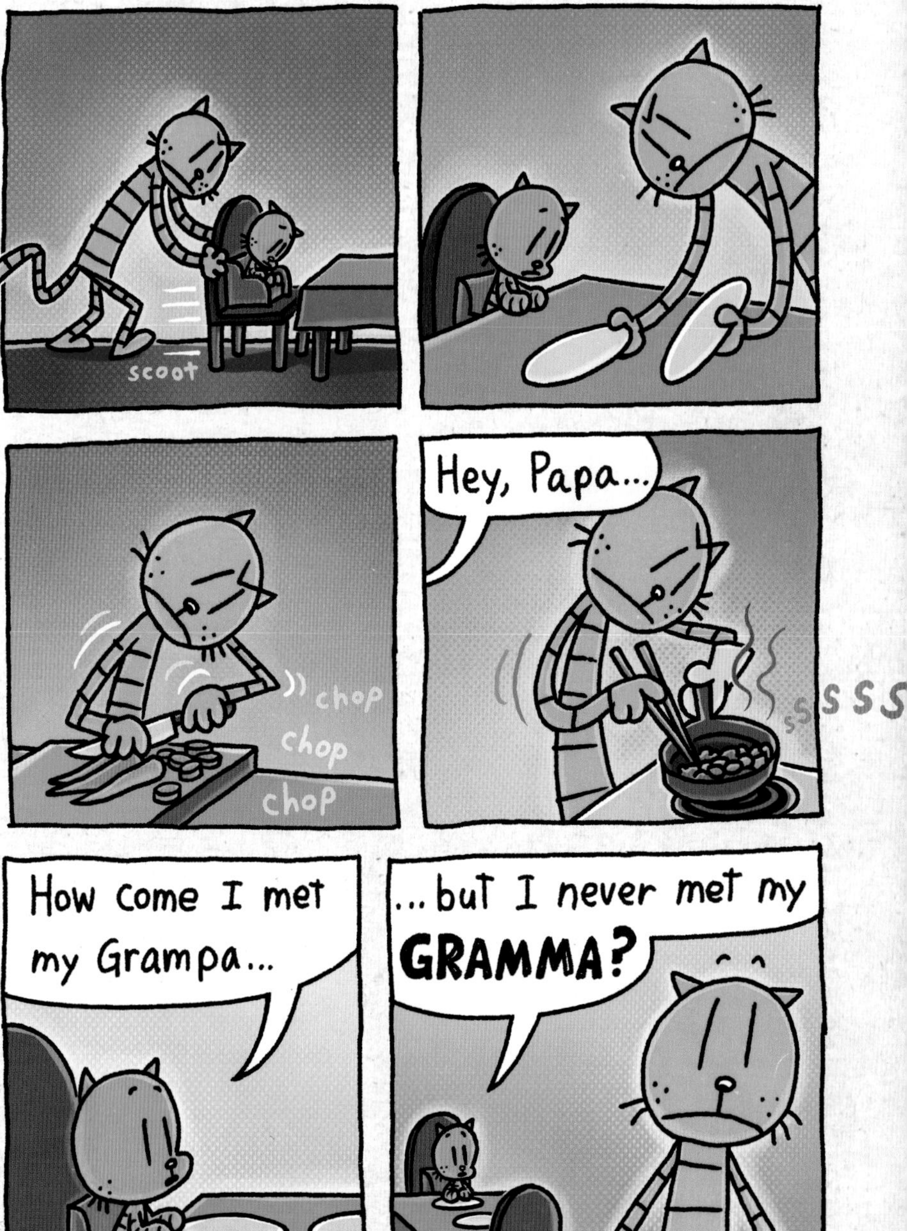
scoot
chop
chop
chop
Hey, Papa...
SSSSS
How come I met my Grampa...
...but I never met my GRAMMA?

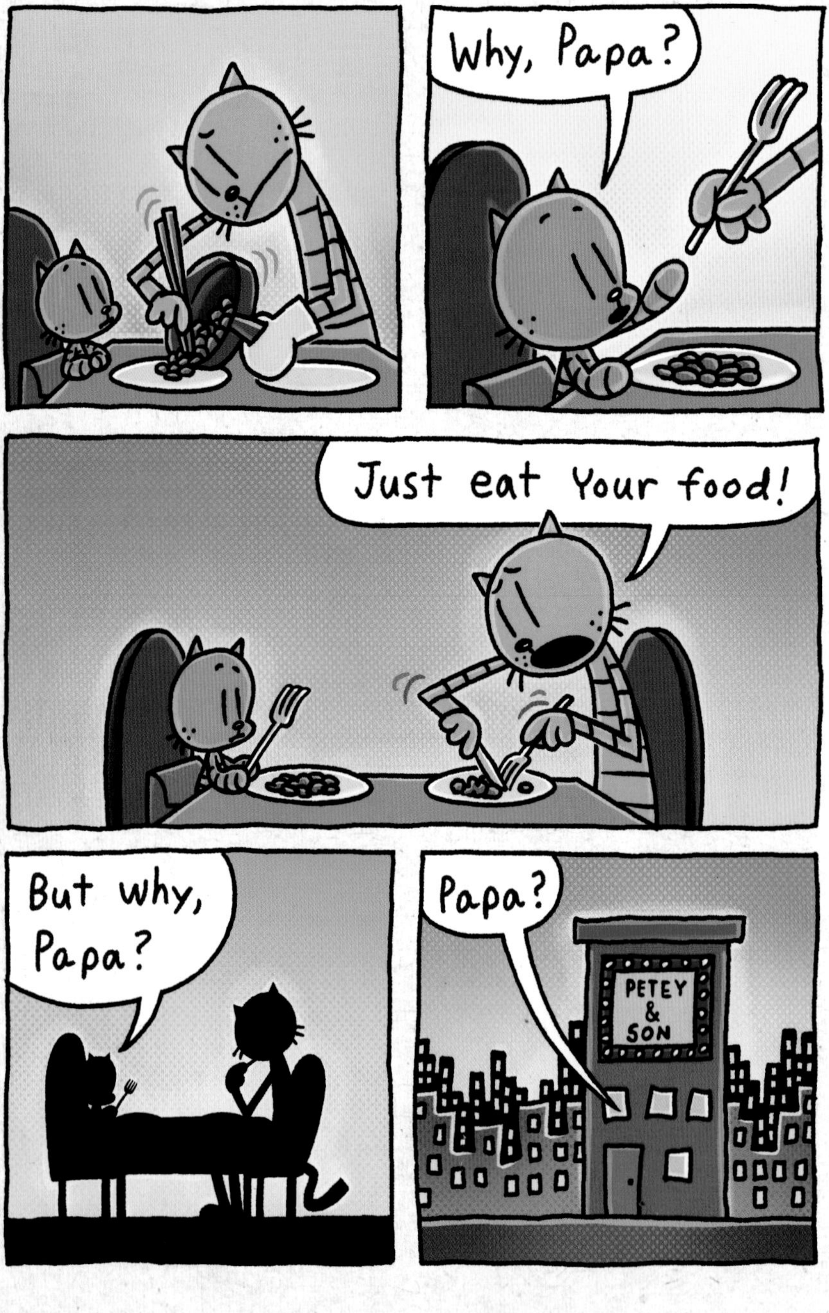

Why, Papa?
Just eat your food!
But why, Papa?
Papa?
PETEY & SON

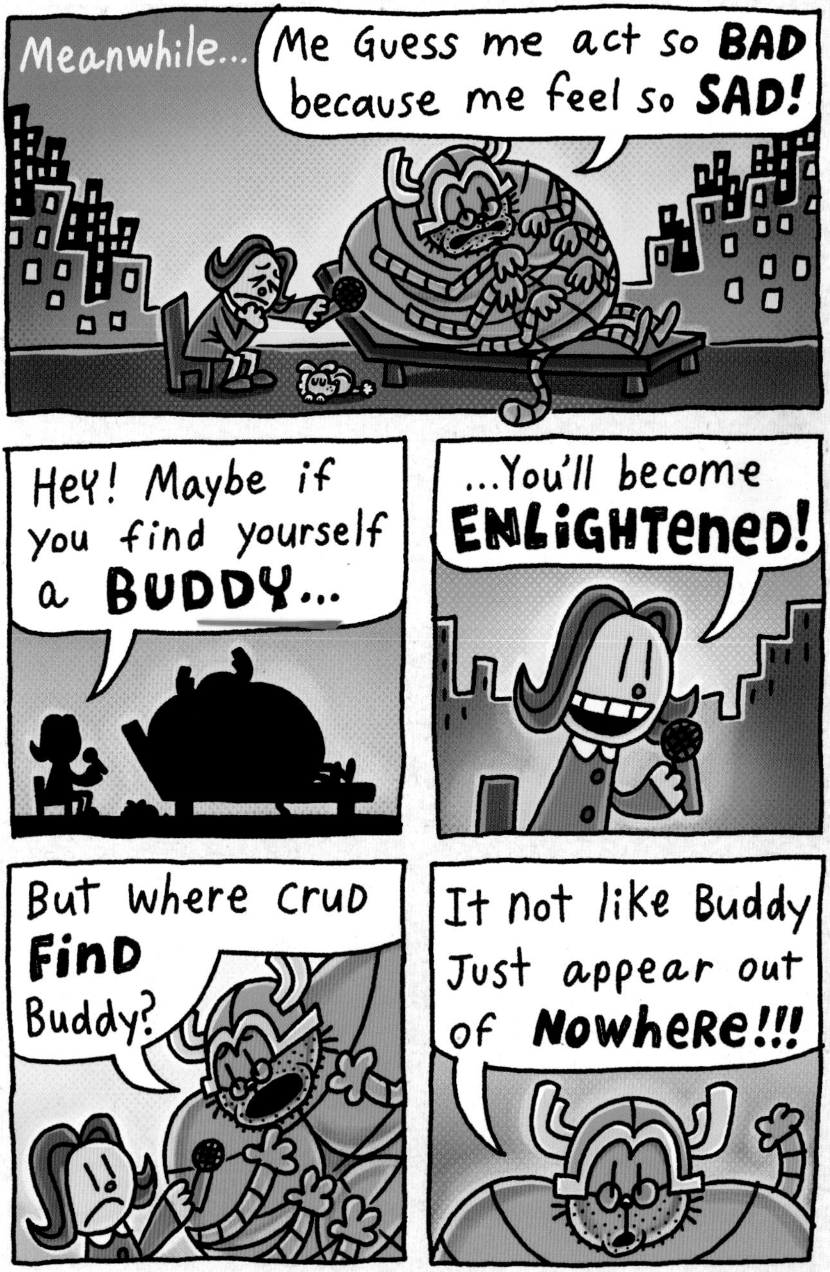
Meanwhile...
Me Guess me act so BAD because me feel so SAD!
Hey! Maybe if you find yourself a BUDDY...
...You'll become ENLIGHTENED!
But where Crud FIND Buddy?
It not like Buddy Just appear out of NOWHERE!!!

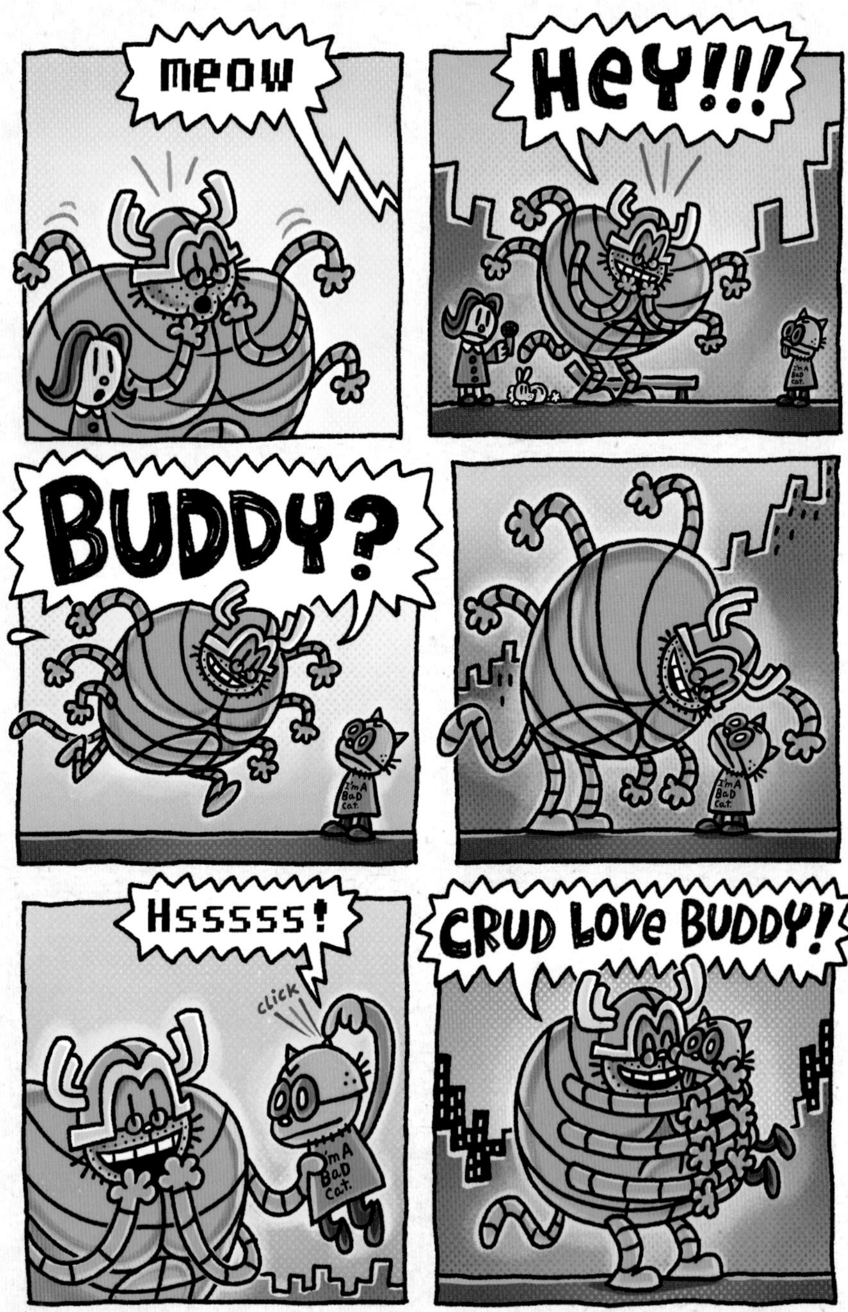
meow
HEY!!!
BUDDY?
Hsssss!
click
I'm A BaD Cat.
CRUD LOVE BUDDY!

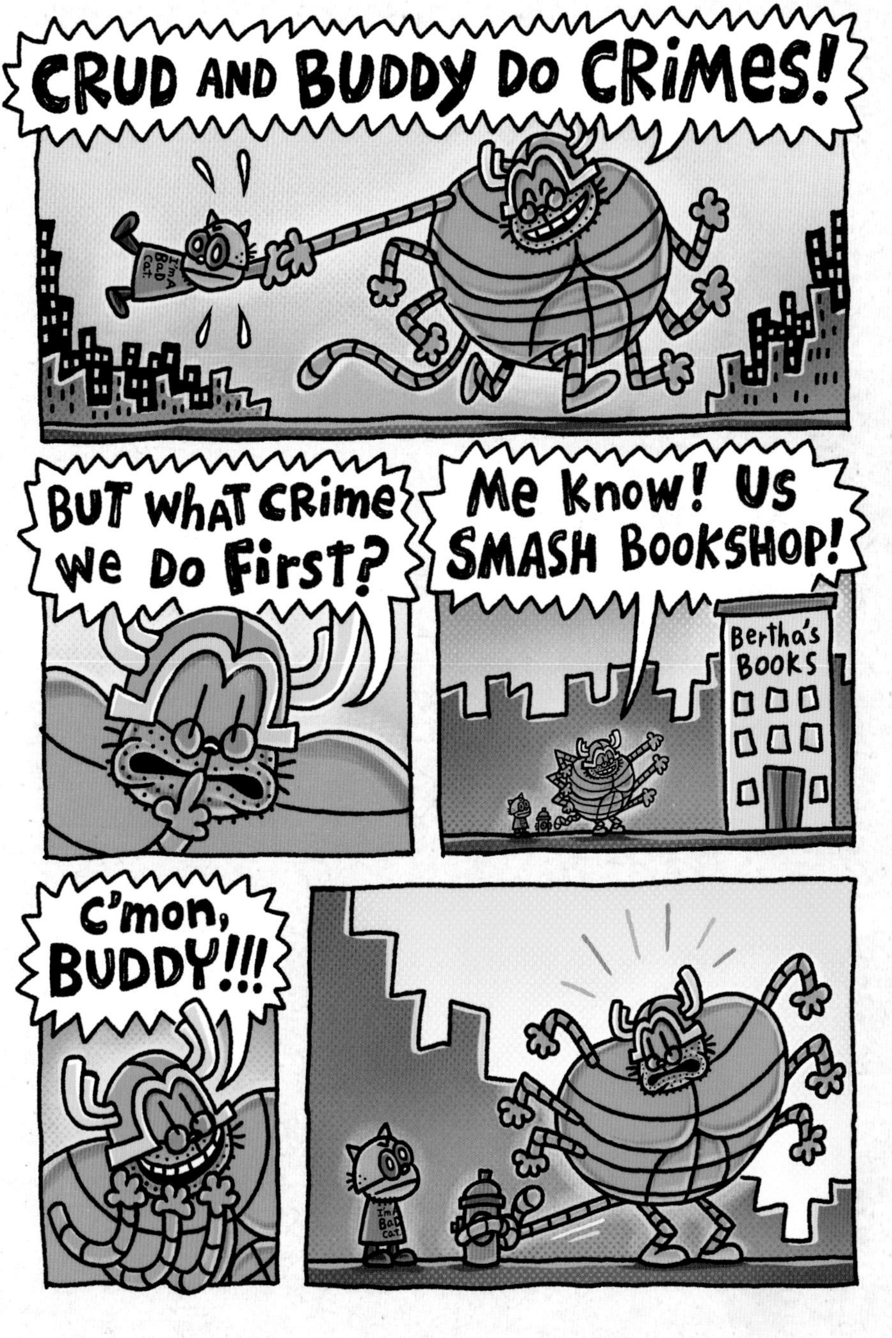
CRUD AND BUDDY DO CRIMES!
I'm A BaD cat.
BUT WHAT CRime we Do First?
Me know! Us SMASH BOOKSHOP!
Bertha's BOOKS
C'mon, BUDDY!!!
I'm A BaD cat.

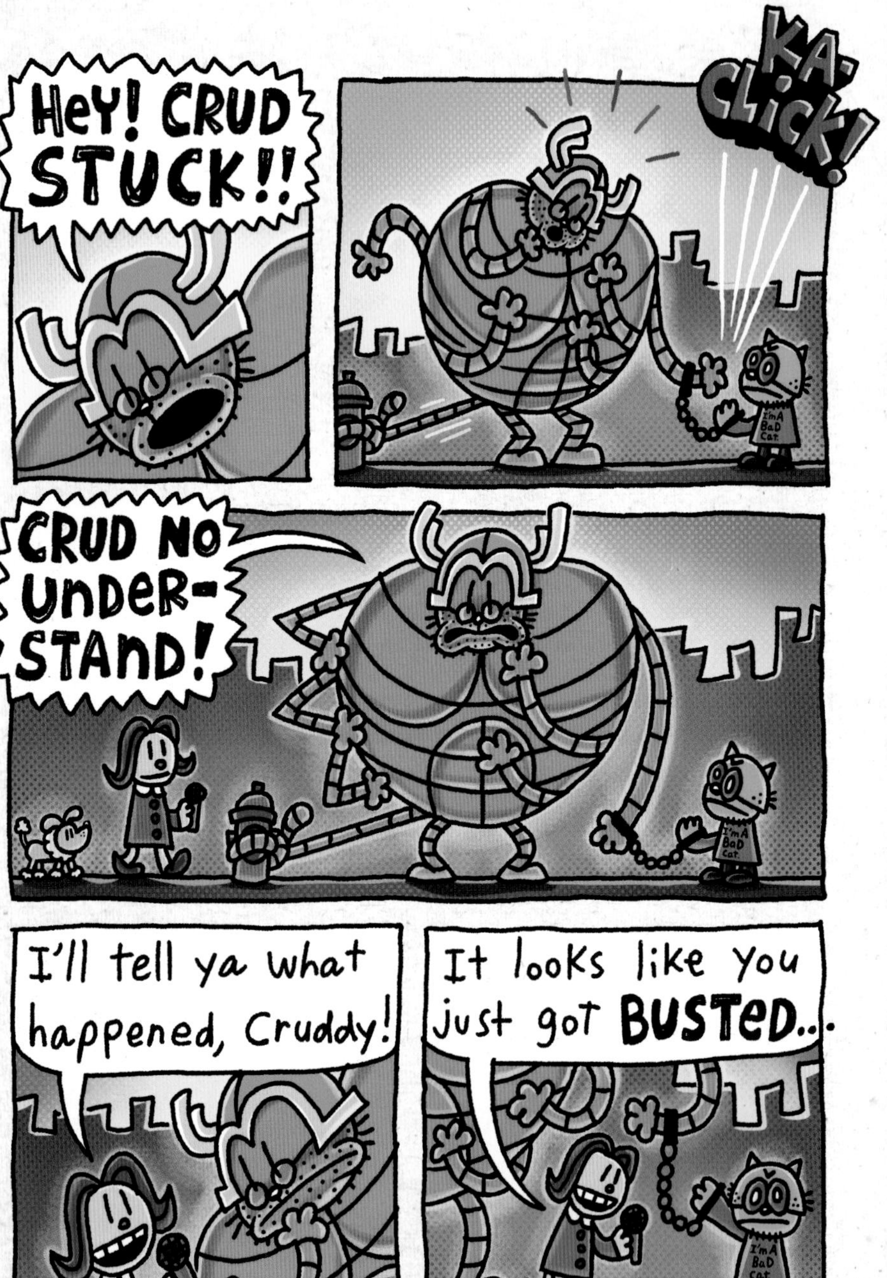
HEY! CRUD STUCK!!
KA-CLICK!
I'm A BaD Cat.
CRUD NO UNDER-STAND!
I'm A BaD Cat.
I'll tell ya what happened, Cruddy!
It looks like you just got BUSTED...
I'm A BaD Cat.

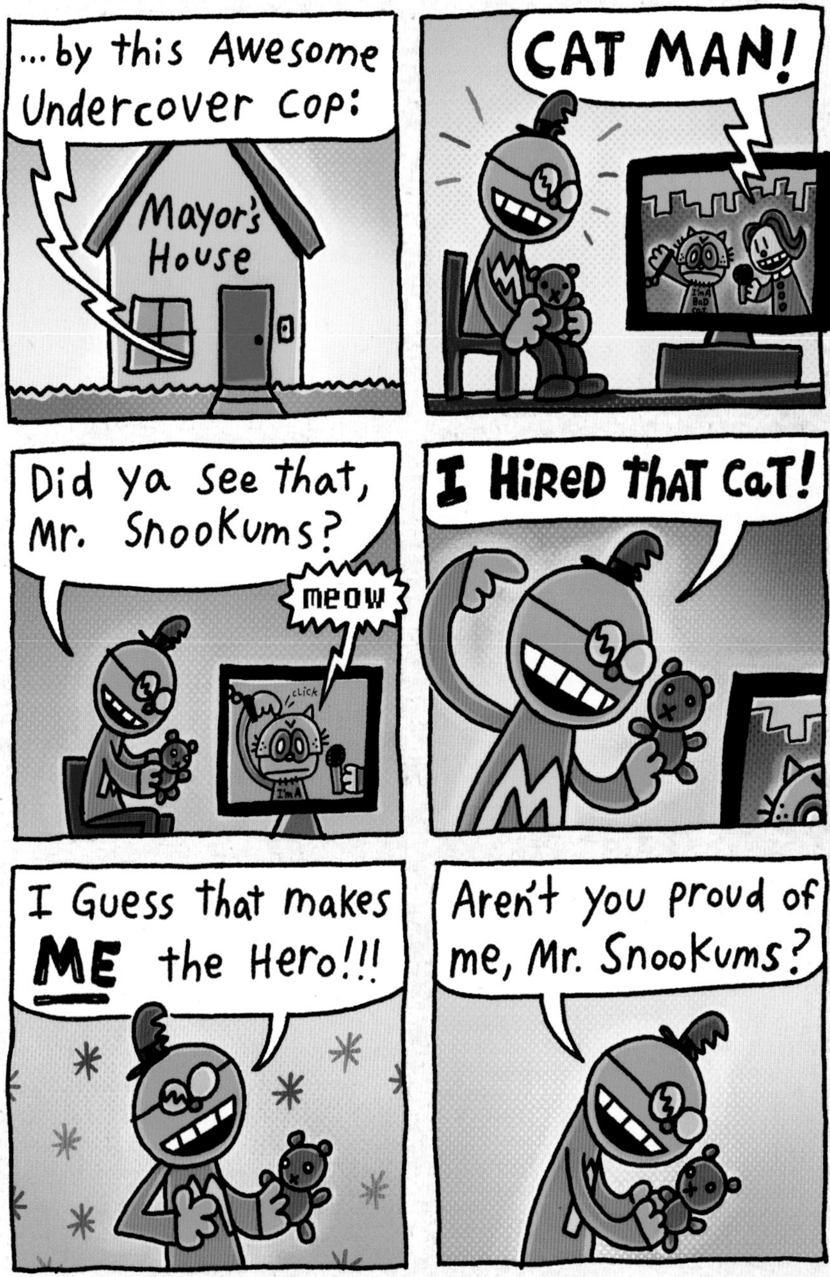
...by this Awesome Undercover Cop:
Mayor's House
CAT MAN!
Did ya see that, Mr. Snookums?
meow
click
I HIRED THAT CAT!
I Guess that makes ME the Hero!!!
Aren't you proud of me, Mr. Snookums?

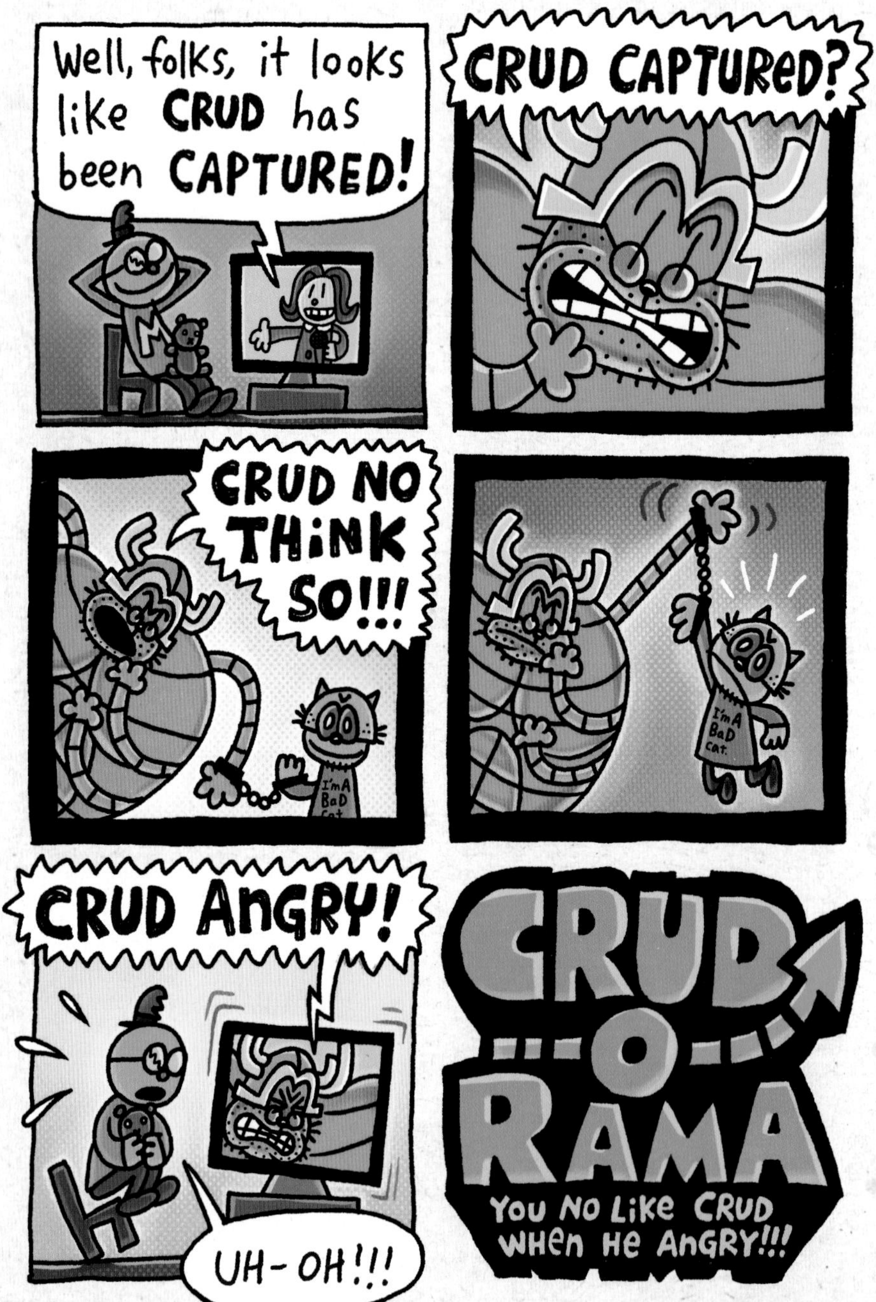
Well, folks, it looks like CRUD has been CAPTURED!
CRUD CAPTURED?
CRUD NO THINK SO!!!
I'm A BaD Cat.
I'm A BaD Cat.
CRUD AnGRY!
UH-OH!!!
CRUD-O-RAMA
You No Like CRUD WHen He AnGRY!!!

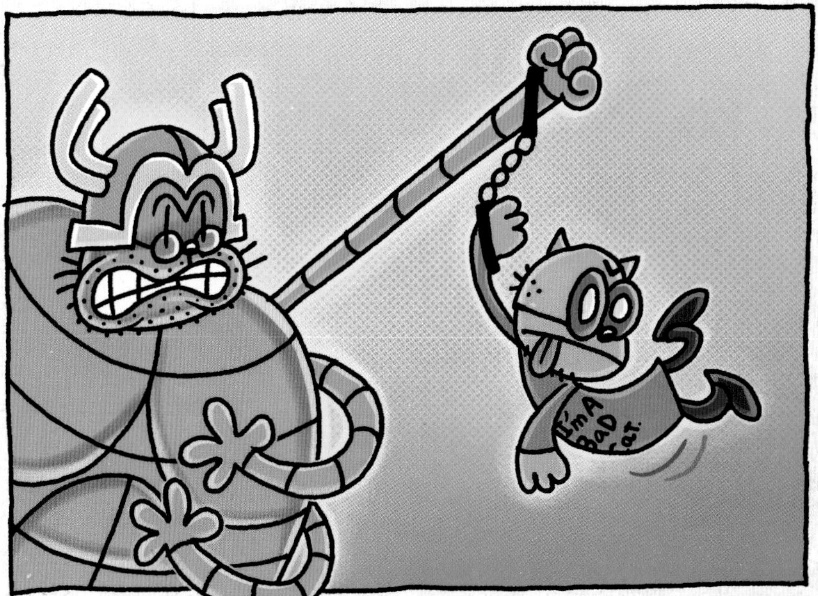
I'm A BaD Cat.

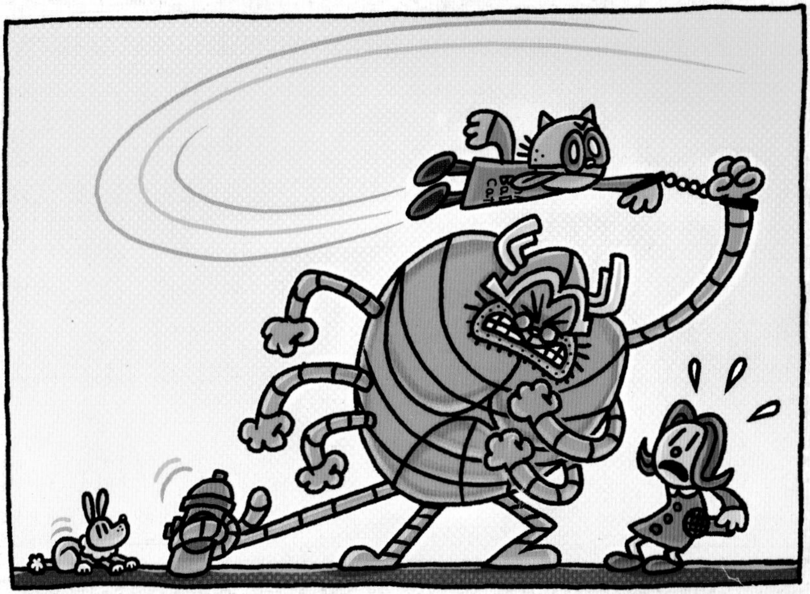

Right Thumb here.

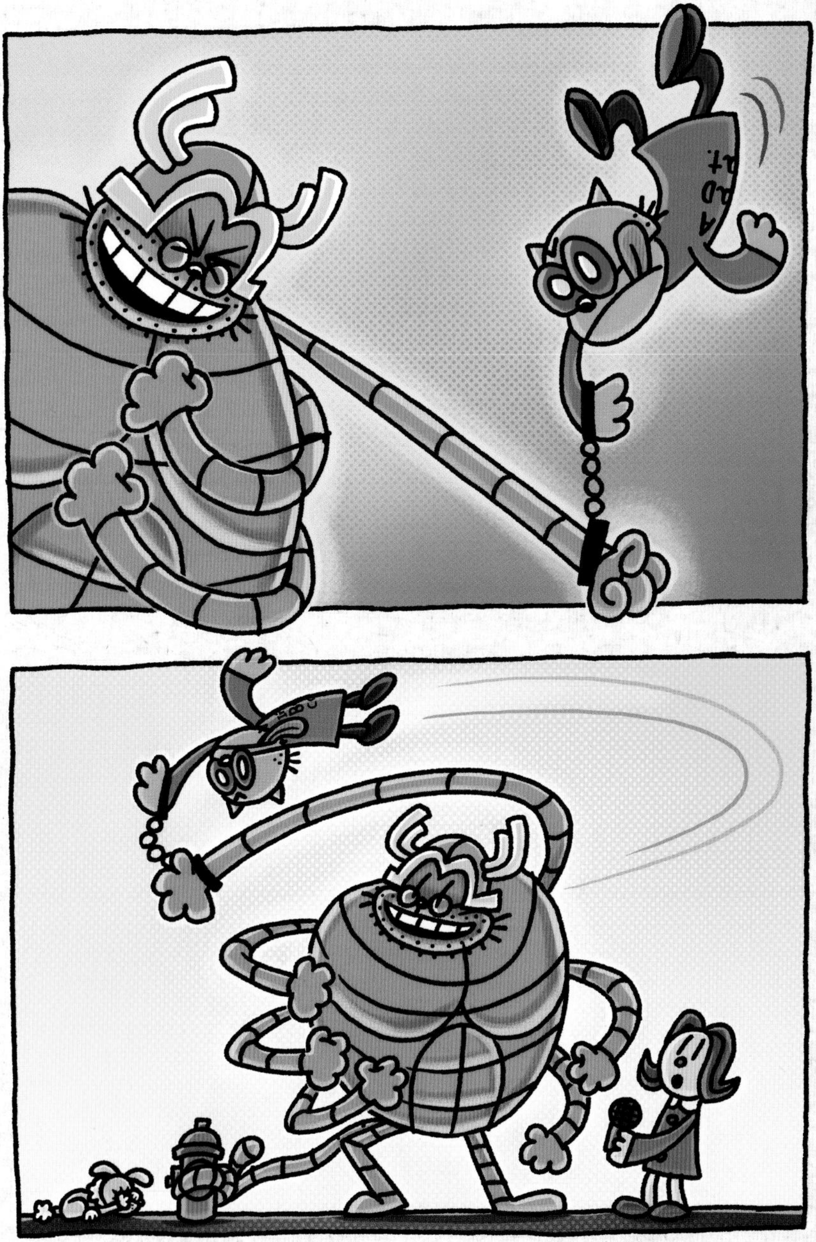

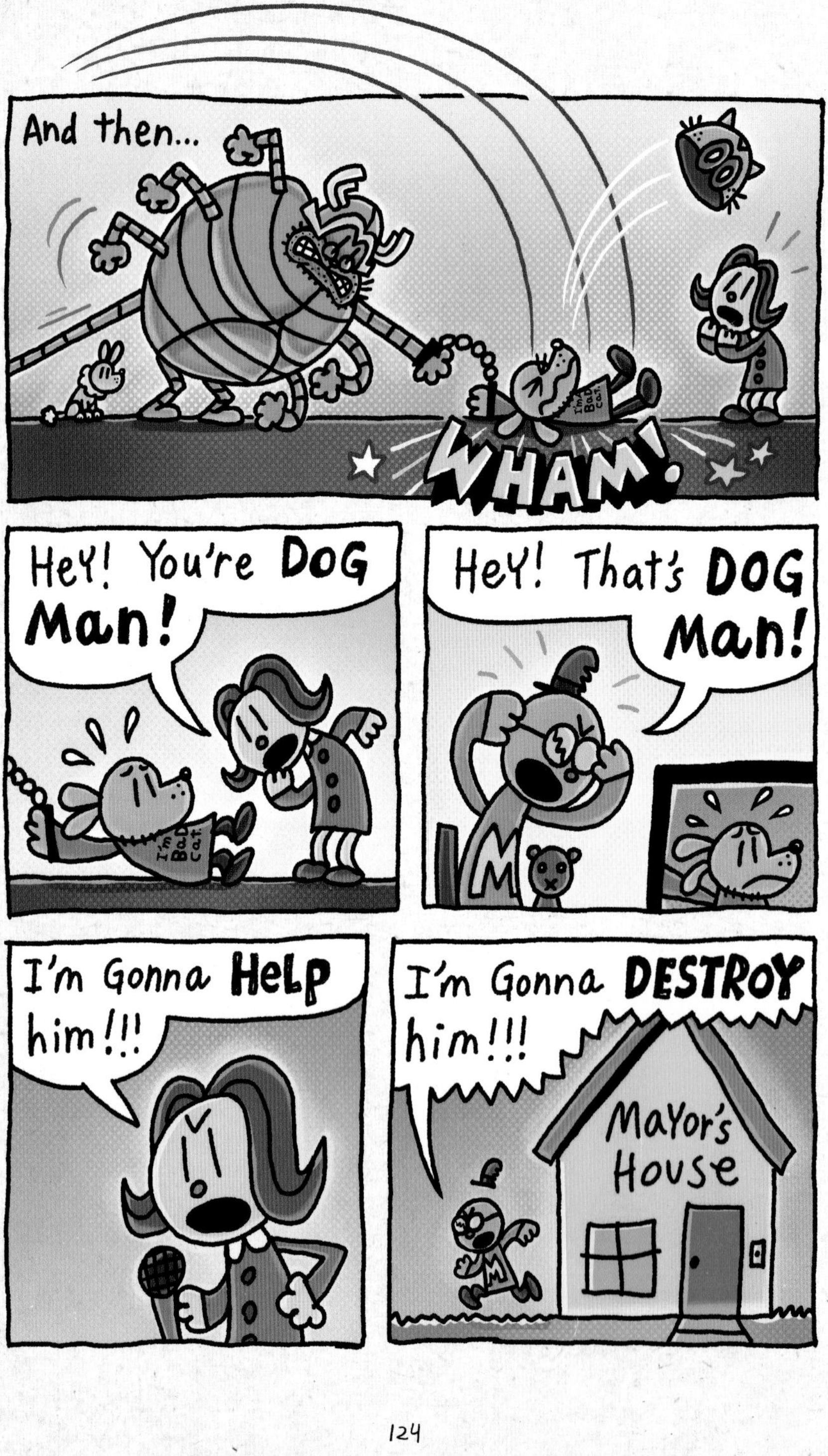
And then...
I'm
Bad
Cat
WHAM!
HeY! You're DOG Man!
I'm
Bad
Cat
HeY! That's DOG Man!
M
I'm Gonna HELP him!!!
I'm Gonna DESTROY him!!!
MaYor's House
M

CHAPTER 8

BIG FIGHT

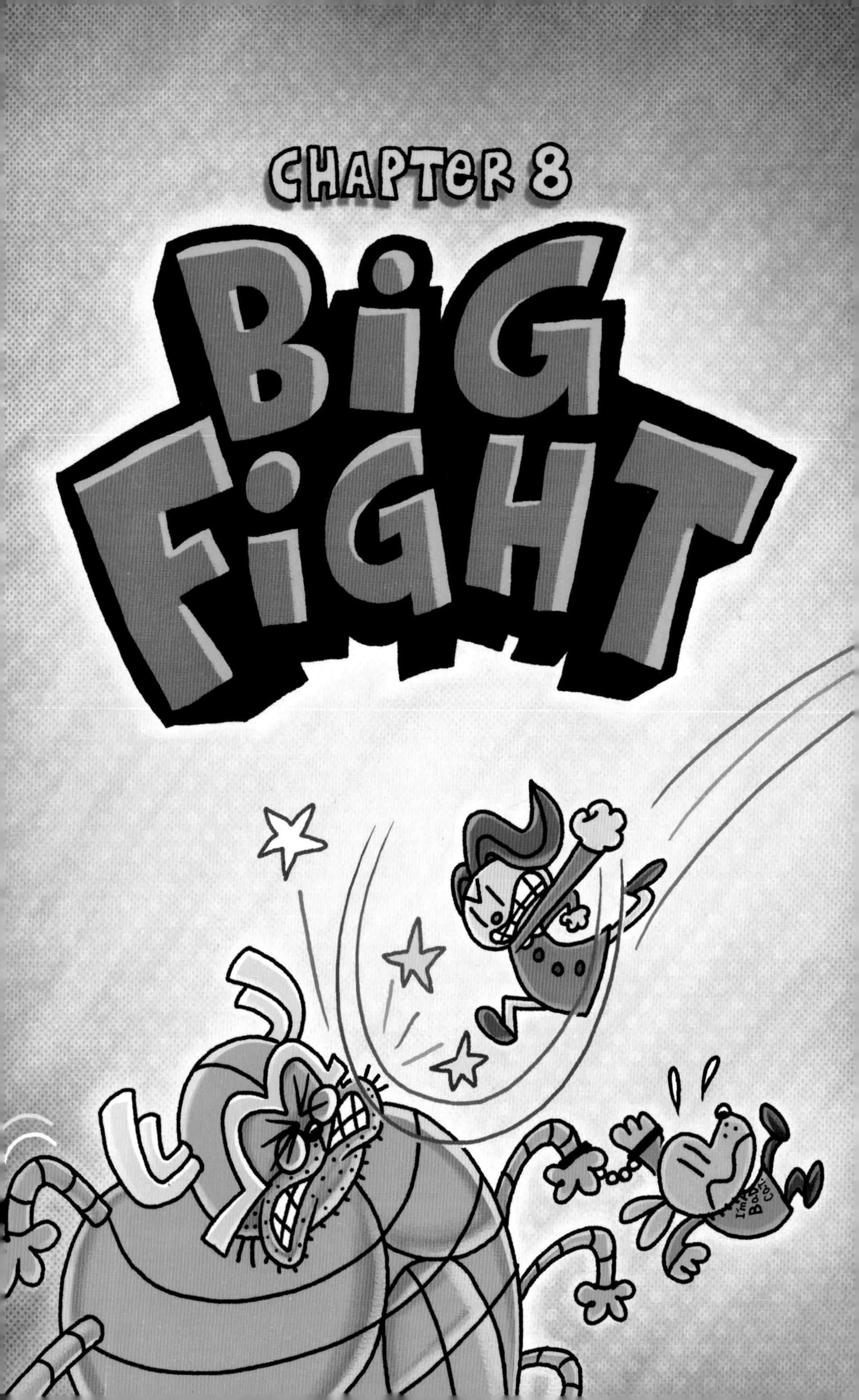

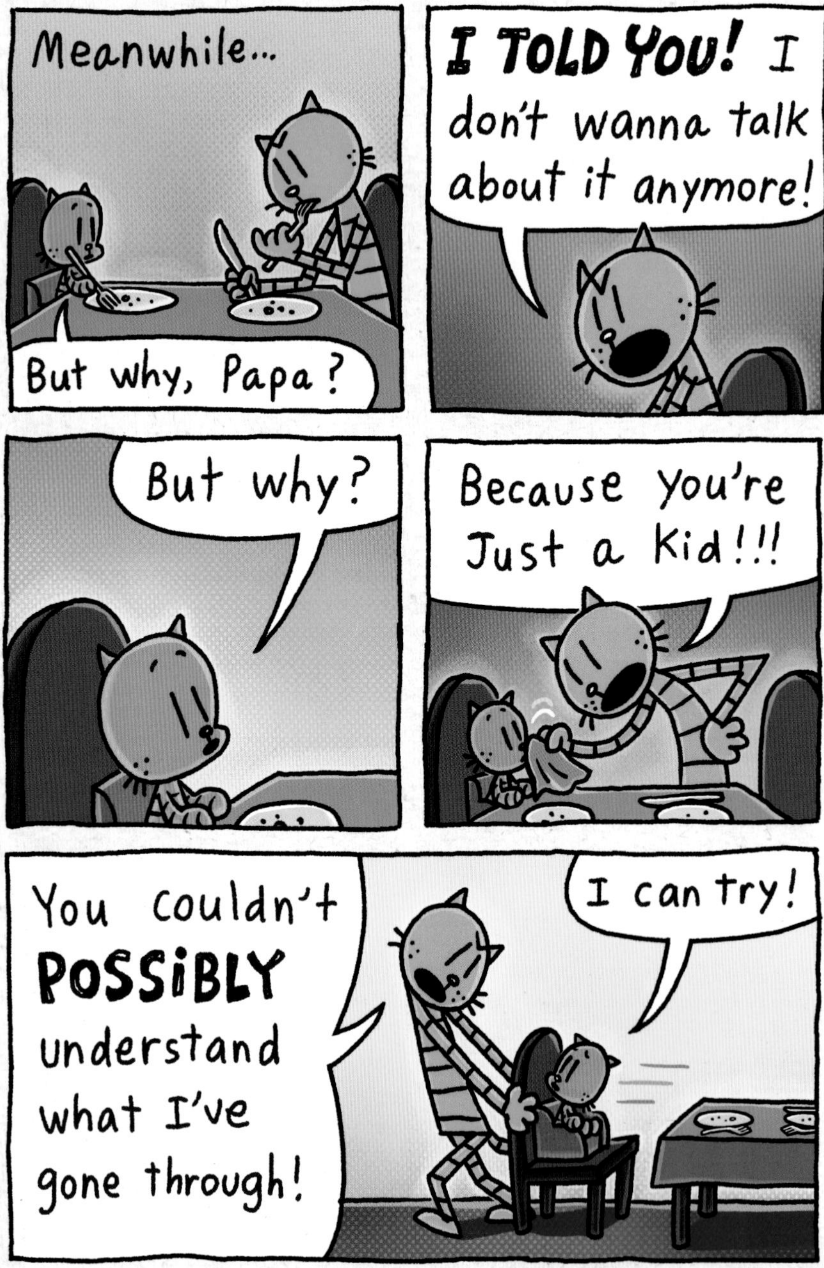
Meanwhile...
But why, Papa?
I TOLD YOU! I don't wanna talk about it anymore!
But why?
Because you're Just a Kid!!!
You couldn't POSSIBLY understand what I've gone through!
I can try!

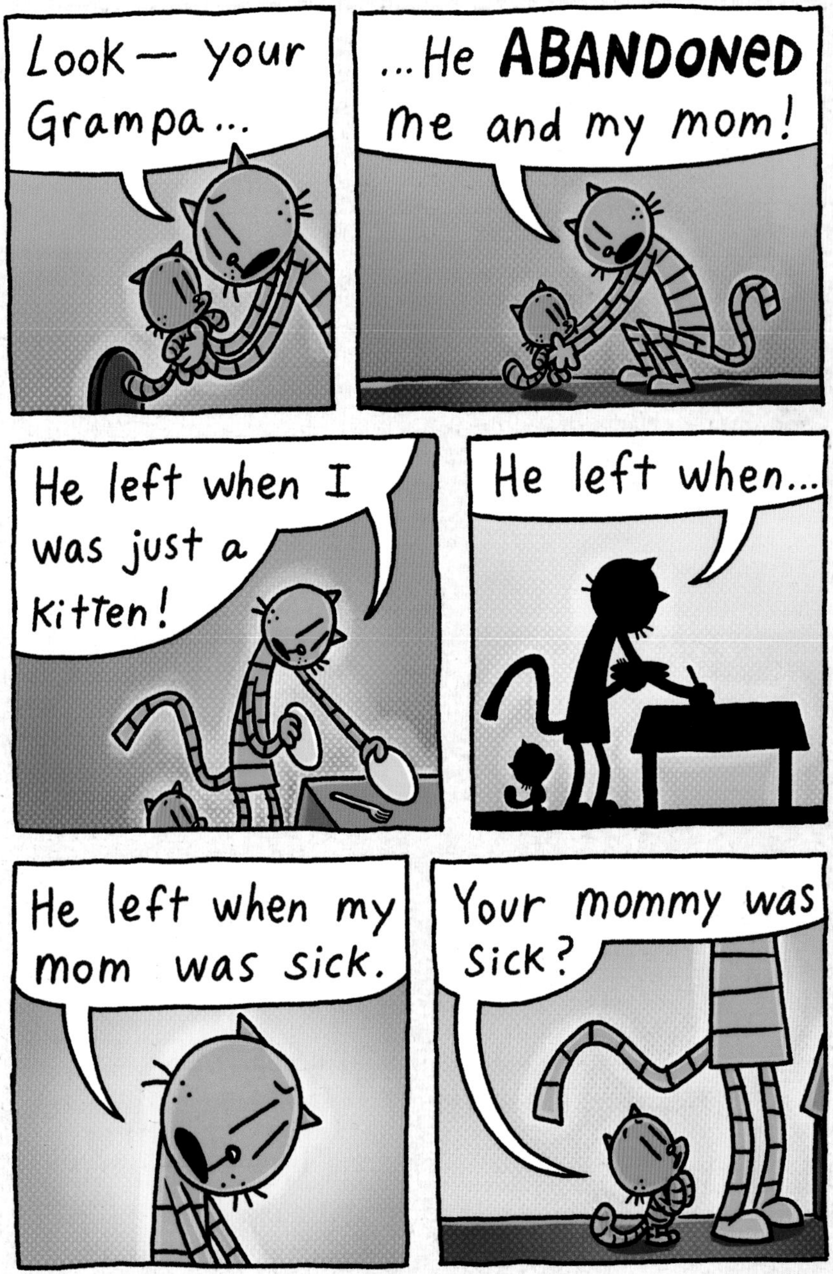
Look— your Grampa...
...He ABANDONED me and my mom!
He left when I was just a kitten!
He left when...
He left when my mom was sick.
Your mommy was sick?

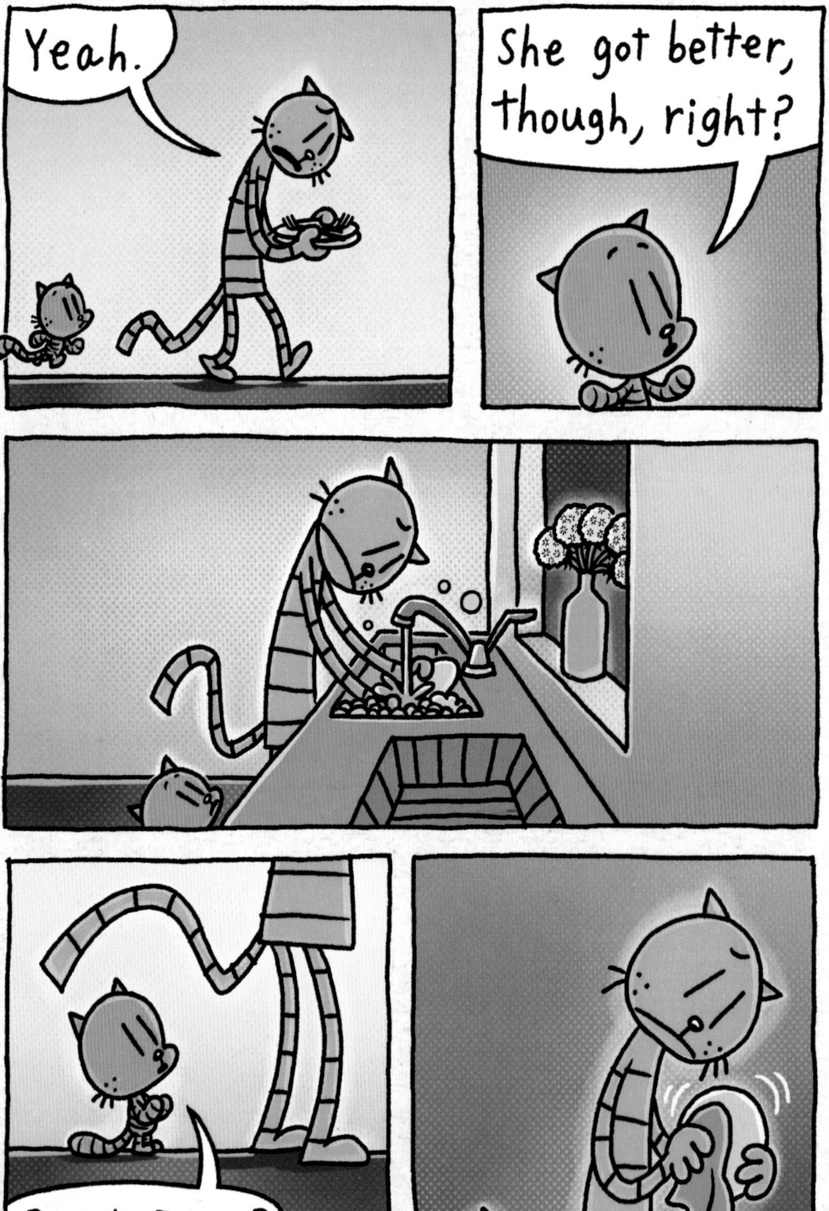
Yeah.
She got better, though, right?
Right, Papa?

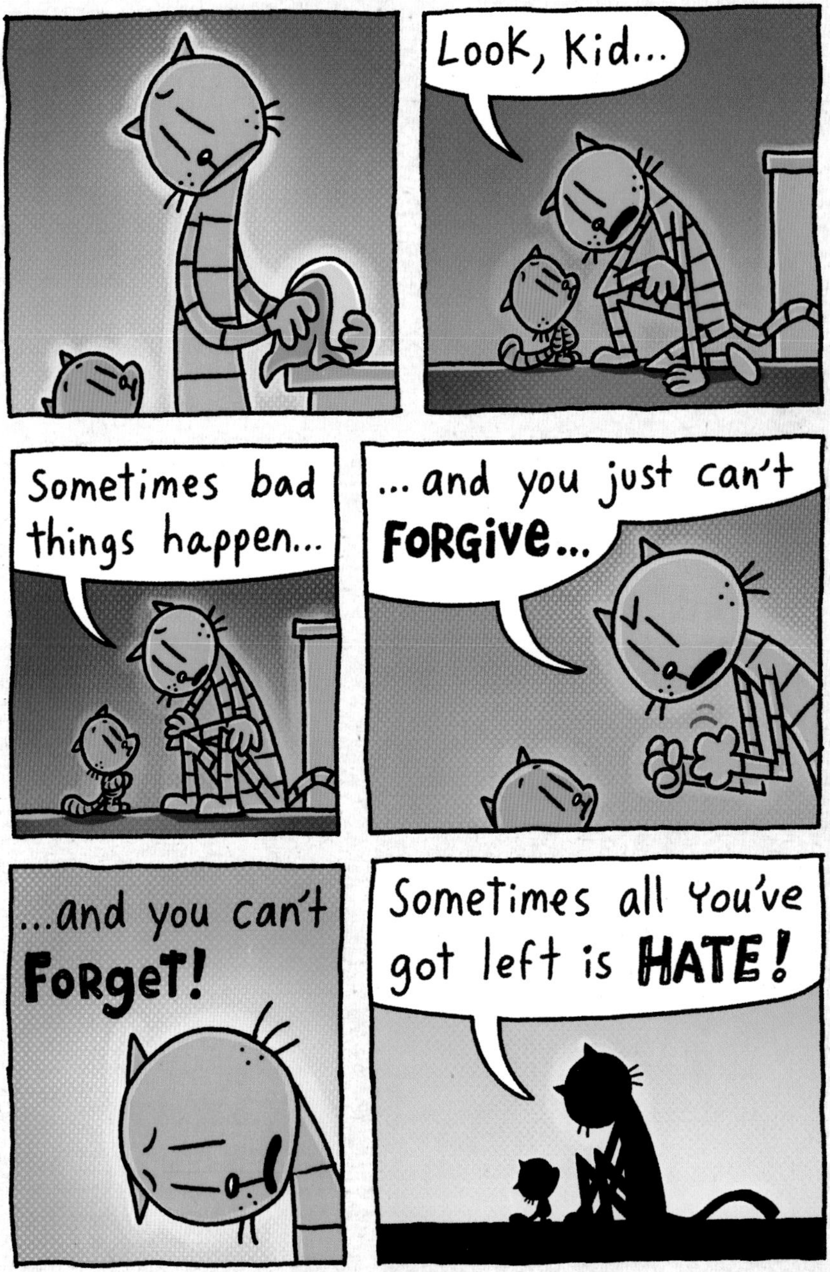

Look, Kid...
Sometimes bad things happen...
...and you just can't FORGIVE...
...and you can't FORGET!
Sometimes all You've got left is HATE!

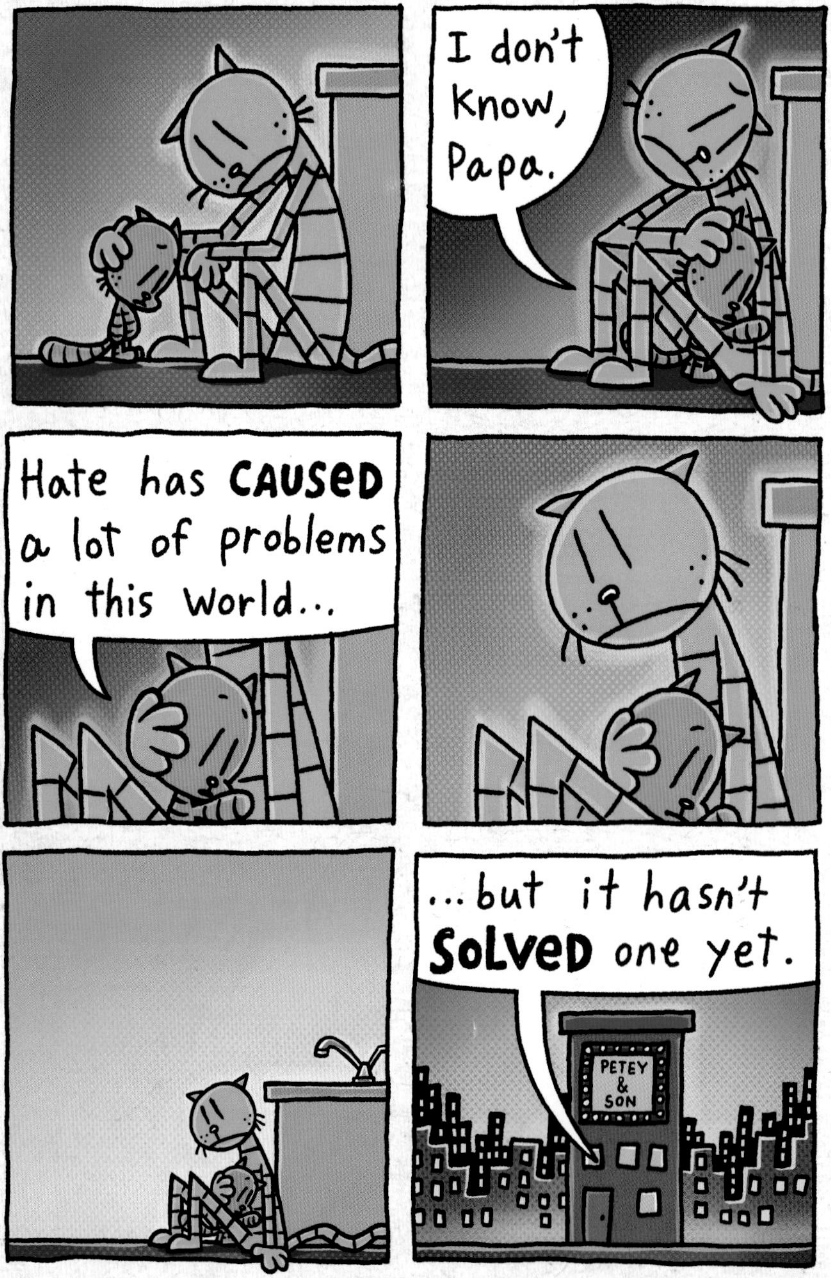
I don't know, Papa.
Hate has CAUSED a lot of problems in this world...
...but it hasn't SOLVED one yet.
PETEY & SON

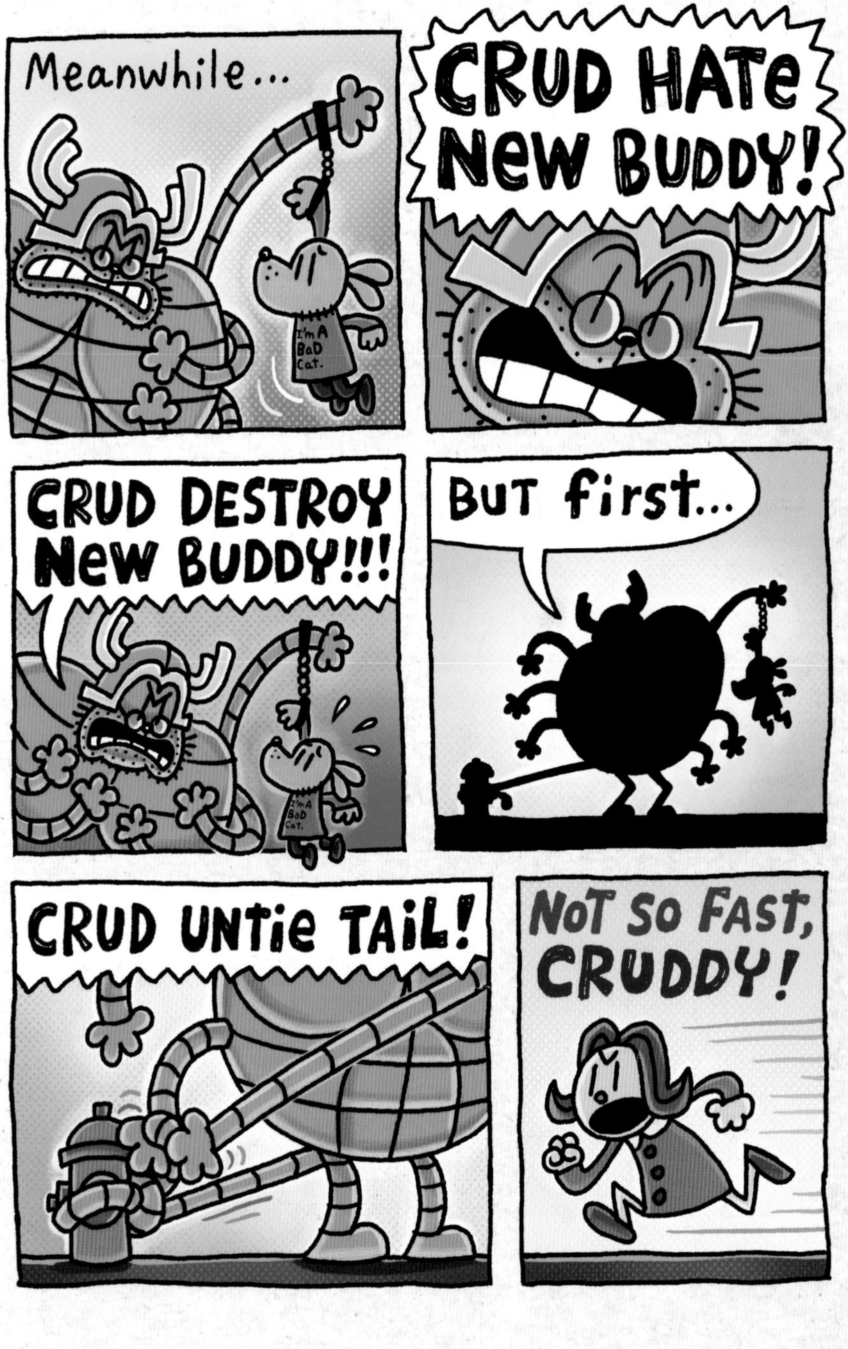
Meanwhile...
I'm A BaD Cat.
CRUD HATE New BUDDY!
CRUD DESTROY New BUDDY!!!
I'm A BaD Cat.
BUT first...
CRUD UNTie TAIL!
NOT SO FAST, CRUDDY!

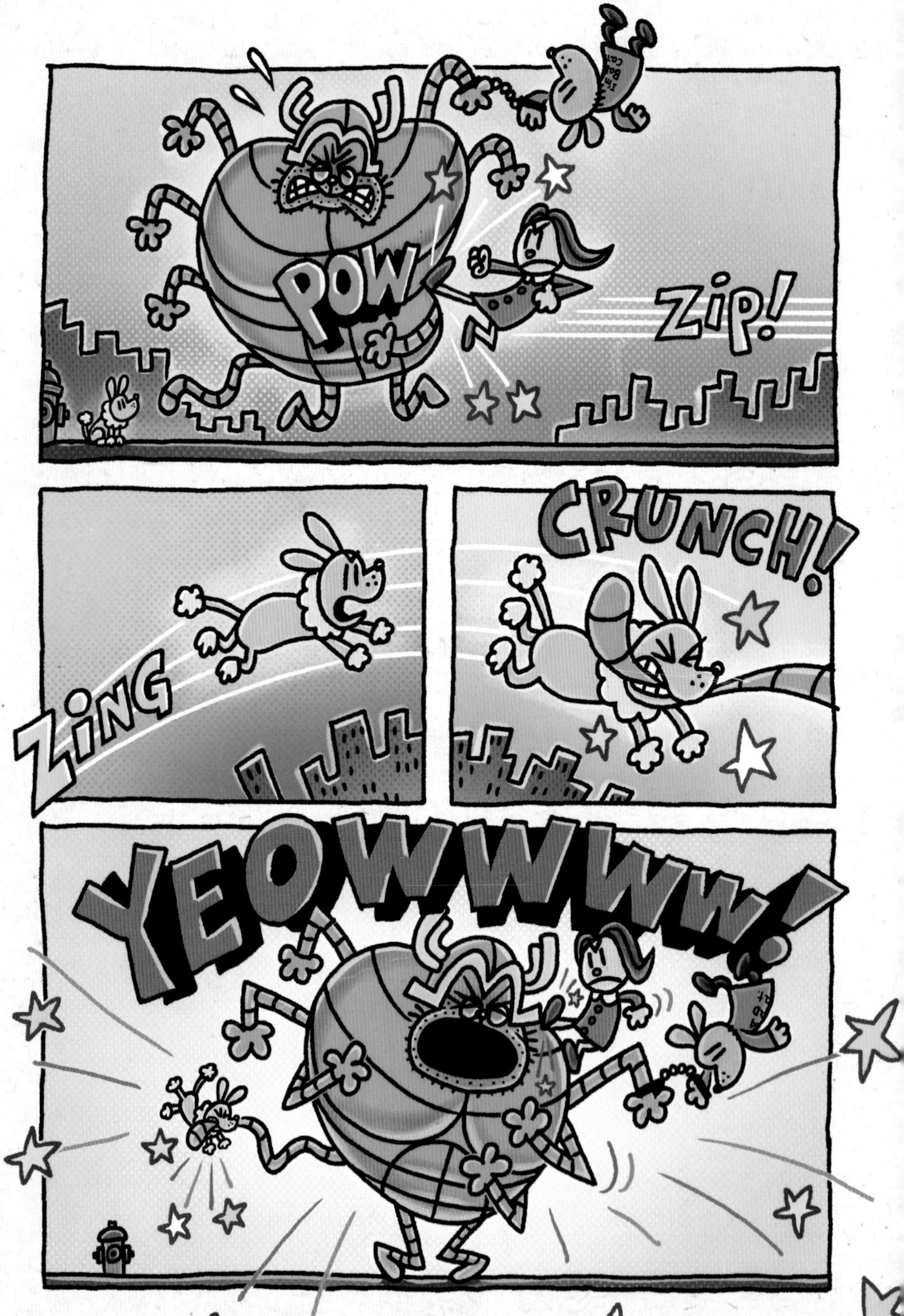
POW
ZIP!
ZING
CRUNCH!
YEOWWWWW!

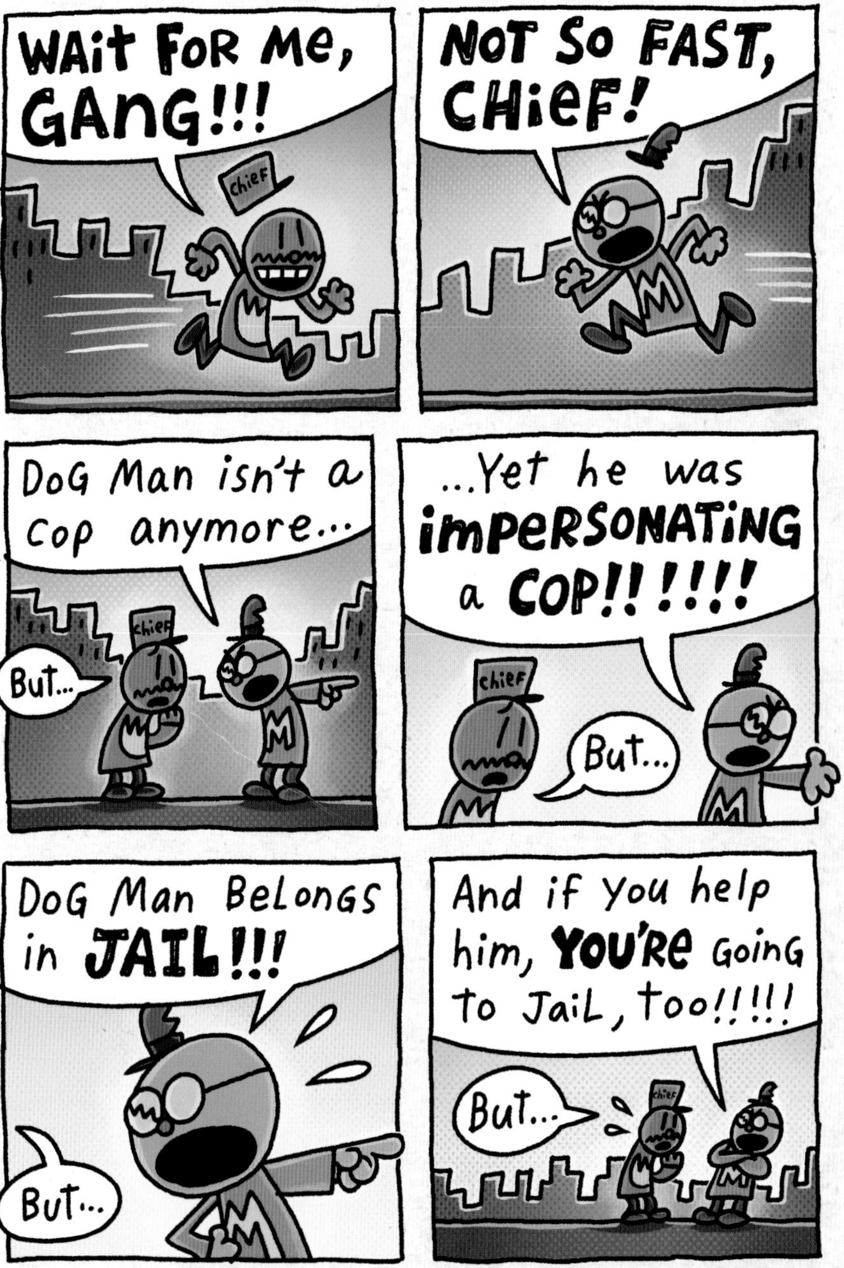
WAit FOR Me, GANG!!!
chief
NOT SO FAST, CHieF!
DoG Man isn't a cop anymore...
chief
But...
...Yet he was impersonating a COP!!!!!!
chief
But...
DoG Man Belongs in JAIL!!!
But...
And if you help him, YOU'Re GoinG to JaiL, too!!!!!
chief
But...

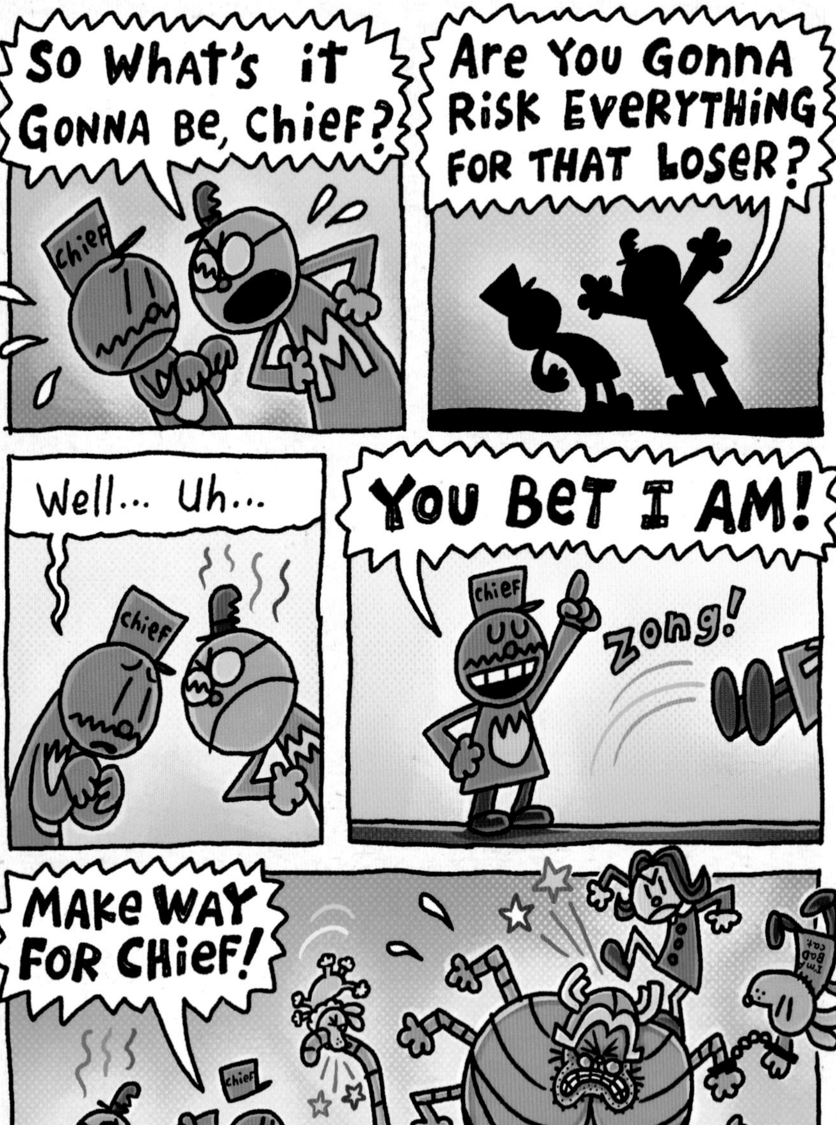

So What's it Gonna Be, Chief?
Are You Gonna Risk Everything For That Loser?
Well... Uh...
You Bet I Am!
Zong!
Make Way For Chief!

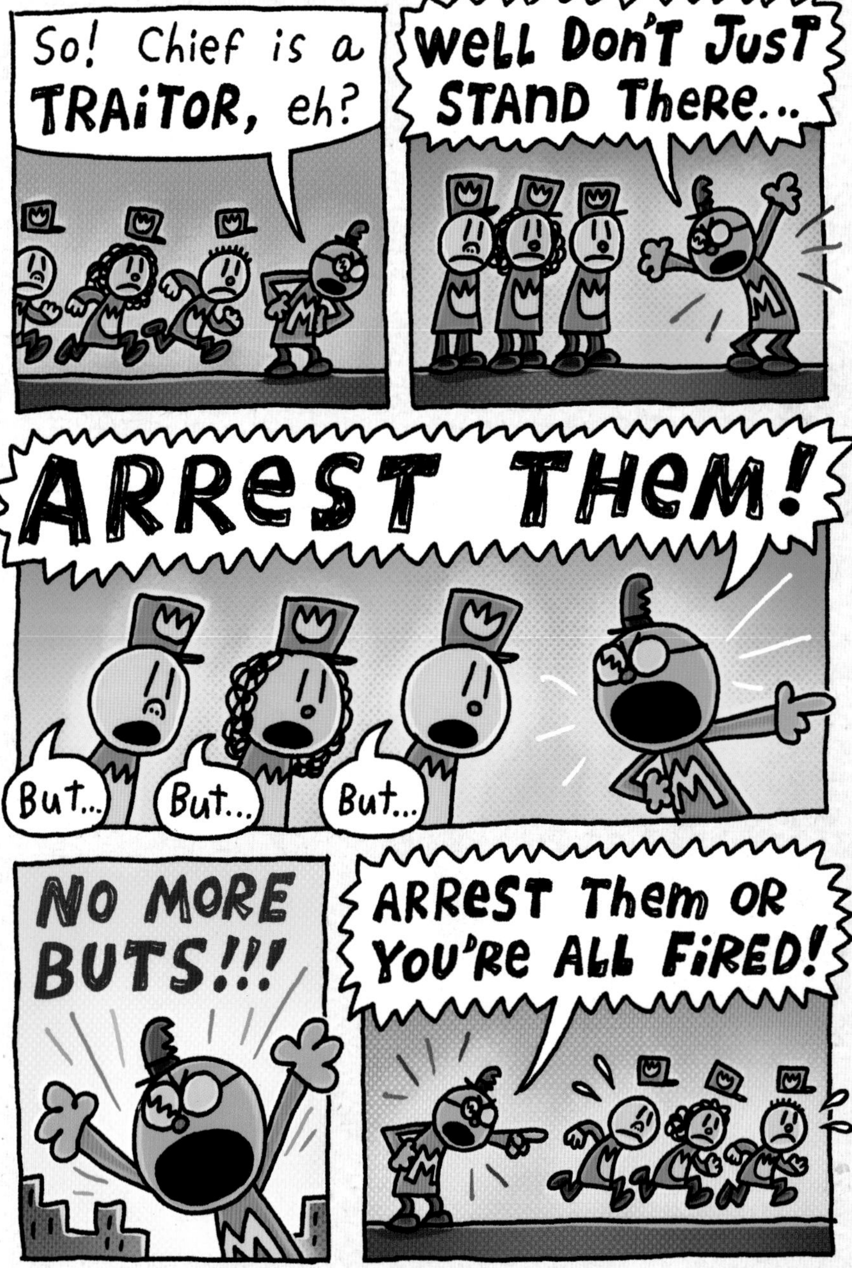
So! Chief is a TRAITOR, eh?
WELL DON'T JUST STAND THERE...
ARREST THEM!
But...
But...
But...
NO MORE BUTS!!!
ARREST THEM OR YOU'RE ALL FIRED!

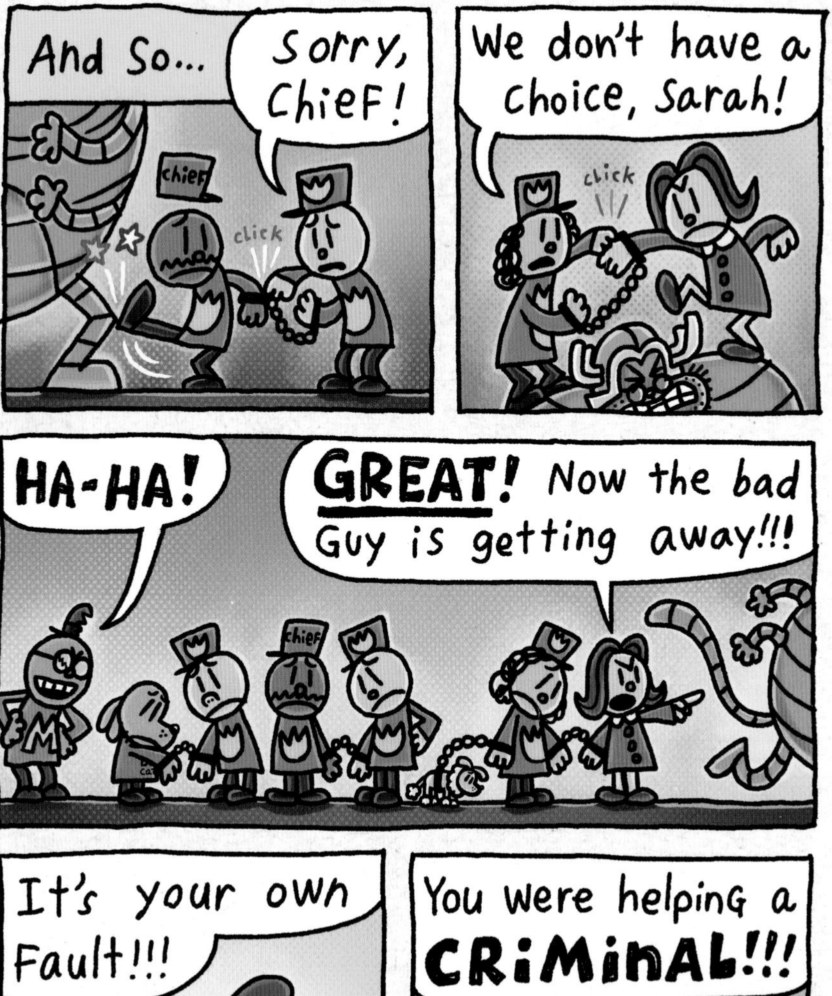
And So...
Sorry, ChieF!
chief
click
We don't have a choice, Sarah!
click
HA-HA!
GREAT! Now the bad Guy is getting away!!!
chief
It's your own Fault!!!
You were helping a CRiMinAL!!!
I'm A BaD cat.
chief

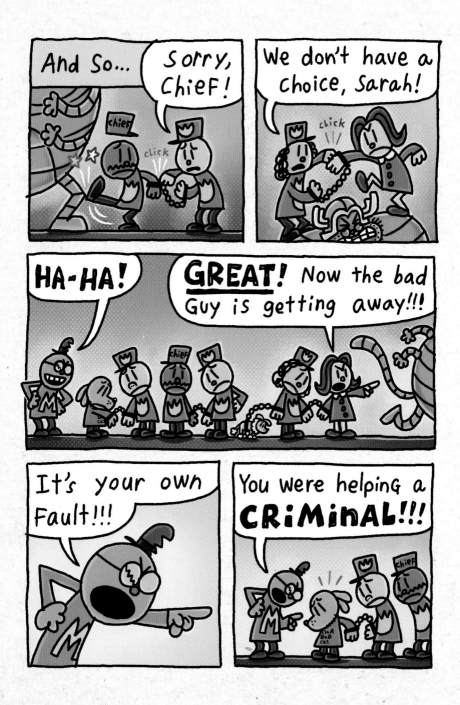

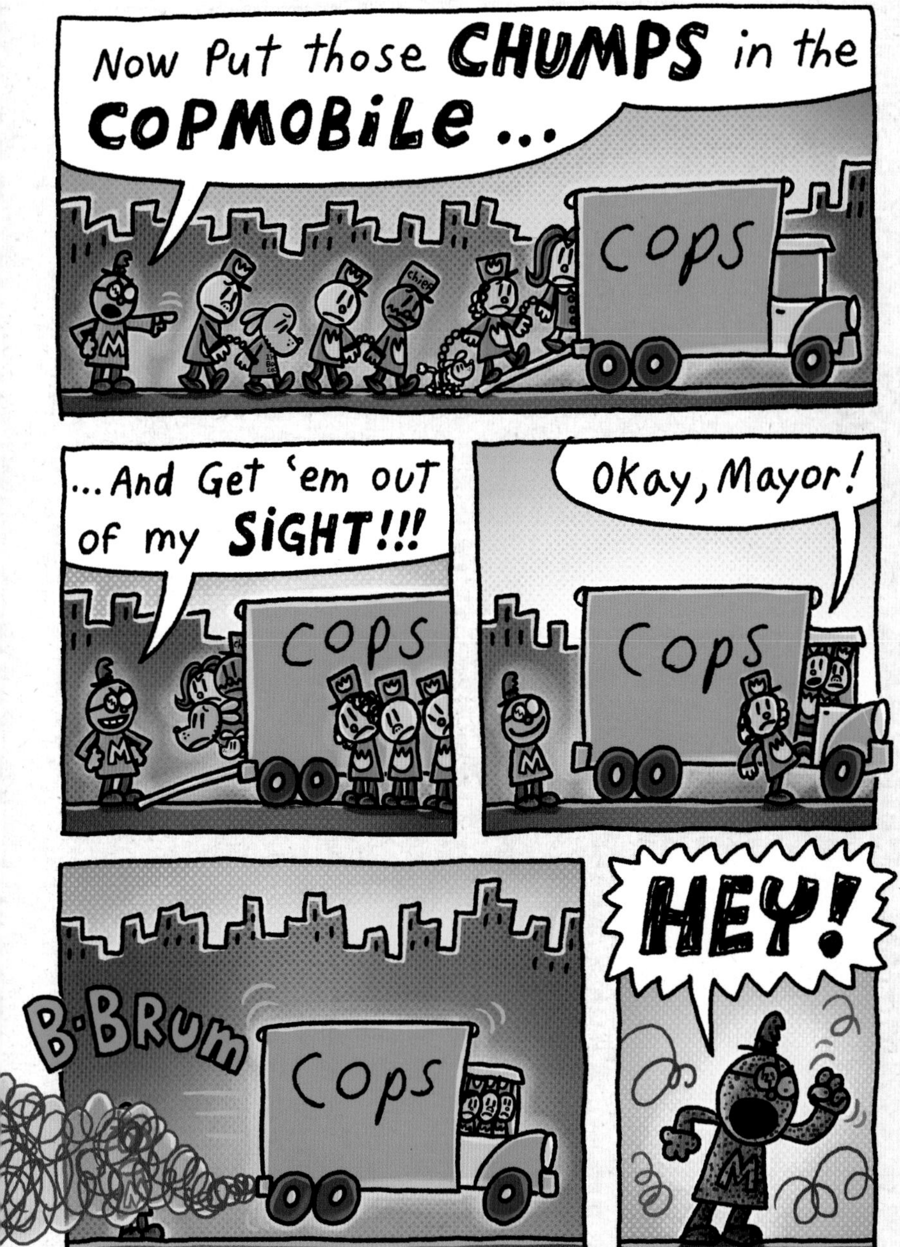
Now Put those CHUMPS in the COPMOBILE...
COPS
...And Get 'em out of my SIGHT!!!
COPS
Okay, Mayor!
Cops
B-BRUM
Cops
HEY!

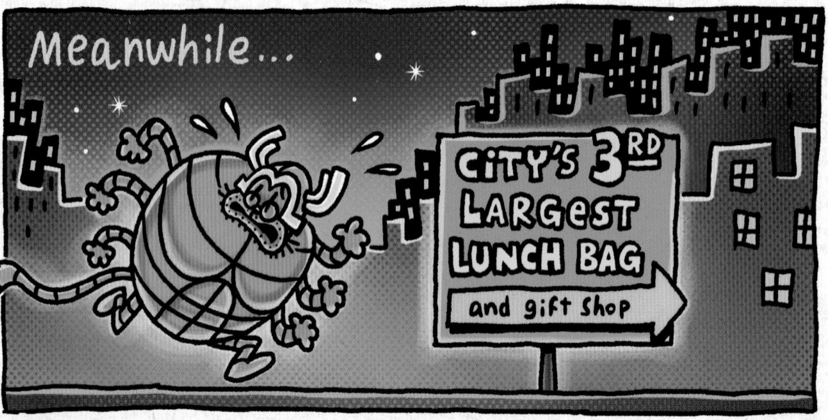
Meanwhile...
CiTY'S 3RD
LARGEST
LUNCH BAG
and gift Shop

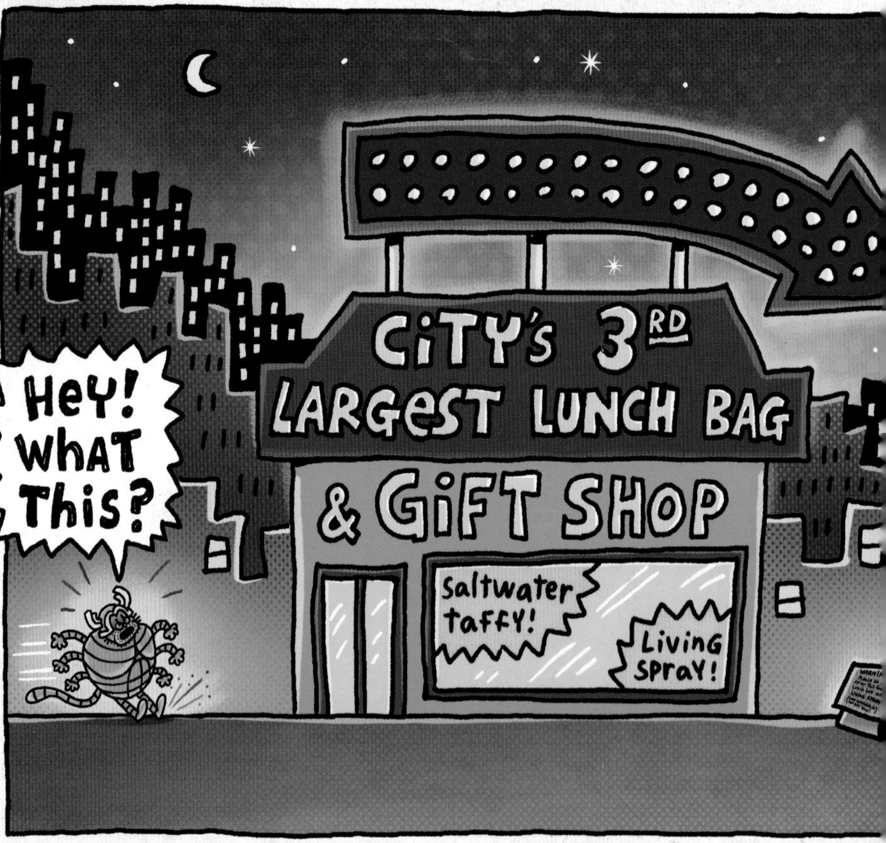
CiTY'S 3RD
LARGEST LUNCH BAG
& GiFT SHOP
Hey! WHAT This?
Saltwater taffy!
Living Spray!

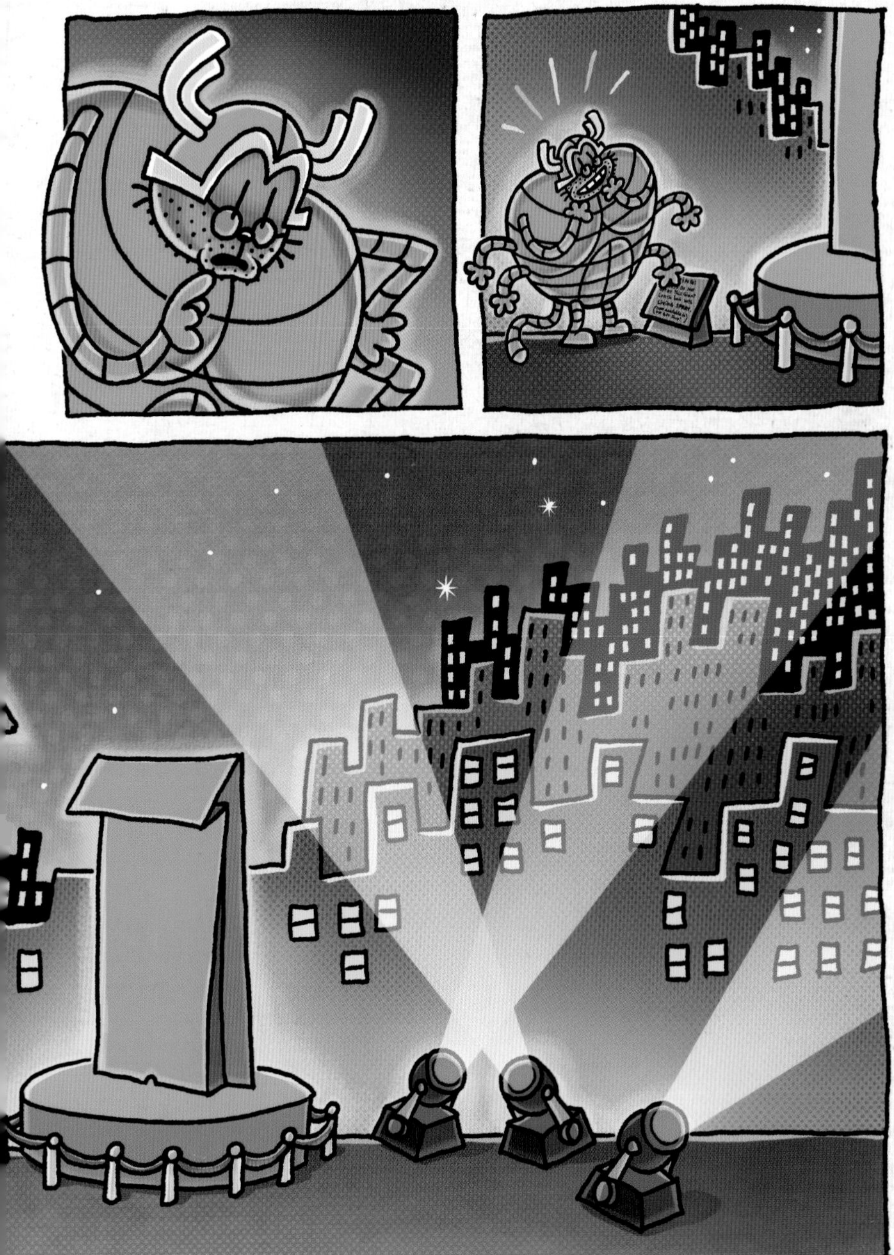

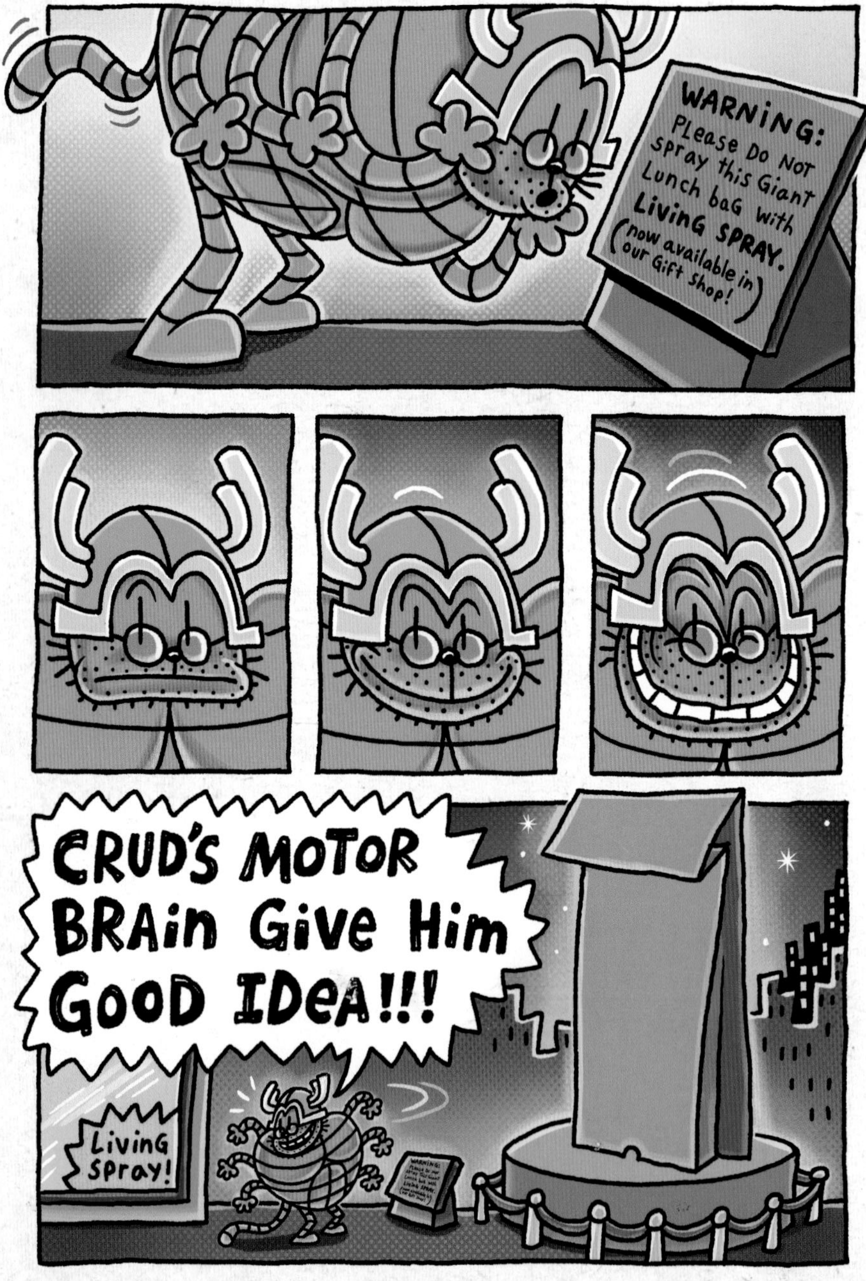
WARNING:
Please Do NOT spray this Giant Lunch baG with LIVING SPRAY.
(now available in our Gift Shop!)
CRUD'S MOTOR BRAIN Give Him GOOD IDEA!!!
LiVinG Spray!

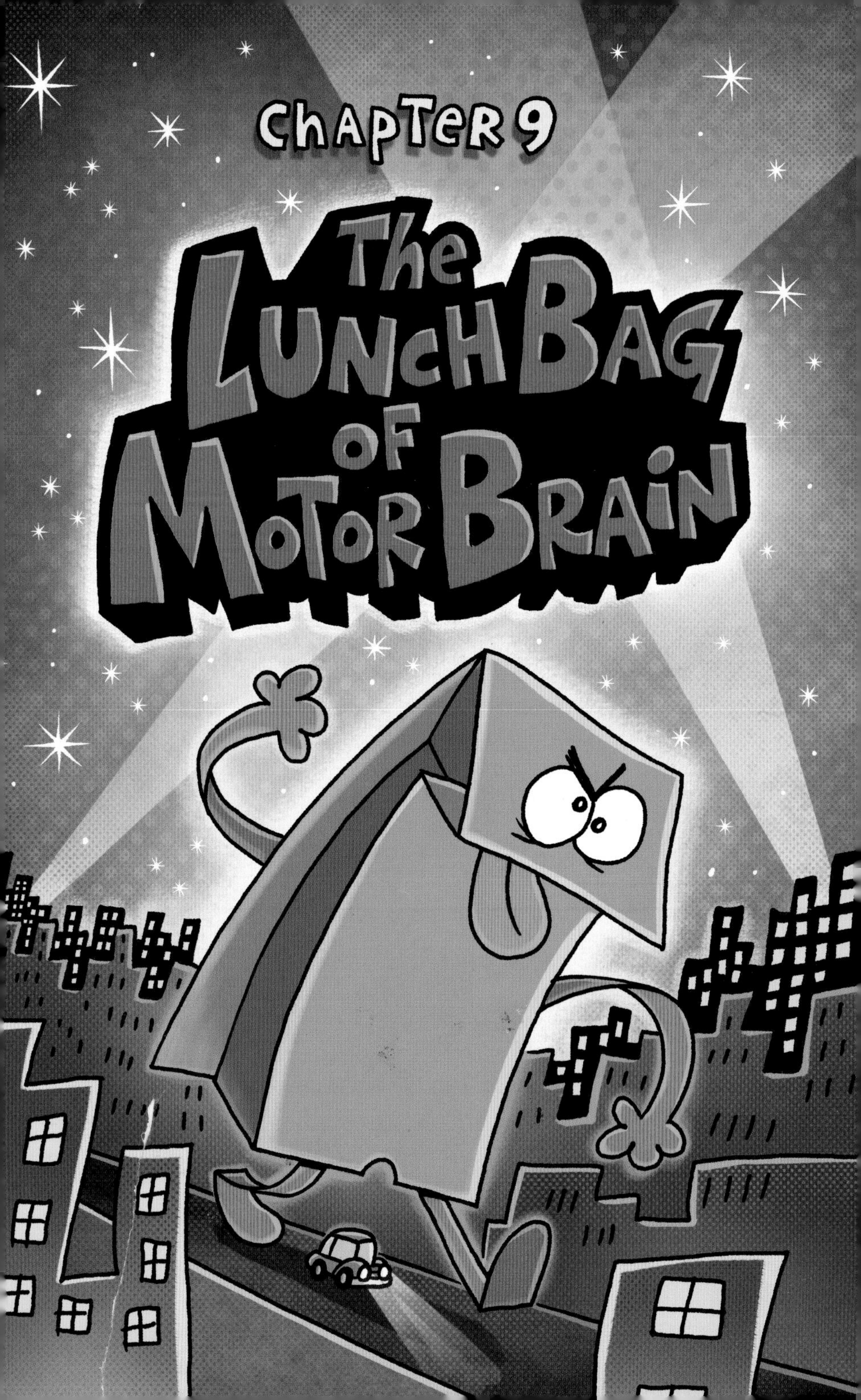

CHAPTER 9
The Lunch Bag of Motor Brain

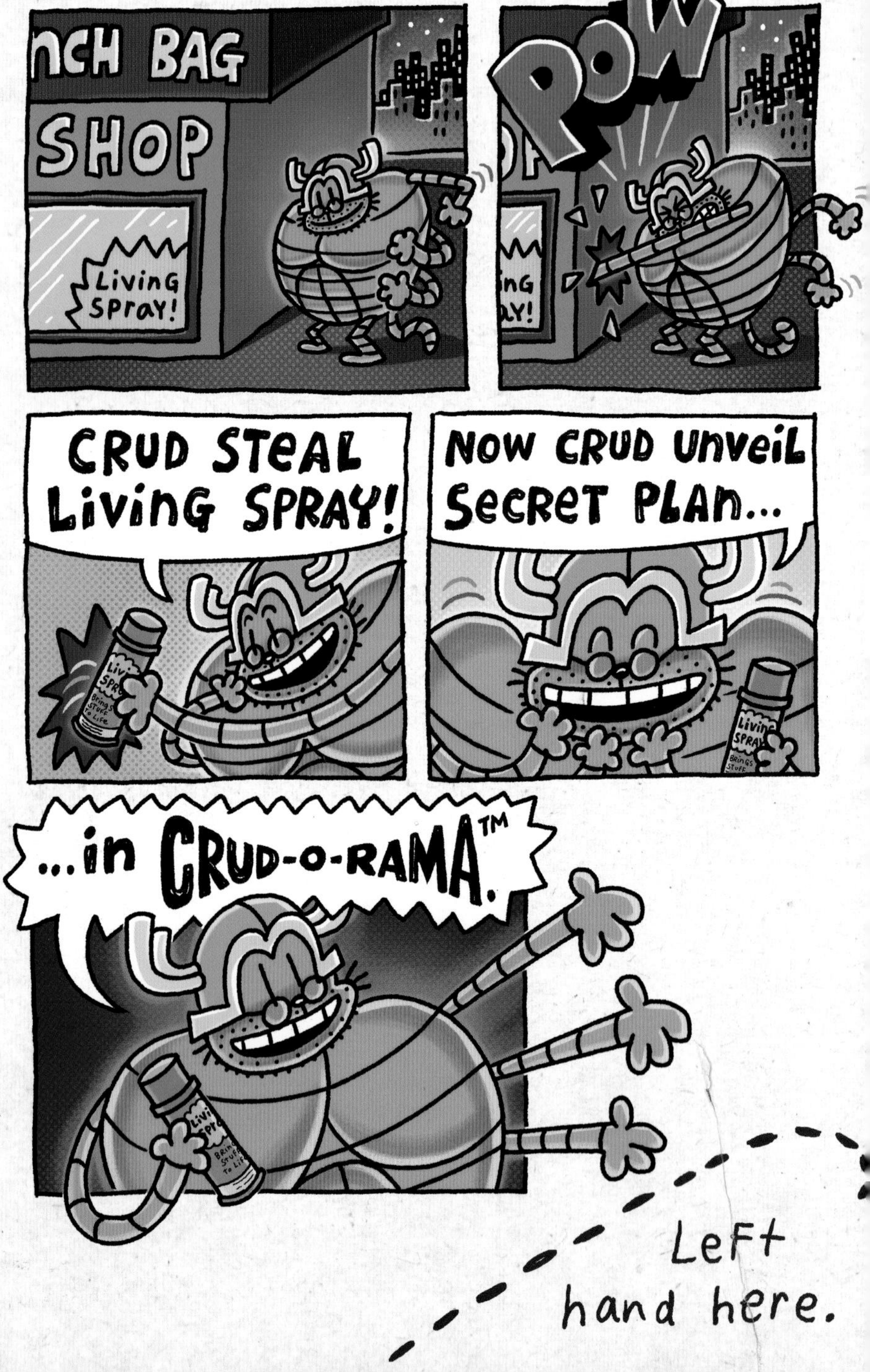
NCH BAG
SHOP
Living Spray!
POW
CRUD STEAL Living SPRAY!
NOW CRUD UNVEIL SECRET PLAN...
...in CRUD-O-RAMA™.
Left hand here.

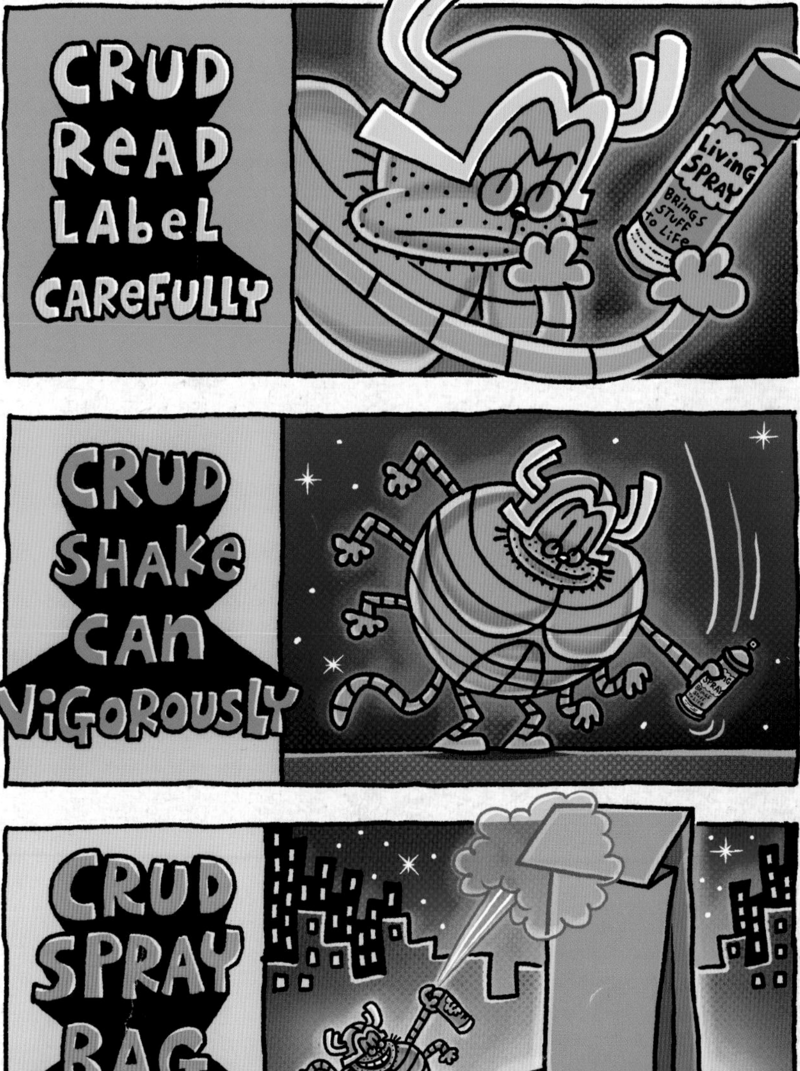
CRUD READ LABEL CAREFULLY
LIVING SPRAY
BRINGS STUFF TO LIFE
CRUD SHAKE CAN VIGOROUSLY
CRUD SPRAY BAG THOROUGHLY

Right Thumb here.

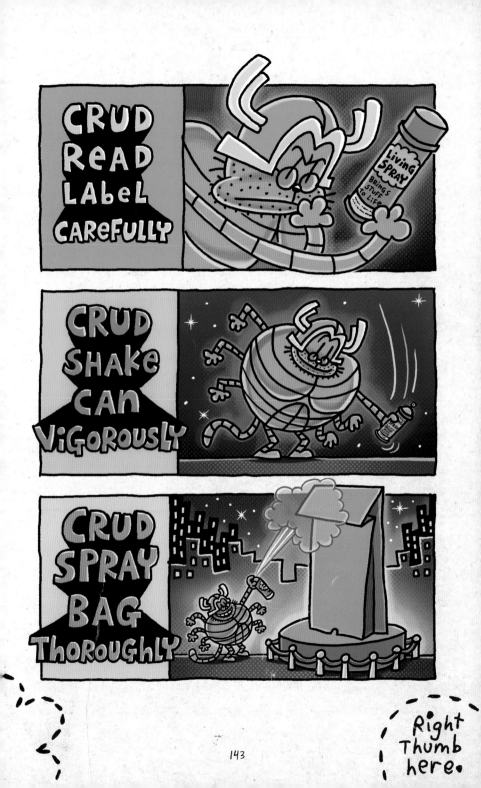

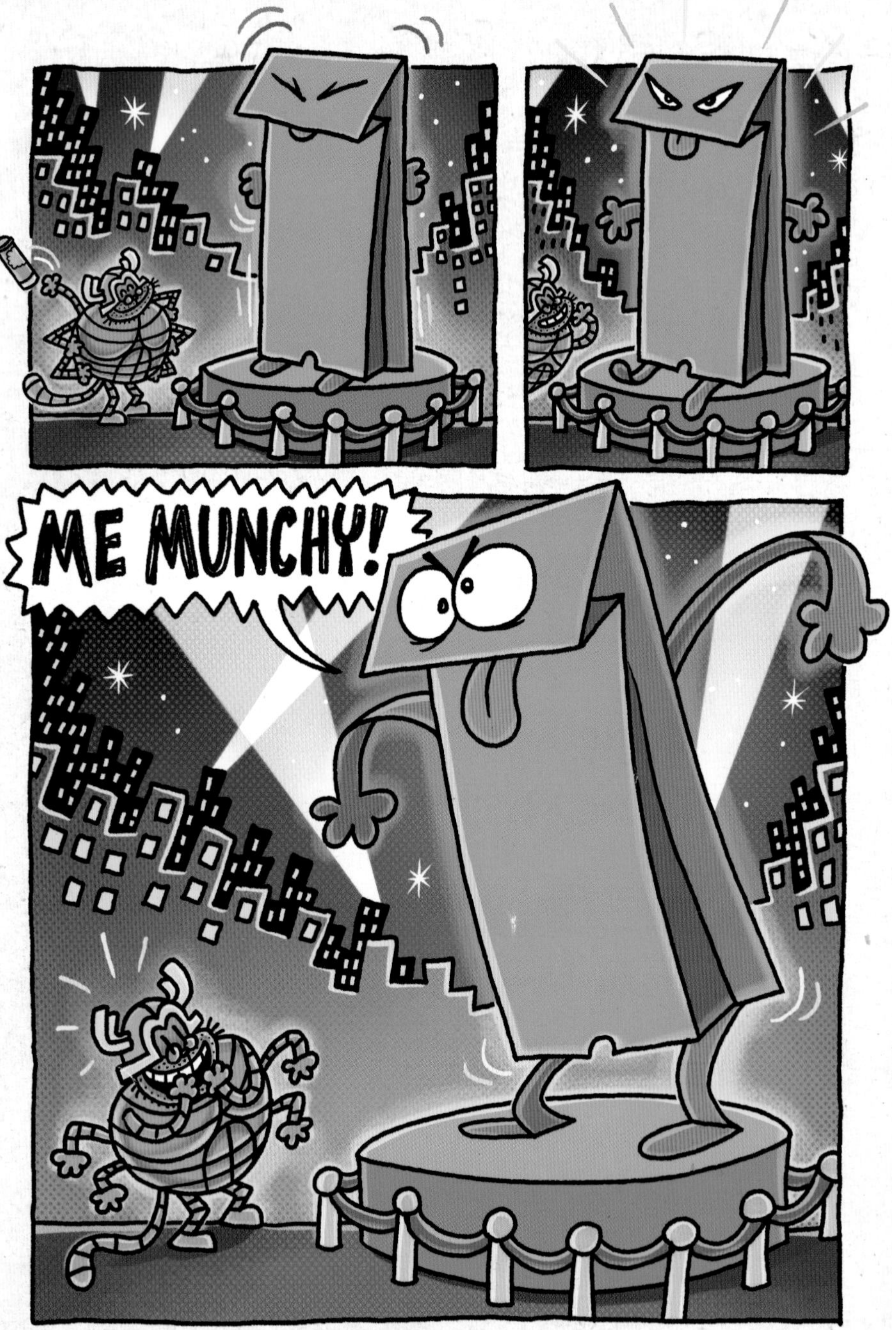
ME MUNCHY!

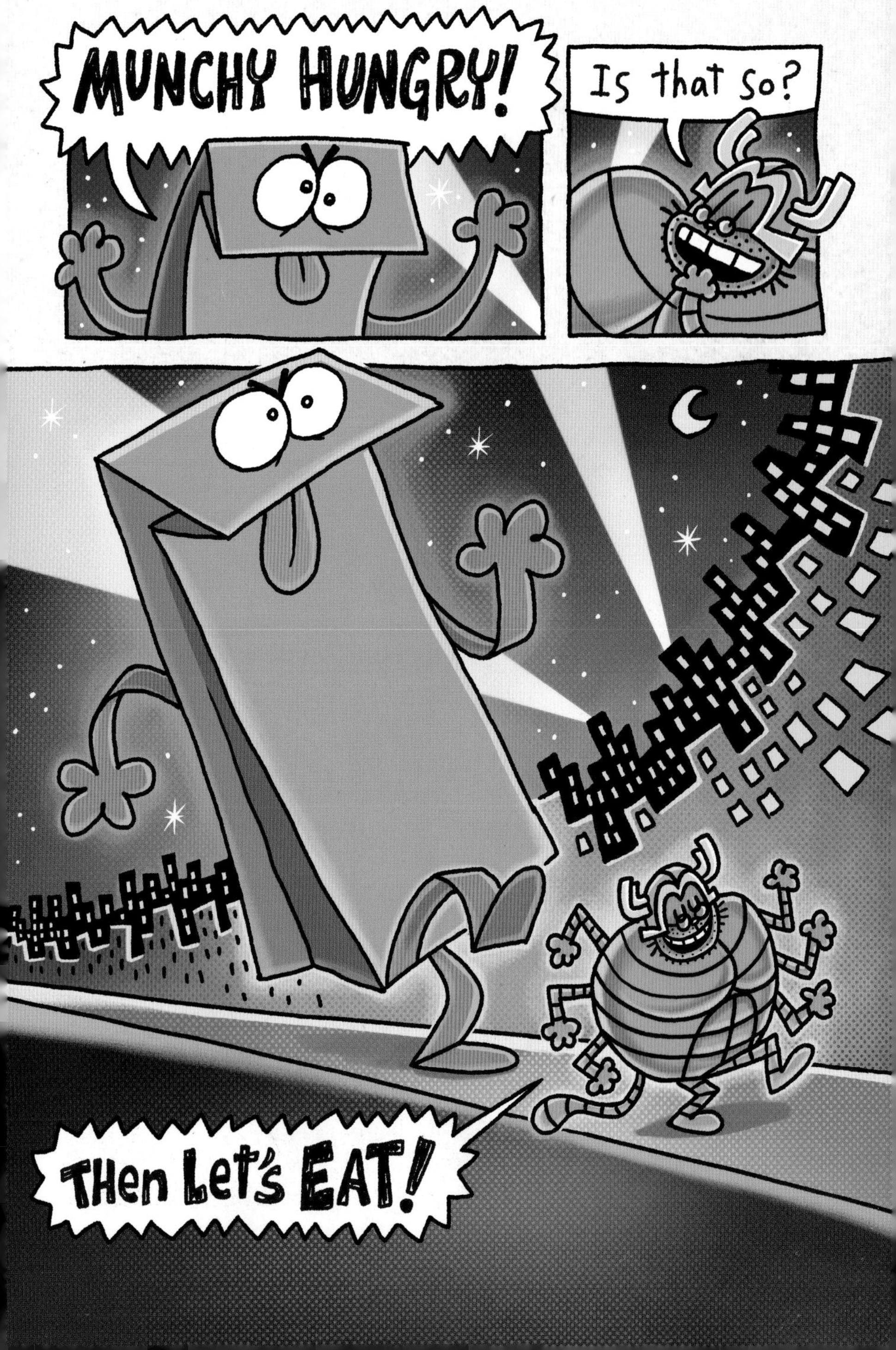
MUNCHY HUNGRY!
Is that so?
Then Let's EAT!

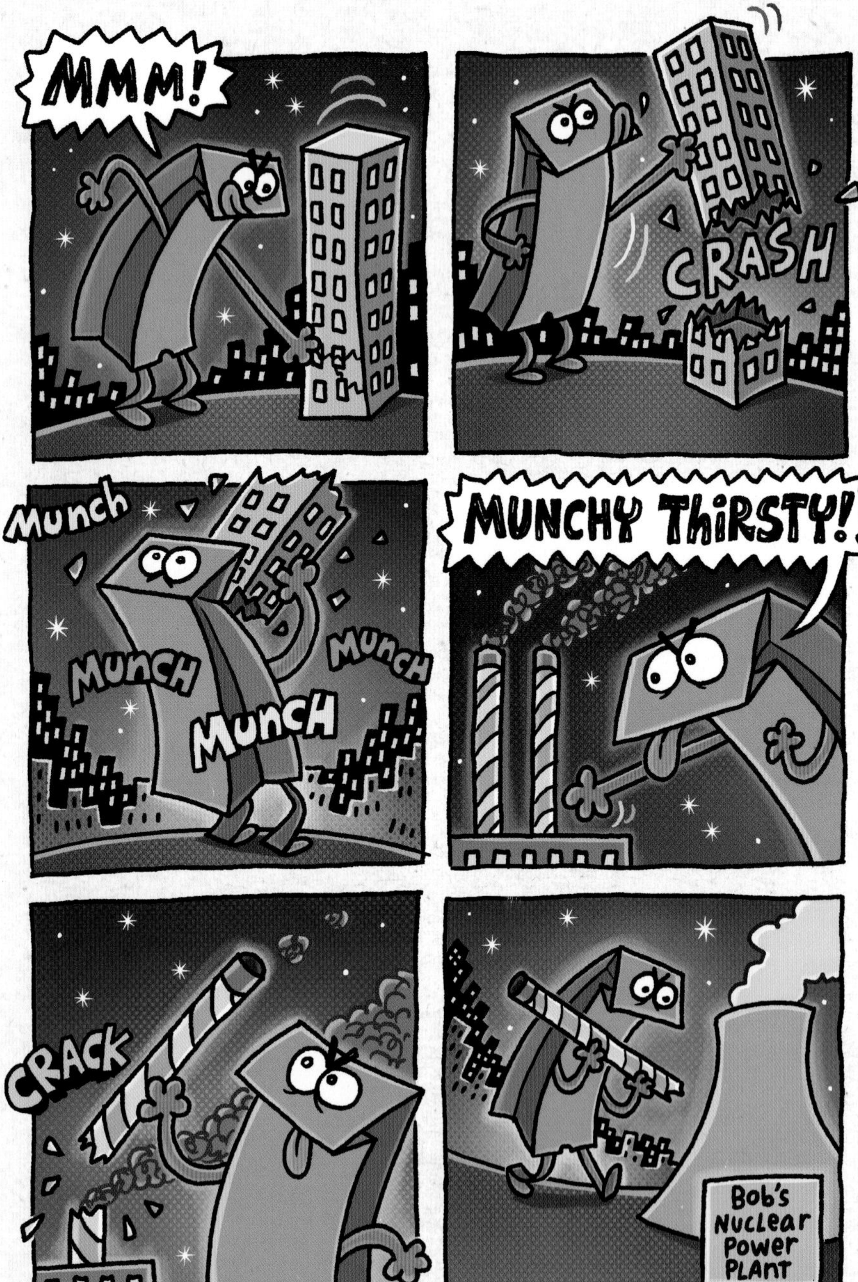
MMM!
CRASH
Munch
MUNCH
MUNCH
MUNCH
MUNCHY THIRSTY!
CRACK
Bob's Nuclear Power PLANT

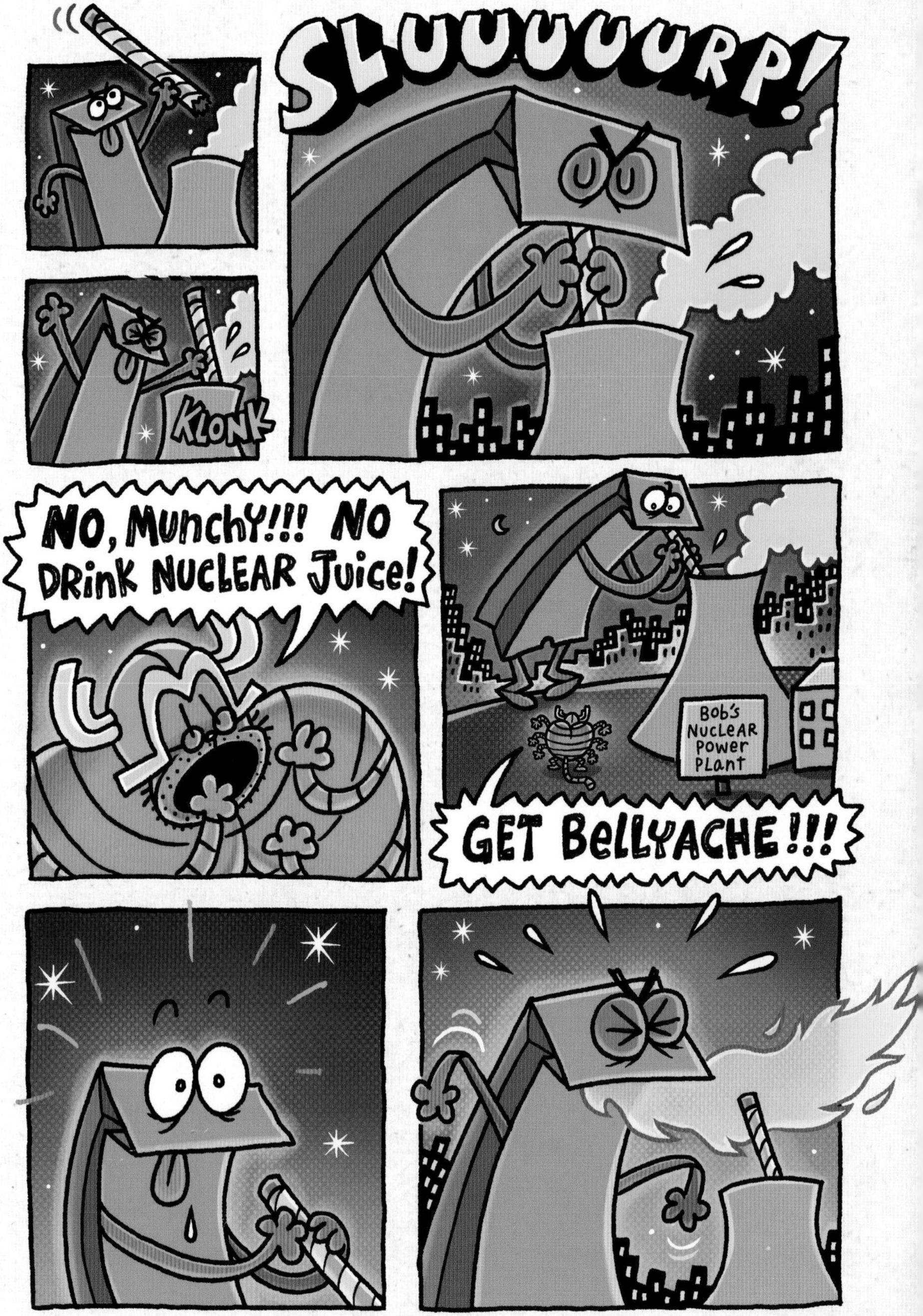
SLUUUUUURP!
KLONK
NO, MUNCHY!!! NO DRINK NUCLEAR JUICE!
Bob's Nuclear Power Plant
GET BELLYACHE!!!

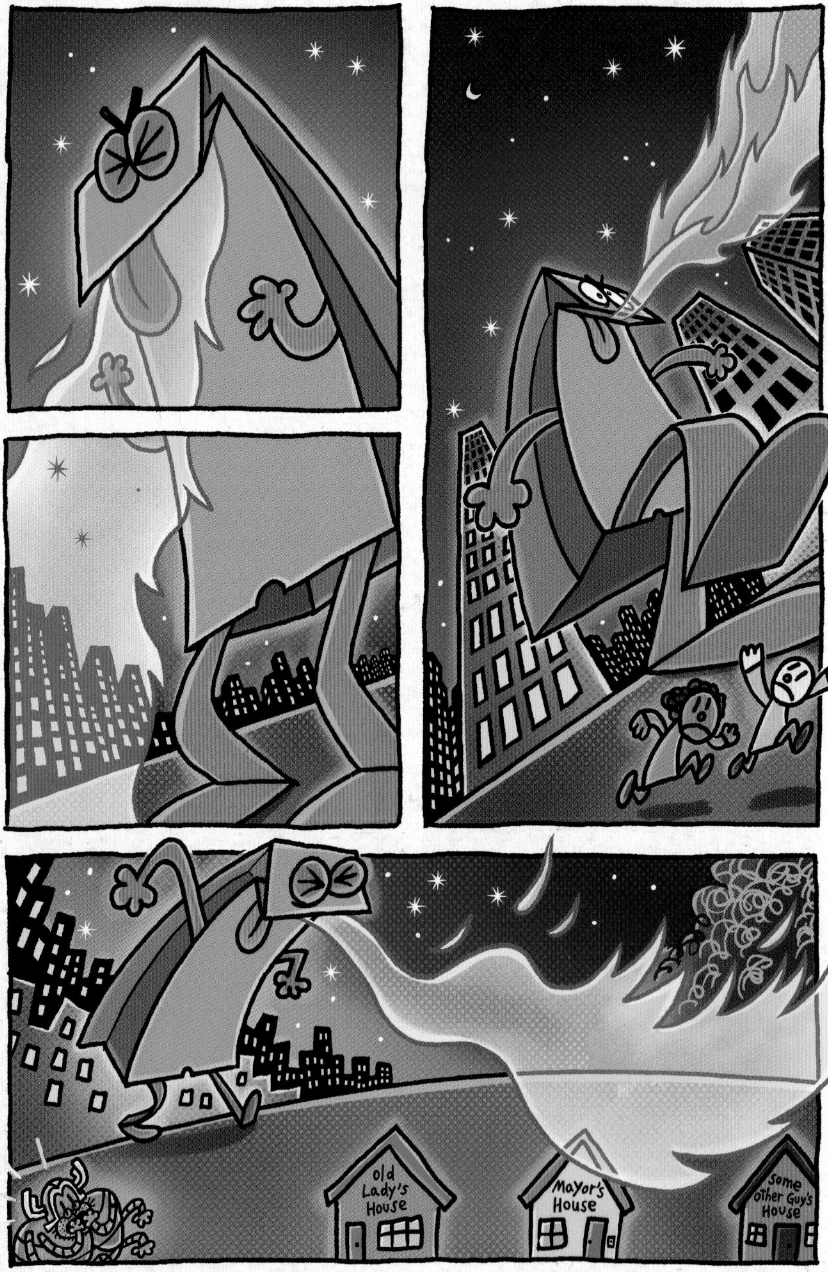

Old Lady's House
Mayor's House
Some other Guy's House

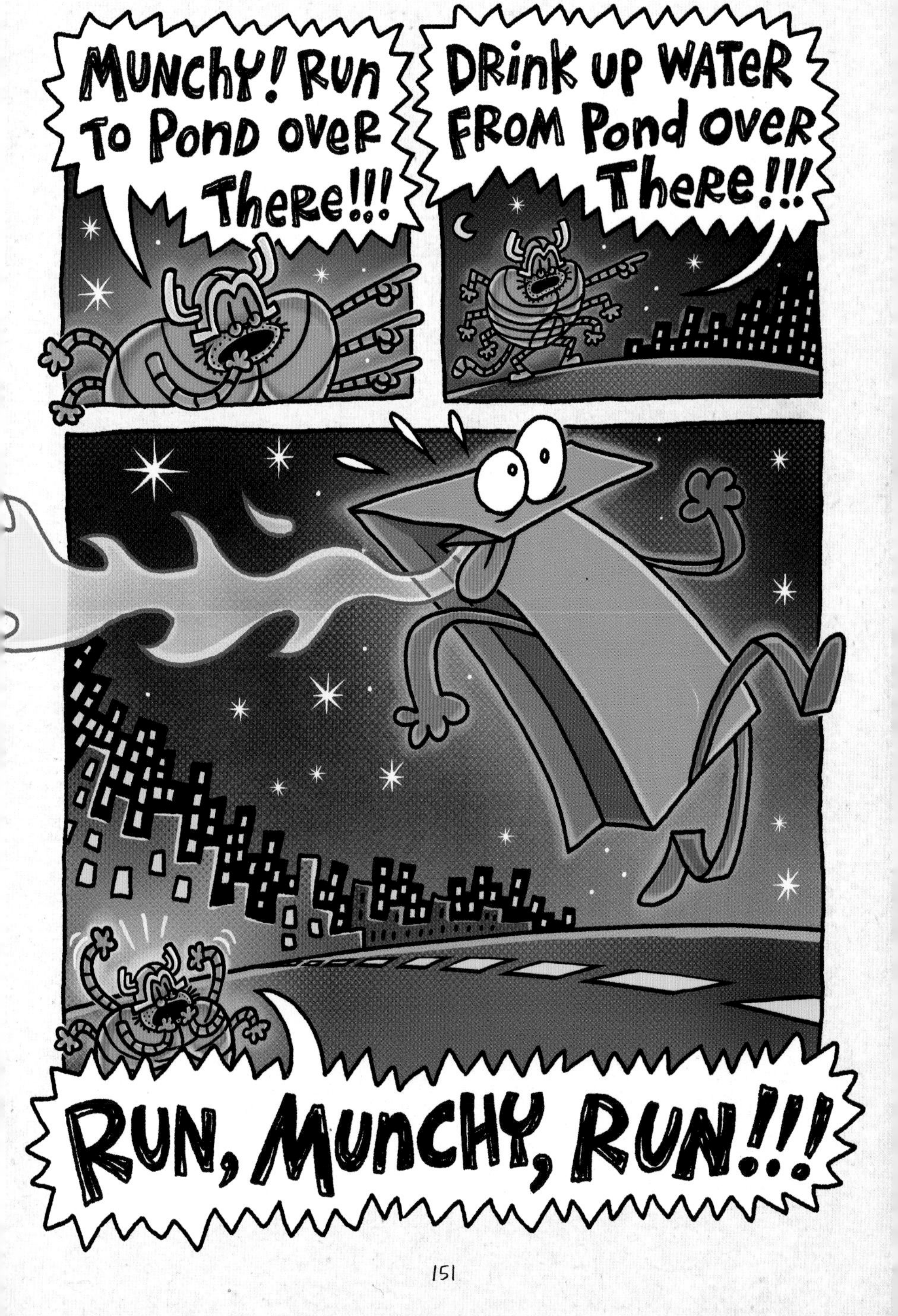
MUNCHY! RUN TO POND OVER THERE!!!
DRINK UP WATER FROM POND OVER THERE!!!
RUN, MUNCHY, RUN!!!

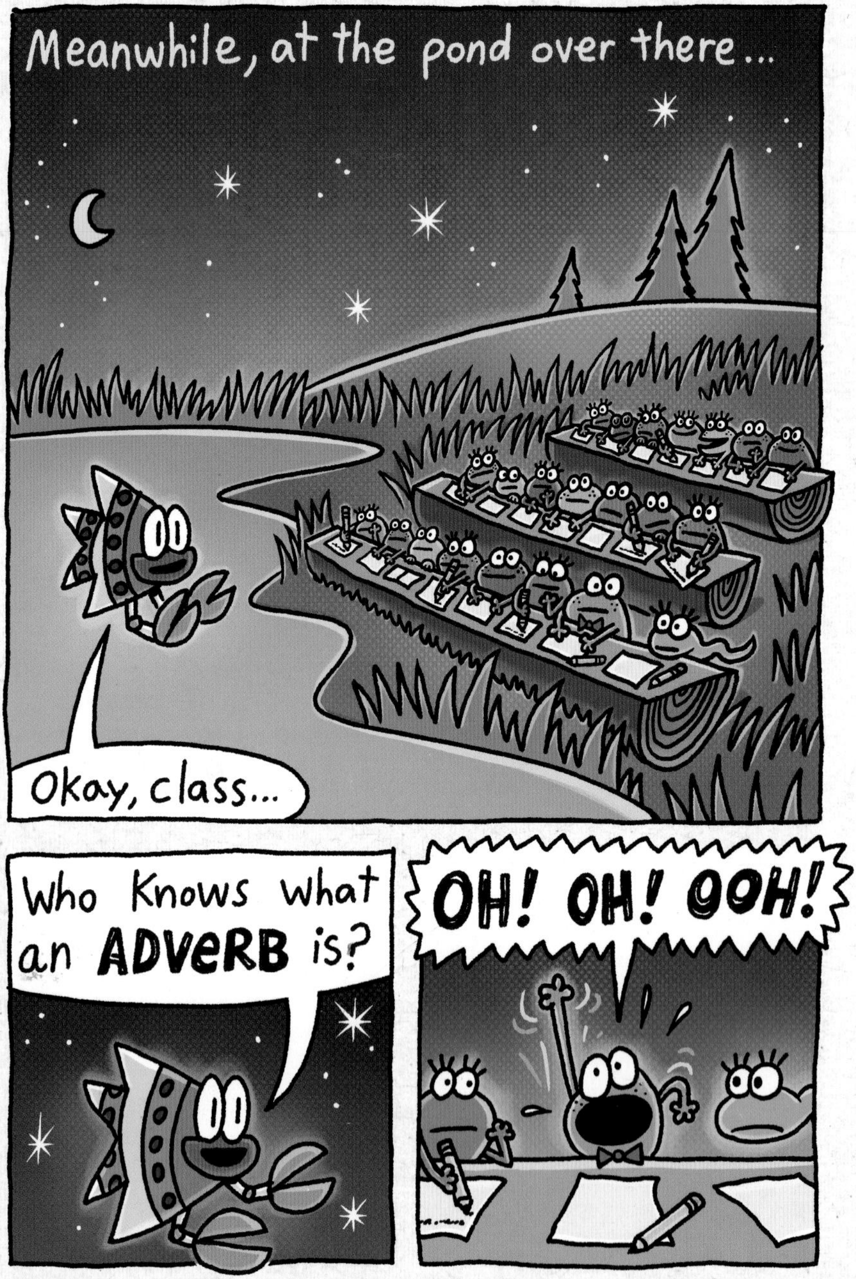
Meanwhile, at the pond over there...
Okay, class...
Who Knows what an ADVERB is?
OH! OH! OOH!

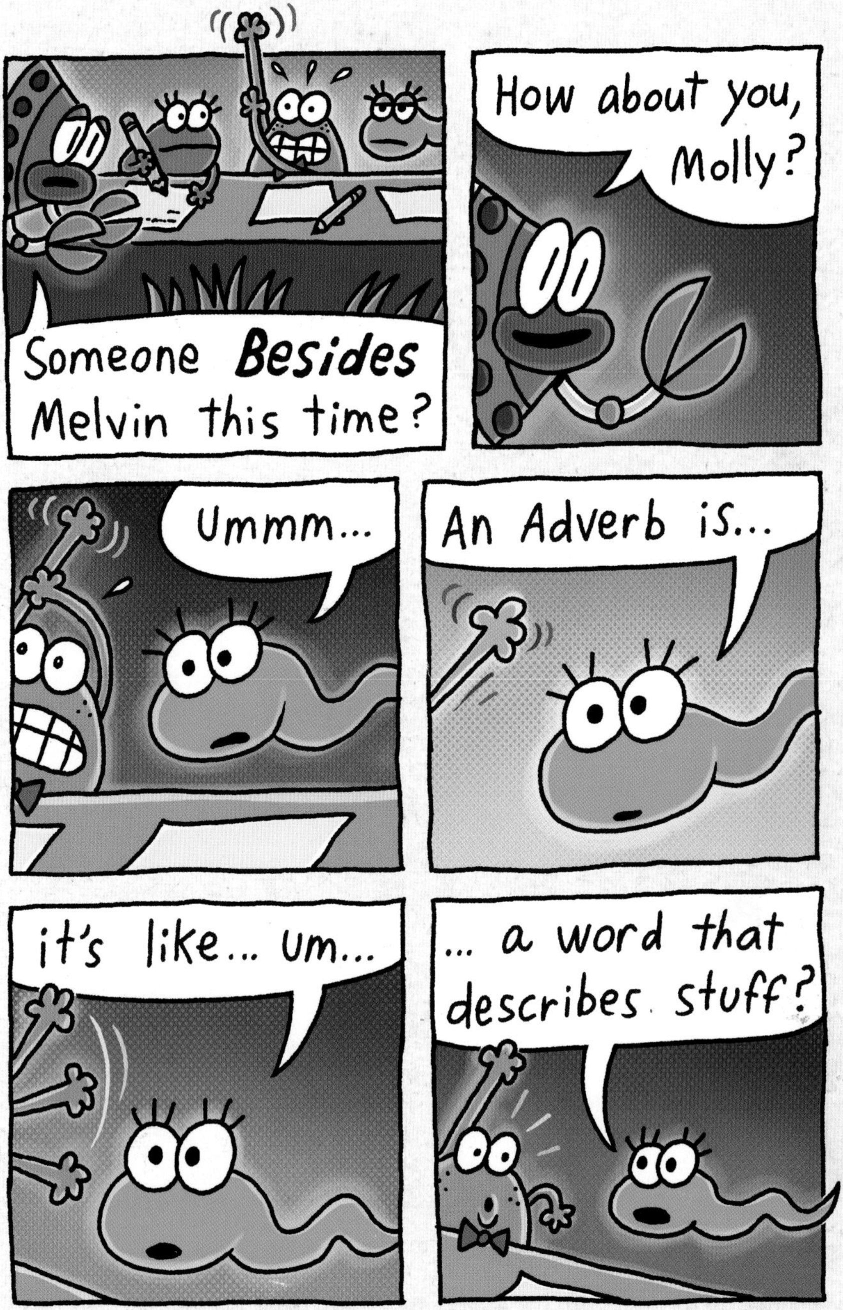
Someone **Besides** Melvin this time?
How about you, Molly?
Ummm...
An Adverb is...
it's like... um...
... a word that describes stuff?

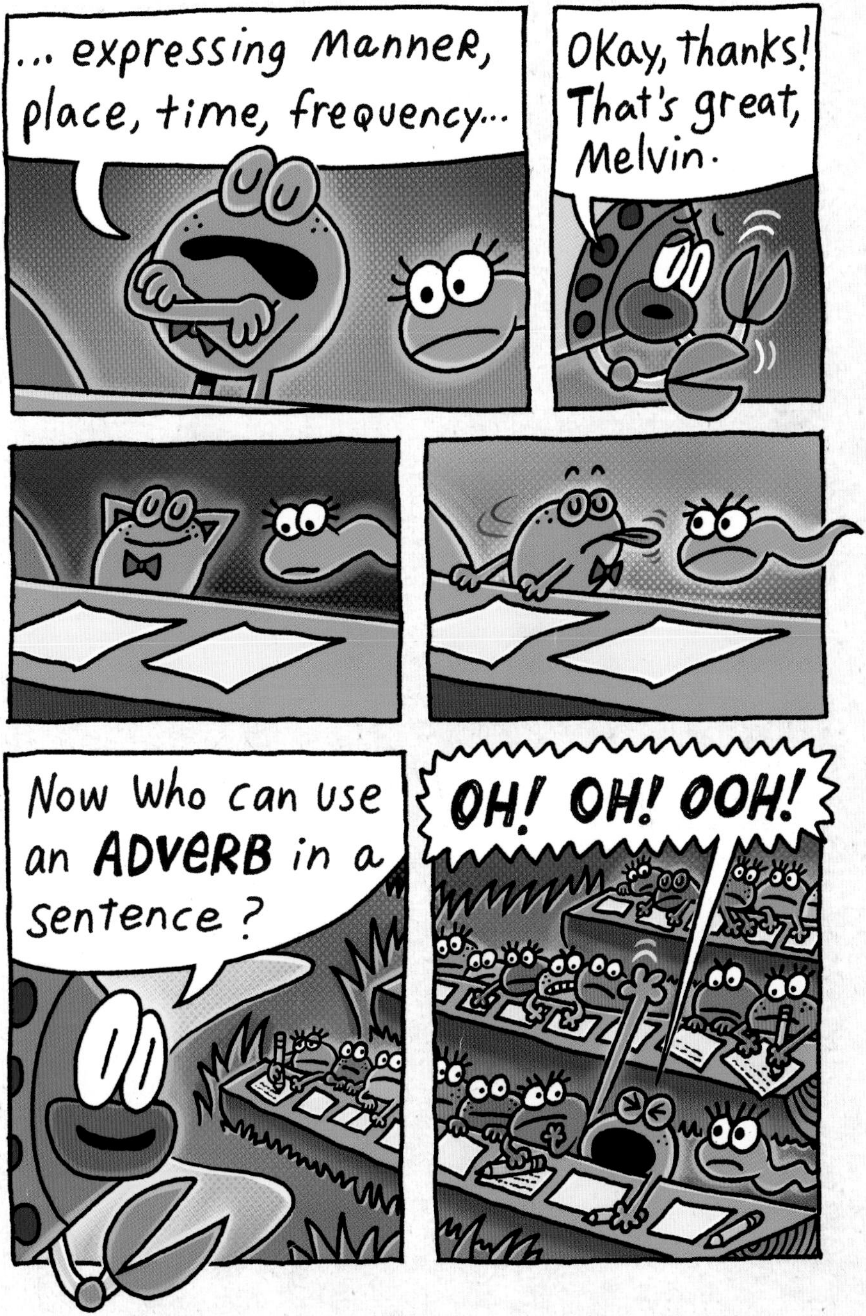
... expressing manner, place, time, frequency...
Okay, thanks! That's great, Melvin.
Now who can use an ADVERB in a sentence?
OH! OH! OOH!

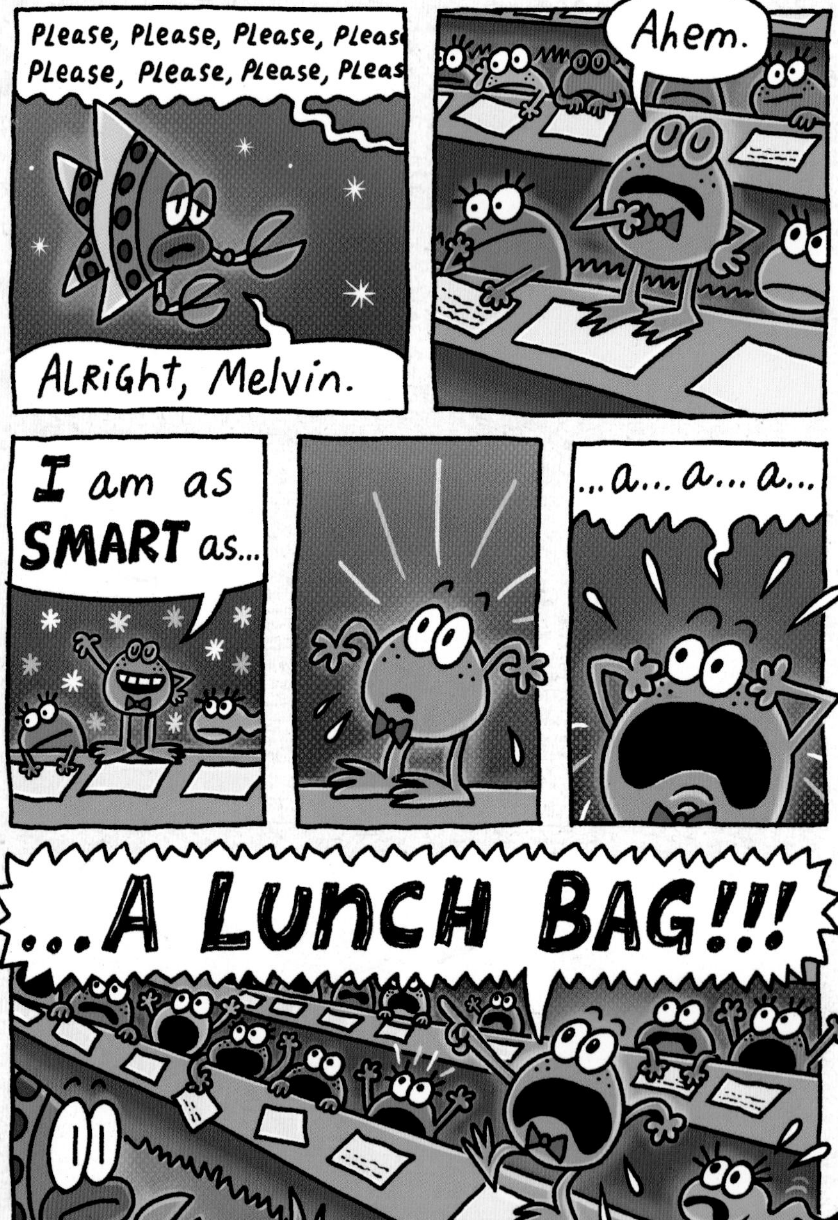
Please, Please, Please, Pleas
Please, Please, Please, Pleas
ALRIGHT, Melvin.
Ahem.
I am as SMART as...
...a...a...a...
...A LUNCH BAG!!!

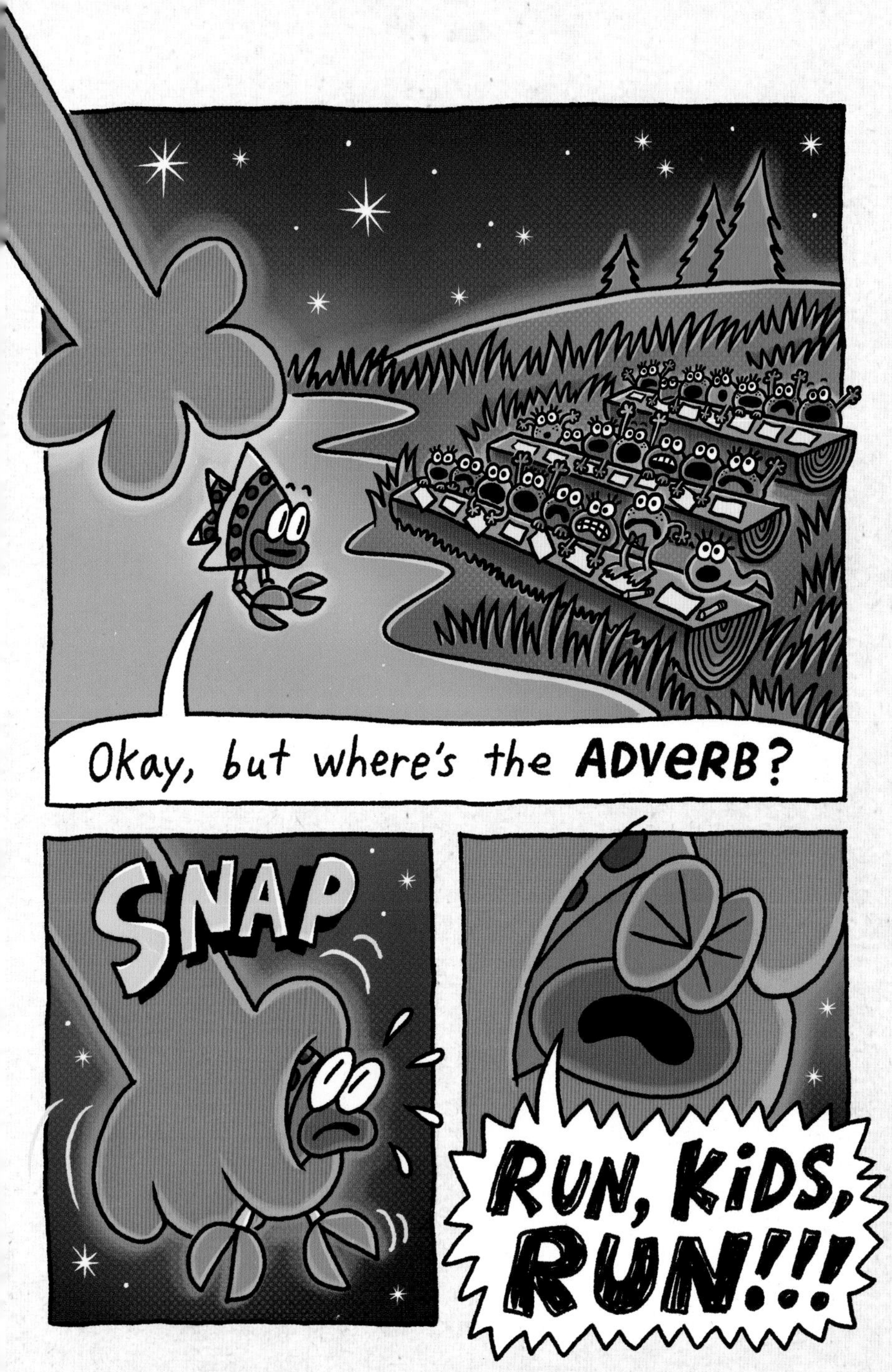
Okay, but where's the ADVERB?
SNAP
RUN, KIDS, RUN!!!

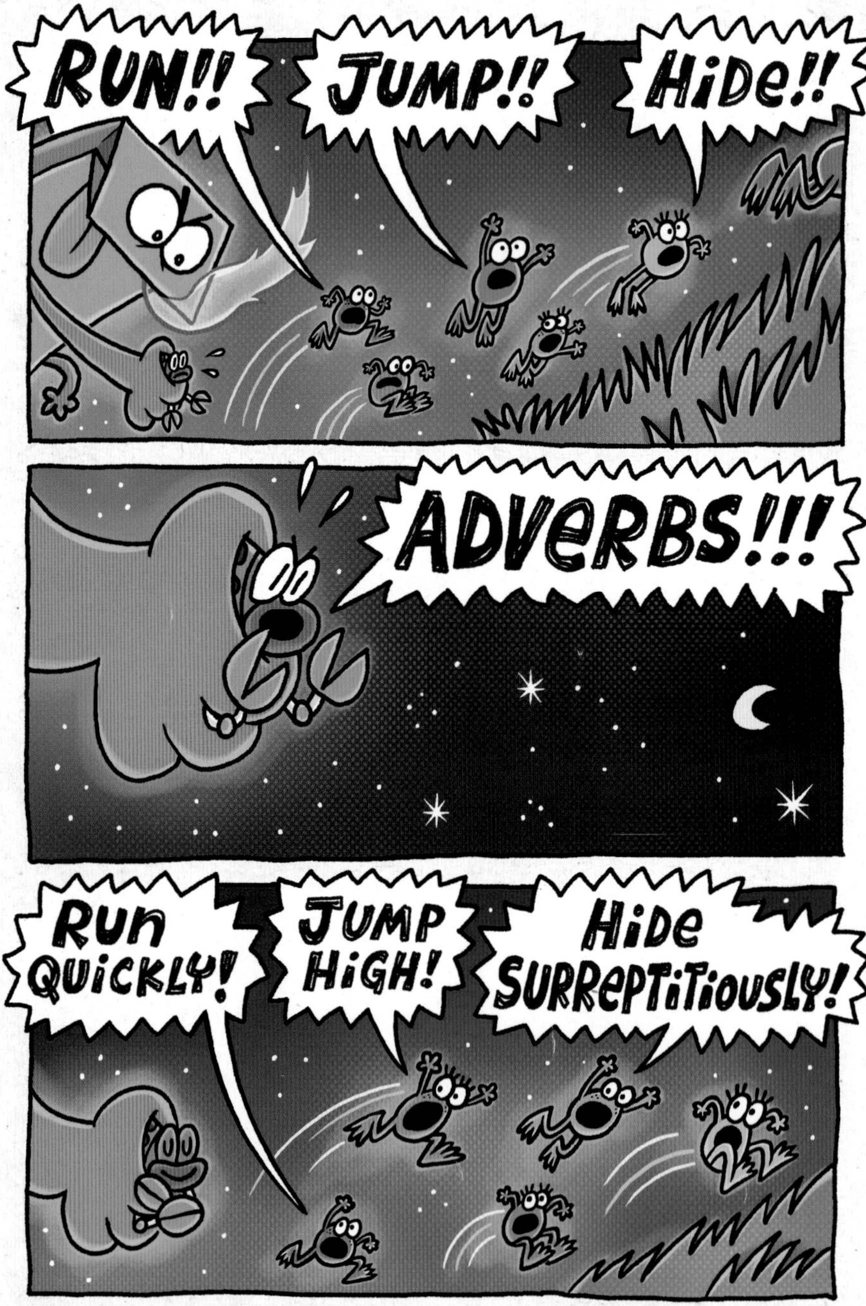
RUN!!
JUMP!!
HIDE!!
ADVERBS!!!
RUN QUICKLY!
JUMP HIGH!
HIDE SURREPTITIOUSLY!

CHAPTER 10

80-HD POWER

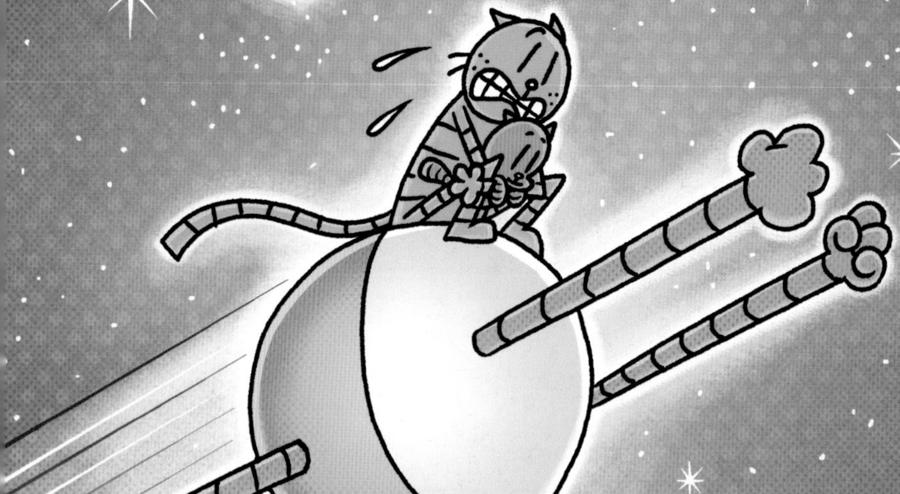

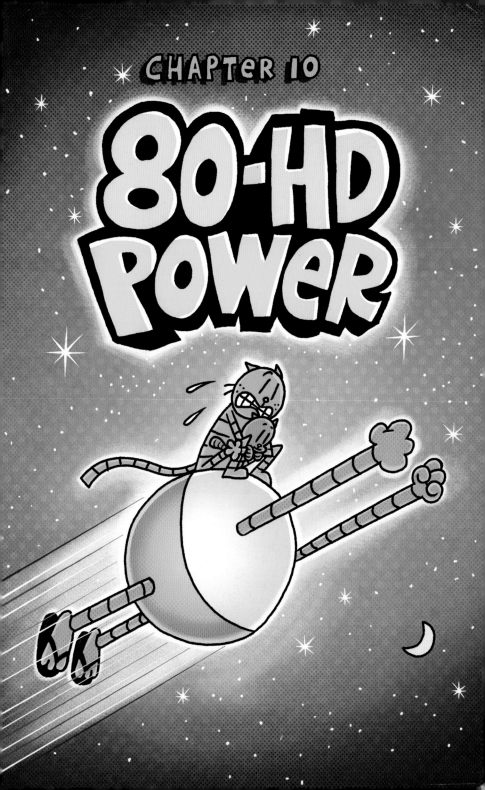

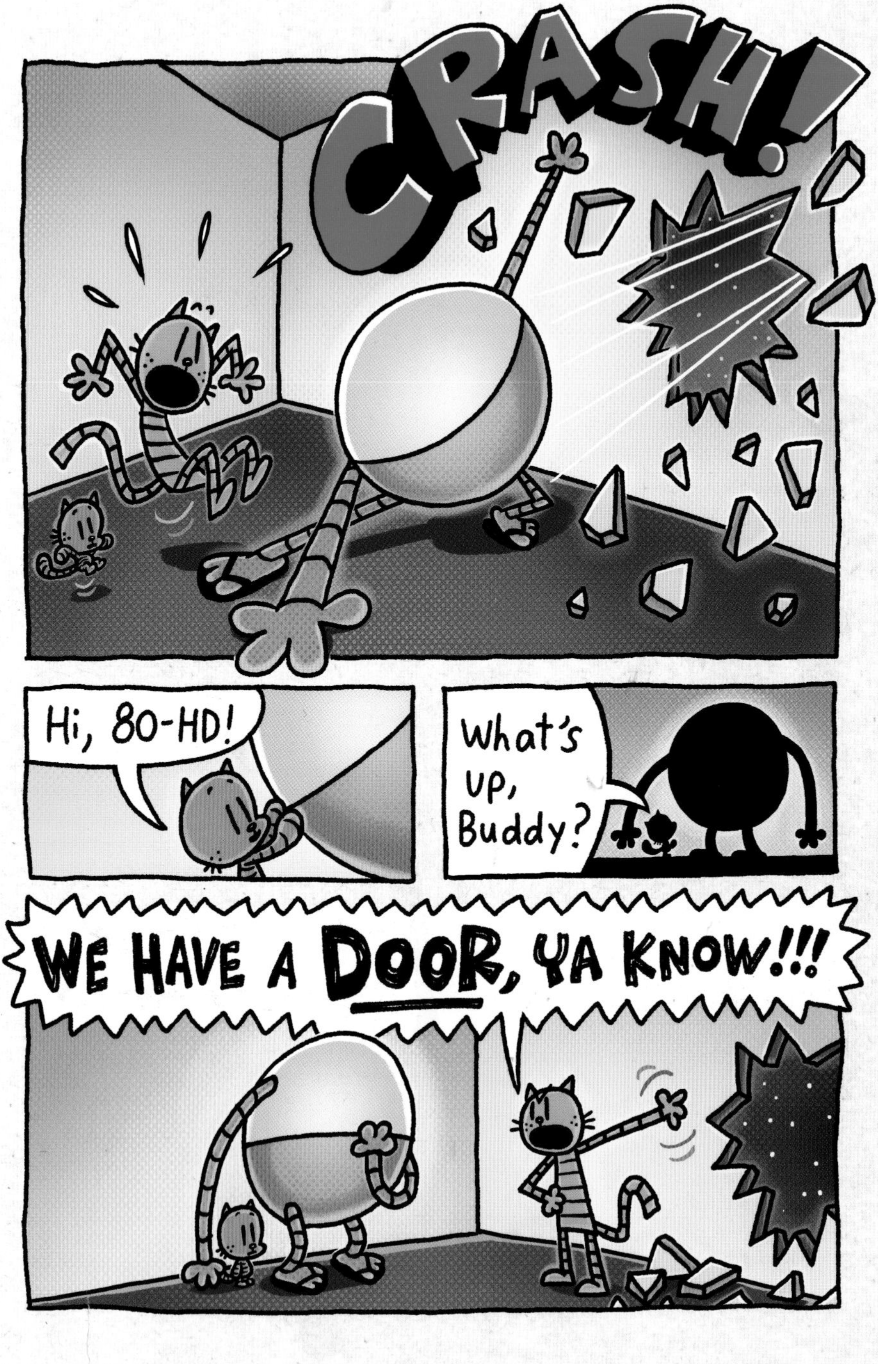
CRASH!
Hi, 80-HD!
What's up, Buddy?
WE HAVE A DOOR, YA KNOW!!!

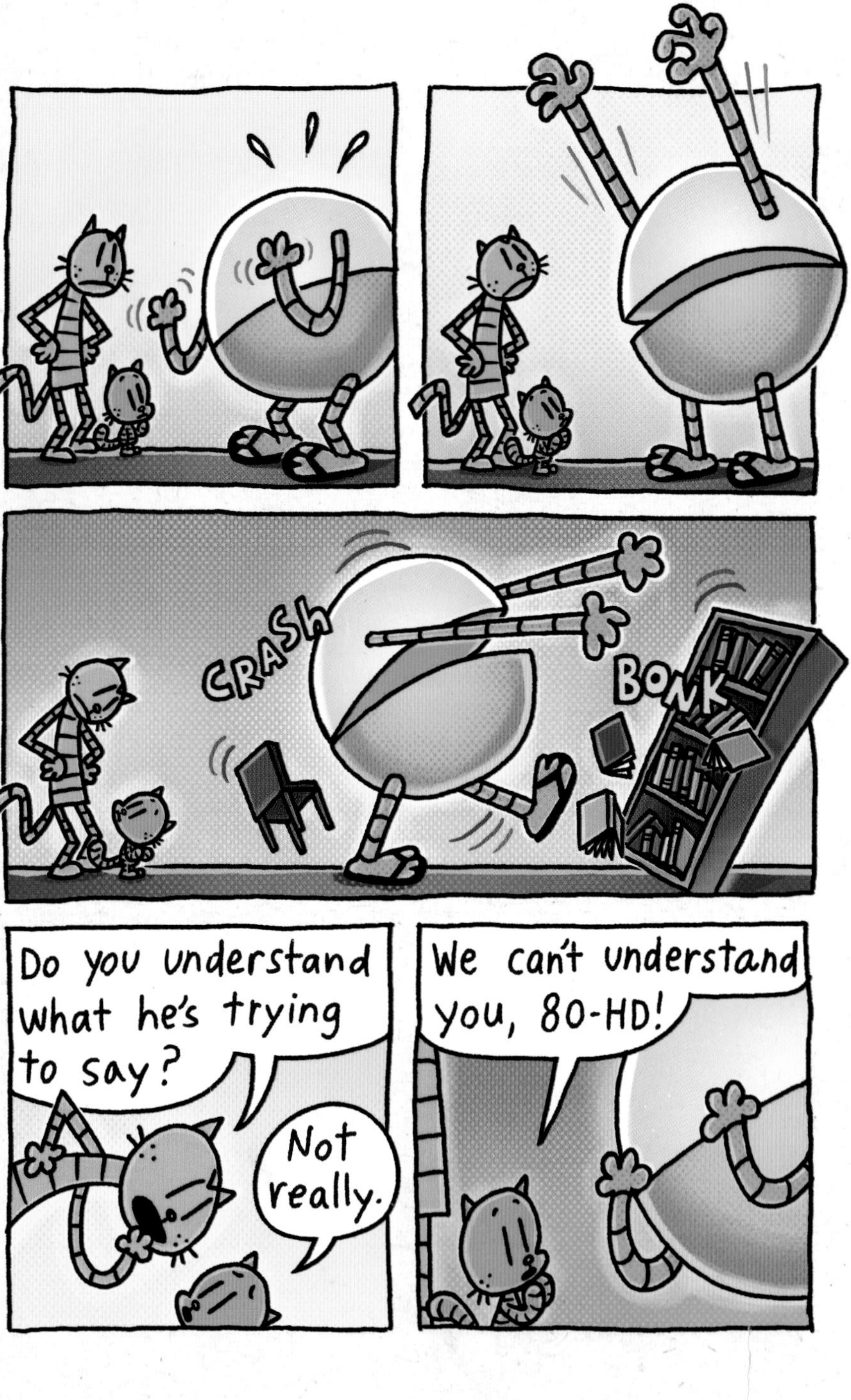
CRASh
BONK
Do you understand what he's trying to say?
Not really.
We can't understand you, 80-HD!

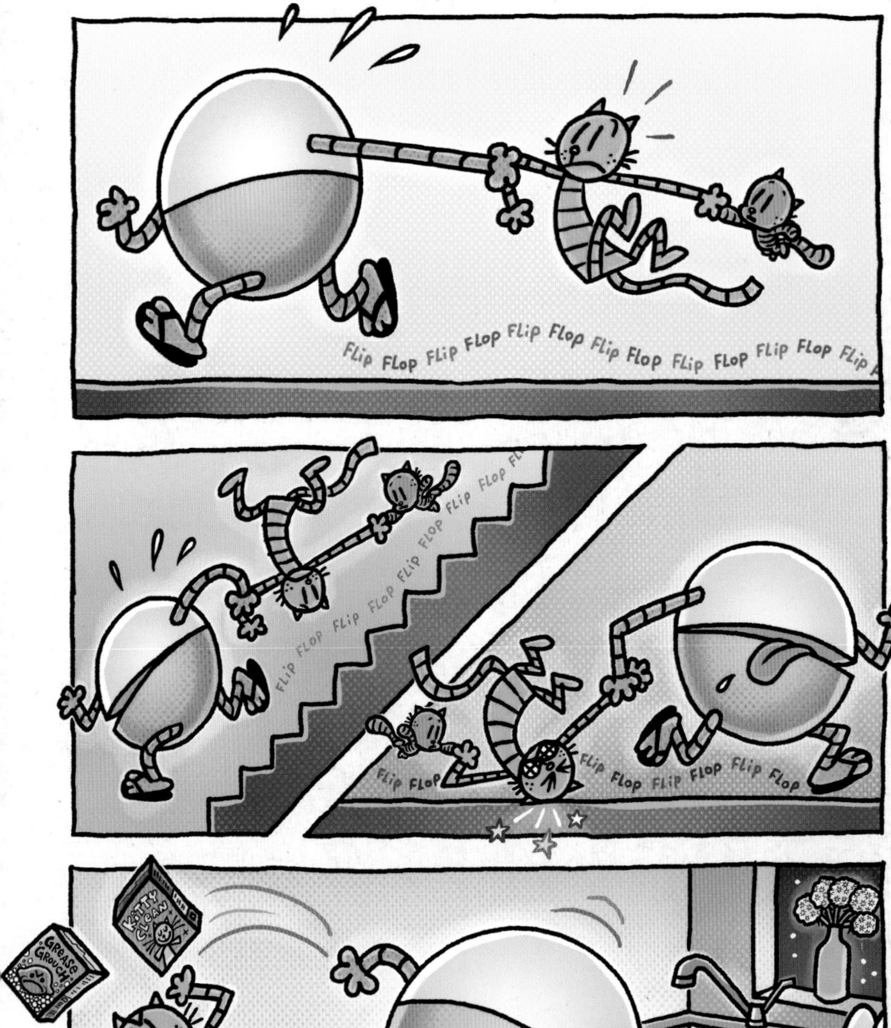
FLip FLop FLip FLop FLip FLop FLip FLop FLip FLop FLip FLop FLip
FLip FLop FLip FLop FLip FLop FLip FLop FLip FLop
FLip FLop FLip FLop FLip FLop FLip FLop
GREASE GROUCH
KITTY CLEAN

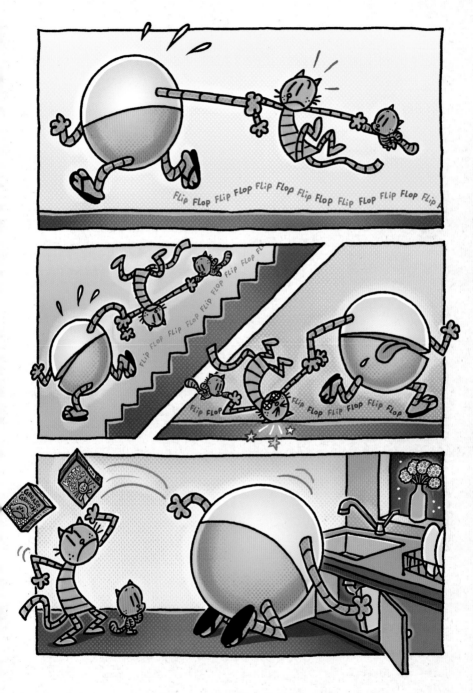

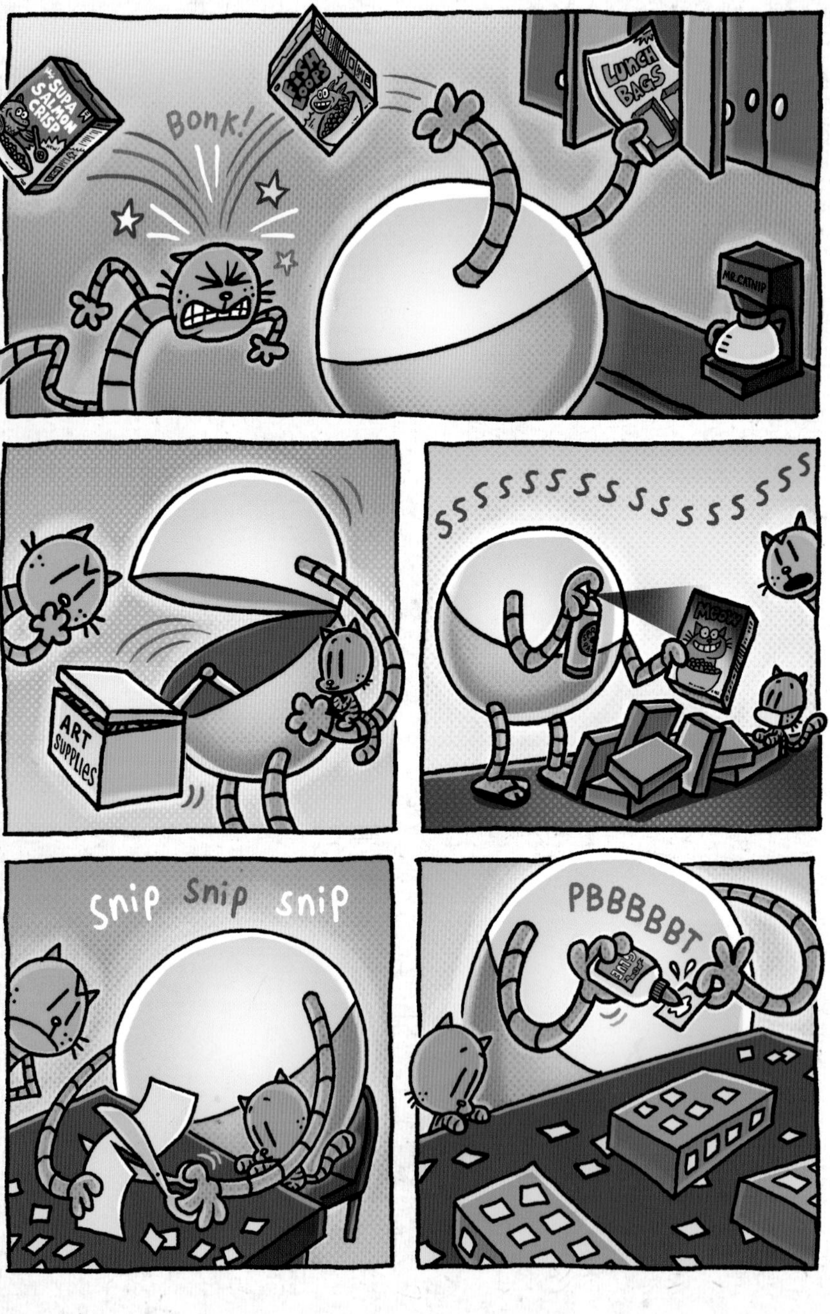
SUPA SALMON CRISP
FISH LOOPS
BONK!
LUNCH BAGS
MR. CATNIP
ART SUPPLIES
SSSSSSSSSSSSSSSSS
MEOW
snip snip snip
PBBBBBT
GLUE

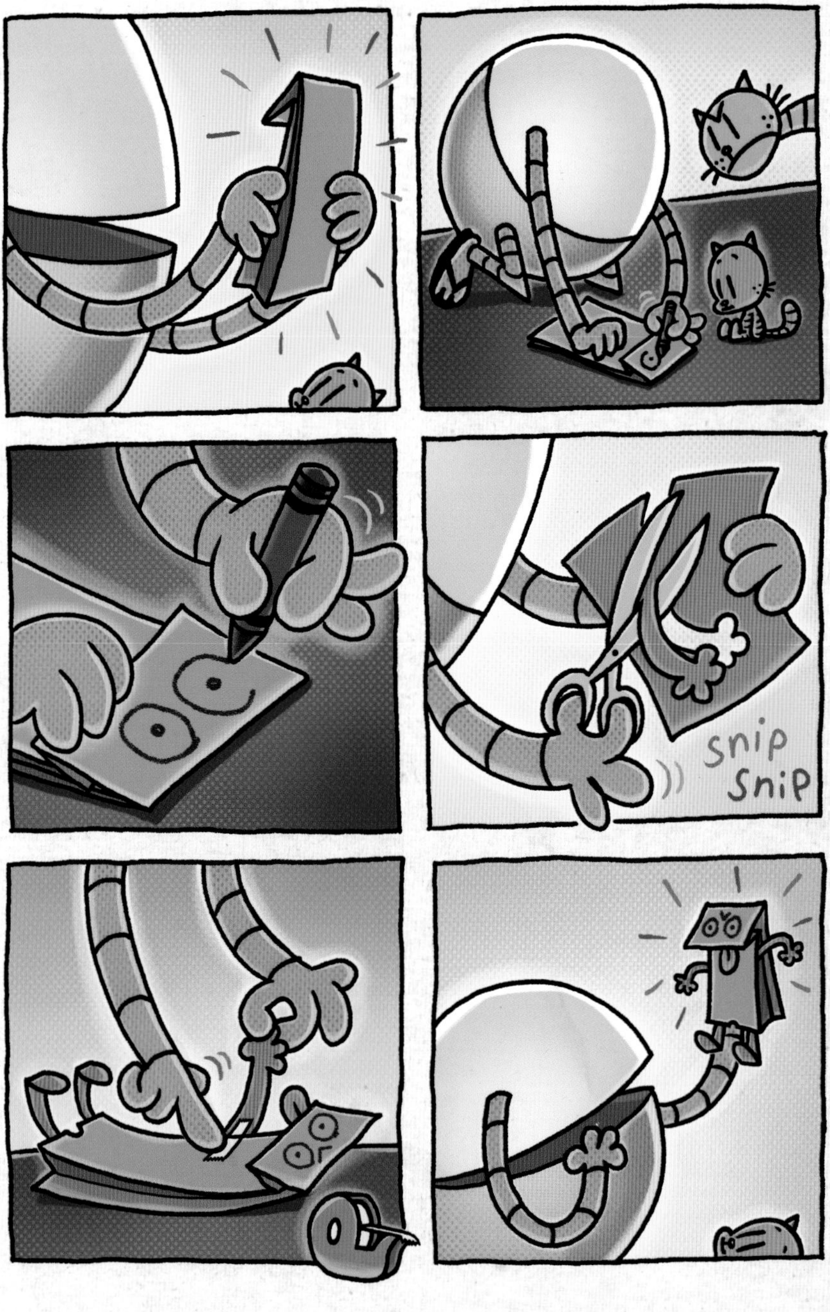
snip
snip

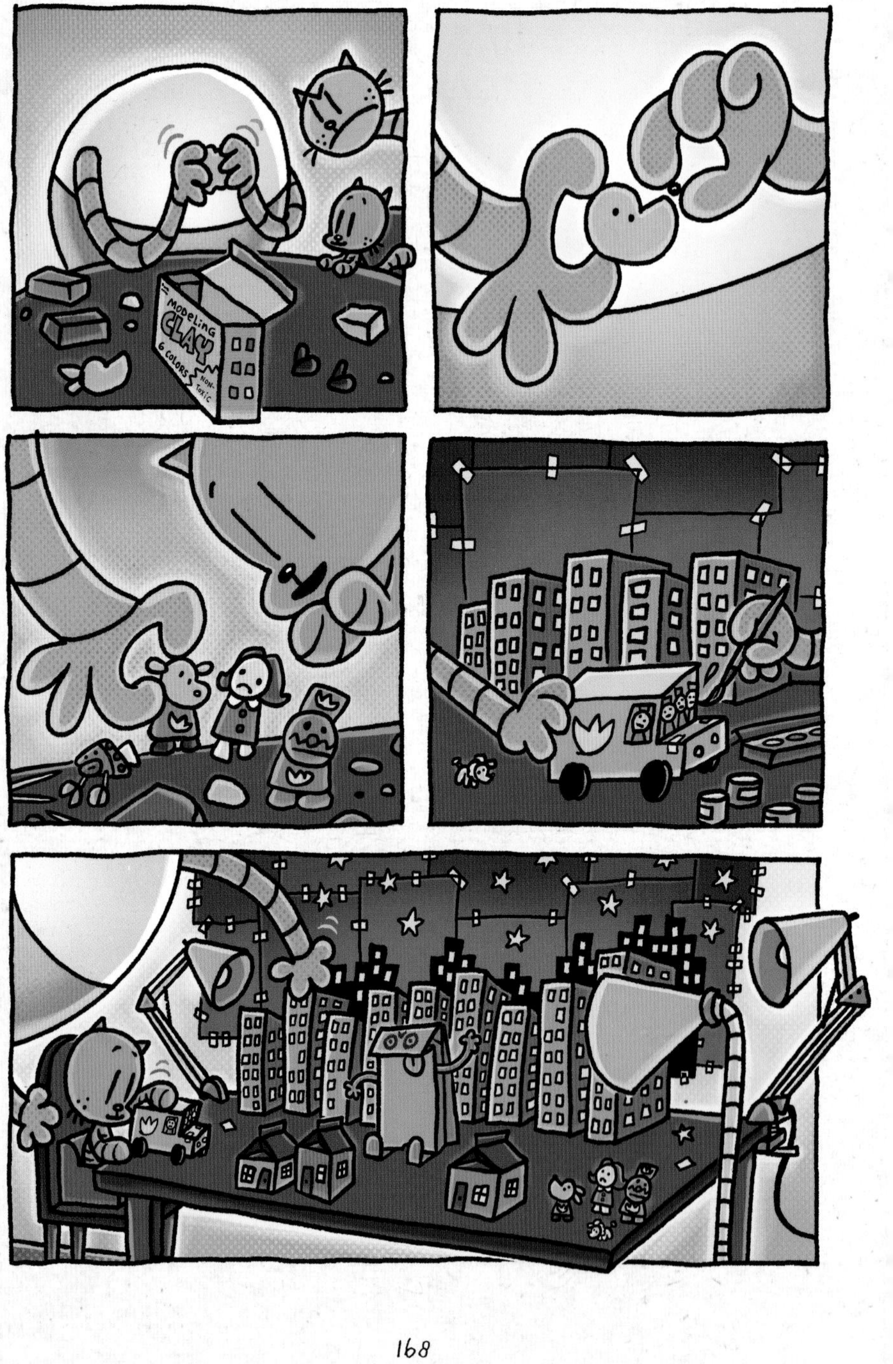
MODELING CLAY
6 COLORS
NON-TOXIC

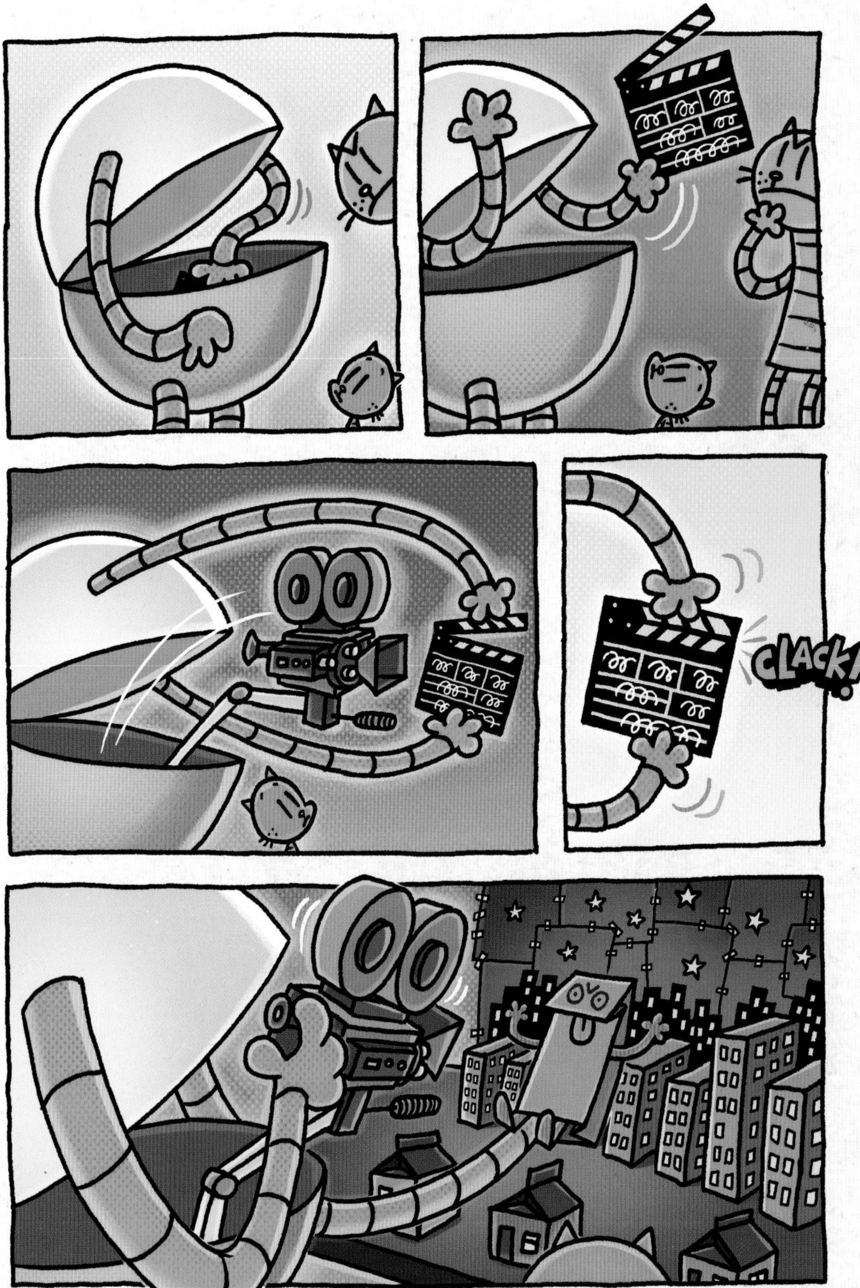
CLACK!

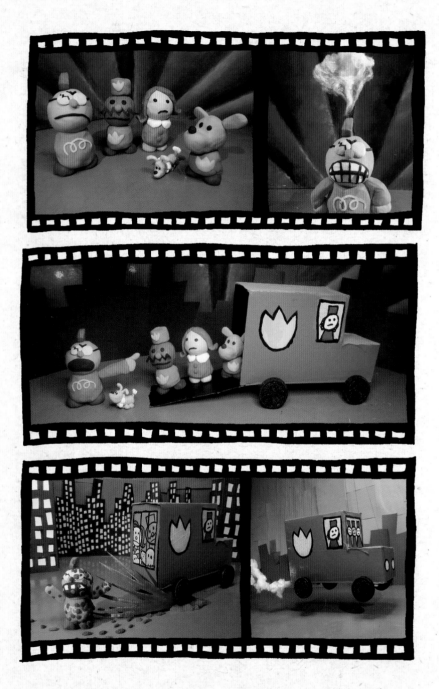

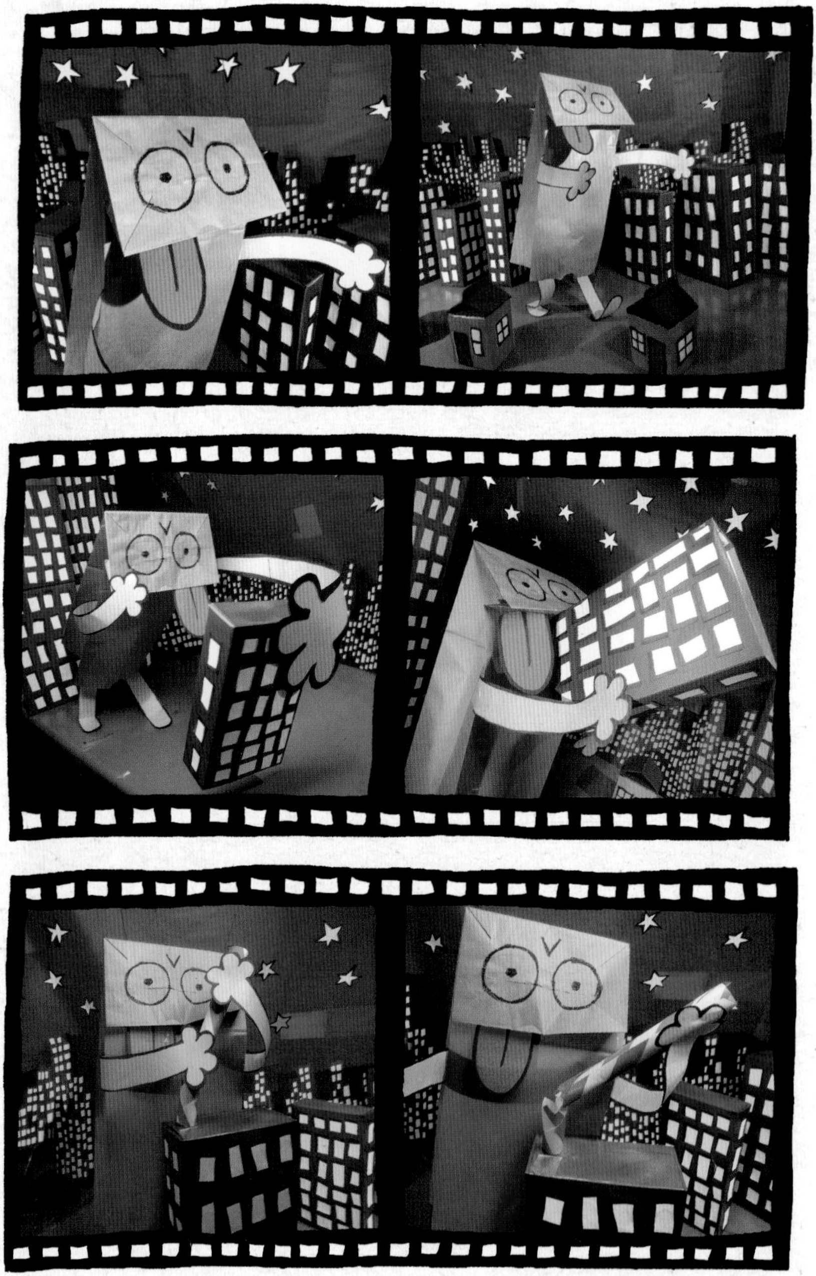

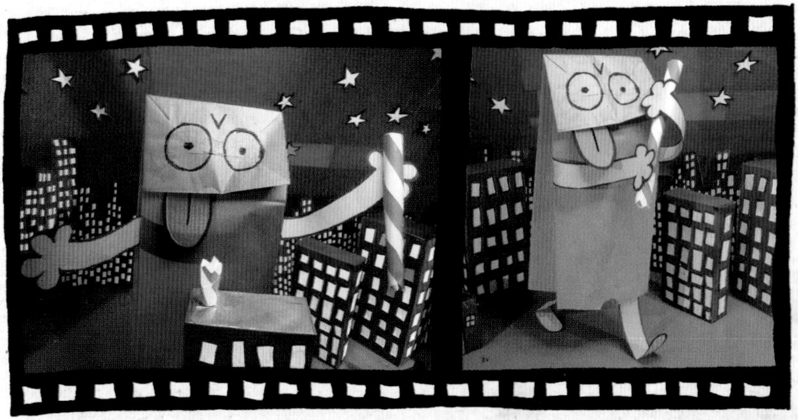

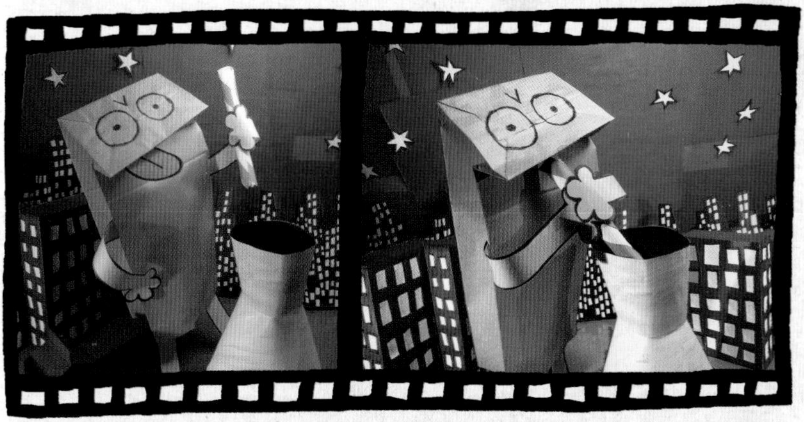

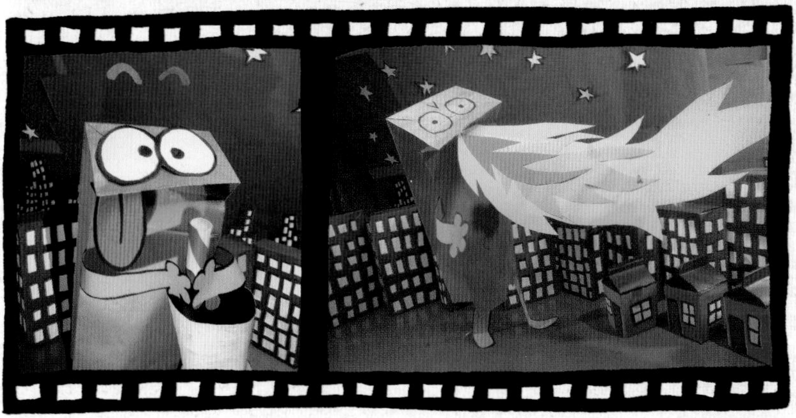

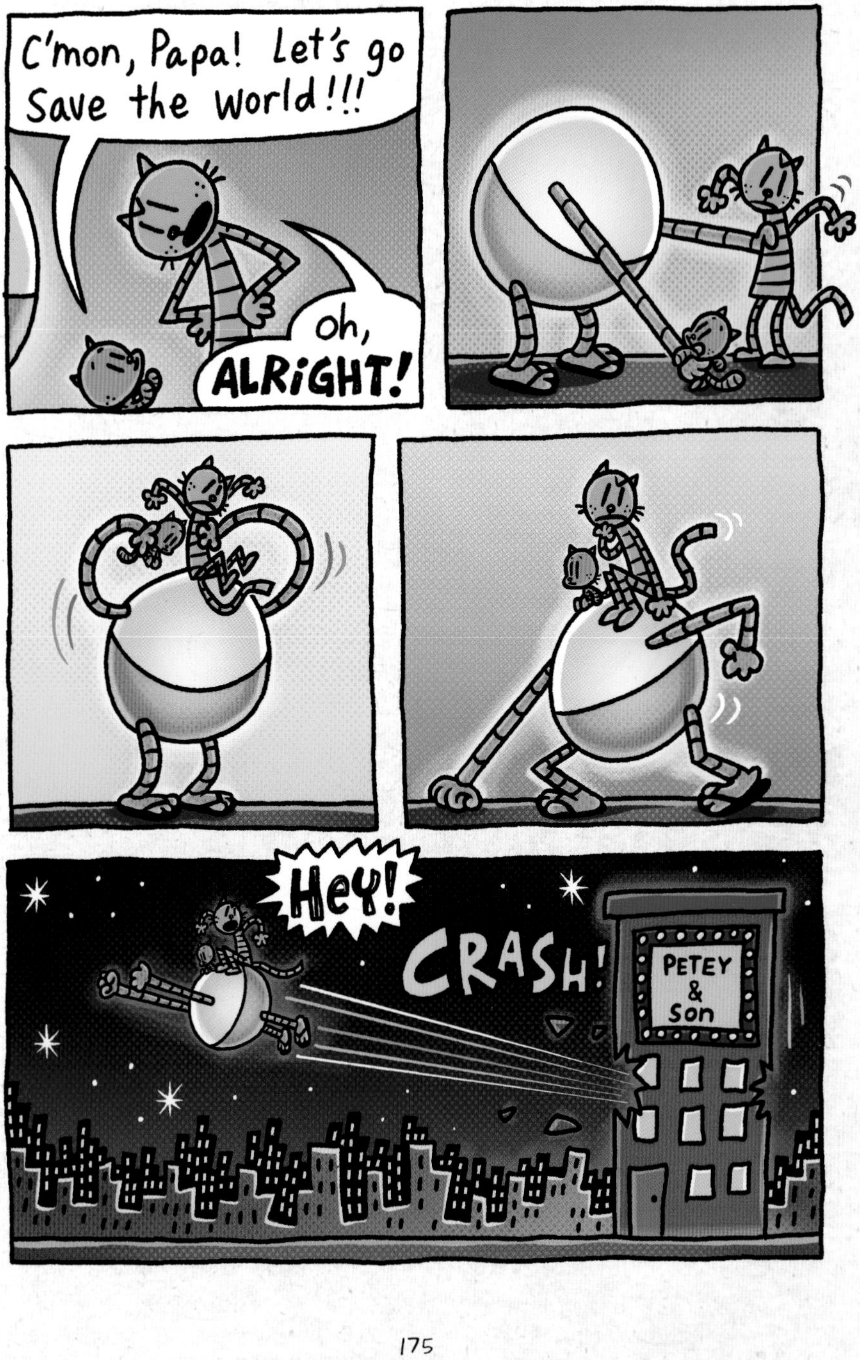
C'mon, Papa! Let's go Save the World!!!
oh, ALRIGHT!
Hey!
CRASH!
PETEY & Son

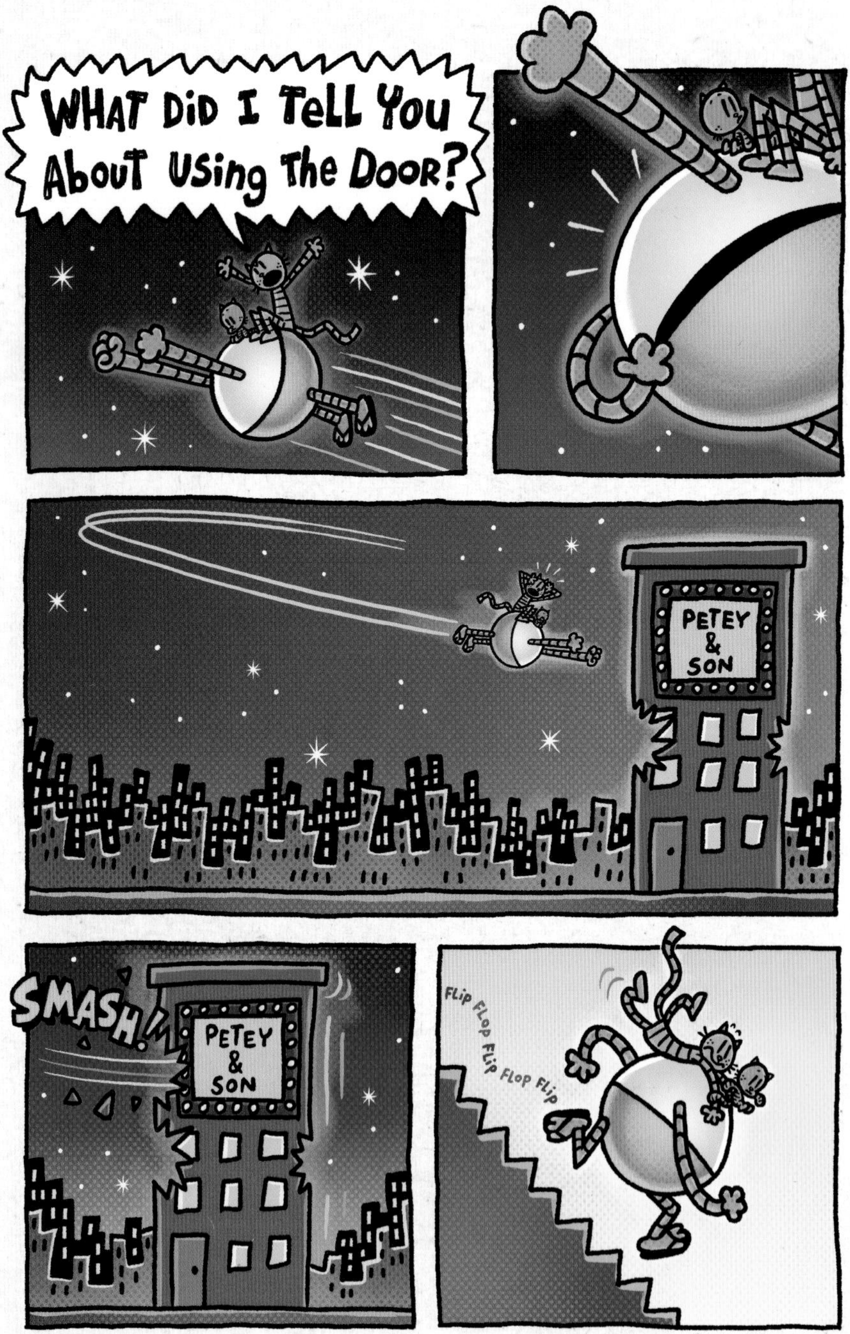
WHAT DID I TELL YOU About USing The DOOR?
PETEY & SON
SMASH!
PETEY & SON
FLIP FLOP FLIP FLOP FLIP

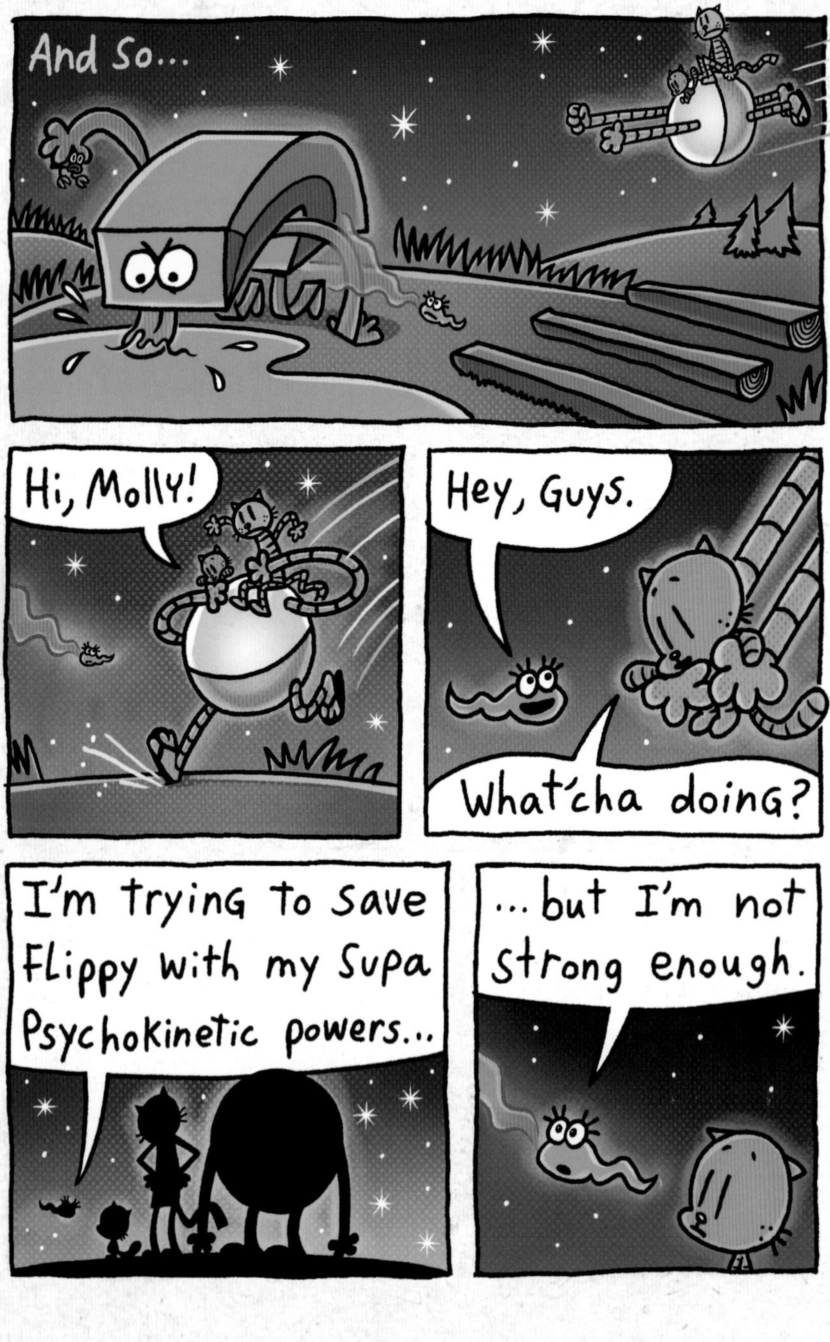
And So...
Hi, Molly!
Hey, Guys.
What'cha doing?
I'm trying to save Flippy with my Supa Psychokinetic powers...
...but I'm not strong enough.

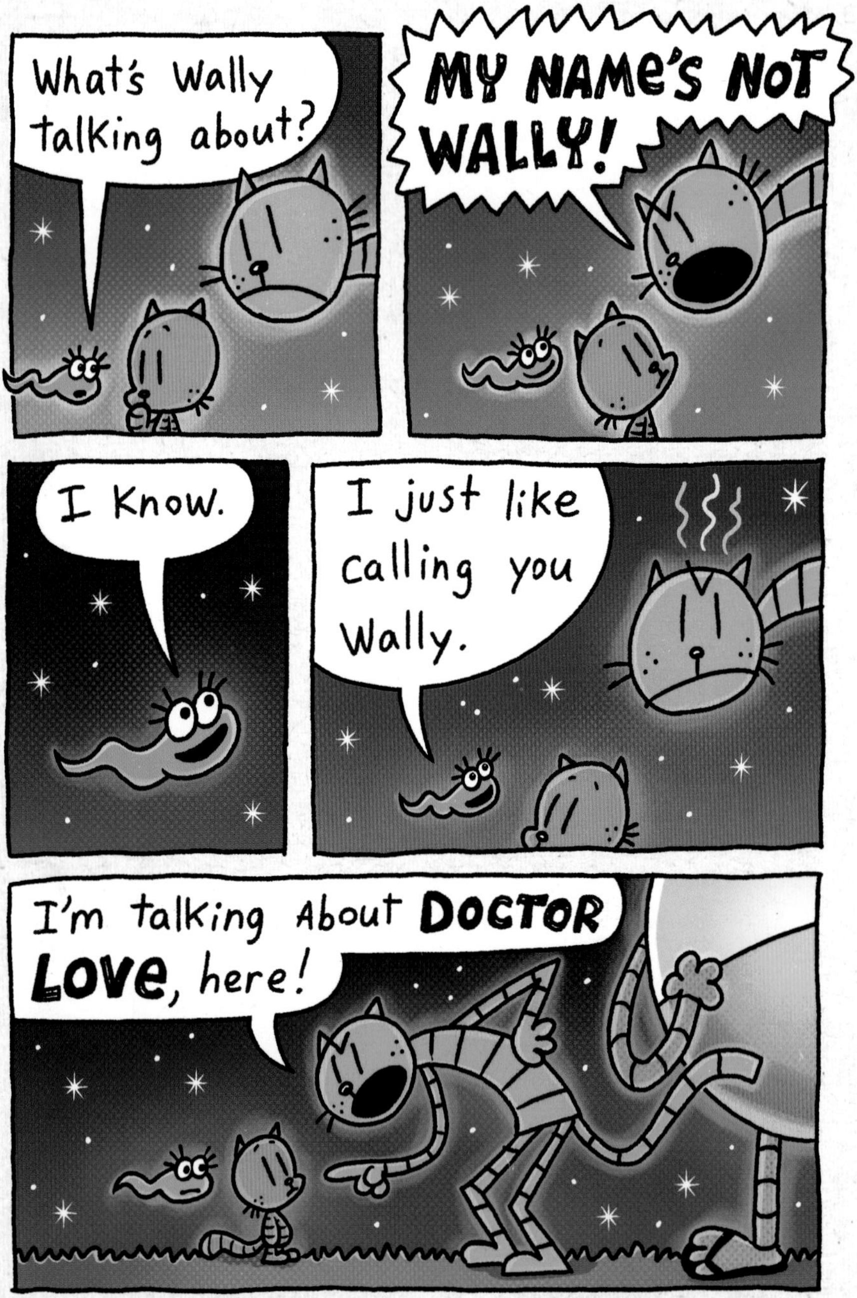
What's Wally talking about?
MY NAME'S NOT WALLY!
I know.
I just like calling you Wally.
I'm talking About DOCTOR LOVE, here!

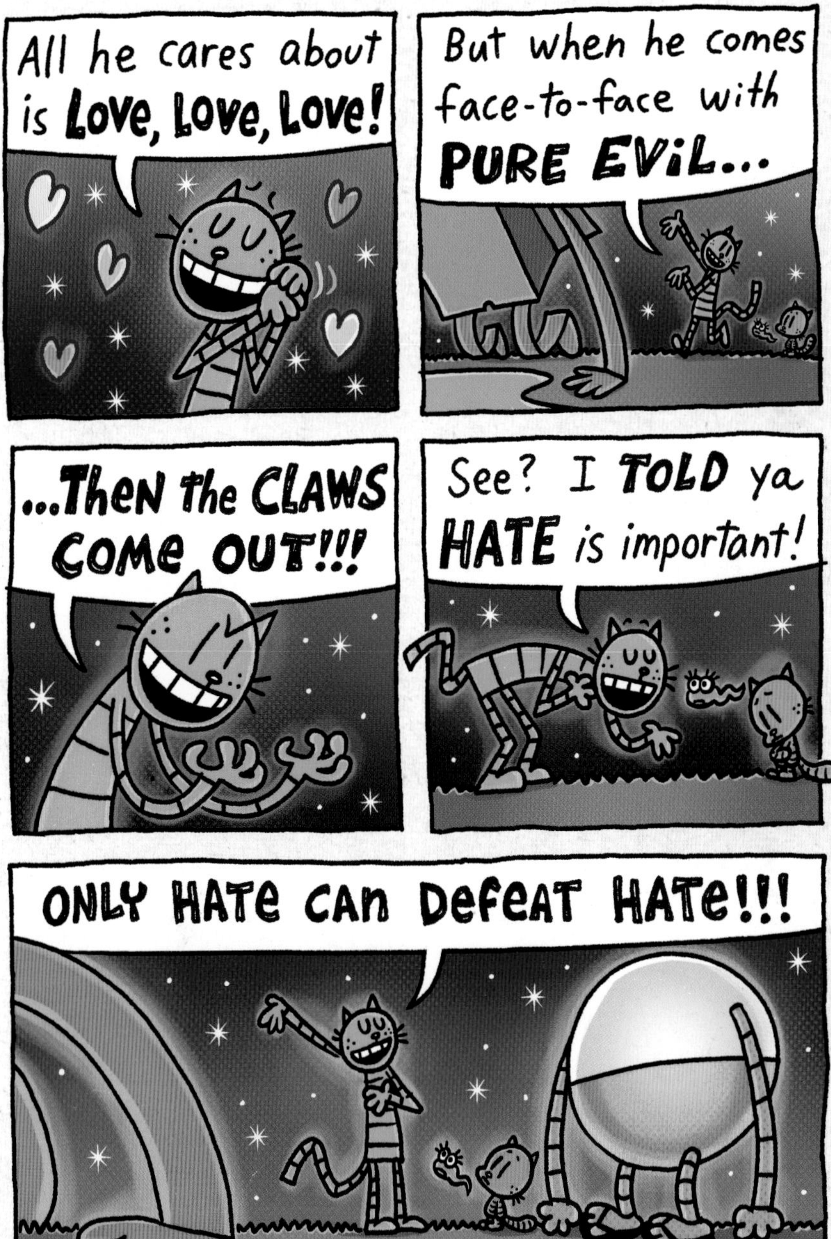
All he cares about is Love, Love, Love!
But when he comes face-to-face with PURE EVIL...
...Then the CLAWS COME OUT!!!
See? I TOLD ya HATE is important!
ONLY HATE CAN DEFEAT HATE!!!

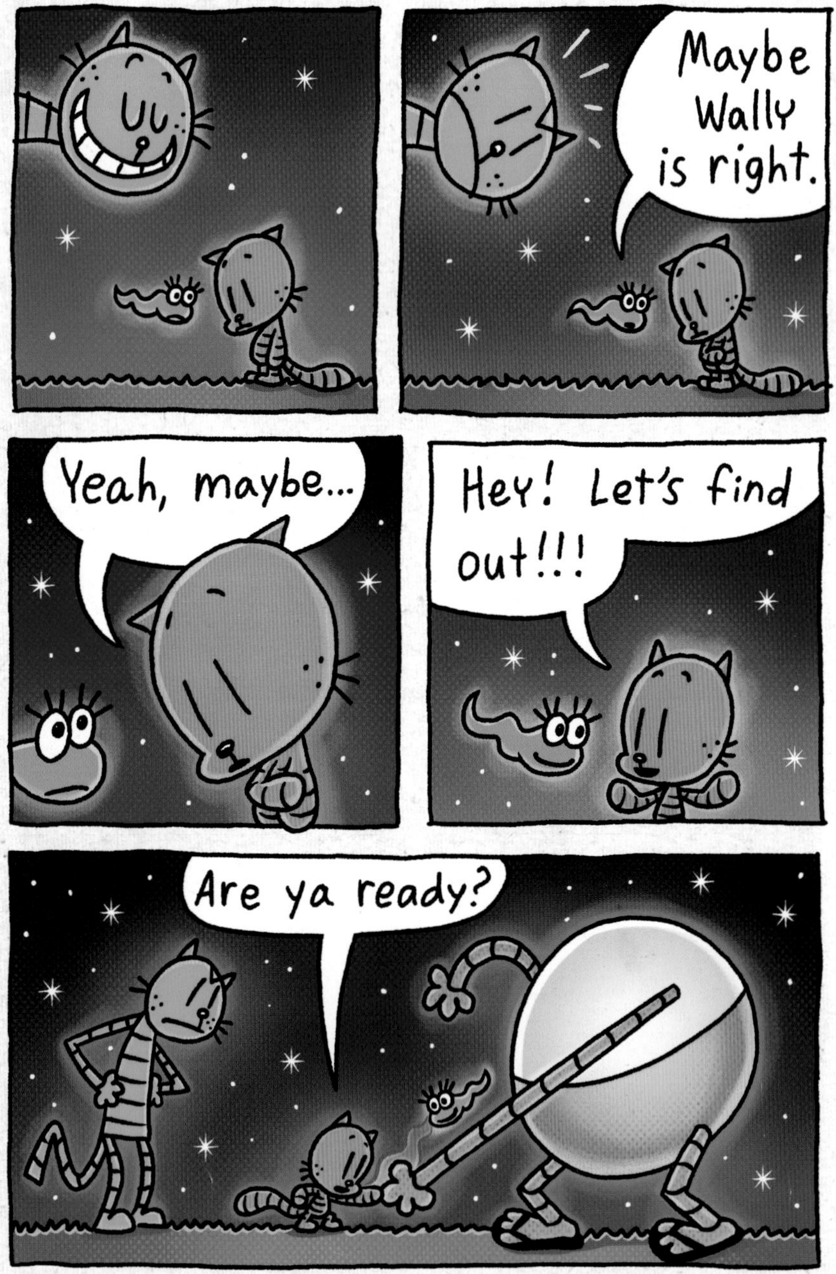
Maybe Wally is right.
Yeah, maybe...
Hey! Let's find out!!!
Are ya ready?

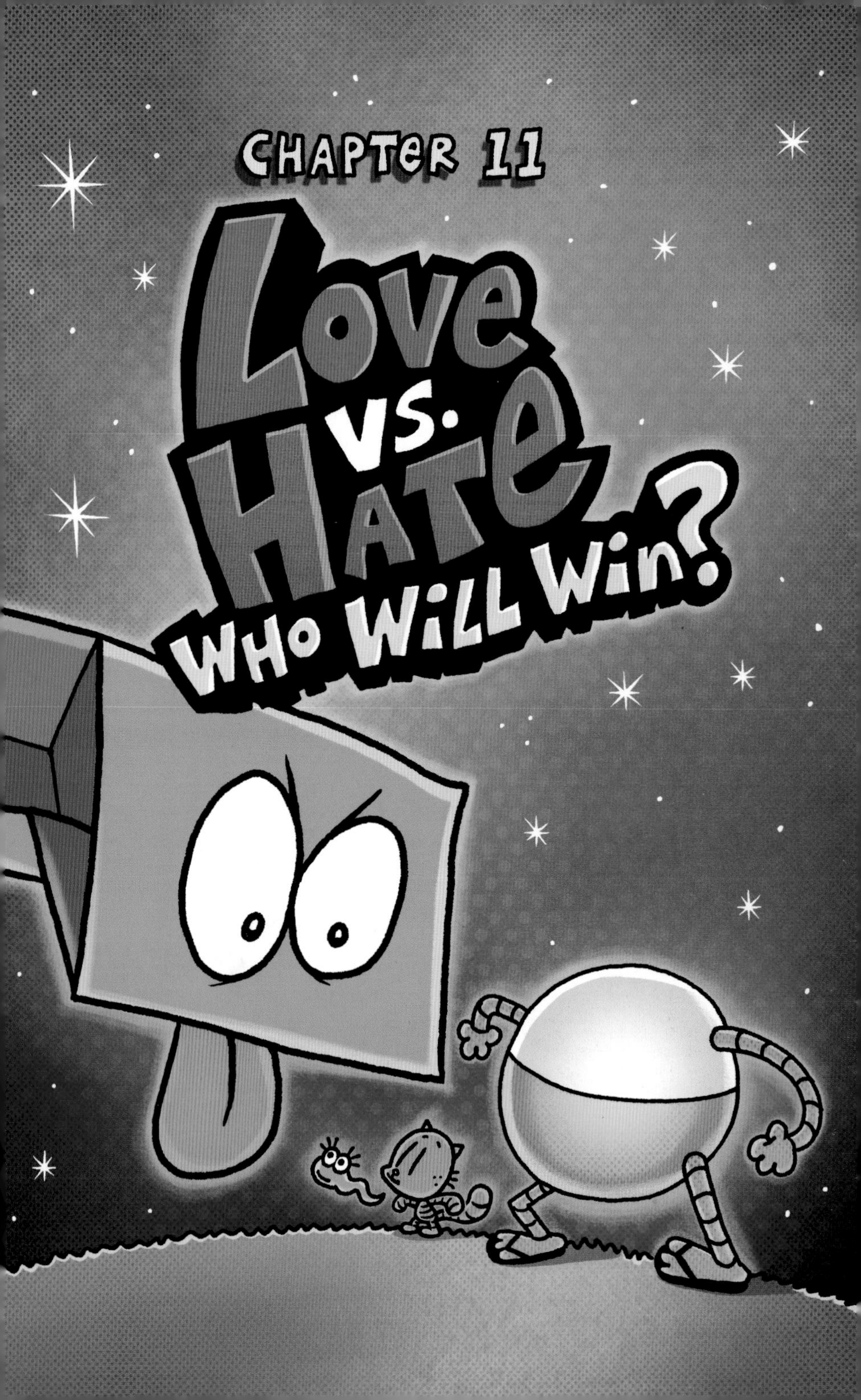
CHAPTER 11
LOVE VS. HATE
WHO WILL WIN?

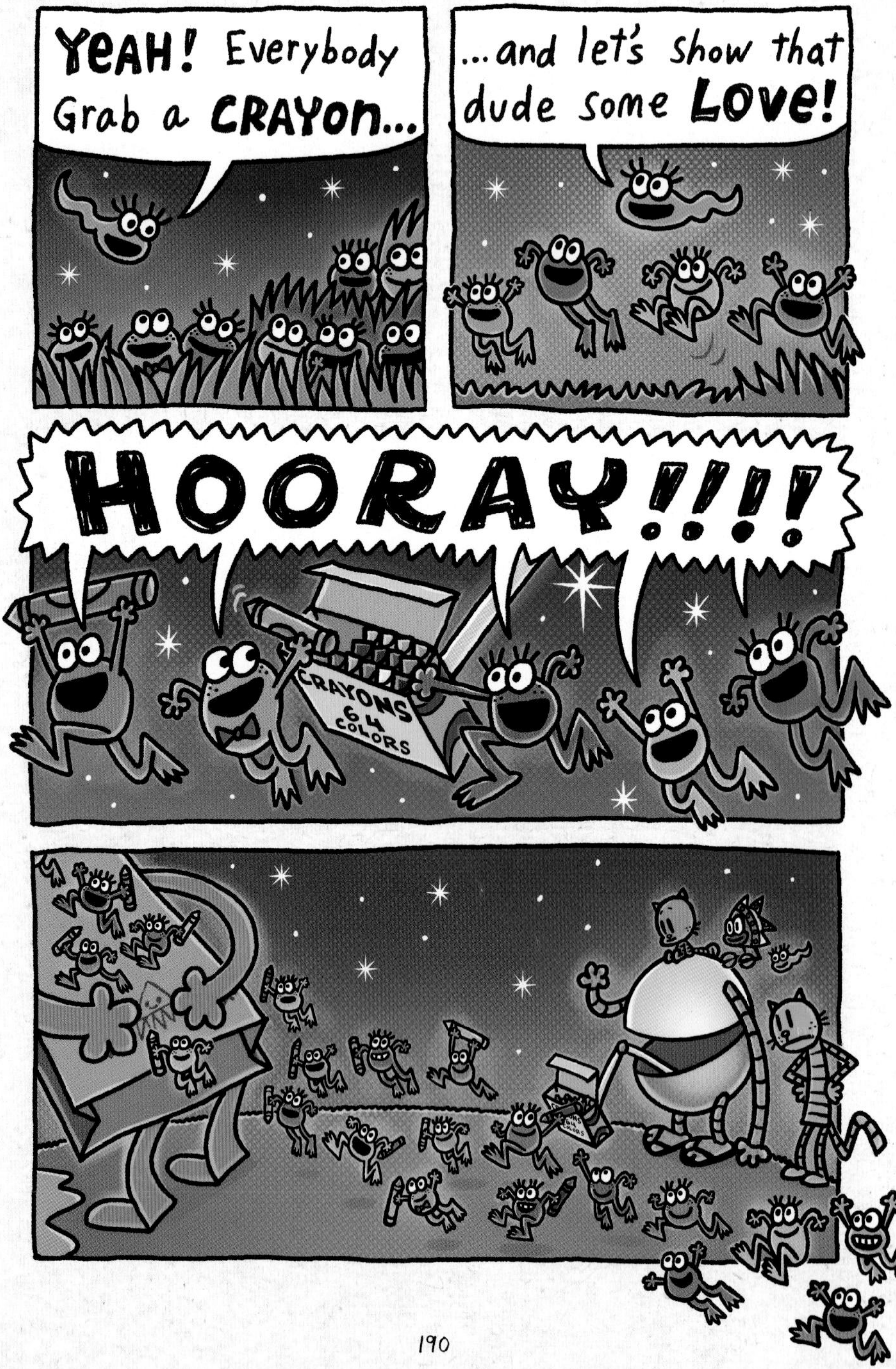
YEAH! Everybody Grab a CRAYON...
...and let's show that dude some LOVE!
HOORAY!!!!
CRAYONS 64 COLORS

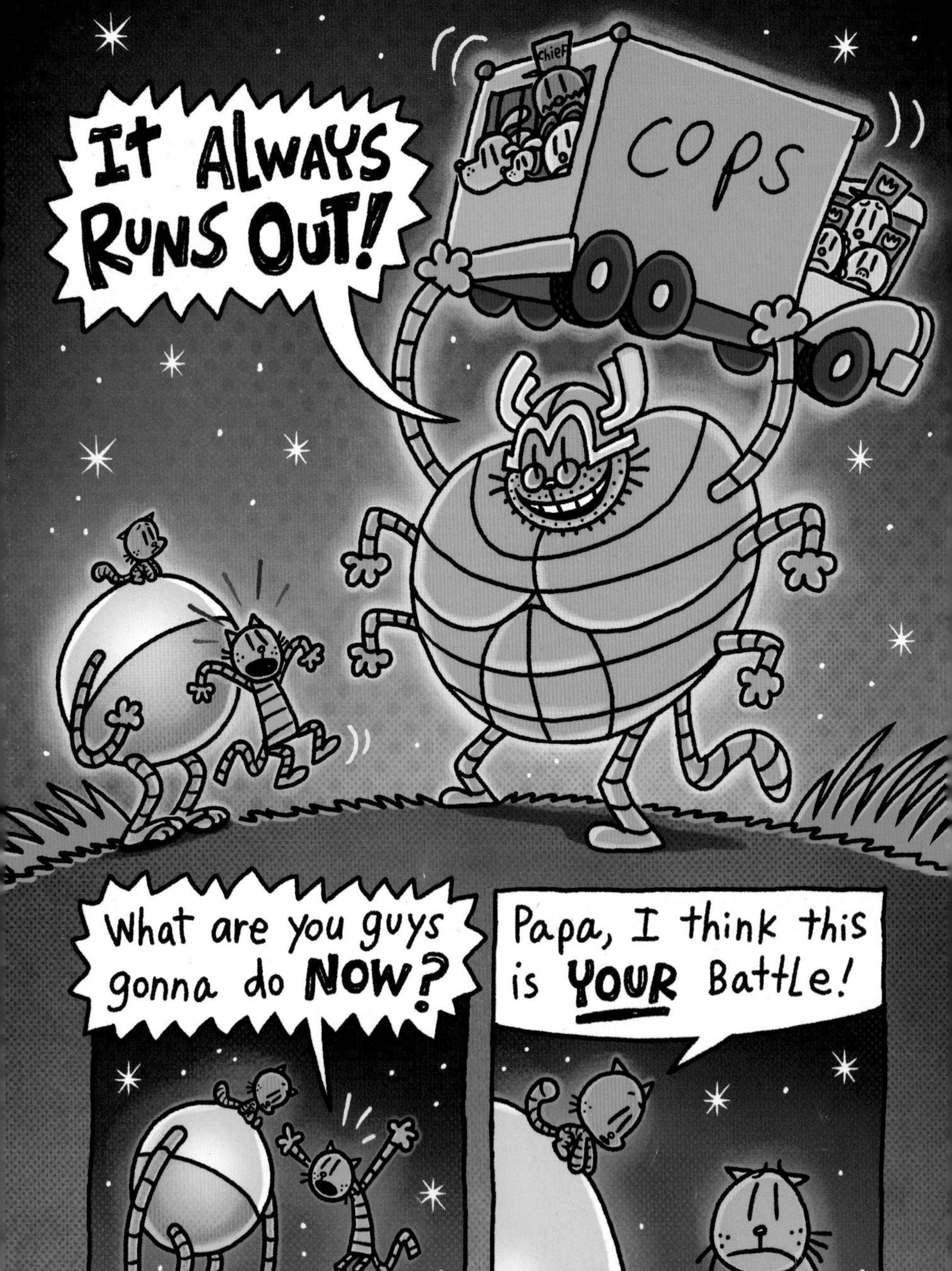
IT ALWAYS RUNS OUT!
CHIEF
COPS
What are you guys gonna do NOW?
Papa, I think this is YOUR Battle!

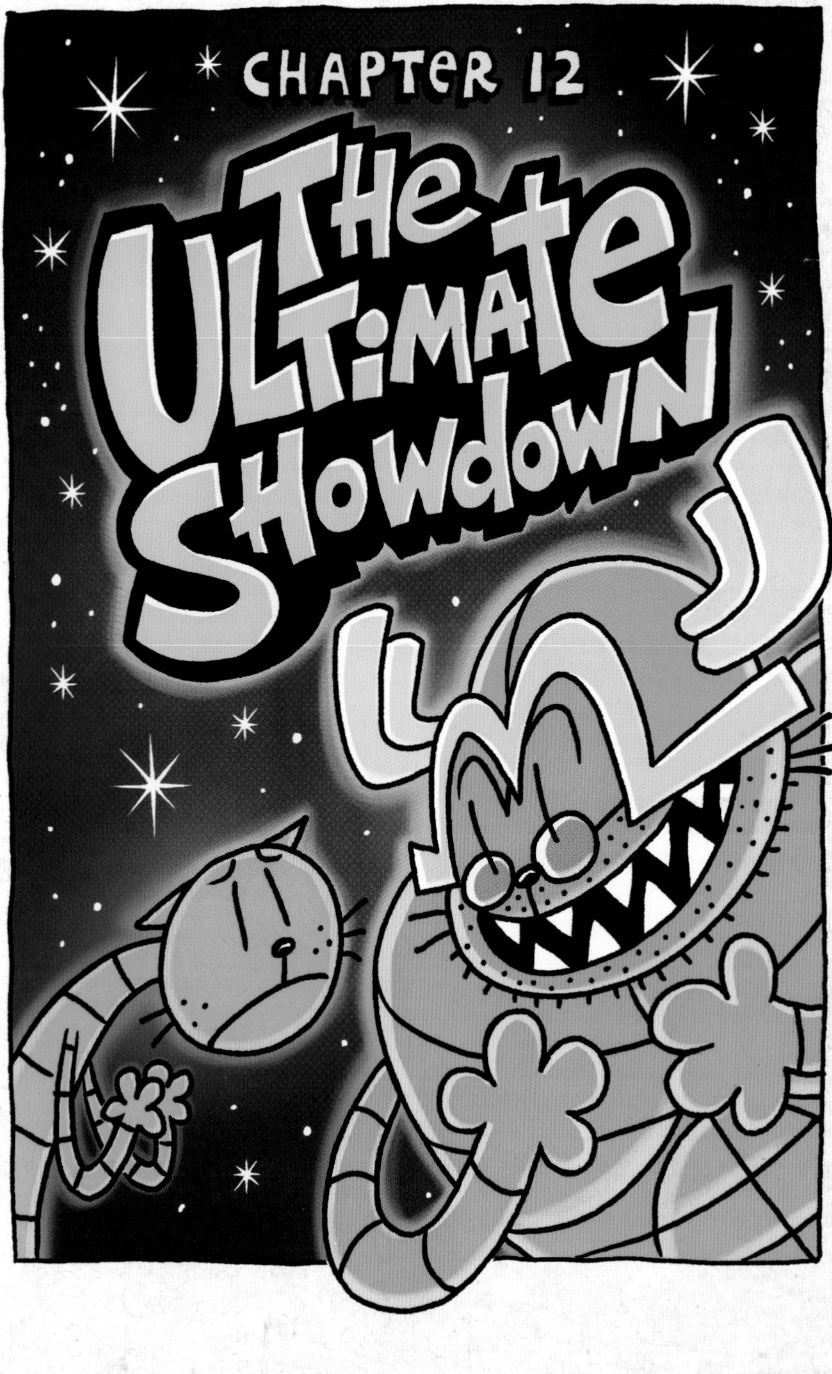
CHAPTER 12
THE ULTIMATE SHOWDOWN

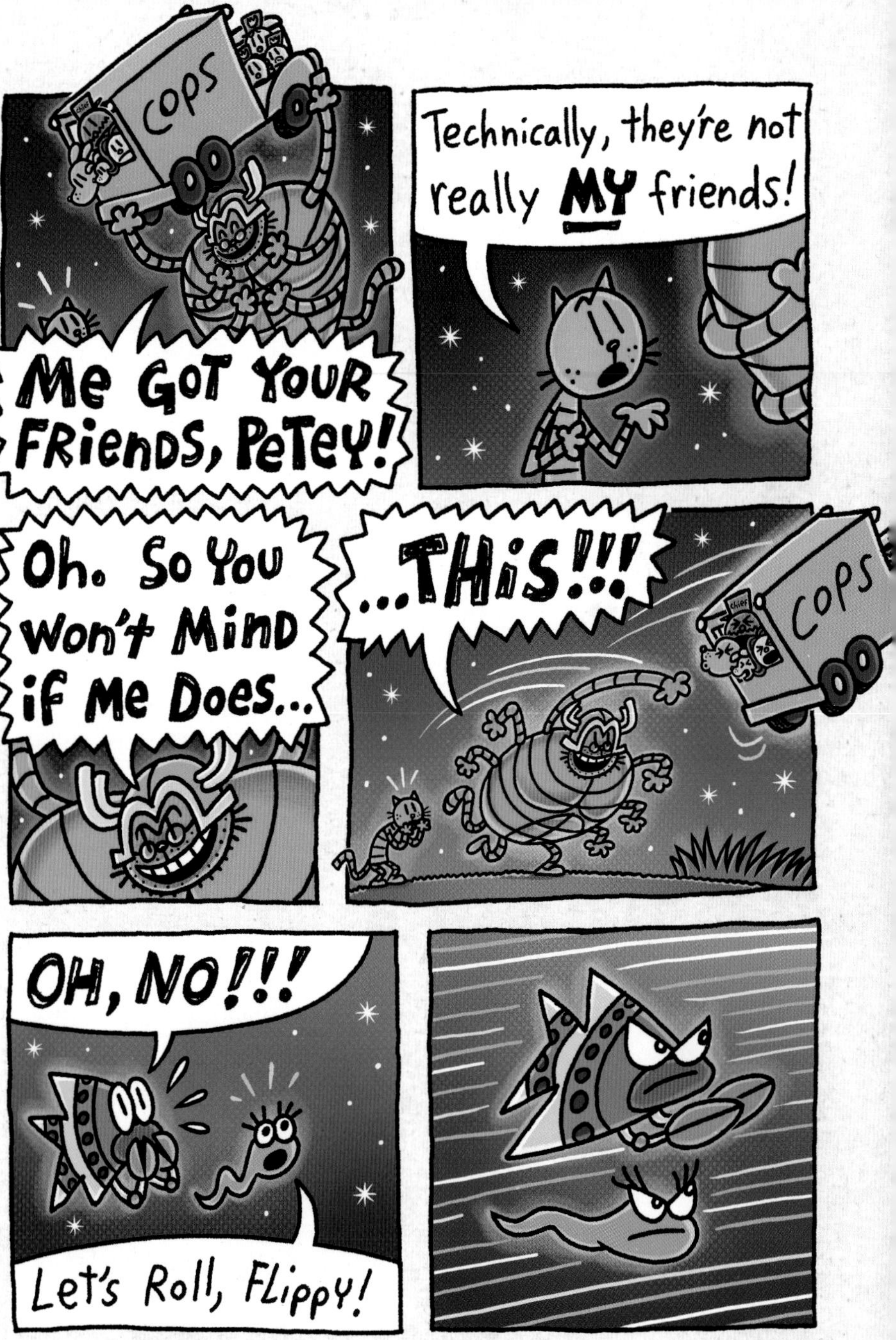

COPS
Technically, they're not really MY friends!
Me GOT YOUR FRIENDS, PeTEY!
Oh. So You won't Mind if Me Does...
...THiS!!!
COPS
chief
OH, NO!!!
Let's Roll, FLippY!

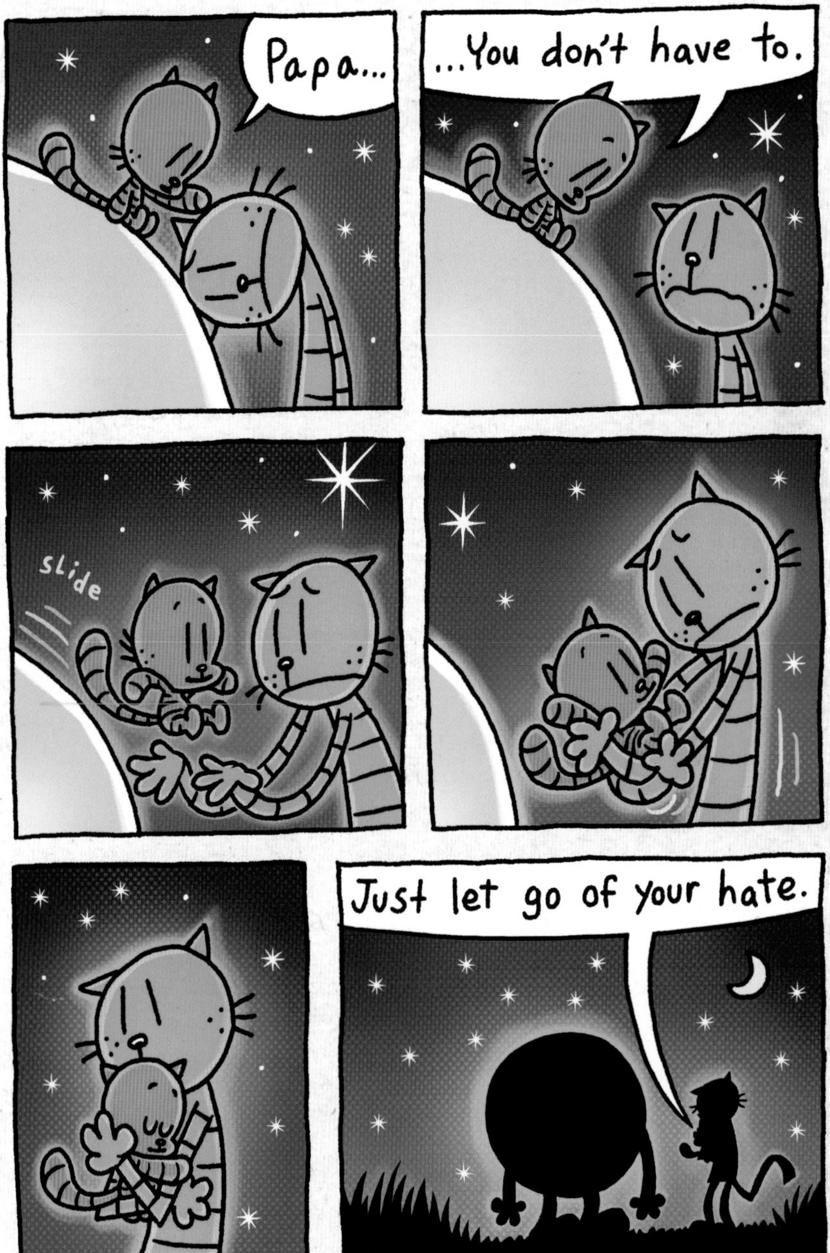
Papa...
...You don't have to.
SLide
Just let go of your hate.

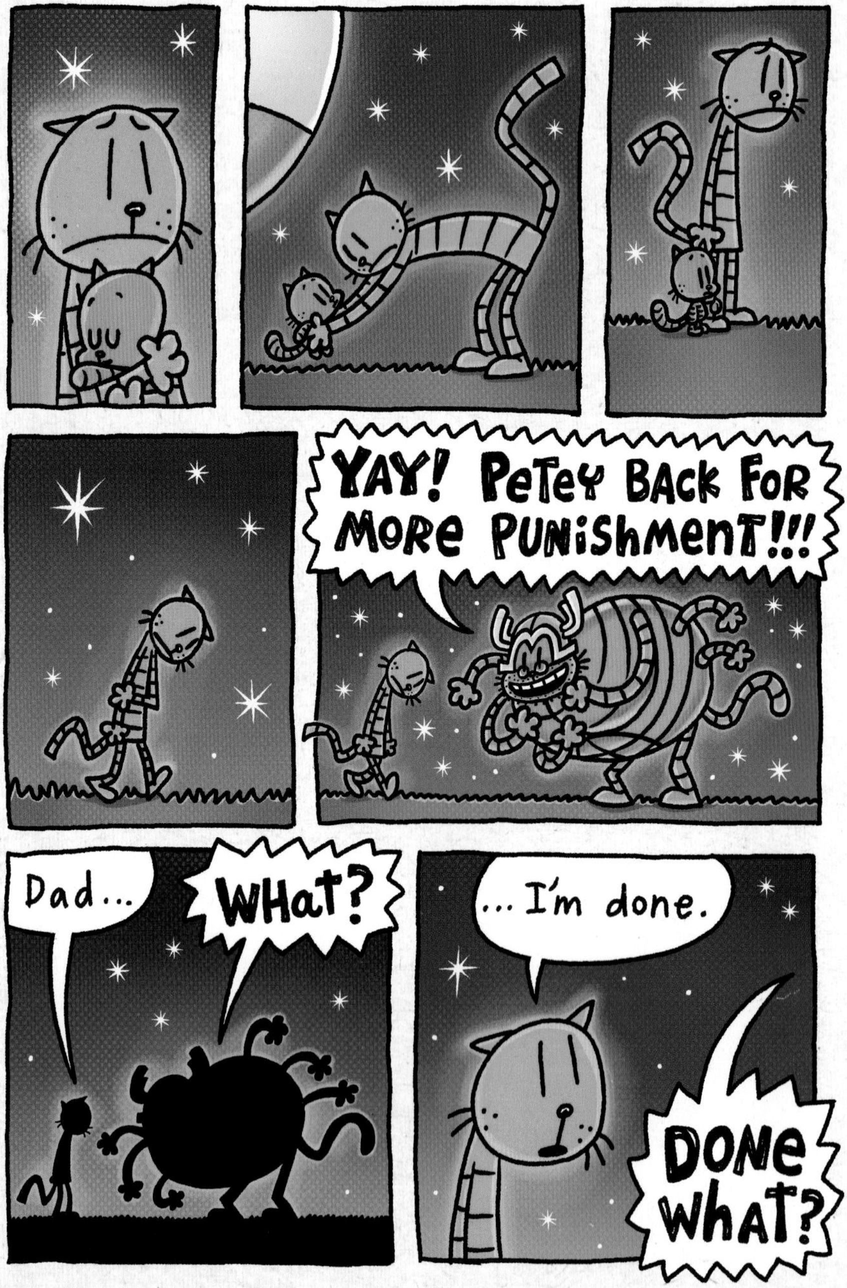
YAY! PETEY BACK FOR MORE PUNISHMENT!!!
Dad...
WHAT?
...I'm done.
DONE WHAT?

CHAPTER 13

Three Endings

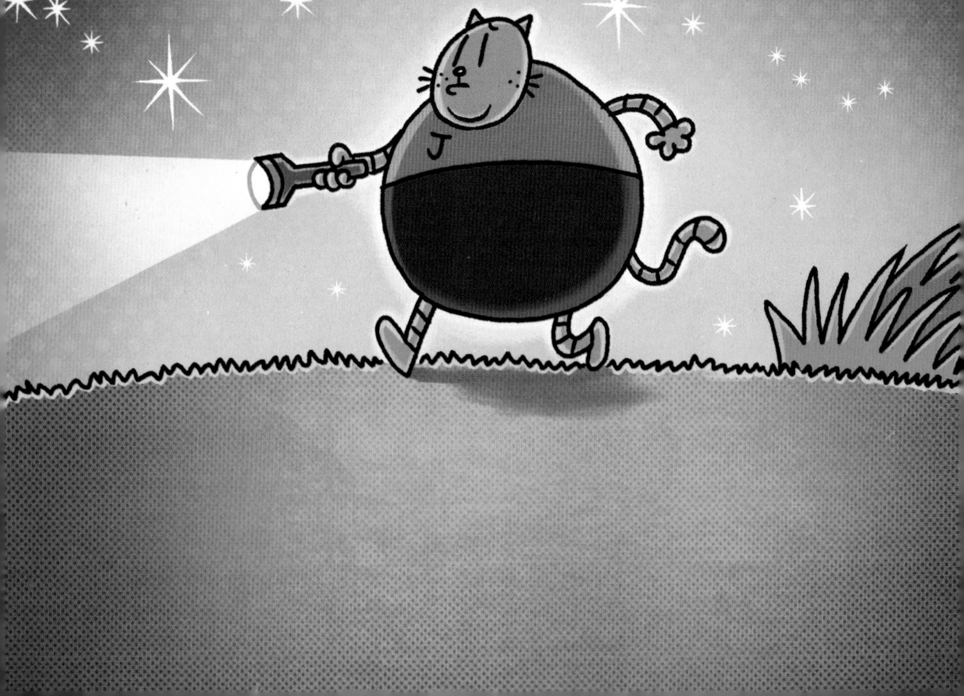

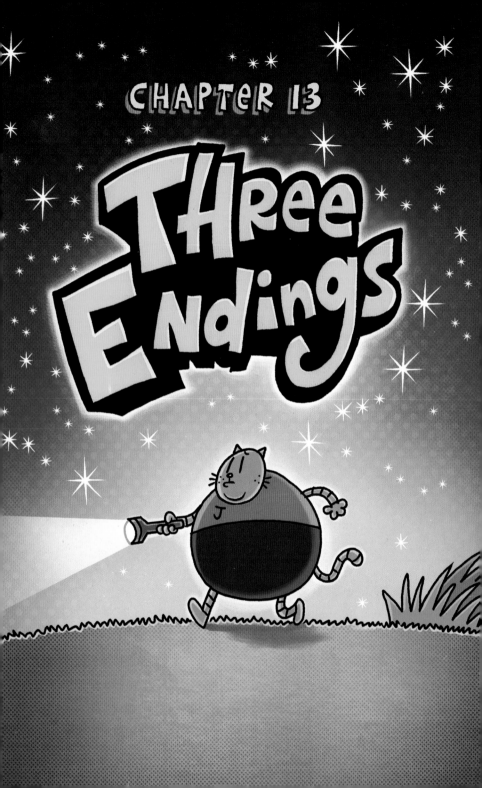

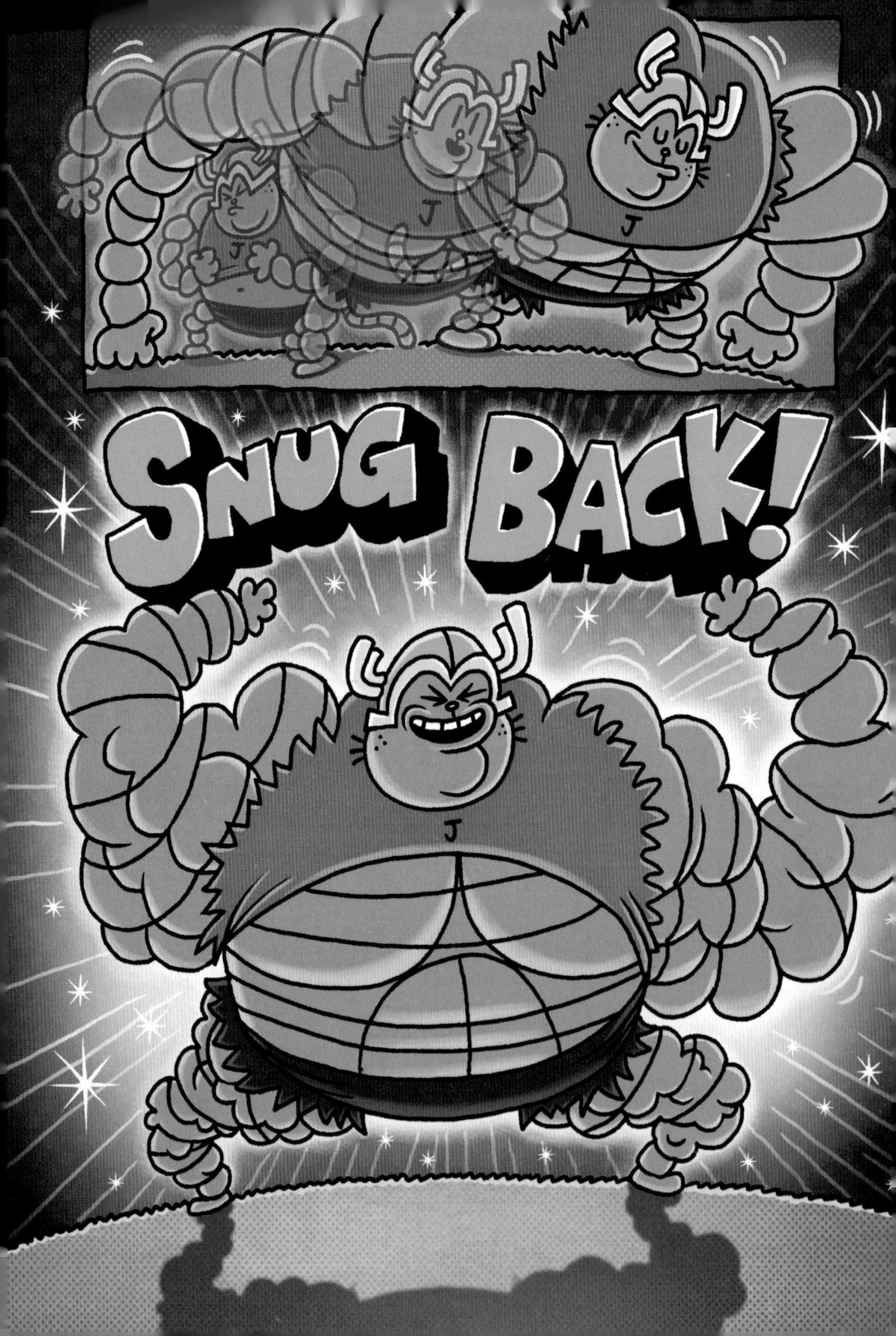
SNUG BACK!

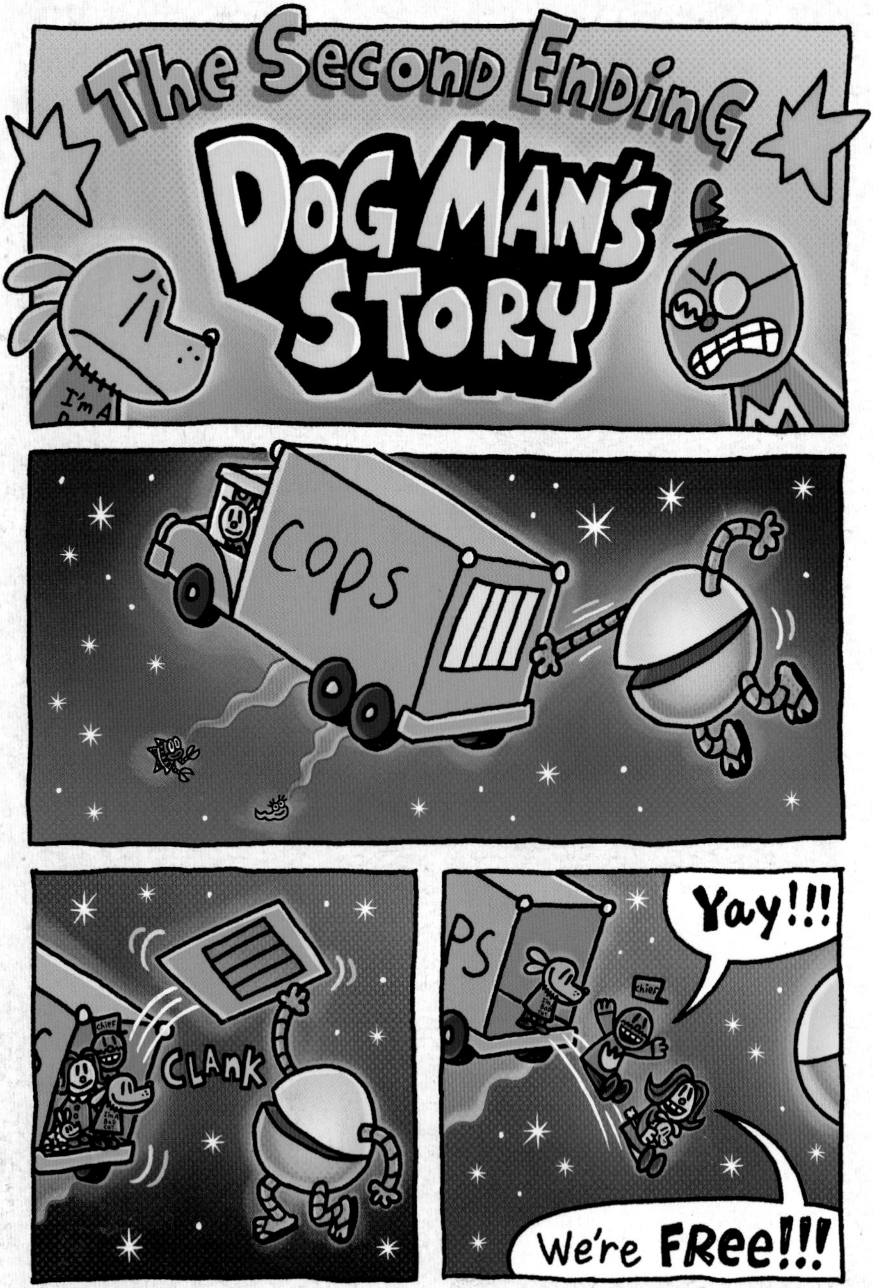
The Second Ending
Dog Man's Story
COPS
CLANK
Yay!!!
We're FREE!!!

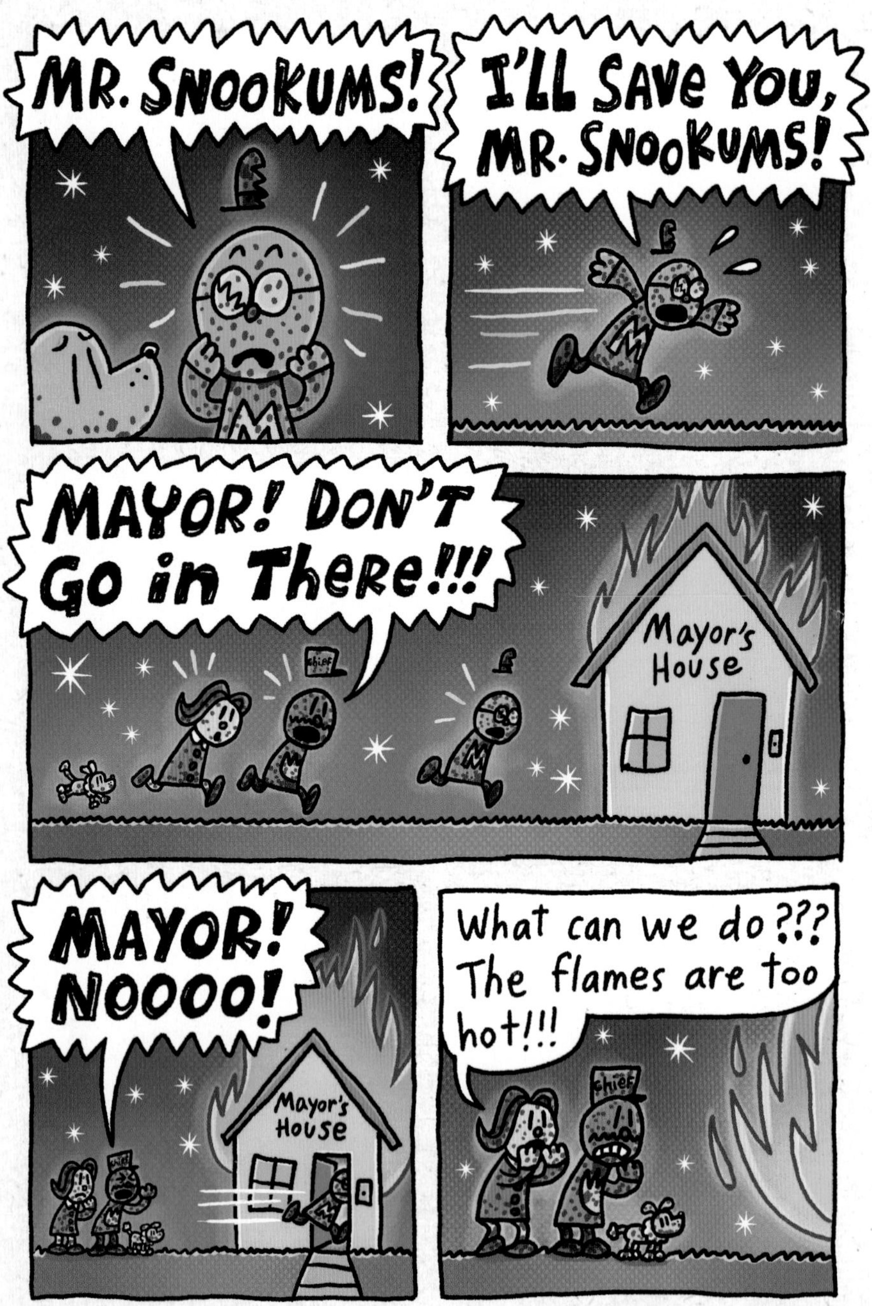
MR. SNOOKUMS!
I'LL SAVE YOU, MR. SNOOKUMS!
MAYOR! DON'T GO in There!!!
Chief
Mayor's House
MAYOR! NOOOO!
Chief
Mayor's House
What can we do??? The flames are too hot!!!
Chief

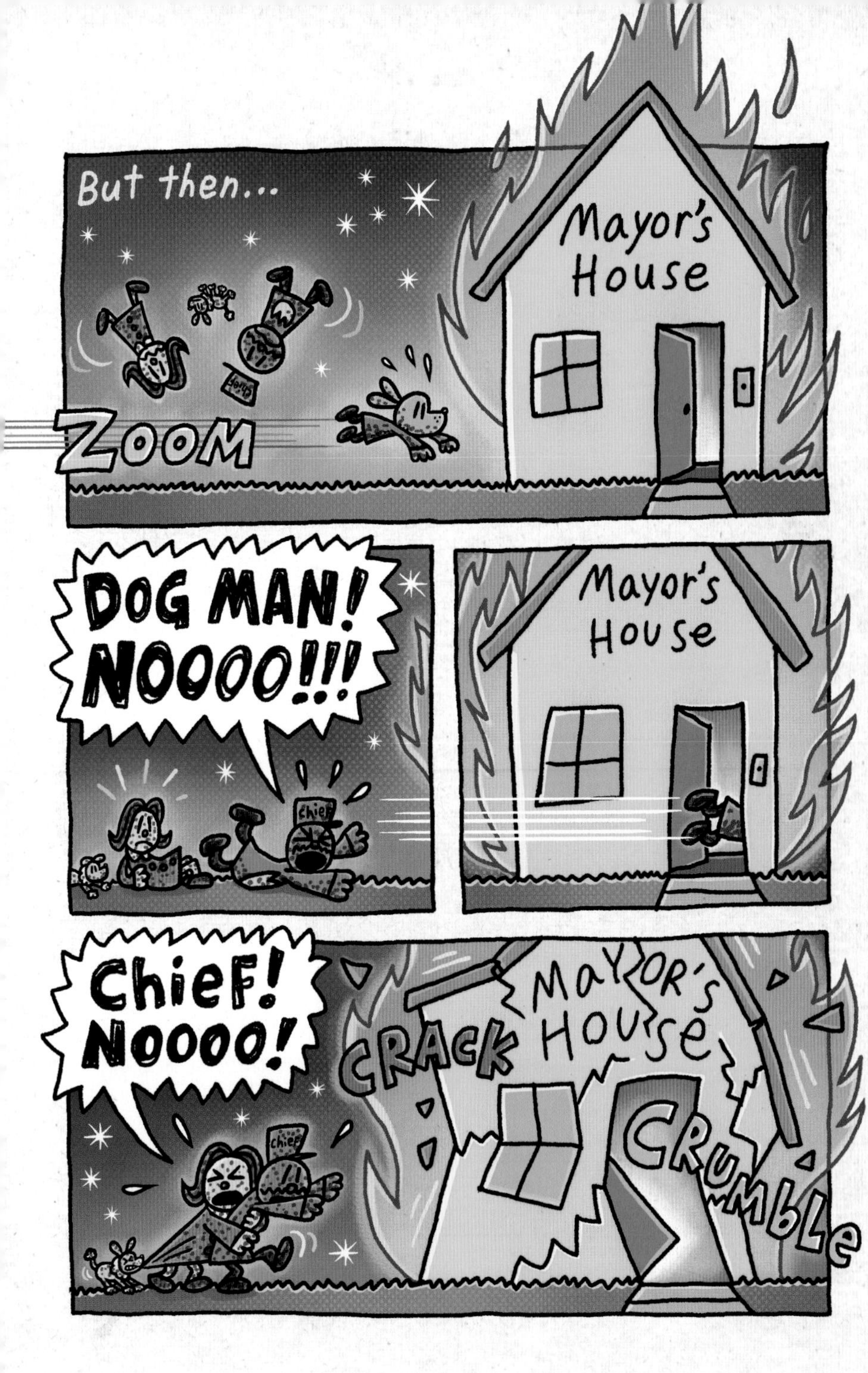

But then...
Mayor's House
ZOOM
DOG MAN! NOOOO!!!
Chief
Mayor's House
Chief! Noooo!
Chief
MAYOR'S HOUSE
CRACK
CRUMBLE

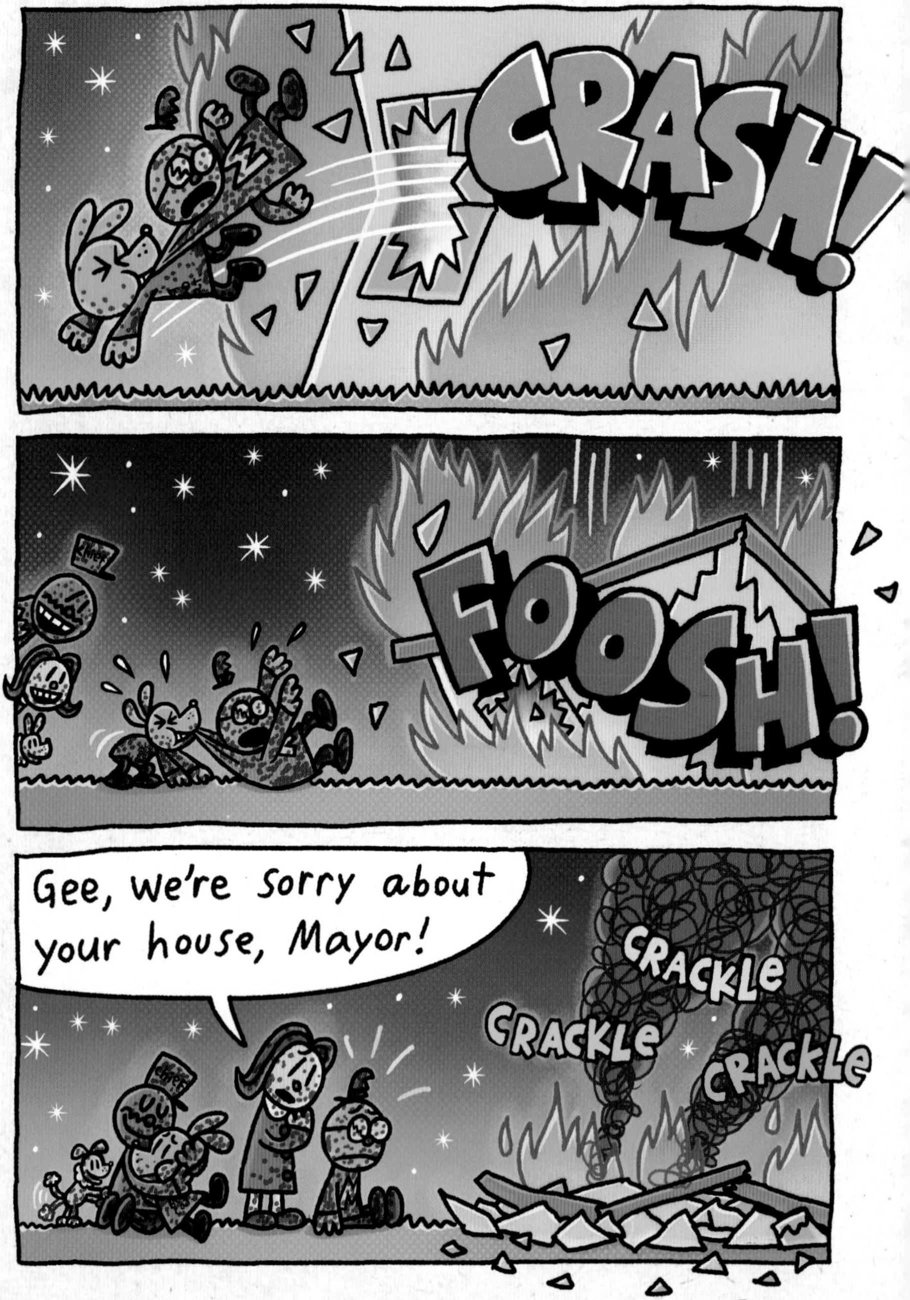
CRASH!
FOOSH!
Gee, we're sorry about your house, Mayor!
CRACKLE
CRACKLE
CRACKLE

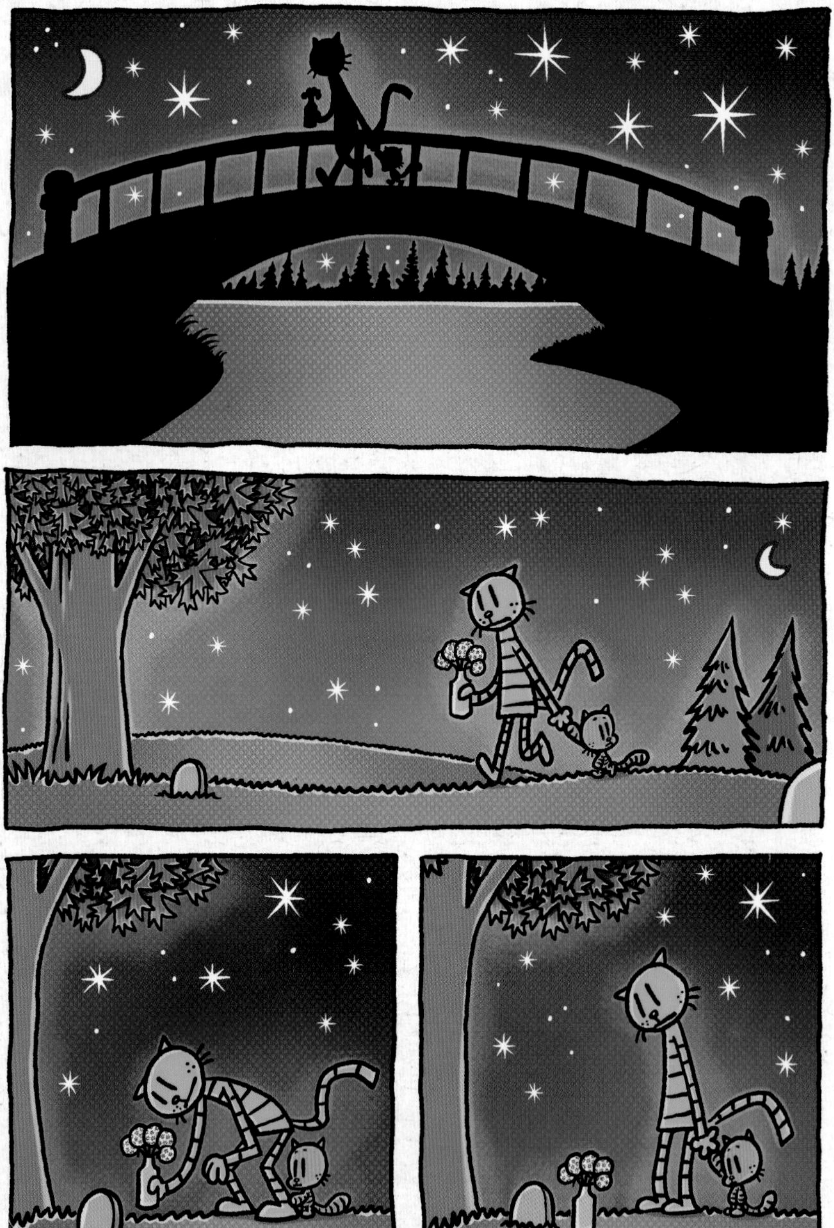

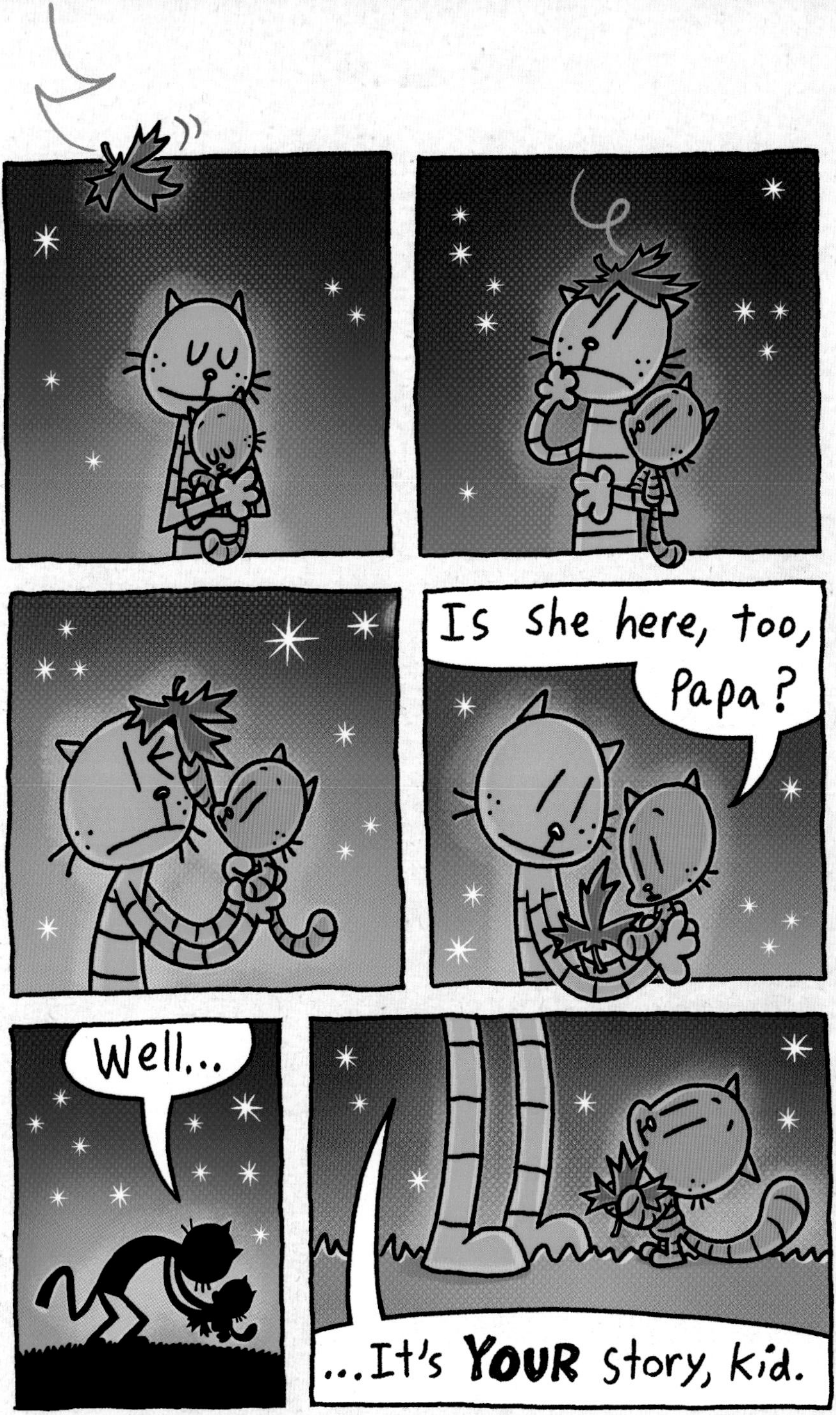
Is she here, too, Papa?
Well...
...It's YOUR story, kid.

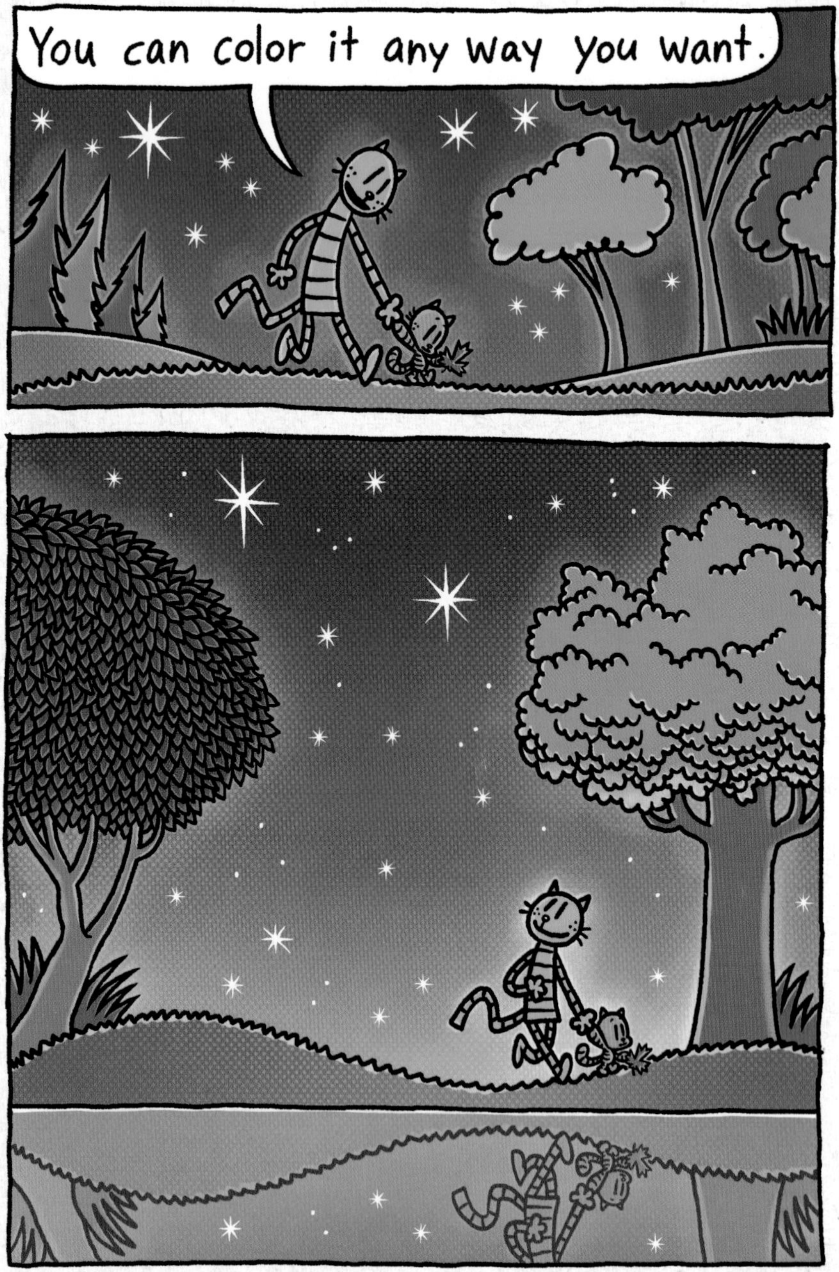
You can color it any way you want.

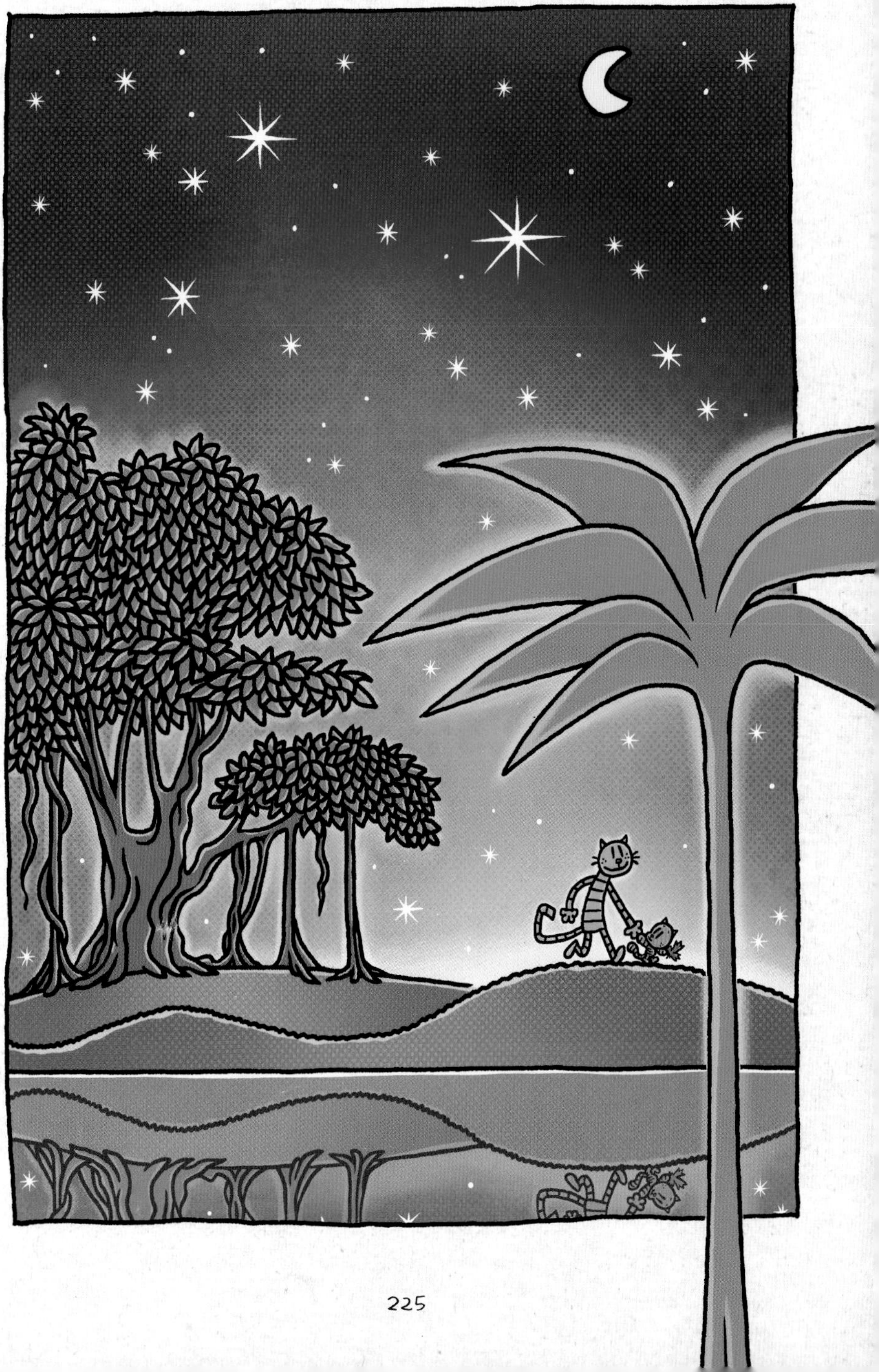

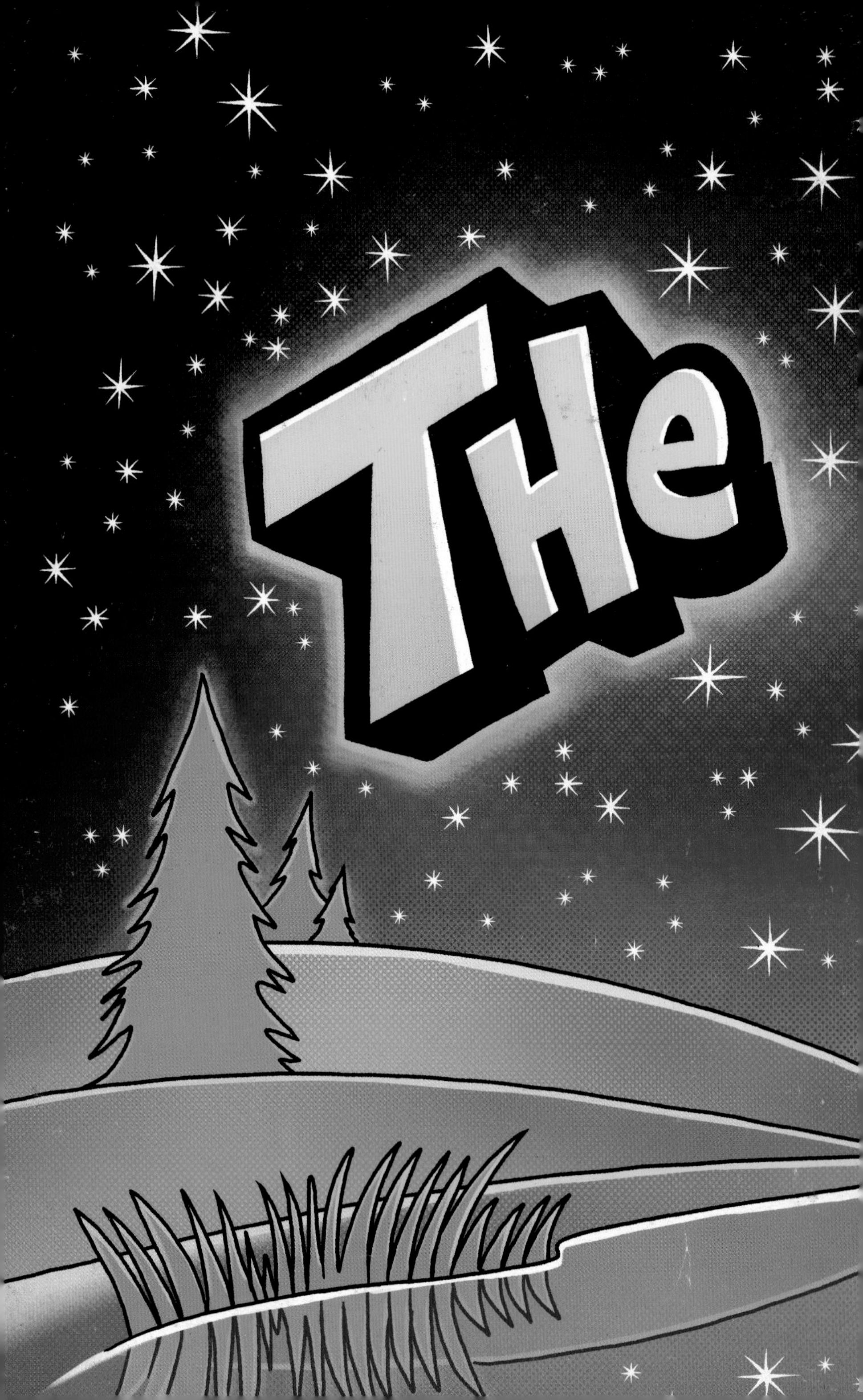
THe

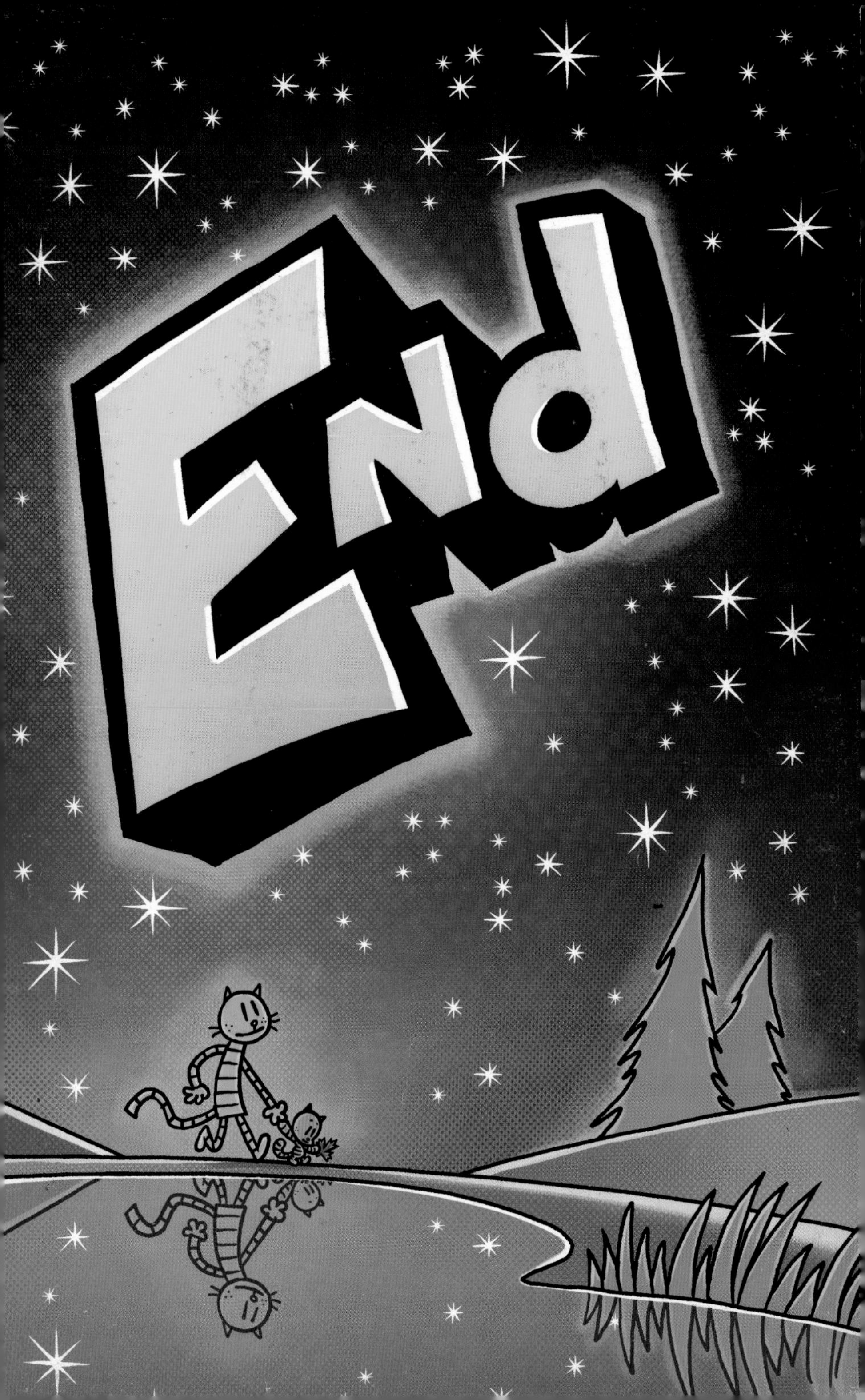
End

NOTES

by George and Harold

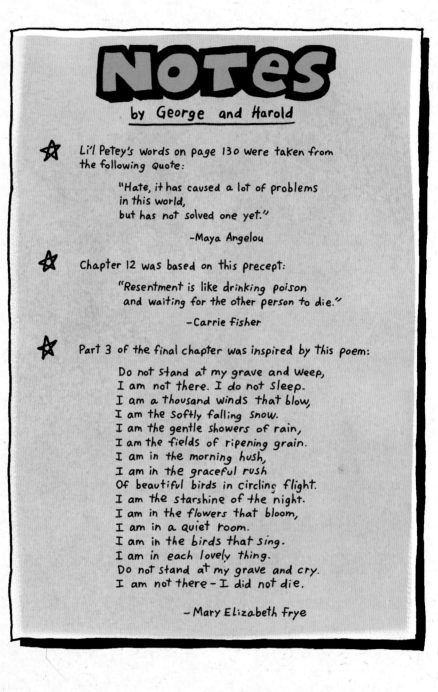

Li'l Petey's words on page 130 were taken from the following quote:

> "Hate, it has caused a lot of problems
> in this world,
> but has not solved one yet."
>
> —Maya Angelou

Chapter 12 was based on this precept:

> "Resentment is like drinking poison
> and waiting for the other person to die."
>
> —Carrie Fisher

Part 3 of the final chapter was inspired by this poem:

> Do not stand at my grave and weep,
> I am not there. I do not sleep.
> I am a thousand winds that blow,
> I am the softly falling snow.
> I am the gentle showers of rain,
> I am the fields of ripening grain.
> I am in the morning hush,
> I am in the graceful rush
> Of beautiful birds in circling flight.
> I am the starshine of the night.
> I am in the flowers that bloom,
> I am in a quiet room.
> I am in the birds that sing.
> I am in each lovely thing.
> Do not stand at my grave and cry.
> I am not there – I did not die.
>
> — Mary Elizabeth Frye

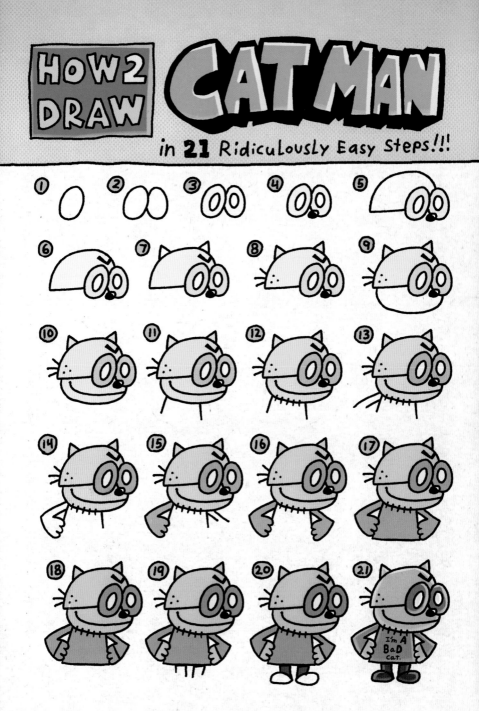

HOW2 DRAW CAT MAN

in **21** Ridiculously Easy Steps!!!

I'm A BaD CaT.

HOW 2 DRAW Melvin The FROG

in 17 Ridiculously easy steps!

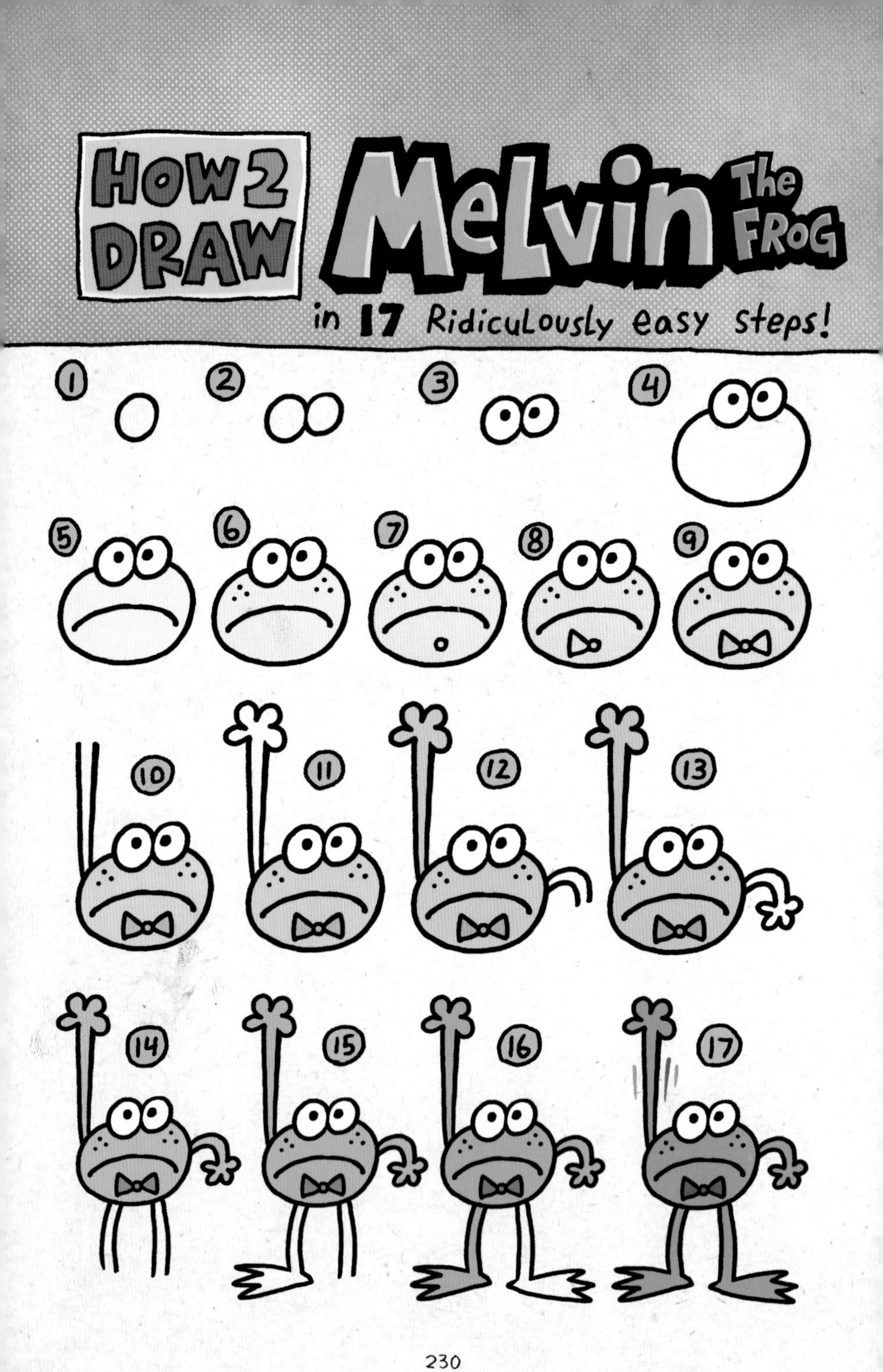
1
2
3
4
5
6
7
8
9
10
11
12
13
14
15
16
17

HOW 2 MAKE MUNCHY The Lunch BAG

in **4** Ridiculously easy steps!

Step 1:

Get Supplies:
- ★ Lunch bag
- ★ Pencil
- ★ Tape
- ★ Construction paper ★ Scissors
- ★ Crayons / markers / colored Pencils

STEP 2:
Draw and Cut out the arms, Legs, eyes + Tongue.

FREE Printable/Colorable template available at: Scholastic.com/catkidcomicclub

STEP 3:

Assemble as shown using tape or glue or paste.

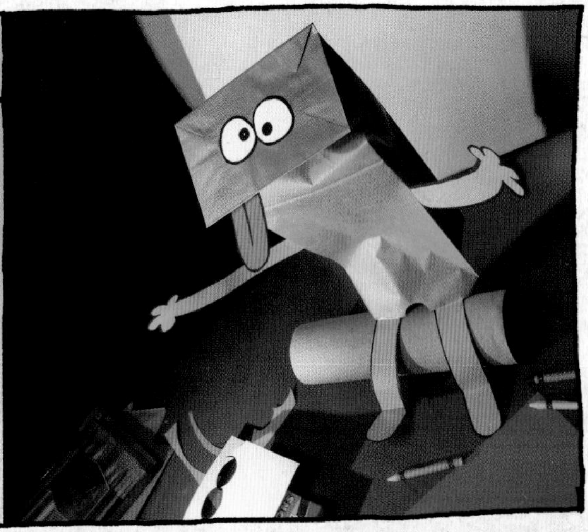

STEP 4:

Take away his eviL powers by filling him up with all the people and things you **Love!** Use pencils, crayons, paint, or whatever!!!

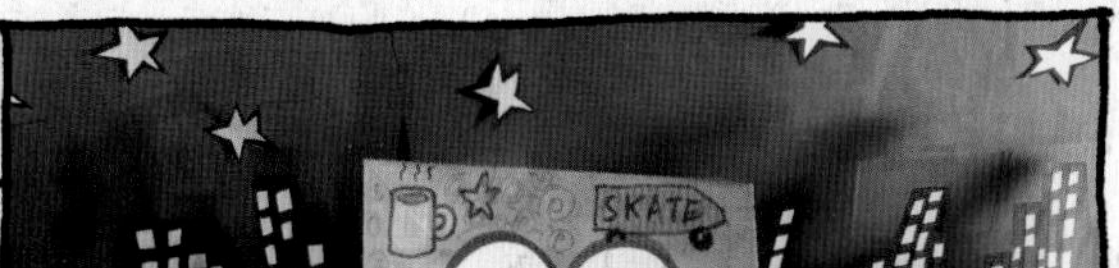
SKATE
COMiX

WRITE... DRAW... Be CREATive!

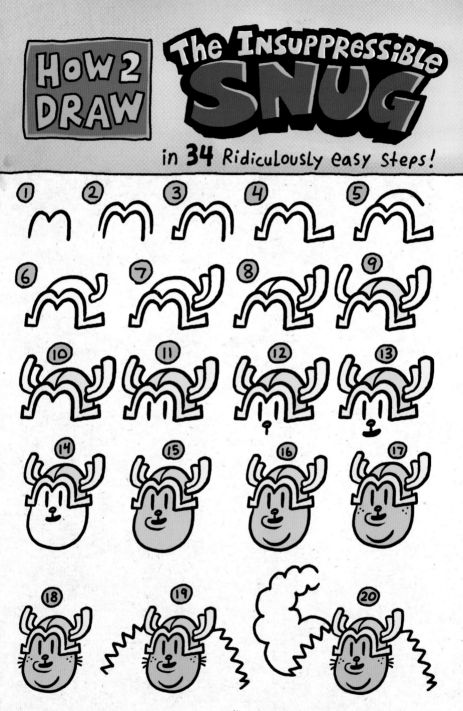

HOW 2 DRAW

The INSUPPRESSIBLE SNUG

in 34 Ridiculously easy steps!

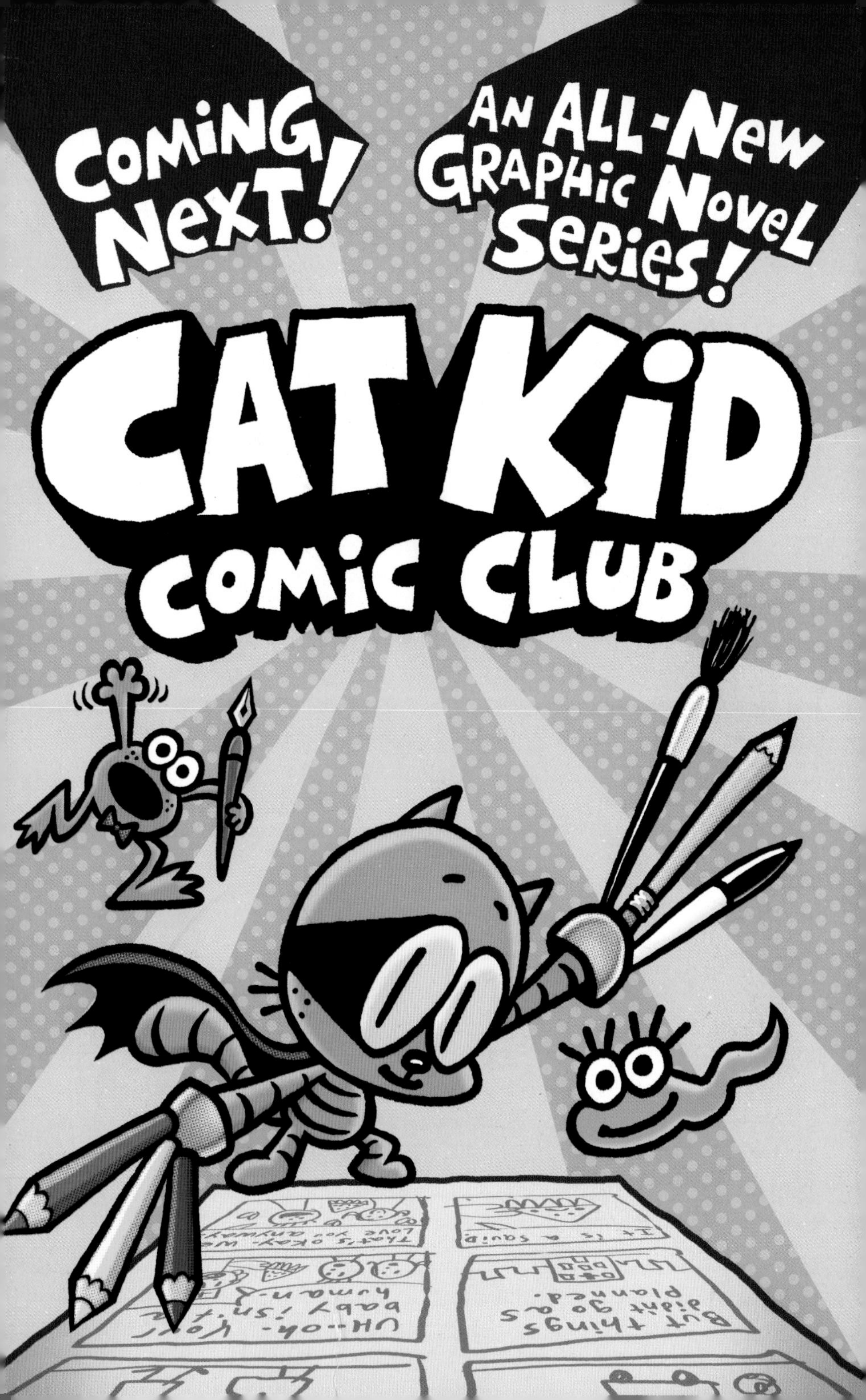
COMING NEXT!
AN ALL-NEW GRAPHIC NOVEL SERIES!
CAT KID COMIC CLUB
It is a squid.
That's okay. We love you anyway.
But things didn't go as planned.
Uh--oh. Your baby isn't human.

GET READING W